WhydahMaker

by

John Best

AUTHOR'S NOTE: Cape Cod, and by extension, the town of Wellfleet, is a wonderful place to live. I know this because my wife and I call it home. None of the characters in this book are real. Many places *do* appear as they actually exist. It would have been wrong to exclude them from the story.

Special thanks to my dear wife, Elizabeth, for her support, the book cover design and one of the many proofreadings that have helped to make the story coherent. Our neighbor, Korynne is another who has made important corrections.

Also, I must thank local Cape Cod author, Elizabeth Moisan, for her great novel, "Master of the Sweet Trade". Her story, characters and local history left me with many ideas for my *own* story line.

Speaking of that, Cape Cod is filled with a wealth of history, legend, characters and, of course, ghosts. All became my "writer's playground". I wish to repeat that all characters in my story are fictional, as are at least half of the places mentioned. I will say, however, some of my friends *may* get the impression that certain characters resemble themselves. Only in your imagination, folks. Enjoy the journey.

John Best
2019

CAST OF CHARACTERS

Elizabeth and Lester Worthy

Viridian Bean (musician and close friend of the Worthys)

Sam Bellamy (pirate and ghost)

Mariah Hallett (Sam Bellamy's girlfriend and fellow ghost)

Persiphone Painestaker (local medium and musician)

May Potowatomie (AKA March Maxtor/ March Madmess)

The Firm:(All ghostlike creatures)
Ishmael Crouch
Faustus Diabello
Morley Enoch
Mendicant Flinch

Assorted ghosts:
Elvis Presley
Napoleon Bonaparte
Marie Antoinette
Mikey the cat

Beetroot (villain from Opus 133)

Sam Bell (descendant of Sam Bellamy)
Mary Hall (descendant of Mariah Hallett)
(both *not* ghosts)

The Ballad of Lester Worthy

A recap of our continuing story, dear readers. This is the third and final episode in the Lester Worthy trilogy, and about time, too! This book can be read without the other two in the series.

"In The Out Door"- We meet a young Lester Worthy and the future Mrs. Worthy at the beginning of their long careers in the perilous quest to teach the Arts to the "adolescent creature". There are many tales to tell, some good, some bad, some funny as all get out and some that bring the reader to tears. Book One ends with the Worthys leaving teaching after thirty two years and "attempting" retirement, to no avail. The story leaves them riding off into the sunset.

"Opus 133"-Book two. We run into the Worthy family peacefully "enjoying" retirement as working artists. Little did they know that a seemingly harmless visit to a flea market would first, send Lester, then, his wife on a happy romp involving Ludwig van Beethoven, a deranged killer and a former American Nazi camp. Really! What sick mind would think up such a....Oh. Everything *almost* turns out well in the end, only this time, no one rides off into the sunset.

"WhydahMaker"-Book three. The Worthy family escapes the clutches of the late, great state of New Jersey, to move to the peaceful, sleepy New England town of Wellfleet on Cape Cod. As these things seem to go, little did the Worthy family know what they were in for. No, I will not give it all away! It's up to *you* to read the book.... *why I did all this in the first place!* Suffice to say there will be dungeons and dragons and evil beings....*I lied....no dungeons or dragons...pity.*

Let us begin. *(I've always wanted to start a story this way).*

Prologue

It was a late April night on the good ship Whydah, now known as the pirate ship Whydah under the captainship of Sam Bellamy; "Black" Sam Bellamy as his victims knew him.

Sam couldn't sleep. It had been a long day and long evening fighting with his crew. Thinking about it all, he shook his head. The captain and some of the crew on his last capture, the Mary Anne, refused to help him pilot through these treacherous waters on his way home. He was forced to arrest them and put some of his own crew in charge.

Good riddance to them, anyway, he thought to himself. Recently, his crew had been nothing but trouble, if not drunk. *Such a superstitious lot*, he thought, and then, aloud, "Damn the Articles!" Being the captain of a pirate ship wasn't as easy as he once thought it to be.

Yes, the Pirate Articles, probably one of the most important and respected pieces of pirate law that existed. The Articles were drawn up at the beginning of any pirate voyage by the crew. It set down all the laws that the entire crew must follow from the captain on down, including punishful acts, and most importantly, how treasure was to be divided. If not all involved were not in agreement and he, as captain, refused to sign it, the voyage was finished before it began. The Articles were an extremely civilized document in a very uncivilized world that the crew took very seriously.

As Sam had found out early on, the captain of a pirate ship served at the will of the crew and the Articles; a contract the crew could use to vote Sam out of "offfice" if he didn't abide by them or win them enough booty.

Originally, Sam Bellamy was the son of a family that ran a major rope making business, supplying rigging for the area shipping. It was a hard, boring job and Sam had enough of the family business, He had been attracted to the stories of Spanish shipwrecks and piles of gold and was smitten withn the idea of striking it rich.

The first vessel he served on left him beaten, brutalized and determined to have a ship of his own. Beginning then as a privateer, a legal form of piracy, he, his ship and crew went in searchh of the lost gold.

When that didn't work out, the crew exercised their rights under the Articles to head into a more lucrative trade: piracy. Under the Articles, Sam had little choice. Anyway, he hadn't made any money by doing everything legally.

So, here he was now, a fully laden Whydah..dangerously overladen, a second ship he had recently raided, their crew in chains and some of his own crew with very bad attitudes.

Sam sighed. He really didn't need to be on watch during these early morning, darkest hours but this was a most trecherous stretch of water. He was unsettled with the prospects of an edgy, superstitious crew...and now, this damned fog.

Earlier, one of the most troublesome of his crew, who Sam felt he should have fed to the sharks long ago, had the rest of them worked up with pronouncements of gloom and doom; disaster waqs waiting for them.

The only disaster Sam was worried about was this fool turning the crew against him. He needed them to be sharp and on their guard in these terrible waters off the Cape. His ship was wallowing like a pig in the unsettled waters.

Home! It woiuld be so good to get home, again. Free from this crew. Free from piracy and back to the love of his life, Mariah Hallett, "Goody" to her few friends.

He had abruptly left her on his quest for gold, promising to secure a future for them both. He was anxious to get back to her. He could imagine her watching each day and night along these cliffs for signs of his return. Yes... gfood to get home and away from this lot.

God, the Whydah was wallowing like a pig for certain... and this damned fog was the thickest he had seen, especially this time of year. Knowing these waters well, he was troubled by the fog, the oppressive, warm air and the dead calm.

Danger signs for sure. It was late April and any form of ungodly weather was possible. He was on his guard. In the dark and fog he had lost sight of the Mary Anne but that meant little. His crew could handle the ship and its cargo of madiera wine.

The wind came up; a whisper at first but rapidly growing in strength as the temperature began to drop. Out of nowhere, the Whydah's bell began to sound furiously on it's own. From somewshere on board, the troublemaker began to yell: "See? Told ya! We's doomed. Hear the bell? It be our deathknell. Doomed, I tell ya, doomed!"

Out of nwhere, the wind suddenly roared out of the Northeast, the worst possible place for hard weather this time of year.

Sam cried out, "A Nor'Easter, boys! Batten down and pull the sails. Work for yer miserable lives!"

Sam hung on for dear life as the ship heeled over under the strain of the wind....now the roaring of the waves signaling the approaching shore. All out of nowhere. He was thinking of Mariah, hoping she was nowhere near the perilous cliffs. Later for that. He had ships to save... and so close to home....

While he was trying to save the Whydah, little did he know that Marlah *was* on the cliffs, where she was most nights while waiting for Sam's return. The are was known by locals as Lucifer's Land, an area so inhospitable, where outcasts and undesirables were banished to live or die by the miserable, narrow-minded, God spouting townspeople. She stood there in the fog and wind, heard the wild tolling of a ship bell, felt the wind turn violent, going from a whisper to roaring fury. She thought she could hear a voice yelling....far below....the wind was tearing at her clothes....

CHAPTER 1

Change is.....

Inevitable?

He woke with a sudden jolt. Where was he? *Oh, crap! I'm blind*, he thought as he broke out in a cold sweat. *Where am I?* His thoughts immediately went back to a mountain top incident years earlier. Then he realized shamefully, *Oh! It's the pillow over my face.* He might have laughed, remembering where he was. It had been another in a very long line of bad nights. Looking back almost 2 years, after the Opus 133 fiasco, the nightmares had become relentless. Terrible dreams. An evil villai.... *BEETROOT!* Long gone but not forgotten. All the death and destruction. The loss of his best friend, Tadpole; more like a brother, really. The turmoil. The notariety. The Nazis! Nazis? In this day and age?

Well, it *was* West Milford, N.J....and the surrounding areas all dancing to the tune of historical weirdness. Another reason for the continuing nightmares, also dancing maliciously through his brain when he should have been sleeping. Enough was enough. Change was coming.

Change was good, wasn't it? Lester and Elizabeth both had spent their entire lives in the Garden State. It was time, wasn't it? Damned straight, it was! Far too many memories here and too many of *them*, bad ones.

Just then, Elizabeth walked in.

"Lester! I heard youi screaming again. Another bad dream?" She looked at him with concern in her eyes.

"Here, I thought I'd let you get some sleep. I was wide awake and you get so little sleep these days..." nShe trailed off, looking at the drawn look on Lester's face. It had been so long for her husband, every night a constant battle with the demons from two years ago. She still cursed the day he found that damned violin at the flea market. She turned to look at the strange lamp it had become, thinking, *"Well! That's one thing that won't be going with us!"*

"Lester, since you're awake, you'd better get up. We have to meet with the realtor this morning."

He looked with interest as he remembered.

"Oh? She has some prospects on the house? Do we have to leave for a showing?"

"No, Les....sadly, not yet. It's probably that she wants us to lower the price...again."

"Again?"

"Again."

Lester sighed. They just couldn't get rid of the thing. It was a wonderful house and had been for almost forty years. Now? Too many bad things went on around here and it was time for a change. His hands began to shake but he noticed and clenched his fists to stop them.

"Well, let's get moving then. Time's wasting and we have money to lose."

No time to lose, Elizabeth thought to herself. As far as she was concerned, they nhad taken far too much time. They needed to get out of here! Ever since the fiasco with the damned Beethoven piece,133, their lives had been in complete turmoil.

Oh, yes, the notariety, the interviews, the news articles were intriguing for a time and they faded pretty quickly as old news. *That* wasn't the problem. *Lester* was the problem. Whatever had happened to him while she was away at the conference had scarred him, seemingly for life. Bad dreams. *Terrible* dreams. Lack of sleep.

He was still blaming himself for Tadpole's death. Granted, Tadpole wasn't *her* favorite person. He and Lester; the two of them always found ways to stir up trouble. Lester was no angel and was very good at starting his own mischief but add someone like Tadpole to the mix....like two kids finding new ways to throw rocks at a hornet nest.

Now, whatever she thought of him, Tadpole was dead and her husband blamed himself. As far as *she* was concerned, if she hadn't arrived home when she did and found Les with that evil, old bitch Karlson, *she* would have been the one in mourning for her husband....ther idiot! If it wasn't one ofther things she loved about him, much to her frustration, at times.

They had to get away from this town, theirt home for so many years. Maybe by moving on, Les could escape the pain and guilt. Oh, they'd miss therir friends, like their neighbor, Carolyn, and a few otherrs who were close but there wasn't much else to keep them here these days. The neighborhood had changed. It was no longer a warm, welcoming community where everyone knew everyone else *and* their business, too.

Now? No one seemed to care about anything outside their own home, job and kids.

Thank God they had discovered Cape Cod so many years ago. They had gone there on a whim one summer to spend a few days, never realizing they would find the place they truly belonged. Wellfleet.

Yes, the people could be a bit....thorny, until they got to know you; even if you were "washashores" and from New Jersey, to boot. The "Jersey" part could be a stumbling block around there. The town? It was as if they had passed back to a simpler time; real, honest.....and so rich in history. The town hadn't changed much in over one hundred fifty years. Neither had the long-time residents. Elizabeth felt comforted by all of this.

She and Les immediately felt they belonged here, something they hadn't felt in New Jersey for some years. Their home state may have felt a bit like this when they were both kids, spending weeks "goin' down the shore" in the summer, but that had changed over the decades, mutating into something that wasn't as welcoming as it once was.

Yes, it was time to move on....for both of them. There was peace to be found on the Cape as well as a wealth of things to do.

In Lester's words:

Hi! I guess it's time for you to hear from me, again. Who? Me ...Lester. Oh, remember now? The guy from Opus? The "Door" thing? You do? You don't? Whatever. In the way of bigger things, it doesn't matter. You're here now, reading, so that's all that matters.

Yeah, it's been two tough years; for me and for my wife, Elizabeth. I never wanted all this to fall on her shoulders. That stupid treasure hunt for that ridiculous piece of Beethovern fluff. *That* was a journey I wish I *never* went on...or involved her....or Tadpole...anyone else, for that matter. Too late now.

Oh, yeah. We all have nightmares about it but, at least we're alive....more than I can say for poor Tad....

At night, I still picture us climbing down from Odin's Mountain, treasure in hand. "Top of the world, Ma!" Yeah, right. Then the shotgun blast. The big, empty space that suddenly appeared in Tadpoles chest. The surprised look of shock on his face as he died; the blood.

I relive it each and every night. Can't get rid of it. Won't leave me in peace. *Nothing* here in town seems to leave me in peace any more. Far too many memories. All my fault. All my fault.

Oh, I took Elizabeth's advice and went to a shrink to see what help I could get. What did I get in return? A lighter wallet, that's what. Pills that made me stupid. Platitudes about PTSD.....I'll get over it, eventually...stop blaming myself....blah, blah.....blah.

I have to admit, though, all that crap seemed to help a bit. I actually thought I was climbing out of the pit I dug myself. Then, one night....I didn't just have a nightmare about it. Tadpole came to me....no, not part of the dream. I swear. He showed up *in* my room....and not just the one time. Every night after.

We talked....well, he did most of the talking. I laid in bed looking through the hole in his chest to the mirror across the bedroom, seeing his reflection...with me looking through to the mirror, looking....

"Mostly", what he used to call me,Tadpole smiled, "Don't blame yourself. Hey! I went along for the ride. I knew what I was getting into. It was exciting, that walkabout....wouldn't have missed it for the world. Too bad that bitch shot me....*her* fault, not *yours*. Some wild ride, huh?" Each night we talked. More and more, about the adventure, how he was dead but didn't feel too bad about it....another kind of walkabout adventure.

Well, you can imagine I didn't take all *that* too well. Did i mention this new development to my wife? Hell, no! This was something I had to handle myself. I did some reasearch on the QT and when she was out doing stuffr, I went to see a psychic. Yeah, that's right. One of *those* veggie-eating, new age quacks. But I'll tell ya, it was enlightening in ways I never imagined. The conversation went something like this:

"Lester Worthy. After talking to you, I not only feel a vibe, but I believe I have some insight into what's happening to you. You come from a very Irish background, correct?"

"Yes, as I've mentioned...a big Irish family....and?"

"Bear with me, please. According to your family history, iin each generation there seems to have been a person who was....oh, let's call it sensitive...with psychic talents."

"Yeah, my grandmother and then her daughter both had, as they put it, *the sight*."

"Exactly! No, in most cases, especially in these old world families, the *gift* is passed on to a female member of the family but since all members of your family are dead, *you* are the last of the line. Sorry to say, I think the gift fell on your shoulders."

"Bummer! How do I get rid of it? I don't want it! Lady, I see and talk to people....*dead* people. *They* talk to me. I can do without this....gift. My life is complicated enough."

"Yes, I've heard about your fascinating story. Read about it, too. You know, it's really a blessing that you have been able to talk to your old friend, Tadpole."

"I wouldn't call it a gift. I want *it* gone. *He* is gone and I want him to *remain* gone, too."

"To put it bluntly? Until he's done with you....fat chance."

And so the conversation went. I never told Elizabeth about it, either. Why make her more concerned than she already was? It was then I got the idea that maybe...if we moved away from this "ground zero" of disaster, things would calm down and we could live a normal life. *That* is how it all began.

Like many, I had become fed up with the state for many years and after sixty four of them, whether or not all of this craziness had happened, sixty four years in one place was enough. It was time to blow this burg.

Soooo, we did some major work and finally put the homestead on the market. We were looking forward to a new start up north in Yankee Land. We were going to miss our few close firends, especially Carolyn, the only person on our street who still mattered,(or wasn't killed off).

"I know she was upset with our plans to leave but she knew she was always welcome wherever we were.

A final blessing? Where we were headed, our land had no grass, hence, no lawnmower! After my last adventure, I hoped *never* to see another lawnmower as long as I lived! (refer to book two). The night before the "big moving day", sleep came easily for both of us. We were exhausted. I figured that maybe....just *maybe* it would be a peaceful one.

Wrong! No Tadpole holding a conversation this time but I seemed to be branching out.

First, there was this black cat that came to me. "Meow, meow, ****ing meow", he said. I never heard a cat say "****ing meow" before, so this got my dream-attention. Before I could talk with this foul mouthed feline, it left my restless sleep and was replaced by a man and woman. Both were dressed in colonial era clothing which shifted over to modern clothes as their mouths were silently moving. As usual, I woke up screaming. Oh, joy. What next?"

Well, as things always seem to happen, once the Worthy's had made their decision, things began to move, both slowly and rapidly. Selling the homestead of all these years seemed like an easy proposition but it was dragging on, taking way too much time as far as the were concerned.

Growing impatient, we said our goodbyes to Carolyn and friends, gave a hearty wave "goodbye" to New Jersey and were on our way, never looking back.

On their way down the street for a final time, Lester saw his obnoxious neighbor, Ahab, roaring around on his newest "uber-mower". Good riddance to *that* as well.
It was off to Wellfleet, Massachusetts and Cape Cod. In one of Lester's unsettled nights, he also heard whispered, the name, *Pirate's Cove*. As far as he knew there *was* no such town on the Cape. Oh, well, another bad dream...forget it. Off to a new life.

Leaving New Jersey was no biggie. Sure, we had spent our entire lives in the Garden State but it wasn't as if there was an invisible barrier keeping us here.

An immense sense of relief? Yes! No more mega- traffic. No more nasty drivers....flashing high beam headlights, blaring car horns, extended middle fingers, extended weapons or foul language; the usual terms of endearment from caring, New Jersey drivers extended to one and all.

Crosiing the "Crapanzee Bridge" was another milestone. Condemned many years befire, it was always comforting to make it across without it bouncing off the Hudson River. Maybe some other time.

Connecticut, the "Reconstruction State", with its multitude of "fine print" warnings reminding you it was hazardous to be driving on these roads and anything that happened to you while on them, was your *own* fault, all passed slowly....way too sloooooowly.

Getting into Rhode Island signalled that this was getting real. The town names got very interesting and we had no idea we were in Wyoming. Funny, that. Once out of Providence, and as long as "providence" didn't intervene with construction or accidents, we waved to the "Big, Blue Bug",*(really? How many cities celebrate a giant ,blue roach?)* and turned towards Cape Cod.

The town names became even more historical and, as we drew closer to our new home, the traffic and blood pressure lowered considerably....except when people began driving in a "Massachusetts frame of mind". Now? We understood where the term, "Massholes" came from. Oh, well. Different from the Garden State, *that's* for sure.

Once over the final bridge and canal, we felt like we were back in the "Cradle of American Civilization." Change was *good*. We were heading to our new home in Wellfleet! All would be well. All would be good. So we thought.

CHAPTER 2

A Rare Moment of Clarity

Author's note(about time, too).

So far in this book, you've been getting the story from all directions. I, as the author, am narrating this tale about Lester Worthy but, every once in a while, I'll want you to read Lester's own words.

Now, how can I do this? Isn't Lester a figment of my own imagination? Not true, not true. Lester and I share some similar roots. We both grew up in a former "Garden State". He became a teacher, as did I. He married an Elizabeth, while *I* married a Betti. O.K., so we *all* moved to Wellfleet, although somewhere in Lester's mind, Wellfleet would become a *Pirate's Cove*. Confusing....for now.

One morning, here in town, I found a 55 gallon recycling bag labelled, *Pirate's Cove*, left on my doorstep. Really a scruffy, nearly useless thing but filled with a treasure to me, or garbage for anyone else, I guess.

In it was the diary of the *missing* or maybe, *final* times of Lester Worthy. I mean, who really knows? I can only pass on what I found and have read. *That* was *not* an easy job! Cataloging the mess was a time-consuming frustration for yours truly.

The man wrote on anything he could find; scraps of paper, drift wood, old animal hides from roadkill. *(Really? Give me a break, Lester)*. Some text was written in pencil. Others in crayon. Some carved and some written on a concoction of berry juice and God-knows-what!

All I can figure is that he used whatever he could find to document this, his journey. My wife, Betti, made me store the "manuscript", and I use the term loosely, in a storage shed. It stank. Horribly. Thanks, a lot, Lester. I guess I should thank him for writing/carving.scrawling page numbers on each one, so the job wasn't impossible, only....odious. I've never read a story while wearing rubber gloves before. Again? Thanks a lot, Lester.

So, to get back to the "clarification" stage of the tale, I will be narrating the overall tale while, every now and then, I will leave Lester's actual....words for you to contemplate and add, at times, my own comments as your "humble" author to help sort things out. Oh, trust me. This tale wraps around your brain like a coiled spring, getting twisted so tight until....boiiiiing! Your credibility snaps. I know *mine* did. Damn you, Lester!

Getting back to the story

The trip north was rife with thoughts of loss, friends, the future...it all danced through the mind when you were making a drastic change in your life. Lester and Elizabeth were no exceptions. While Lester drove, Elizabeth looked out the window at the scenery passing by. Their two cats, Shadow and Critter, either slept, complained or watched the scenery as well. When he glanced over, he could guess the many conflicting thoughts that went through his wife's mind. They probably weren't much different from his own. The cats? Who knew?

Except, Elizabeth was also hoping against hope that her husband would finally stop torturing himself over the New Jersey fiasco. She was deeply worried about his health and sanity. He brooded so much about the death of his old friend. All *she* thought about was that old *bitch*, "Addie" and her damned shotgun. Oh, well. Soon, she was taking over the driving. She looked over at the two cats, who were presently sleeping peacefully. *If only Lester could do the same.*

She took over the helm, relieved to see Lester finally dozing off next to the cats. *This has to be a good thing*, she thought. *Maybe now, the heaqling can begin.*

First, the cat came to Lester in his dreams. "Yowl, meow, meow, ****ing MEOW! He thought, *really, cat? Such language from a cat? You from Jersey or something?*

"****ING, YOWL! JERK!"
Huh, thought Lester.
Don't mind the cat, much. He don't mean nuthin' by it.
Suddenly., here was a rather tall, dark haired gent standing next to the cat. Dark hair, weather-beaten complexion of someone long in the elements,

Old, odd clothing. No, wait! The clothing kept changing....old...modern, old, modern.

You be goin' to Pirate's Cove, that be th' right o' it? To make yer homestead.

It was a simple statement of fact, not conjecture. In his dream, Lester just listened.

Oh, we goin' t' be grand friends there. ARRRRRRRR!

Arrr? Lester thought back at the stranger.

Considering.....what?

Arrrrr, we be talkn' later, we will. Don' mind th' cat. He talk big, sometime.

Lester woke up with a start that made Elizabeth suddenly look over to him.

"You O.K., Lester? Everything alright?"

He sighed and stretched.

"Yeah, Liz, just woke up. Not used to getting much sleep. Big surprise. All good. It's all good." *Or was it*, he thought?

A pirate? Really? Now my dreams include pirates? Lester tried to look calm for Elizabeth as he sat there, anything but calm. The scenery whipped by on Rt.95 as he contemplated his sanity. *And that damned, foul-mouthed, talking cat....what was that all about?* He looked over at his two, adorable, sleeping felines perched next to him.

He looked out the windshield as if he was looking into his future. E*nough of this. Things are going to be different for us. A new life. No more angst. It's the quiet life for us both when we get to Pirate's Cove....no, wait a minute....Wellfleet.* So he thought.

They rounded the exit ramp in Providence that led away from their former life and towards the Cape on Rt. 195. As always, when they passed the sign reading, "Welcome to Massachusetts", they *all* breathed sighs of relief. Blood pressures went down. Tensions eased. Even the cats began to stretch and purr. Life began to ease. In two hours they would be at their new home.

Taunton, Fall River, (40 whacks and all), New Bedford, (visions of Ahab), and finally, turning towards the famous Cape bridges, Bourne and Sagamore..Lester hated those bridges as he hated heights but, over time, he had come to an uneasy truce with his dislike. It was his way to get home, so he learned to deal with them.

Crossing the Bourne. he watched the canal from the corner of his eye. Impressive, but God, he hated driving this bridge. Finally! Onto the Cape, proper. We had become "used" to this unique highway, Rt. 6, for many years. Now? Our main drag. Safely through "Suicide Alley",next the damned rotary, (why do they still tolerate these things?). Through Eastham, next stop, Wellfleet and home! Maybe now, no ore bad dreams, No Tadpole, pirates or foul-mouthed ghost cats. Farewell, New Jersey! Hello, Cape Cod!

Elizabeth sat in the passenger seat looking out the window. She was looking forward to their new home. She loved the Outer Cape. She loved Wellfleet, tolo. This was going to be an adventure.

CHAPTER 3

Wellfleet/Pirate's Cove?

I didn't get what all this *Pirate's Cove* stuff was all about. We were going to live in Wellfleet. It is a very historic town. steeped in the history of this country, one of the reasons we love it. For us as artists, it also has the reputation as *the* gallery town. It may be small, with only two main drags but it is chock-full of galleries and interesting, intimate stores that are so much better than the "big box" variety in the cities. Restaurants, breakfast nooks, bars, Mom&Pop stores and lot's of local color. There's the tourists, (tolerated, mostly), the washashores, (like us but tolerated a bit more unless you're from NJ, then you are watched quietly but with suspicion) and the locals, most of whom are shell or shell fisherfolk and store owners.

In the winter, it's basically the locals who hang around and even then, it's divided into those who have enough money and *can* escape the Cape winters, those who are stuck here or those who are crazy enough to enjoy the peace, quiet and beauty. Guess where Elizabeth and I fit in?

We've had several peaceful, enjoyable days and nights getting fully settled. For those nights, there have been *no* spectral visitors, thank you. Restful sleep can be wonderful. This particular cold, wet morning, we decided to head into town for breakfast at the one small diner open this time of year.

As we stepped inside, shaking off our coats, locals looked up suspiciously or curiously and went right back to their morning papers. Another town tradition. One person would buy a paper and, after reading it, leave it for the next patron.

Music was blaring from a radio at the bar.

"You're listening to station WPDQ, Waaaay Outer Cape Radio! I'm your morning show host, March Maxtor! You can call me March Madness. ARRRRRRR! Your Cape pirate, playing the finest in pirate, local music! All the music that fits, we play! And here's a cut from our own, punk-bluegrass group, DeadBass, called, "If you don't love us, walk east. Keep goin', keep goin".

As heavy metal banjo came blasting in a tortured blaze of sound, we sat at a quiet table and waited for a waitress to appear.

While waiting, Lester and Elizabeth sat taking it all in. The locals. The warmth of the place. The absolutely miserable weather outside. It all seemed so.....normal and relaxing; comfortably laid back in it's normalcy.... except for the music.

Lester was riding high, happy in the relief of getting a few nights uninterrupted sleep with no.....visitors. He was enjoying breakfast out with his wife, watching everything, listening to all the conversations going on around them. To his left, he heard.....

"Yuh, yuh can always tell the time of day to the second. Yuh don't need no watch, daylight, nuthin. If ol' Wally, the town drunk is headin' towards the Minesweepuh Bar, it's mohnin'. If'n he's headin' back north, it's dinnah time." Eyuhs, all around in agreement.

Lester was almost gleeful in his enjoyment, listening to these conversations. On his other side, he started seriously listening to a small group of shellfishers who were having their morning"coffee and tall tale" session. Lester started to take some notes on his napkin. Elizabeth looked on, a bit amused.

"What are you doing, Les? You seem miles away."

"Shhhh, Liz. I'm taking some notes. This is priceless."

What Lester wrote down went a bit like this:

"Yuh know ol' Larry?"

"What abou 'im?"

"Yuh heard he lost his ystuh grant license? Damned shellfish wahdens."

"But Larry was poaching on someone else's grant, wasn't he?"

"Yeah. but that ain't how ol' Larry see's it. Says he's goan get his license back an when he does, if it takes 'im till; he dies, he's a-goin tuh get back at tha' wahden an the town fuh all the grief. He says....when he dies, it'll be in his will fuh his ashes tuh be dumped in the oystuh beds."

"Damn! Prob'ly kill all the damn oystuhs!"

"Hell, all o' Larry gotta do be piss on th beds....prob'ly kill the whole damn bay!"

Everyone had a chuckle and the stories continued.

"Hey! Yuh heah about Johnnie and his guhlfrien', Matilda?"

Questions and nods all around.

"They's goin' up front o' hahdass judge Narragansett." The local leaned fohwahd...forward and lowered his voice.

"They was 'rested ovuh in Wellfleet the othuh mohnin'. Seems ol' Johnnie was drivin' with no plates on his truck. Claimed they rotted off when he got pulled uvuh. Fact is, he nevuh had none. Then the cop found he had no license...no insurance, too."

"Yuh's" all around the table....and a few knowing smiles.

"Then, the cop saw thuh lobstuh pots in thuh back....all illegal, too....buckets of poached lobstuhs as well. I tell yuh, the cop, he weren't no way happy 'bout all that. Top it off, gave Johnnie tickets fuh speedin' an' runnin' thuh only damn stoplaht in thuh 'Fleet."
More laughter.

"That weren't enough, thuh cop was a gonna 'rest Johnnie until his girlfrien' Tilda jumped outa thuh an' beat thuh crap outa thuh cop. By thuh time all was said an' done, thy both were 'rested and dragged off. Cop none too happy, neither."

All around the table, laughter broke out and sniffling, too. One guy, faking tears, sniffled....

"Makes a damn 'Fleetlan proud, don' yuh think?"

"Eyuhs" all around the table. Lester sat there holding his laughter in. All Elizabeth could do was say, "What? What? Lester, I don't get it. What's going on?"

"Oh, Liz. Nothing....nothing." Wiping his eyes, "I'm really going to enjoy living here."

At that, their breakfast arrived. Lester glanced past Elizabeth to the next table. He drew a quick gasp. There sat....a pirate.....1600's dress, long, black hair, tri-corner hat, beard. He smiled and waved to Lester. Real? Maybe? But why...until a young woman in colonial dress appeared next to him. Then, suddenly, they both faded.

Lester sat, fork of food halfway to his open mouth, staring, in shock.

"Lester? What is it? You look like...," She stopped before she finished....*you've seen a ghost.*

"Nothing, Liz. It's nothing. Just a bit of gas...too much coffee and hot sauce. I'm O.K.."

Then Lester felt something rub against his legs. *A cat? Not Liz.* He was afraid to look under the table. *What the Hell is going on here*, he thought, *at least if it's a cat, it's not cursing at me...*

"Hey, Lester, we're done. If we stay any longer, you'll only drink more coffee. Let's go on home."

"Yeah, good idea." He smiled to his wife and got up, looking around....peering under the table. *No cat....no pirate...no girl, either...just a few locals giving me the stinkeye.*

"Les, lose something?"

"Nah, let's go. Good breakfast, though"......(looking at ther disapproving locals and smiling). "Good company, too."

As they got up to leave, March Madness came blaring back on the radio.

"And now, everyone's favorite local punk ukelele band, *The One Chords*, doing their popular, "One Chord Rant". The song blasted throughout ther room.

"We know one chord. We play it well.(play it, play it, play it) We fake the rest. We do it well.(We fake it, fake it, fake it). We fake it good. We do it well. If you don't like it, go to Hell! (go to, go to, go to.....)"

Lester thought as they left, ..*cool radio station....gonna like it 'round here.....****ing ghosts leave me alone, that is.*

They walked up the main drag in town, past the quaint stores, shops and galleries. Lester stopped abruptly, hearing,

A sheep? He thought....*no, a goat....definitely a goat....wtf?*

"Les, what is it?"

"Did you hear that?"

"What? The dog barking? Why?"

"Nothing. Daydreaming, that's all." *I hope.*

CHAPTER 4

Meet the new Life.... Same As The Old Life

(not)

Another, annoying author's note

Yeah, me again, referring back to what I like to call the "Lester Manuscript" or "Manuscrap", depending if I'm downwind of the bag. I mean, really? What I have to do to bring this story to light.

At this point, Lester still finds himself in the dark about what's going on. On one hand, he's left the stress of his old life behind. He and Elizabeth love the town of Wellfleet

It was bad enough that the dreams began again but now? Seeing a pirate-like person, a woman in a shawl and a cat with questionable vocabulary, all appear out of nowhere was beginning to shake the man up. Poor Elizabeth was starting to seriously worry about her husband's sanity or health but she was willing to "wait things out a bit" and let everything settle. Her dear husband *was*, after all, a musician...and that particular species of human had it's....eccentricities. She would wait....and watch.

If you haven't begun to guess who these apparitions are, you aren't familiar with Cape Cod lore. You'll figure it all out. *That* is your job, *not* mine. Anyway, *you're* the reader. *Your* home doesn't stink after Lord knows what all Worthy wrote on to give us this story. Back to the story while I go find the air freshener.

Over the next few weeks, things began to settle down for Lester and Elizabeth. While his dreams of pirates, ladies in period clothing and foul-mouthed cats still gave him nightly entertainment, at least, they no longer interfered with his days.

Life was settling down. Elizabeth was happy with their new lives, although the occasional nightmare, with Lester throwing wild punches and screaming at some miserable cat, made for lively nights . She felt there was hope this would all quiet down with time.

As artists,they began to develop their own individual skills and having a good time doing shows and meeting people.

They occasionally traveled back to that *other* state to visit and do shows but home was here. One couldn't live here without getting enfolded in the history and style of life on the Cape. You lived and breathed ther history of the place, all the time. And the people...
Ahhhh, the people, *not* the tourists, the locals. From what they discovered, the locals were basically warm, loving folk to a fault but were cautious concerning washashores. They took a *long* time accepting them as permanent parts of their lives. Once they did, you could tell. In the beginning, you were welcomed into their homes for whatever reason but, getting them to enter *your* home remined them of vampire stories where the creatures couldn't enter a home unless invited. When neighbors finally crossed the threshold into *your* home as guests, you could consider yourself truly accepted. Tourists? Not so much.

It really was a wonderful place to live. Lester and Elizabeth became wrapped up in becoming part of the community, practicing and exhibiting their art.

Lester, though, as back in New Jersey....there was a restlessness that oozed back into his every day existence. He needed to do something....*anything*...which translated into *getting out in the real world and doing music...stuff.*

Elizabeth accepted this about Lester. For years he had played out; socially, for fun, in country bar bands, clubs and basically whatever attracted him at the time. She knew it let off steam and eased the "frustrated musician" psyche of her husband, hoping , as well, this would ease the tension caused by the damned nightmares. She knew they were not only back, but getting worse, no matter what *he* said to the contrary.

Worse? Any music he was doing these days was "hermit-like" up in his studio "cave". He needed to get out and work with people; other musicians. Now, to figure out a way.

As these things happen, they were out to dinner one night and ran into a populkar, local bluegrass band. The "picker" in the band saw Lester "air-picking" along with him from the table; not showing off, unconsciously air finger picking on the table top.

On a break, he came over and sat down with them.

"Hi, theyuh". He pointed to Lester's hand. "You have to get out theyuh and get some playin' in. Ah can tell when a guy's been uhway from playin' too long."

Lester smiled sheepishly. "Kinda obvious, huh? Can't help it. The fingers start moving and itching to join in."

Elizabeth smiled and nodded.

"Well, I tell yuh. Two things. Every Thuhsday night theyuhs a music jam somewheah heah on ther Cape. Heuhs a phone numbuh tuh call. Also, Friday evenin's, theyuhs an Irish session ovuh at an Inn in Orleans. You should go sit in."

"Hey! I appreciate the info. Who knows? Maybe I'll do just that. Thanks."

Lester did exactly that....went home and thought a *lot* about it. Maybe this was what he needed to return to some kind of "normal". Elizabeth had been right. More was going on with Lester besides simple, bad nightmares, which were becoming *very* real. The recurring characters, extended conversations, the pirate, the girl... that damned cat, too. And he'd remember everything the next morning and *that* wasn't normal.

If that wasn't bad enough, he was beginning to see those same apparitions wherever he went during the day. Not all the time, but they'd show up in the damnedest places, nothing he could hear but he could see the mouths moving and the gestures....*really* not normal. *Maybe there was a local psychic, medium, witch doctor up here he could talk to?* Time to find out.

Lester waited for times when Elizabeth was out meeting with gallery owners. After he went through every ad and phone book he could find, he found someone local who sounded interesting.

Persipone Painestaker ran a quiet little business on a secluded, dead end of Old Holler Road just outside of town. Her advertisement stated, "You may not know you have a problem but when I'm done, you will!"

It sounded good to Lester, so off he went one afternoon when he was alone. At all costs he didn't want to cause his wife any more worry with his "issues". Trying to keep any secretsa from her was difficult.

Now, Percy, as she was known to her friends, had some unusual techniques to get at your "inner" issues. She would listen patiently, asking questions, then sit and ponder while playing her banjo, getting in touch with the spirits in question. Really? Who would make this stuff up? Of course not....this is Cape Cod.

Lester finally arrived at Percy's home, amazed that such an impossible place to find could exist on such a narrow piece of land. After turning onto Old Holler Road, he became hopelessly lost in a warren of "not-so-recently-paved", (meaning during the time frame when paving actually was used in some part of the last century), roads and those that were merely sandpits *resembling* roads.

At any minute, Lester epected to hear bankos ringing out to the theme of Deliverance. Following the "simple" directions, *left at derelict, flourescent green VW bug*, and such, he finally, and gratefully found her home. Yes, he thought he detected the sound of a banjo.....

"Greetings, Mr. worthy, I'm so glad you could come. After hearing your concerns, I was sure I could help. Please, come in and call me Percy."

"Thank you....Percy. You live in quite an....unusual part of Wellfleet."

"Yes. I like the isolation here. It suits me. Please, come in and sit down. Tell me everything."

They sat while Lester unloaded the last few years on Persipone; the Opus 133 mess, the death of his friend, the nightmares, the visions of pirate, woman and black cat leading to their actual appearance to him.

"Well, you've given me a lot of information to work with, Lester. Give me time to absorb it all and....get in touch, so to speak."

At that, she picked up her 5 string banjo and began humming and strumming quietly to herself.

Lester was thinking, *Oh, please.....not Deliverance*, which is what she started to play. *Damn*. Then, suddenly, it took a quick turn to Foggy Mountain Breakdown, as Percy furiously picked up the pace of her playing. *Not that one, too...I hoped to never hear that one, again....oh, well....if it's the price I have to pay for some clarity, so be it.* Persipone abruptly stopped her playing.

Looking up and refocusing on Lester, she put down the banjo and said, "Lester, there's more going on here than you know. I need to go in depth for a bit. Bear with me."

After that, she picked up her ukelele from the wall.

Oh, God! Not a ukelele! Why? Always a ukelele? How bad is this?

Lester cringed to himself while he listened to her as she hummed and strummed to herself.

Please God, please....no! Not "Tiptoe Through ther Tulips"....anything but that!

No, it was only, "Somewhere Over the Rainbow." Percy was channelling her inner "Izzy". After some time, and torture to Lester, she again stopped and gently rehung her instrument hack on the wall, patting it, lovingly.

Really? Thought Lester.

Persipone sat back down, gave Lester a *very* serious look and sighed deeply.

"Lester, I have been in touch with the spirit world. Trust me, it took some doing. What's going on here is deeply entrenched in our Cape history and now, *you* are entangled in it, as well."

This got Lester's attention. "And this means....what, Percy?"

"Lester, the trauma and grief from the past....adventures and the depth of your brooding left you open to the spirit world. That, and ther fact that you already have a familial connection to that world; the line of seers in you mother's past...all this has finally opened the doors widely to your latent....*talents.*"

"Hey! Not my doing! Not my idea to become a spook-magnet!"

"Well, at the moment, not a lot you can do. Otherwise, deal with it."

Persipone leaned forward, gazing sternly into Lester's eyes.

"That's not all, either." She shook her head at Lester's confusion.

"You truly have no idea what you've unleashed, do you?"

At that, she began to explain in depth; the history. The *whos* and *whats* of what was happening to him.

"You already know some of the history and legends of this Cape, don't you? Especially those concerning the pirate ship, Whydah? Sam Bellamy? Mariah Hallett? If not, there are several books I suggest you read, one especially, by author Elizabeth Moisan, "Master of the Sweet Trade". Granted, it's fictional but fiction based on fact."

Lester gave Persipone a skeptical look.

"You're kidding me, right? A pirate ship? A pirate? ARRRRRRRR, and all that? This is the earth-shattering revelation you have for me?"

"Lester, you don't *really* understand. This Cape has a long, *long* history. Yes...and legend...and ghosts....*lot's* of ghosts. Whether or not they are real, many people *believe* and, because of that, I think many have become real....in *our* reality. Now? With the discovery of the actual pirate ship, Whydah, anything relates to it must be taken seriously."

Lester stood up, pushing back his chair.

"Ms. Painestaker, I came here looking for some help, maybe insights....closure, whatever to help make all this go away and let me get on with a peaceful life. *This?* This stupid story of pirates, women and ghosts? I'm not *that* gullible."

"Lester! Believe what you think about it. You're having dreams at night and visitations by day. There's a pirate.... and a woman with him..."

"Yeah? And don't forget a foul-mouthed, black cat that can speak!"

"I *told* you! Cape Cod is filled with legends., ghosts and realities. There is a famous, black cat ghost legend and it's from an Inn two towns away. The bad language? I have no idea where *that's* coming from."

"There are possibilities *here*; Sam Bellamy....Mariah Hallett....even the cat *and* remember *your* families psychic history. Don't take it lightly. The stories of your recent past and the stress....who knows what has been awakened in you. *Think* about it, *please*? And come back to me if you have *any* more questions. If I discover anything, I'll call you."

"Persipone Painestaker, thank you for your time and effort...and your music. Yeah, I'll think about it. *All* of it. Now? I've got to get back home before my wife finds me missing and panics. By the way? How do I get the f*** out of herer and back to civilization? Yeah, yeah, right turn at the VW bug....got it. Bye, for now.":

Off Lester went, snaking his way back through the torured roads leading back to the highway and home, hoping to be home before his wife, thinking....*pirates, ghost woman...that damned cat,**** this! I can never, never tell Elizabeth. She'll think Ive lost it for sure.*

He got back home minutes before his wife. He was just inside the door before she pulled in.

"Hi, Les. You're all dressed up? Where ya headed?"

"Nah, nowhere. I was going to gas up the car but decided it could wait. You caught me before I could change. Glad you're home, Liz."

And so, ended anotherr interesting, confusing, possibly *disturbing* day for the Worthys, newly of Wellfleet. Washashores they may be but they had become entangled in their new world in ways *one* didn't know and the *other* wouldn't even consider,.

Pleasant dreams, Lester. Hang in there, Elizabeth. It's going to be quite a ride.

CHAPTER 5

In Other Words

Author's note (again)

This whole, "Whydah, Bellamy, Hallett" thing....an interesting quirk here on Cape Cod. Up until they actually *found* the remains of the dread pirate ship, Whydah, I felt this was one of those touristy-legend-thingies to impress the visitors.

Now, as far as I can figure, nothing is clear concerning bad-ass-Bellamy or his true love, Mariah Hallett. History or legend? Who can tell? There *are* several great books written on the subject, the best being, in my estimation, "Master of the Sweet Trade", by Elizabeth Moisan. Good story.

Ghosts? Bah! Such stories abound here on the Cape, as many stories as grains of sand. "Humbug", I cry! Then, again, I'm going by what I absorb here from the locals and what I also absorb from the vile, disgusting Worthy manuscript! Back to the story......

It became harder for Lester to hide his growing problems from Elizabeth. The dreams, becoming more like reality, with Sam Bellamy, Mariah Hallett and even that damned cat...the goat, too, all showing up. Lester still didn't understand what the goat was all about but, at least, it didn't talk or curse like the cat did.

Elizabeth was used to the bad dreams by now. Lester worried she would draw a serious, "sanity line" for him if he began explaining the daytime visitations, silent though they might be. Watching mouths move, though as their bodies faded was disturbing at the best of times.

"I need a life", said Lester, talking to the wall.

"What was that, Les?". Elizabeth called from across the room.

"Nothing, Liz, nothing. Thinking of things I want to do....may get involved with the music, again."

She came over and hugged her husband.

"Well, it's about time, Les. Day after day, month after month. It's you, alone up in that studio like some deranged hermit. Playing everything....alone, talking to the walls, alone....the computer...

to whatever you talk to up there."

"Yeah, I know. I *know*. You're right....as always, Elizabeth. Hey! Would you mind if I checked out that punk bluegrass band, DeadBass?'

"Finally! About time!" Elizabeth smiled. "*Finally*! The hermit leaves his cave! *Please*, by all means. Don't ask to go, though. I have no interest to hear any band called DeadBass *or* punk bluegrass music. Go have fun. Give me a rest."

Author's note: Yeah, I know. You're getting annoyed with my interruptions. Get on with the story, already! Well, guess what? *This is* part of the story, too.

Lester Worthy, for all of that, was very organized. He *did* number everything in the "manuscrap"., whatever it was written on. The documentation of this tale is, disgusting as it may be, orderly, once you sort through it all and disinfect *everything*.

Every once in a long while, Lester must have come across some *real* writing paper, even if the writing tools were of questionable origin. During those times in the story, I got a clearer view into the mind of one Lester Worthy. When these pages come to light, dear readers, I plan to let you read his own words and follow the story through his own perspective. *This* is one of those chapters. So, say hello to the person behind it all....for the moment.

"Hi, there. It's me, Lester. I hope some day, someone reads all this and makes sense of it all. By the way? No, I'm not crazy! I don't *think* so, I mean...lot's of people have bad dreams, right? What gets me upset is that when you wake up after a night of....them....dreams, that is, you kind of remember little bits and pieces? Then, they all fade away leaving you frustrated trying to remember anything about them, right?

Me? I've been spending every....single....night....having discussions with a pirate, his girl friend, a black cat.... thatn talks....a *lot*...sometimes a damned goat....doesn't talk....what's with the goat, any way? The goat goes bahhhh, baaaaah, baaaaa....on and on.

I don't know which is worse, the cat or the goat. Never mind. I'm *not* crazy! By morning? I remember *all* of it. Everything!

That either means there's something wrong with me or the whole thing is real.....no! I'm *not* crazy!

At least, during the day, the cast of characters show up once in a while, hang around, look like they're talking....or baaaaah-ing and fade away, again. It's not like it was....me not getting any sleep or drinking waaaay, to much coffee. *That* would be crazed. I sleep like a rock. Really. *NOT*...crazy. No! No way!

Elizabeth was right to force me out of the house. Good for both of us. Just from the music angle, seeing other musicians and talking to people would give me a better perspective on living here on the Cape. I love the place. Great,(but different from New Jersey) people. Time to get out and have a life, again. Maybe that will give the ghosts the hint to take a hike.. Tonight, I'm off to the Minesweeper Pub to hear that punk, bluegrass band, DeadBass. Should be fun; seems like a nice bunch of guys.

Ahhhhh, the Minesweeper. If I hadn't spent all those deformative years playing backwoods country bars, I might have been intimidated...but in a different way. In the old days, it was NJ rednecks, bikers and wannabe country yahoos. Here? It was all local color, fisher-folk, bikers and the occasional, daring tourists....all exceot the last not *exactly* trusting unknown types invading their space. What the heck. I was here for the music and when DeadBass started their set, I was soon forgotten.

Speaking about forgotten, it was amazing. The music kicked in and all my memories of past times slammed back down hard. I had forgotten about the power of the music and of performing. Yeah, I was hooked again. Maybe....just maybe, it was time, as Elizabeth put it, to emerge from my cave. On a break, I talked with one of the band who remembered me from an earlier gig.

"Well! Back again. Did you check out those sessions I told you about? No? Too bad. You really should.

"I can tell a person who isn't comfortable sitting on *that* side of the table."

At that, he slipped me his card and wrote a phone number and address. "This is where this weeks session is going to be held. Give a call. Go. It's not that far away. You'll regret it if you don't go. Well, back to work!"

I planned to take him up on it. I hadn't felt this good or excited in a long time. I turned to grab my drink...and turned to face a certain pirate-type-ghost in the chair next to me.

Gloating at me, he smiled and took a slug from his ghostly mug of beer.

"See? Told ya it be the right move to make, didn't I?" He saw the shocked look on my face.

"What? Aye, I can talk. Ye expectin' an, ARRRRRR, Matey? Ya gettin' in th' swing o' things hereaaaaarrrr ya? That suit ye better? ARRRR?"
He laughed at that and shook his head.

"I be tellin' ya. Been 'round for lot's of years. I can sound any way I damn well please to talk. Dress as I wish, too. May be a ghostie but I learned things over time. You'd be amazed. You *will* be amazed as time goes on. ARRRR! We be mates, now. We be sailin' on th' same tide....so to speak. Arrrrr."

"You....you can talk?"
More laughter. He swigged the rest of his beer and faded, as did the laughter when he slammed down his mug. I looked around to see if anyone noticed....what?
Nothing, of course.

Everyone was listening to the blast of unusually loud and crude music....
"I play my ****ing banjo. Electrified to ****. You don't ****ing like it? Ya can go and ****ing ****!"
Absolutely...charming. Bet WPDQ plays *that* one a lot.

I stood up, a bit shakey but determined to show up at that next session, pirate interventions or not.

Thursday night came with great anticipation. Elizabeth was glad to get her pacing husband out of the house. I spent most of the day trying to decide what instrument(s) to bring. I figured, probably too many guitars...and my banjo playing was kinda rusty, enough to embarrass me. Fiddle? Not going there...Been too long and and I needed serious help getting my playing "perverted" from classical to wherever I was heading.

So! I took my "in your face", chrome dobro, an instrument that looked so good, it didn't matter *how* I played. Next, I chose my "old standby axe, my sax. No matter what, my old friend could play without my conscious thought, if need be and would still make me sound good. All decided.

"Go! Have fun. I won't lock you out." Liz gave me a big hug and shooed me off into the night.

Well! It was quite a night for making impressions. I tell you! Amazing stuff. Whever you looked. Whatever room in the host home, different groups of musicians were hanging, playing amazing music.

Yeah, I made my way from room to room. Dobro here, sax there. Both in the same room at times, somehow making it all fit. *DAMN!* Over in the corner, my old pirate buddy...dressed real piratey....smiling, tapping his foot... giving me a thumbs up...cheeky bastard. What could I do? Put my head back into the music and realized, from what I heard some people saying, I must have been playing some wild shit. (Told you about me and my sax.... never really needed me.)

I turned to one of those conversations when I took a breather. Two charming, (and tall) ladies who smiled and introduced themselves.

"Hi, I'm Viridian Bean and my friend, Cassandra Parkhouse. We're both fiddlers. We came tonight just to listen for as change. *Now,* who are *you* and *why* haven't we heard about you before tonight?"

"Ohhhh, I'm really nobody in particular....Les...Lester Worthy...but you can call me the "Phantom Musician", I guess."

At that, I saw old pirate Sam Bellamy seated in back of the two ladies, crack up at that, playing air...something... mouthing...*lame, boyo, lame...but funny as hell...go for it!*

Back to the ladies. "Uh, yes. My wife and I are new here to Wellfleet. Someone told me I should drop by and sit in. It would be worth my time."

"Well, as far as we're concerned, *you*, Mr. Lester Worthy, are a pleasant surprise. Come to more of these and stop being a phantom. Maybe next time, we'll join in, too."

At that, they got up and left. Sam, thankfully, was gone, too. Looking at my watch.....p*ast midnight. God! Where did the time go?* I told Elizabeth I was only stopping for a little while. She'll kill me! Thinking that, I figured, *well, I'm dead, any way, so maybe I'll have another drink and play a tiny bit more....and...*

Lester eventually left the session, his mind dancing with all the music, the chance to play with real people once again.. All the great people. The classy ladies, Viridian and Cassandra. Deemed like such great people.
Be nice to run into them again. Who knows? He put it all out of his mind and danced to the music in his head as he drove back to town, a smile on his face.

Elizabeth woke when he got home and was overjoyed to hear her husband had some *fun* for a change.. Maybe this was what he needed to climb out of the strange hole he dug for himself and for *them*. He did *not* mention a certain ghost named Sam.

Over the next weeks, Lester went to as many sessions as he could find. Lot's of music. Lot's of new faces. He hadn't seen either Viridian or Cassandra at any of the sessions, so they faded from his memory.

What became clear to Lester though, was an instant love fr Irish fiddle music.

While he himself was mostly Irish and had put up with all that came with it as a kid, especially aroind St. Patrick's Day, he had never gotten involved with the music. When a drunken family got *into it* on St. Pat's,it got a bit embarrassing. This was different. The music was fascinating.

Lester would come home after a session, look at his old fiddle, (the one in a single piece), thinking....

Ya know? It's about time I did something about this. He took the time and hunted down a promising fiddle teacher.
Big disappointment. *Big* mistake.

It was obvious after one lesson that he either already knew too much...or far less than the teacher wanted to deal with. Yes, Lester had classical training and a *major* music background. Also true, he had a "musical black hole" for the Irish fiddle.

As Elizabeth put it when he practiced, "Les, the cats have left the area. Your playing sounds like a cat being tortured or killed. They are not impressed. Neither am I. I wasn't aware a fiddle could make such sounds."

"Funny. I'll get bettert I know it. *You* know it. Just an uphill battle....been a long time since I did any fiddle playing."

"Well, Les? Me and the cats hope it happens soonest."

The lessons with that teacher didn't last. Abruptly, after a second lesson, she handed him a card.

"Lester, I think I've taken you as far as.....I can." (Which he translated to mean: as far as I can stand it.)

"Here is the name of another teacher I think will be far better for you. Get in touch with her." She quickly packed and left. Looking at the name, he saw: *Viridian Bean*.

When he called and saw her again for a first lesson, he thought, *are all female fiddlers so tall?* He hadn't remembered that fact from the jam sessions until she walked through the door.

"Hi. I'm Viridian. I remember *you*, Lester. Hard to forget when you played up such a storm at that session."

"Yeah, maybe....but....**you're** going to be my teacher? Look....sorry about how that sounded. I'm surprised, that's all. I wasn't expecting a teacher I actually knew. Kindfa odd, ya know? We're new here and I haven't *really* met anyone local....yet, here you are."

"Small world, huh?"

So, the two of them sat down to work. The first lesson, shakey but the second was much better. Better enough that Viridian stopped playing and stared at him.

"Lester, I'm not gonna take your money."

"Why? Not good enough? Damn! I knew I shouldn't have picked up this damned fiddle again. You have no idea the trouble this fiddle has...."

"No! No, Lester. Not that at all. After two lessons, I don't think I can teach you much. The improvement in only one week is, well....it reminds me you've played before and all you needed was to remember."

But I don't know any of this Irish stuff, Viridian. Help me."

"I don't think it's much of a problem How about this? Why don't we simply get together and play each week. Maybe, we can help each other and have fun at the same time. What do you say? Deal?"

"Deal."

So it began. Both Lester and Viridian *and* Elizabeth had found a new friend. Over the weeks and months, Lester and Viridian found that playing together created a magic neither had ever run into before with other players. A bond was formed. They not only challenged each other to play better, but as funny as it sounds, *things* happened while they played off each other, bouncing ideas back and forth. The music would take on a completely different life. The both talked to each other through their instruments in ways neither had heard before. Elizabeth and Viridian also found much in common. They, however, used actual words not notes.

As time passed, Lester and Elizabeth came to believe they had truly found a home here. Thanks to Viridian.... *maybe* life was getting better for the Worthys. Elizabeth breathed the first sigh of relief in a long, long time. Uh-huh.

CHAPTER 6

Wa-a-a-ay Outer Cape Radio

'This is your host, March Maxtor, comin' to you from WAAAAAAAAY Outer Cape Radio on WPDQ. We're *so* far outa the Cape, we're not even on *land* like tha*t other* P'Town station."

Ahhhh, yes. WPDQ radio. If there is an *alternative* to alternative radio, WPDQ is it. Known for playing music no other radio station would touch, WPDQ was.....*loved*, I gues you could honestly say, by local musicians who never got a chance to be heard anywhere else. In some cases, there was a very good reason for this but not always.

The station was located offshore in Cape Cod Bay, utilizing an old lightship they had salvaged, refloated and equipped, much to the dismay of ther other, land-locked stations that had to put up with rules, regulations and any or all local and county codes; business, music, ethics. Just about all of that was blatantly ignored by WPDQ. The other stations kept hoping for a really violent storm and sinking. A Viking funeral for WPDQ wouldn't be out of line either, as far as *they* were concerned.

Possibly the biggest, sharpest in their collective butt was Ms. March Maxtor. Nobody knew what the "March" was short for, if anything but on the air, she was known as March Madness. A louder, more grating, annoying pimple on the behind of sane, local radio broadcasters could not be found to exist.

"Yes, my waaaay outer friends, you're listening to my favorite show, "The Silkie and the Harpy". Since *I'm* the DJ, I *have* to like it! No, really! I *love* doing this show, playing for you the finest in music everyone else has tried and *failed* to have banned from Cape Cod radio. Well, maybe not the finest but surely the most fun to listen to, even if it's only once! I mean, even *I* have *some* taste.!"

The lady was, without a doubt, as annoying as the usic she played but, every once in a while, she *did* bring some valid musicians to the attention to the listening public. Her listeners loved her for that....though, even the Coasrt Guard thought about using WPDQ as a target.

"And now, fellow Outies and those living across the border in Truro and beyond....for your listening enjoyment....The Uni-Chords....formally known as the One Chords. Why? Who the **** knows? They just *are*! Here are ther Uni-Chords, our own punk, ukelele band, performing, "I Love to Make Your Ears Bleed!"

The Uni-Chords, formerly the One Chords, Dead-Bass, the heavy metal bluegrass band, Proudfoot Roachstomper,(singing God-only-knew-what, but enjoyed by the many hard of hearing) and many others mwho had "made it" on WPDQ in ways no sane musician had in the past. It was their "moment in the sun".... or shade....or dark...wrapped in brown paper packaging to protect the innocent, but *there*....doing their thing. Only on the Cape, I guess.

Who could have guessed that our own, humble (but psychotic), radio station would play such an important role in the story of the Worthy family and Viridian Bean? Only time, and the story line, would tell.

"And now, my rabid listeners! Coming up is a P'Town favorite! Proudfoot Roachstomper singing his country classic, "My Momma is a Cowboy!" But first, a word from one of our fine sponsors, Ms. Persipone Painestaker, the Painless Psychic....also available for weddings, bar mitsva parties and exorcism wine tastings. Now, back to Proudfoot!"

"Ohhhhhh, my Momma was a cowgirl, home, home on the range...
Then she came to Ol' P'Town, home, home of the strange....
Now, she's a He and a cowboy to boot...
She's still my Momma...Ahhhhhh don't give a hoot"....

Ah, yes....WPDQ, The Silkie and the Harpie Show. The motto? "Whatever fits, we play it. If it gives you fits, we play it more."

Authors note: The only thing more disgusting than organizing Lester Worthy's notes was listening to WPDQ.

At least I didn't need to wash my hands, just my ears. Way back then, you may ask? What does he mean? Patience. We'll get there eventually, dear reader, yes, we will. Eventually.

It is also interesting to note that in spite of Ms. Maxtor's popularity, no one actually knew her by that name or would recognize her in person. She never let herself be seen in conjunction with WPDQ. I couldn't blame her.

In real life, March Maxtor, AKA March Madness, led a quiet life, one May Potawatomi, an accomplished percussionist, also an outspoken "carnovegan". The carnovegans were omnivores whose platform was, "Hell! I'm hungry! I'll damn near eat anything!"

May, in her every day life, would sit in on music sessions, a welcomed player, who would scout out new, "talent challenged" prospects for her radio station. Yes, *her* radio station. May had saved her pennies, so to speak, over the years and quietly purchased the old lightship, "Leaky Toilet" and stealthily turned it into the minor juggernaut known as WPDQ, a Cape Cod Bay fixture *not* sorely missed these days. All this information wasx to be found in Lester's trash ba...journals. Now back to the story.....

"Yes! That was Proudfoot Roachstomper, performing his not-so-popular-in-the-real-world single, "My Momma is a Cowboy." And *now*, our own Charlie Darwin and the Evolution, performing their non-starter, "Cause I's Wicked". I have *no* idea what this song is about but the grammer is sooooo WPDQ, sooooooooo now, here it is!

"Cause I's wicked- I is.
I's mighty wicked.
Anyhow, I can't help it."

March turned away from the soundboard, getting up to stretch her legs. Holding her aching back, she did some bending exercises. She waved to her crew on the other side of the sound booth. They were the only people who really knew her....*and* her real name. One being her husband, Rolf, the station manager.

She loved her husband but wasn't thrilled being stuck with his last name....Potawatomi. *What kind of background did someone named Rolf Potawatomi come from?* She always wondered this and Rolf wasn't very forthcoming with clear answers.

She sighed and stretched some more. *So what?* She thought. *Listen to what I'm playing. I should question the name Potawatomi?*

March/May....whatever, both loved and hated the stuff she foisted on the listening public. Yes, some of it was good, evem great; music that was being ignored by the other local stations. Most of t? Crap. Hardly classified as music but, ohhhh so popular. Money kept rolling in on fund drives and from unusual sponsors, so who was she to question? She could live with the station motto: *We play anything that fits....ANYTHING!* It paid well enough.

She looked out a porthole towards the shoreline and the outline of buildings that defined her beloved Provincetown. *Yes*, she thought, *WPDQ was her baby. The show, The Silkie and the Harpy was as well.* She laughed every time people from the major Cape station yelled about it being a horrible knockoff of their popular Celtic show. *Too ****ing bad.*

She was looking forward to the next few days. Tonight, she was playing, (undercover, of course), at another Irish session. Who knew what lurked there to be discovered and brought to WPDQ? The next morning she was leading a group of Carnivegans in a march against a tofu bar recently opened in town. Again, she sighed as she turned back to the soundboard and her show. Charlie Darwin and the Evolution was ending it's rant. *Life was good.*

CHAPTER 7

Vermilion & Viridian

It would be unjust not to include more information concerning the two important women in this story, Elizabeth and Viridian. They both play important roles and would be bad form having them play second fiddle to a foul-mouthed-ghost cat.. Wouldn't it?

Elizabeth, as Lester's long-suffering wife, has quite a background. Once in a while called "Red", (but not more than once by anyone), has bright red hair that has aged well over the years, altrhough she doesn't think so. A very quiet, private person, she still has the heritage of a fiery, Italian temper. With a last name of Gambinocalimarimafiosa, there is no doubt. There is also little doubt that when married to Lester, Worthy was a far more comfortable name than Gambinocalimarimafioso.

The point? Oh, yes...the point....although quiet and even tempered, Heaven help anyone, (especially Lester), who manages to push the wrong buttons. It was all the "family values" embodied by her family; that and growing up in the late, great Garden State of New Jersey.. There is something in the way Italian, New Jersey families ingteract that can make one shudder. When the family got together for dinners, conversations were held at top volume with screaming matches and empty threats thrown back and forth across the inches separating them at the table.

Not Elizabeth, though. She was the quiet one....but she had no choice but to absorb the "finer" family traits. Mostly, they remained subdued. Let's paint Elizabeth "Vermilian" for the story's sake. (Much safer than "Red").

Now, Viridian has a much different story, growing up as an Iowa farm girl. Her family ran a successful farm until they got the bright idea to expand the business. Combining several farms, they grew tomatoes in one, wheat in another, mozzarella beasts (whatever *they* are) on another and pepperoni critters on the last. The idea was to create a one-stop pizza farm empire. Growing pizzas was not the smartest business move, although it sounded good at the time.....one of the reasons Iowa is *not* known for it's pizza.

Traumatized by it all, Viridian grew up hating tomatoes and spent many a dark night hiding from tomato dreams that sent her screaming to the mustard gods in her sleep. This was understandable and to make matters worse, the family started a mushroom farm as well. Mushrooms sent Viridian screaming to the lettuce gods in her dreams. So tragic.

Elizabeth was a well-travelled lady who experienced many areas of the country while growing up, sadly settling in New Jersey for an eternity until moving to Cape Cod and Wellfleet.

Viridian? She travelled to so many places around the country in her quest to escape tomatoes and mushrooms that they could have named towns after her in most of the fifty states, (which would have easily overtaken all the towns named after mills and mill fords....

Lester? It only figures that Lester went nowhere in his life, but that was Lester in a nutshell; boring. He *did* make one smart move, deciding to move to Cape Cod.

All in all, it was quite amazing that these three people came together as friends. The "twist" in the mix was Lester, who always managed to bring out the best and worst in people. The "est" was simply what Lester did. The "worst" was something he managed to elevate to an art form.

Elizabeth was the stabilizing influence for Lester. Viridian was also a quiet person but with the fatal flaw of being very, *very* willing to be led into mischief; musically speaking in this case. Lester? The nitro to her glycerine. Oh, it was an interesting combination and soooo important to this story.

Green & Red....Alive & Dead...

And so, the days progressed in Wellfleet....not yet quite the "silly season" with thousands of tourists underfoot; peaceful enough to actually *want* to stroll around town.

Viridian was walking down Main Street one day, taking in the sights. She absolutely loved the old buildings and the landscaping everyone seemed to cherish in the community. Oh, the flowers! She loved this time of year before *they* showed up. She enjoyed stopping in all the small stores to say *Hi* to everyone. She knew them all and they, her.

A daily stop was down by the harbor, not for anything in particular, just to take it all in, make friends and say hello to all the dog walkers. During the quiet moments, she thought about her new friendship with both Elizabeth and Lester. They looked to be great people. She was amazed by Elizabeth's art work and by Lester's almost insane devotion to his music.

She still wasn't too sure about getting sucked into working with him as a duo. At times, circling Lester was like entering the field of a musical black hole. Who knew where you would wind up if you got sucked in? Still....it was an interesting thought...the two of them working together. Lester seemed excited with the idea. Maybe she should....

Looking at her watch, she sighed. Lunch was almost over and she had to head back to work; one of the great perks of working in a small town. Nowhere in Wellfleet was more than a few minutes walk from anywhere else. Well, back to work. Such a lovely day.

At the same time, Elizabeth headed into town from another direction. It was such a lovely day and Lester was off doing whatever. She shook her head. For someone she knew so well, he was acting even more strangely and secretive than usual these days. She couldn't figure it out.

Retirement was supposed to be relaxing, wasn't it? Sure, they had their art business that kept them hopping but even that didn't where Lester's head was at recently.

That whole thing with the Beethoven piece...and that horrible Beetroot! She shuddered whenever she thought of that monster. Good riddance to him! And that horrible, Neo-Nazi neighbor. Elizabeth hoped that time, and getting totally away from West Milford, New Jersey would help snap Lester out of his funk.

The nightmares were pretty bad but, hey, she suffered a lot of stress after the Opus 133 mess, too. *She* was the one who wound up killing that miserable, old witch, not *him*. It wasn't always about Lester, was it? But...thinking about it....these days?

Maybe it *was* just that. She sighed again.

That was why she had to get out of the house and walk into town. Such a pretty, little town. Everything was so close you almost didn't need a car to get around. At least not before *they* began to show up. Yes, we were recently like *them*....tourists but Wellfleet had become our home and *they*....became the enemy....by default.

She loved all the well-tended buildings and gardens. She loved smelling all the wonderful flowers as she strolled from gallery to gallery, checking out which ones might be interested in their craft and art work. She also might find something so attractive that she couldn't avoid buying it. Elizabeth knew Lester felt the same.

Lester....oh, damn. Lester. What was going on with him? It was almost as if he was distracted by someone else talking to him when there was no one there. Maybe she'd have to find him some help, after all. She hoped not.

After leaving the last gallery, Elizabeth wandered her way down to the harbor. She sat for a few minutes then decided to walk arfound it for a bit, taking in the fresh, salt air and marvelling at how lucky they were to be living in such a gorgeous place. Wellfleet. It felt as if she were travelling back to another time and place. They both needed this little town.

She was happy they were beginning to make friends here. It wasn't always easy, what with the New Jersey attitude meeting the typical New England mistrust of "foreigners" from out of state. At that, Elizabeth thought about their new friend, Viridian. She liked her and was glad that Lester hit it off withn her as well. She would open up a whole world of local musicians for Lester to meet. He *desperately* needed to find other musicians to work with.

Viridian seemed just the person to drag him out of his cave-like studio into the real world....and Lester was actually beginning to talk about working with her as a music duo. Who knows? She .looked down at her watch. Wow! She was here for two hours. Time to get back home and see what her husband was up to.

It was a beautiful day and Lester ws tired of hanging around the house. Besides, he was driving Elizabeth crazy. The good news was that damned ghost of Sam Bellamy was off somewhere and leaving him alone. Also, he hadn't seen that damned cat in a few days. At least his two real cats didn't curse him out all the time. Who knew if they could see this ghost? He hoped not. What nasty habits could they pick up?

Lester hoped, *none*! They coukld get in enough trouble on their own. Oh, well, he sighed and strolled into town. Hey! *He hadn't even seen that damned goat, either... even if it wasn't there.* "Good!". He said aloud. "Things are looking up."

He didn't appreciate the thought that he might be going bat-shit-crazy. Even worse? He didn't like the thought that if he *wasn't* going bat-shit-crazy, these ghosts might *really* exist. Now *there* was something he didn't want to think about. "Enough!" He spoke out loudly enough to startle one of the early tourists who probably did think we *was* bat-shit-crazy.

Cool, Lester, be cool. All is well and gonna get even better as the day goes on....such a beautiful day. He loved Wellfleet as did Elizabeth. This was going to be good for them both. Lester loved the galleries, but even more? He loved the history that seemed to live and breathe all around him. This town hadn't changed all that much in the last hundred years or so.

If pirate ghosts *did* exist, *this* was the place to find them....just not around him or taking an undo interest in his life, thank you very much. Lester loved the buildings. He had seern pictures of the town from so long ago and nothing had really changed. Even the building that was badly tilted off-center and leaning in the old picture, was exactly the same today. It sort of made sense. If the "tilt" on a building worked, why change it?

To him, that *was* a powerful thing about Wellfleet; change wasn't necessary or necessarily a good thing. The history was important and the world needed more places like Wellfleet to keep things in perspective. The outside world moved too fast and it was a dangerous place out there.

He shuddered as he thought about that fiend, Beetroot... but...all that was behind him...*them*. He and Elizabeth had new lives here and he was damned surew going to try and make it better.

Thinking this, he cautiously looked back over his shoulder....just in case....nope... no ghosts. He made his way through town, thinking....thinking...and found himself down by the docks and the harbor. Looking around, he took in the panorama and thought again of the history. Maybe he'd sit for a bit and chill.

Looking at some of the fishing boats nheading out he thought about his new friend, Viridian, and his plans to start a new music duo. It was time. He hadn't worked with someone in years. Every time he did, it ended in a train wreck and him swearing never, *never* to work with another musician again. But now, there was Viridian.

Oh, he had worked with several musicians who he felt were musical "soulmates" but they never stayed the course....or maybe *he* didn't. Who knew? Did it really matter in the long run? Viridian? She was different. Here was someone who could grab onto any crazy, musical idea of his and turn it to a new direction, which he would instantly twist it around, answer and throw it right back at her. Most times, something beautiful and totally unexpected would be the end result. It was difficult to explain, but they were like two halves of the same musical entity. They simply *had* to work together! Lester had plans....

Yes, he had plans. He stood up, realizing he had been away, deep in thought for a long time. *I'd better head on home before Elizabeth sends out the cops to search for me. Looking around again,* he thought, *yes....there's something about this town that draws you into it....*He headed on home.

At the same time, although Lester had no idea, Sam Bellamy was sitting on a bench just a bit down from him. No, he wasn't interested in bothering Lester at the moment. Plenty of time for *that*. And time was something he had plenty of. Plenty of time on his hands.....time.

He knew this town so well. *Very* well. The whole damned Cape, too. For two hundred and fifty years, give or take...but who was counting anymore?

Where else was he going to go, any way? Or fit in? Could he? Even if he tried?

Enough of that. He both loved and hated this town. In many ways, the people were as narrow and opinionated as they were back in *his* time. Ohhh, they may have fancier clothes, new toys and new ways of talking, but deep down? They could be as mean-spirited as they were back...then. It was tough going being a pirate back then... even worse if your were caught. He could attest to *that*. Now though? There were modern day pirates everywhere, only *these* were well-respected members of the community. He laughed at that and shook his head, although no one could see or hear him... unless he wanted it so.

Back then? They would all have been hung, drawn and quartered, burned at the stake, drowned...you name it. Now? Heads of Industry. Heads of Government. Bah! Hell! He *knew* some of these modern pirates and was forced to depend on a few. Big time. For a very....long.... time. Some day, though...

A miracle to remain sane over all the centuries. At least he had Mariah, sweet Mariah....even that damned cat. How had it latched onto them from that old Inn, anyway? Didn't matter much. The cat was entertaining and gave them something to laugh about until *he* found a new project. Lester Worthy was his best, new prospect for fun in a long, long time. He was going to savor this.

Sam looked out over the harbor and directed his thoughts out over the bay to Great Island...or *Really Big Island* as it was known ...elsewhere, visible in the distance.

Since he was a ghost or a "not-quite-living" entity, he could basically travel anywhere he could think of....and-right now, he was focused on Great (or the other) Island. The site of the old Pirate Tavern, "Higgin's Bottom O' The Barrel Inn". Ahhhh, yes, he spent many a day or night there; drinking,laughing with his associates, planning... always planning. *Big* plans.

Wdell, mostly they worked out. Only took one not to.... *Wonder what happened to Old Higgins? What did he think after we wrecked that morning?* He sat and stared

Mariah appeared next to him and put her hand gently on his shoulder. The cat? Well, he sat there dockside, mournfully looking at all the fish and birds. Nice sweet, crunchy birds. Couldn't get 'em. Couldn't have 'em. Didn't need 'em. Still, hard to get such thoughts out of a cat's head. Birds and fish. Didn't seem fair. At least Sam and Mariah finally rescued him from that !##@! closet in that !###****#! Inn! Having them as company was ****ing good!

He thought about this imbecile, Lester. *Calling me Garfield....who does he think he is? What does he think? I don't read the comics? He might not need birds or fish anymore but, even dead, still a cat with desires.* Sam and Mariah, plus a host of others were friends he could call on and he too, had plans for Mr. Lester (meow) Worthy. Oh yes he did.

Such was a day here in Wellfleet. An easy day. A simple, homey, New England day with everyone moving about, many on the way home. Many things to think about. Many plans to put into motion Such a lovely day. Tail lashing, he faded away.

CHAPTER 8

The Die Is Cast...

(Die...Get it?...
Oh, Well.)

Lester sat in his studio, guitar on his lap. No, not playing, just thinking, thinking.....he had come to a major decision, well, at least for *him,* you could call it a major decision.

"Yes! I'm gonna do it! I'm calling Viridian and asking her to form a music duo with me. The way we work together, how can she refuse?"

That decided, he went back to work on some new songs for them even though he had no idea if Viridian would say yes to the band idea. Lester was kind of like that, jumping off at a new thought and acting before working it all out. He couldn't wait any longer, so excited he quickly called Viridian.

"Hey, V! I've got a great idea! how about we form a band together?"

"Huh, Lester? What? A band? What are you babbling about?"

"Look, you know as well as I do we not only work well together but something wild happens whenever we *do* work together. It's unpredictable. It can be exciting....O.K., so it can be a disaster, too. But people who listen to us seem to like what we do. What do you say?"

Viridian sat silent at the other end of the conversation for a minute. The silence stretched out and Lester thought he made a big mistake; a biggie, springing this on her. Finally, she sighed and answered.

"Sorry about that. You took me by surprise. I'm in the middle of work here. Thinking about what you said? Yeah, it's true. We have fun playing and I haven't had this much fun in a long time, sooooo....whu not?"

"Great! Let's start rehearsing next week on some new stuff."

"O.K. but I've got some ideas, too, on where we might get to play. We've got to get known around here before any place will take us seriously. I'll get to work. See you next week."

Lester hung up, so excited he ran downstairs to tell Elizabeth.

"Viridian and I are gonna be a band! We're gonna go out and play places and stuff and...."

Elizabeth stared at him silently for a second. She was used to this kind of enthusiasm but hadn't seen it in so long, thinking, *welcome back, Les, my husband... it's been too long.* Speaking out loud, she said, "Les, it's about time. You've been hiding up in that music cave far too long. We're so new here and this will get you out meeting people. Make friends. I'm happy for you." Thinking to herself, Y*es, and not talking to someone who isn't here....including an imaginary cat...*

"Go with it. You two really *do* sound great together. Anything I can do to help, just ask."

"Yeah! We can practice...and play out.... and...and.. we'll do an album together! *You* can do the album cover..."

Lester babbled on and on.....

Viridian sat there after putting down the phone. She was fighting a cold...and a headache....and the guys at work were driving her mad....but still, she thought as she sat in front of the computer...

Les doesn't have a bad idea. This could be a lot of fun. Thinking that, she also knew that Les could be a handful. He had so many ideas, writing constantly and difficult to keep up with. Rehearsals with him? They could bounce around in twenty directions before they settled down to real work. It was tiring but when you came right down to it? More times than not, something very unexpected and special came out of left field leaving them both laughing with the excitement. Elizabeth would call up, "What was that you just played?" With them yelling back, "We don't know. We just made it up."

Oh, yes, this was going to be fun. She liked Lester a lot, too. Yes, fun. He wasn't like any of the other musicians she knew; egotistical fools and so full of themselves. She was going to enjoy this rehearsal...and she knew *just* the place to ask if they coiuld play there.

Meanwhile, somewhere else on the Cape, Sam and Mariah were sitting on the bayside dock of a well known restaurant. The place was always packed by midday but nobody noticed trhem. Of course not. They didn't *want* to be seen but boy, if they did....what fun it would cause.

That wasn't on their minds though. The cat spoke first.

"Look, I don't know why you pick this place. I have real, bad memories of a closet here.

Look...Garfield...or was it Heathcliff? What did he call you?" Mariah smiled warmly at the cat. She knew he hated whatever name Lester gave him but she enjoyed teasing him from time to time. Secretly? She guessed he enjoyed it too, but would never admit it.

Did they even know his real name, anyway? Some day, she'd force him to tell them.

"Meow,****ing meow, Mariah! How's that for an answer? ****!"

Sam focused on their conversation. He had been deep in thought, again, staring out over the water to other places, other times....

"Nice mouth, cat! Can you two pipe down for now, please? I've got a lot on my mind."

"Sam? It's about....them....isn't it?"

Them being Crouch, Diabello, Enoch and Flinch. What could be said about these four? They sounded like a law firm, because, in reality, they were simply not a *normal* law firm.

C, D, E&F had been around in business for generation upon generation upon....well, to be honest, they had been around longer than Sam, Mariah, the cat and many others.

Crouch, Diabello, Enoch and Flinch were the lawyers and business management firm for those who were.... extra-human in nature.

"We are a full service firm and manage your well-being and lives....forever and ever." They meant it, literally.

Never was a claim more true than with C, D, E & F. Were they human? Maybe. A loooooong time ago. Maybe not. Were they paranormal, ghostly beings? Maybe, maybe not. That...they were ...something else? Definitely! They represented the ..".timeless".

You see, or not, (depending on the wishes of their clients), their *clients* being in various stages of afterlife or "other-something-lives", and couldn't handle their own, real world business....being not too delicately....dead, almost dead, still-hanging-around-in-spite-of-not-being-alive....or whatever.

    These souls were unable to do real world things for themselves, being ghosts...or something. Oh, they could scare the crap out of the living, be seen...or not; even talk to the living. Handle a stock transaction? Not really. Manage their financial accounts? Not possible.

Author's note: From what I've gatherd and scraped up/off....quite literally from Lester's notes, ghosts *claim* not to be able to force people to do things against their will, but, as usual, according to Lester, there is some "fine print" involved. Although they can't force you to do what they ask, some of them, especially the older, more accomplished of them *can* take over the operation of your body without permission for short periods of time. It's all in the details....or so he says...said...whatever.

    Entities such as Sam Bellamy came into being knowing where they had kept their treasures, in whatever form. Not being able to do anything about it, they would approach the firm of C,D,E&F to recover and invest their wealth for them....in perpetuity...and I mean f-o-r-e-v-e-r. Again, you might ask, *what could these souls possibly need with money, wealth or investments, etc.?*

    Think about it. Many of these spirits have watched their "living" relatives grow, survive, flourish and eventually die and yet, the families continued on. A firm like C,D,E&F would help the spirits provide for their still-living families or, if they really loathed them...provide for some well-needed entertainment as they worked from the sidelines, so to speak,to vex and destroy them.

    If a client wanted something done for or to someone, C,D,E&F provided the necessary services....*whatever* those services entailed. Crouch, Diabello, Enoch and Flinch were *not* above any manner of crime or murder, if asked.

As I said, this was a *full* service firm for *all* time. One did not mess with Ishmael Crouch, Faustus Diabello, Morley Enoch or Mendicant Flinch. Sam, however, was having some second thoughts about their reliability after all this time had passed. Their clients never usually confronted these account managers....ever. Due to his history as *the* Black Sam Bellamy, pirate, he had a long understanding concerning evil. Yes, he had been, (and still was in his faded heart), a pirate and had done many, many despicable things, both in life and after. But these *people*? The firm gave *him* the creeps and that was hard to do if you were a long-standing, charter member of the spirit community.

"Mariah? Really. What *are* these creatures we have to do business with? I know, I know. What choice do we have? We need them but they make me very uncomfortable I go to their office. Me!"

"Oh, Sam....my Sam. Be at ease, my Sam. They've never done anything to hurt any of their clients...ever. They can't. Think of their reputation."

"Yes, and think what would happen if they actually crossed *any* of us. What we could do to *them*."

"But could we, really? After all these years? We still don't know *what* they are. Can they even be harmed in the long run?"

"Maybe not, Mariah...but if they ever crossed *me*...I'd be happy to make their 'short-term' as uncomfortable as possible."

"Well, I guess I canna put it off no longer, Mariah. I best go an' see 'em. Business is, after all, business."

Mariah sighed. The cat simply purred. The people around them went on with their meals, totally clueless about who had been with them. Sam faded from view. As he did, another appeard next to Mariah.

"Is this seat taken, dear Lady?"

The cat looked up, scornfully.

"Napoleon? What the **** are you doing here? (The cat was never polite).

"You horny midget! Don't you have some part of the world to go imagine pillaging? ****ing little creep! Get the **** lost."

Mariah turned and gave Napoleon a disgusted look.

"Corporal, I don't know why you keep coming by to vex me. If Sam found you here bothering me...."

"Ha,ha! Madame, he will never know. I am here on business and saw you sitting here alone....such a waste. Cherie, come away with me. Leave that dusty, old pirate behind. We will fly away together..."

"No, we won't Corporal. Sam is *mine* and *I* am his. The Cape is ours, *not* yours. Please leave."

"Meow, ****ing meow! How are you still here? This isn't your neighborhood."

"Ah hah! But I have business with the Crouch, Diabello, Enoch and Flinch. There are travel exemptions, you know... Adieu, mon Cherie", as he faded from sight.

"Little shit", said the cat.

Back on the home front, Elizabeth was trying to concentrate on her art work as the radio was blasting out the latest obnoxious mix from WPDQ.

"Yaaaaah, this is March Madness bringing you the most current, the most local, *the* most underrated, underheard and rarely, the finest in local Cape music. What do you expect? It's the Silkie and the Harpy Show! We play whatever fits or gives you fits. Who cares?"

"Sheesh, said Elizabeth. "How does Lester listen to this crap?" She looked up at the ceiling and yelled, hoping he would hear her.

"Lester! **Please** lower that God-awful music. I'm trying to work here!"

She didn't know how he could concentrate on all the things he did while that... *music* was blaring away. Another thing that amazed her about her husband.

Thinking about her husband, she was relieved he had found a music partner and friend in Viridian. Maybe now, he would return to normal...or whatever had always passed as normal where Lester was concerned. The man was hard to keep track of at times.

Things were stirring all over town. At the same time, across town on Old Holler Road, Persipone Painestaker was feeling troubled. Something was very, very wrong. Some*thing* was coming and she couldn't quite put a uke pick on it.

Today, it was the ukelele that was helping her to channel her thoughts...and those thoughts? They weren't good. Plucking away fitfully on, "This Land is Your Land", somehow seemed unsettling under the circumstances. Suddenly...

"Yo! Mama! How ya'll doin' pretty Lady?"

In popped a rapidly solidifying apparition. Standing in front of Parsipone and looking at her with a big grin, was a middle-aged, overweight person in a gaudy, white jumpsuit. In one hand he held a peanut butter, bacon and banana sandwich.

Percy dropped her ukelele. Her mouth wide open, she stammered..."Uh...uh...eee...Elvis?"

"Correct in one, baaybee. In the flesh...huh ha! Well, maybe not."

"But...but...you're so....fat?"

"Huh! Ya'll cut me to the quick. Did *I* make any comments on your tiny guitar playin'?"

"No, but why are *you* here? I don't understand. I felt something was coming...but...*you*?"

"Nah. Just passin' through....have business with a guy...well, kinda a guy. Ah heard ya'll and stopped in tuh give ya a head's up. Somethin' is comin' your way and it aln't *me*."

At that, in popped another soul. Elvis turned.

"*Napoleon*? What ya'll doin' in hear? Dahym! Getting crowded in heah."

"Mon cherie....are you listening to this fat, old has-been?" At that, he turned to Elvis.

"I am just passing through. I had business with C, D, E&F, as I assume you do, as well?" He then turned who was looking more than a bit upset.

"Sady, mon cher, I must be going. Things to do. Worlds to conquer."

"Ya'll have luck with that, shorty. Later dahrlin'"

At that, they both popped out of existance, leaving Persipone speechless asa she sank back in her chair.

"I....I must be losing it". Talking to herself as she reached for her ukelele.

"Yes. Mama always told me if I kept going, doing what I do, someday it would get me in big trouble....but...Elvis? And Napoleon? Why?"

She began strumming, "This Land", again when suddenly, a *third* apparitrion appeared in front of her. This one, however, dressed as a pirate and he did *not* look happy.

"Arrrrr. I be th' one ye have been worryin' about, Lass."

"Arrrr, really?"

"It be what a pirate be sayin'. Allow me to introduce meself. The name be Sam Bellamy." At that, he doffed his hat and bowed to Percy.

"Now that we be introduced proper-like, let me get a bit less....formal." With that, Sam's clothes changed to a conservative, three piece business suit, his voice and manners changing, as well.

"Yes, Ms. Painestaker, we can *do* that. Do you think we can't learn things over the centuries? Now, why I'm here, and yes, you were correct. You have every right to be fearful. Consider it a warning. You *will* stop meddling in my business."

This time, Percy carefully laid down her ukelele, mesmerized by Sam.

"*Your* business? What business? I don't even know you...well, I know *of* you but..."

Sam interrupted. "*My* business? Lester Worthy is *my* business and *I* am his....even if he doesn't know it as yet. To put it in modern terms, *back off or else.*"

"But...but...what could a person such as Lester Worthy bne to you...I mean, *Les Worthy*? Important to...*you*? His name says it all, doesn't it?"

Sam leaned closer to her as his clothing and face took on a more familiar, threatening, piratey look.

"Ye have been advisin' th' wretch, Lass, and I canna have that. Master Worthy be mine to do with...a plaything, perhaps ta wile away th' boredom. If ye knows what be good for ye....cease and desist, ya hearrrrr. arrrrr?"

He returned to modern dress.

"Consider yourself fair warned, Ms. Painestaker."

Again he changed.

"If not, Lass? Thar be consequences, arrrrr."

At that, he disappeared.

At that, Persipone passed out, sank to the floor and knew no more until later that evening. Upon awakening, her first thought was, *I have to call Lester and warn him.* Totally forgetting Sam's warnings, she put away her uke and grabbed her banjo from the wall.

"*This* calls for some serious mojo." She began playing, "Dueling Banjos" from the old classic, "Deliverance". The voices would tell her what to do. Now, more than ever, she needed *their* advice. They always had before and will, again. She played on into the night. She would call Lester in the morning.

CHAPTER 9

Taking Care of Business

It was a nondescript office in a nondescript building where we find the headquarters of Crouch, Diabello, Enoch and Flinch. Oh, we're not talking about some shabby, flop-house-chic building. On the contrary, C, D, E &F were located in a very exclusive neighborhood but their building and offices were meant to avoid undue attention, at least by the mortal world....unless necessary.

Sam appeared at their doors as two clients were leaving. Napoleon was first.

"Zees....people. Zey geev me le creeps". Looking at Sam, "Good luck, mon ami." He popped from sight. Next followed Elvis, waddling from the doors. He turned back to the office and said, "Gennle....men, thahnk ya'll for your time. Be seein' ya." Turning back to Sam, "Well, that went well...and heah, Ah thought dead folk were creepy. Ah's say, give 'em Hell, Sam...but...well, ya know." Elvis faded from view.

The secretary looked at Sam, didn't smile....exactly, and said, "Mr. Bellamy, you may go in now. The gentlemen are waiting for you."

Crouch, Diabello, Enoch and Flinch sat around the end of a long conference table. Mr. Crouch beckoned Sam to sit down at the far end.

"Mr. Bellamy, *please* have a seat. It is always good to see one of our charter clients. What may we do for you, today?"

Sam remained dressed in his 21st. Century business suit. It seemed fitting, even though the four partners were dressed more like undertakers than lawyer/accountants; somehow fitting, though, knowing these four.

"I was in the neighborhood and wanted to check on my investments and have you handle a small problem for me. First, my account. How are things doing for me? I know the economy is deader than you guys."

Mr. Crouch chuckled a deep, graveyard chuckle; full of dust, gravity and coming from six feet under.

"Ahhhh, Sam. Such droll humor. Let's see now." He opened a ledger that appeared in front of him and studied. (No computers needed for *this* firm.)

"As far as I can tell, finding ways to invest treasure hoards in multitudinous ways is a far better hedge in our present....dead economy. We have our ways and your funds are doing famously. You have enough to handle any monetary issue ad infinitum. Your family, living, that is, if you had any, would be good for generation upon generation upon....well, you get the idea. In other words? We are very, very good at what we do."

"So glad to hear it. Mr. Crouch, I'm pretty sure there are some descendants of mine and Mariah out there somewhere, should we ever decide to approach them...in *any* way."

"Yes, yes. Of course. That was rude of me. My apologies. Now...you also mentioned a ....small problem. How may we be of service?"

Sam leaned forward, his hands now folded on the desk.

"Well, see....I have this interesting *project* I'm working on."

Mr. Diabello looked down at his notes, his finger moving down the page.

"Let's see, Mr. Bellamy. Could this mmmmm project have a name, Lester Worthy? Mmmmmmmm? Interesting."

Sam. first frowning at Mr. Diabello, smiled an innocent smile.

"I can see you gentlemen are as thorough as usual. Yes, I've made Mr. Worthy a project of mine. Consider him a work in progress; a mere....entertainment to while away a few years of boredom. Nothing more."

"Yes, of course...and will this *project* require some funds to be withdrawn? To the usual earthly bank in the name of some mortal?"

Sam sat back, relaxing. "No, no funds are required... at this time, at least. One can never tell. It's nothing like that. There *is* a small problem concerning my project I would like you to handle....discretely, of course."

"Of course, of course. Handled with the utmost delicacy, as always. And what is this ...*small* problem?"

Sam leaned forward again, frowning. "There is this woman...this seer...a Persipone Painestaker."

Mr. Enoch and Mr. Flinch bolted upright, Flinch hissing.

"*Painestaker*? *That* damned woman, again? She has caused us much trouble, lately." Enoch continued,"And using those damned instruments! She could make the devil cringe and an angel scream for mercy. Miserable busybody!"

Yes, that's the one. Well, she has begun to intefere with my...project; giving him silly notions, filling his head with the idea he should beware of me. I went to her to persuade her to back off and leave Lester Worthy to *me*. I thought I got the point across. I was wrong."

Mr. Flinch looked down at his entries and began to laugh in his thin, reedy voice.

"*Oh*, yes! Ha! You made *quite* an impression on her.... so did those other two idiots, Bonaparte and Presley. Why, when *you* left, she picked up that accursed banjo and began her incessant meddling, not to mention that dreadful picking. Oh, you scared her off. Ha!"

Mr. Crouch looked to Sam.

"Well, it looks as if you are correct. You have a small problem and it was smart that you came to us for help in....resolving things. I can assure you, we will calm Ms. Painestaker and convince her to apply her *talents* in other areas. For the usual fees, of course."

Diabello, Enoch and Flinch all nodded in agreement, especially excited where money was concerned. Sam rose.

"Well, then. Thank you, gentlemen. I'll be hearing from you. Good day."

Later that evening, the new duo was hard at work. Les' wife ran for the hills to escape the noise. Their band, WhydahMaker, was about to accomplish it's name if they didn't start sounding better but they were working hard to do just that.

"Ya know", Les said as he put down his guitar, "I think we're getting the hang of this song."

Viridian smiled sarcastically at him. "Maybe we should go back to a more...traditional approach? A little less on the grunge and more on the traditional? Just sayin'."

Yeah, yeah. You're right For some reason, "Banish Misfortune" doesn't work as well as I hoped.

Two fiddles? Maybe fiddle and guitar? *Yes*. Really. I think we're trying far too hard to be different."

"But don't you want to make a big impression? People here need to be hit over their heads to get their attention. Don't you get it?"

"Lester, *when* we get their attention, I don't think you'll be very happy with the *kind* of attention they'll give us. I keep telling you. We have to live here, remember?"

"V, V! Look! I want people to know WhydahMaker is *here* and we're for *real*. You get way too cautious. I mean, looka at the stuff they play on WPDQ. *Those* people take serious chances and the people seem to love 'em. Don't they?"

Viridian gave him a serious look of disbelief. "You're kidding me, right? You're not messing with my head, again? *Why* do you think WPDQ is located offshore? You think it's due to *love*? They ask for trouble each and every day. You're talking about going down that same, dark road."

Lester scowled at her but she knew by now he was really taking it all to heart.

"Lester, how many of the groups they play on WPDQ have you actually *seen* or heard playing around the Cape? I rest my case. Now, let's get serious and work on a set that folk here will want to listen to."

Away in her workshop, Elizabeth breathed a sigh of relief when the music changed and the decibel level returned to human levels.

Meanwhile, in another part of Wellfleet, down Old Holler Road, Parsipone Painestaker feverishly played her ukelele while wildly mumbling to herself.

"He's coming, oh, yes. *He's* coming, oh, dear...oh, my... he's on his way. No! Wait! It's a *them*, not just a *he*. They are on their way, too. What to do? What to do?"
Strum, strum. Pluck, pluck, pluck. Mutter, mutter, fret.

"And *He*, the *other* one....has no idea what's going on...ohmygodohmygodohmygodohmy...."

Over in a corner, unseen, a certain black cat sat cringing...if a long-expired feline would deign to cringe at anything.....

and silently complained to himself about the quality of the music these days. He knew, of course it was better to remain unobserved by this musically challenged mystic, otherwise things might become too much for here, especially in her current, deranged state of mind. It *must* be deranged....considering what she was playing.

Oh, well, he thought, *entertainment, after several centuries is where you can find it...or whatever this was he was hearing.* The term"caterwauling" came to mind but he was far too dignified to go any further with the thought.

Back at the Pirate's Cove harbor, Sam had returned to Mariah. One second the side of her bench was empty, the next, there he was back in his old pirate garb.

Mariah continued to stare out across the harbor to the island where the old Pirate Inn had stood so long ago; only here, it was "Really Big Island" as opposed to "Great Island" in the real world.

"You're back. You're wearing that old outfit. I can tell. Must be because the meeting went well. You only dress appropriately when you're at ease."

Sam sighed and stretched his legs out. "At ease, Lass? I'm not so sure but I do feel more comfortable in clothes I'm used to. The meeting? I can never tell with those....four. I *think* all's well and that things will be handled carefully. Our accounts are all in order. So *they* say."

Mariah turned to face him. "Oh, Sam...I don't know why you still deal with such entities. We don't even know *what* they are, except they are very, *very* old and very, *very* powerful."

"Mariah, we both have living descendants from those times, remember? This way, if we find they need anything...(then he paused and a nasty look crossed his face), or if we need to...do anything for them *or to* them, we have the funds and means to do the necessary."

After all this time...and we are still at the mercy of that treasure." She hugged him. "Maybe that's why we're still stuck here and can't move on."

"No, Lass". Sam saind smiling. He turned to her. " I think it's more because we're so tied to this land;

to the sea, to our deaths."

She shuddered. "And those wicked, wicked people."

"You notice, don't ye? They not be 'round here. Yedinna see 'em? Not since th' likes o' them passed. I can only guess they ha' moved ont' their own, *just* rewards. Good riddance ta' 'em,"

"I guess you're right, Sam." She paused a bit. "And what will happen to that lady? Painestaker? She means no harm, really."

"May not, Lass, but she makes a cargo hold o' trouble with her meddling. I asked Crouch and his unholy crew ta' keep an eye on Ms. Painestaker and discourage her from continuing ta' cause me grief."

"Can't you just leave poor Lester Worthy alone? Wouldn't that stop the trouble as well?"

Again, came the slightly wicked smile. "An' wha' would be th' fun in tha', Lass? Dear, *dear* Lester Worthy is mine. My own lil' project; a mere plaything ta wile away the time.
We all need a bit of distraction now and again, don't we?"

Mariah pulled Sam close to herself again and hugged him ferociously. "*Some*times, I think Lester Worthy has become more important to you than *me*!"

"Now, Lass. Don't ye worry. You're mine. I'm yours. Always have. Always will be." Sam looked down at his feet, seeing his friend sitting there.

"Garfield! Where ya' been, my lil' catly one?"

Tail lashing, "I choose to ignore that. My name isn't ****ing Garfield, you old, dead pirate! It's------- and well you know it, you !*&####!. I hiss at that ****Worthy for calling me that ********name! May his claws all fall out!"

"Not Garfield? Was it Heathcliff, then?"

"Hissssss, spit.!"

Sam and Mariah both laughed at the lightening up of the conversation. The cat? Well, even long dead, still a cat who wouldn't show that he really, *really* had gotten to like....maybe even *need* these two. To top it all off? He didn't *not* like Lester Worthy. O.K., maybe he wouldn't go that far...but the man was...a bit...*interesting*...for a pitiful human. It would be interesting to see how things progressed in Sam's little game. Purrrrfect fun for, as well, a *slightly* interested feline.

   They came strolling down Old Holler Road late the next evening. All was pitch black; as they liked it. Mssrs. Enoch and Flinch had been sent on an errand for the firm; to persuade one Persipone Painestaker from continuing her studies, especially of anyone of interest in the Bellamy case *or* their firm.. They were certain they would be able to dissuade her....in a civilized manner. After all, what could go wrong?
   As they knocked on her door, Mendicant Flinch pondered life, (or whatever it had become). He and Morley Enoch went back for centuries, *many* centuries.
   Faustus Diabello was much older....*much* older. *His* time could be measured in eons, his origins were as vague and faded as the number of years he had walked the Earth. Ishmael Crouch? He shuddered at the thought of *his* name. There were *no* records of; Mr. Crouch; maybe there never *were* any, as he had existed for so long. One thing for certain? You did not mess with Mr. Crouch. You did *what* he said, *when* he said and to *whom* he said....without question...ever....and *ever* was a very, *very* long time.
   He sighed, shuddered and knocked again with a bit more authority. *Maybe*, he thought, *she wasn't home*.... but then he heard that damned instrument. By the Gods that are and aren't! How he hated the sound of *that* instrument!
   Percy had been plucking away at her banjo when the first knock came. Although it sent a chill up herb spine, she continued playing, deciding to ignore whoever was at her door. She was meditating and on to something big!
  So, she thought, *maybe I'll get to the bottom of this whole mess,* and continued playing the theme from "Deliverance", her version, (and a dubious one), of chanting "oooooooommmmmmmmm".
   Again, the knock came with more authority this time. Persipone stopped playing, sighed, and put down her beloved instrument.
   Who would be at my door at this late hour?

She thought as she went to the door. As she opened it cautiously, she questioned, "Yes? May I help you?"

Peering through the crack to the darkened porch, she saw these two, very odd, people. One was short and slightly rotund in a bloated sort of way,(Mr. Enoch), and dressed in clothing she couldn't quite place.

Maybe, she thought, *old sailors costume? No, that wasn't it...military? No, not that, either.* Whatever, oddly, how he dressed seemed to be constantly shifting from one style to another. So very strange.

The other, (Mr. Flinch), was dressed a bit more conventionally, in an older style, three piece, pinstripe suit. *Did I think older? How about a lot older. Very odd.*

The two gentlemen smiled disarmingly to her.

"We are Mssrs. Enoch and Flinch, representing the esteemed firm of Crouch, Diabello, Enoch and myself, Flinch. I doubt very much that you have heard of our firm."

"Very....old firm." Mr. Enoch added. "I doubt it very much but, rest assured, we've been in business for a very, *very* long time. and represent many souls, worldwide."

"*And* beyond", Flinch added, smiling even more. "May we please come in? We're here on Firm business that concerns yourself."

Percy opened thew door for them. "How oddly you out that. No, I haven' heard of your firm. What possible interest could you have in *me*?"

"Oh, we won't take much of your time. Please let us explain. Mya we sit down for a minute.?" Mr. Flinch pointed to the living room. Mr. Enoch rumbled something unintelligible. Pandora ushed them in. "Of course. Where are my manners? Please have a seat."

Mr. Enoch grumbled. "What a ....charming home. Oh! You play instruments? Are they musical?" He pointed to the banjo with utter disdain.

Percy smiled, a bit confused by the statement.

"Why, yes, I'm a musician and all of these are my *musical* instruments." She waved lovingly at her wall of instruments, stopping at her banjo.

She heard Mr. Flinch whisper to himself, *I doubt it.*

"Did you say something, Mr...?"

"Flinch. Mr. Flinch. No, I was simply musing on the extent of....musical....uniqueness arrayed before me. Amazing. Simply....amazing. I am *such* an afficionado of fine.... musical instruments."

Mr. Enoch rumbled to life as they sat down.

"Let us get to the point, Ms. Painestaker. Then, we can leave you in peace to get back to....whatever it was you were doing."

"So eloquently. I might add."

"Yes...so...eloquently.

Mr. Flinch took over. "We are here representing a client....well, really a client of a client....of a *past* client."

"Or passed client". Mr. Enoch grumbled and smiled.

"Ahhh, yes. As we've said, we represent many, many souls worldwide, from humble individuals to large corporations. This particular client, who must remail nameless...."

"As is his wish for many, time-worn reasons." Mr. Enoch added. Mr. Flinch nodded in agreement and turned back to Persipone, again smiling.

"You must forgive Mr. Enoch. He has quite an...*antique*...sense of humor about him. Our client is from a local family with a long and distinguished history. Historically, they have become involved with this story."

"Legend".

"Myths....surrounding that old pirate ship, The Whydah, which sank off our coast so long ago. Our client has become aware of your interest in him....sorry, I mean his *ancestor*, Samuel Bellamy, the captain...."

"Pirate".

"*Captain* of the Whydah.. He and his family would appreciate people, such as yourself, not stirring up old gossip and legends concerning, oooohhhh, pirates, ghosts, treasure and the like. Let sleeping dogs lie, so to speak.

"or cats....especially cats."

"Don't listen to Mr. Enoch. He gets a bit...irregular this time of night. Low suger. Our client knows your reputation as a famous, local seer and has been hearing rumors of you talking to, mmmmm, how to put it? Spirits? Especially of the long deceased Captain Sam Bellamy. For the sake of the family, he would appreciate you backing away from your pursuit of this nonsense."

Persipone sat there in disbelief of what she was hearing.

"Gentlemen, I am a seer; a channeler of spirits. It is what I do and very little control over how or when it works; or *who* and what may approach me from the spirit world. Again, it is what I *do* and have little control over it."

Mr. Crouch smiled, a bit more sternly. "Well, please? Try." He rumbled a bit. "Our client is quite emphatic that you *do*."

Mr. Flinch joined in, leaning forward. "Seriously. Ms. Painestaker. It will be well worth your time...."

"Or what's left of it", came the grumble.

"If you simply let this issue rest in peace."

"Seriously, Ms. Painestaker. Our client has made this request in good faith and hopes you will honor his wishes."

As if on cue, both Enoch and Flinch stood at the same time.

"Ms. Painestaker, we're sorry to have troubled you this late in the evening." Mr. Flinch smiled disarmingly.

"Yes, we do our best work after dark", grumbled Mr. Enoch.

A bity unnerved, Persipone walked them to the door, showing them out into the night.

:"I will what I can to please your client but, gentlemen, I must follow my heart and my calling. I hope your client will be satisfied with that."

"Of course, Ms. Painestaker. Of course."

"Yes, you follow your heart....wherever", with a quiet grumble, sounding like distant thunder. Mr. Enoch and Mr. Flinch turned and walked off into the night, rapidly fading from sight.

Persipone, still shaking, quickly closed and locked the door, leaning back against it. She had much to think about on this night and she didn't think she'd get much sleep.

On her way to the sofa, she absently took her ukelele from the wall, sat down and began to absently strum. Deep thoughts came creeping. Dancing. Visions. She joined them in the dance and sleep came fitfully.

    Their rehearsal over for the night, Viridian packed her instruments and headed for the door.
    "Not a bad rehearsal, Les. A little strange, maybe, but....well, we'll see how things go. You usually make even the weirdest ideas work. Elizabeth? You can come out of hiding now. We're done. Sorry."
    His wife came down the hall and took off her headphones.
    "I thought I heard someone call. I *did* hear some of what you were doing. Are you *sure* about some of this? Lester can get carried away with some of his more radical brainstorms. Some of what you were doing? Kind of extreme. Just...for me? Don't let him get carried away and drag you into something stupid."
    They both laughed. Viridian turned at the door.
    "And *why* would you possibly think that? I won't let him too far off the leash. Really! Have a quiet night, Liz."
    Upstairs, while Lester was packing, he suddenly realized he wasn't alone. There sat Sam in his pirate garb.
    "Yes, Lester, don't get too far off the leash. Mind the Lady."
    He did a slow circle around Lester.
    "You know, you two don't sound half bad together but you could use a bit of advise about your music choices."
    "Oh, *really*, Bellamy? And what the Hell d*o you* know about the music? Old, dead pirates are now music critics?"
    "Well, now that you mention it." Sam sat on the edge of a guitar case. "I *do* have some ideas....a bit more fiddle, maybe a little squeezebox....a lot less electric guitar... and by the way? Some of those *lyrics*!"
    "You *are* using my good name and that of my dear ship. I do not take kindly if you harm either."
Lester turned sharply to Sam.

"Really? *Really*? Your good name? *You*, a pirate? With a pirate ship? Sam Bellamy! *Black* Sam and the dread pirate ship Whydah! Don't make me laugh. *You*, my dear pirate, are long dead. Your ship is dead and drowned. Both are sorry excuses for figments of *my* imagination. So, if I were you, I'd leave my opinions to myself before I ignore your presence all the way back to the grave. *You*... and your ship of the damned. I do what *I* wish and not at the commands of some pathetic hallucination. Me! Not *you*!"

Sam moved close to Lester, leering, face to angry face. His accent changed drastically.

"Matey, If I be ye, I be careful 'bout what ye say ta th' likes o' *me*! Dinna take meself to be some damned harmless night bogeyman scare o' yer own. Ye be wakey, wake and na' dreamin'. Ohhhh, we be ta-gether in this, we arrrrr. Haaarrrrrrrrrrrhahahahahahahaaa."
He faded from sight.

Elizabeth called upstairs. "Lester? You O.K.? Who were you talking to?"

"Oh, just mumbling and trying out some new lyrics. One of the cats showed up and started to mess around. I'll be right down."

"*Arrrrr, yerself, matey, arrrr, we be not done....arrrrr,* Lester thought to himself as he went down to Elizabeth.

CHAPTER 10

The Plot, As They Always Say, Thickens

It had been a very long night for Persipone Painestaker. She playerd her banjo. She played her ukelele. Nothing helped give her the clarity she needed. Back to banjo and Deliverance, again and again until her fingers bled.

The sunlight pouring through her window and striking her face startled her. *My God*, she thought. *It's mid-morning. What have I....why am...my fingers?* Suddenly, it all became clear to her. She realized the danger that lester was in and the disaster that was brewing...and not only for *him*! This was big and things were set in motion that would hurt a lot of people here in town and beyond. She *must* call Lester, *immediately!*

Lester was sitting at the table writing a new song when the phone rang. He didn't like being interrupted when he worked. "Yes?" He answered angrily as he picked up the phone.

"Lester? It's Persipone....Percy....Painestaker? It's very important that you listen to me and do *exactly* what I say! *You* are in serious danger. What you decide to do about it will affect many others."

"You're kidding me, right? Danger? What's new with that, Lady? I've been shot at, threatened with all kinds of mayhem. I taught thirteen year olds, for God's sake! And drummers! So don't tell *me* about danger!"

Persipone was getting desperate. "Lester, *please* listen to me. I know this all sounds crazy but I'm really, *really* good at what I do. I am a powerful medium and you are the focal point of powers you can't imagine." She gasped a breath and continued before Lester could interrupt.

"Sam Bellamy? Mariah Hallett? Even a cat? They're *not* your imagination playing with you. Trust me! They! Are! Real! Spirits, yes! Powerful? You have *no* idea and *they* have become interested in *you*. No....that's not quite true....You....*amuse* them, especially Sam Bellamy. God knows what he has planned for you but it can't be good. And that's not all! There are otherr forces getting involved; older forces so powerful, even Sam Bellamy's ghost can't imagine!"

"You're joking, right? Me? Oooooooooo....forces of eeeevil coming to get me? Hahahahahahahaha! Good one, Persipone. As far as I figure, it's me going 'round the ****ing bend, not ghosts or demons or powerful spirits. Lady...you're cracked. Ya know what? It's that damned banjo of yours. Gone to your head. You can only plat that damned Deliverance theme so many times before you lose it....that, that and that miserable ukelele! Now! You? Leave me alone. I have work to do. GOODBYE!"

He slammed the phone down and went back to work. *What a nutjob...and here I thought Wellfleet was gonna be a saner place to live.*

Percy sat there staring at the wall, he rmouth open as she heard the phone slam down. *He has no idea what was coming, who...or even what.* She sat thinking, staring at ther phone.

Persipone had a difficult life as did her parents. Her Mom and Dad both had been psychics with immense powers, which she inherited. They, however, didn't need props or questionable musical instruments to channel their powers. All they had to do was think...or touch something...and it all became clear. But *they* were long dead. Tragically. Killed by forces they had summoned during their work. Percy was only a small child when it happened. She hadn't even started school yet but she reememberede that terrible night. Her parents were working for a client when they summoned up....something....or maybe, even some...*thing*s. Persipone never saw what they were but she saw her parents get thrown across the room while still in their chairs, smashing, bodies broken, crashing against the wall, then falling to the floor bleeding and beyond hope or help.

All Percy remembered hearing was her mother whispering before the end....what sounded like four names...or was she imagining it? She couldn't tell. Anyway, it was too late for her parents. and then, she found herself alone.

She was moved to a nearby relative here in Wellfleet. The town had an extremely close community.

and while the tragedy was discussed endlessly and the rumormill cranked on, as in all small towns, Persipone was swept up and cared for.

Soon after she started school, maybe it was only in kindergarten, a guest performer came by to play for the class Little Percy was fascinated by the instruments, especially guitar, fiddle and banjo. The banjo *really* got her attention.

In the middle of a song , (you can probably guess which), Persipone stood up in class as if in a trance and blindly walked her way up to the musician, who stopped playing to stare at this tiny apparition standing in front of him.

"Give me *that*!" Percy yelled, her tiny voice suddenly becoming the loudest thing in the room. Everyone sat, silently in shock. With her tiny, child hands, Persipone ripped the instrument from the musician's hands. Her strength was amazing. Even more amazing? She began to play Deliverance...and much better than the musician!

He, the teacher and the entire class sat in awe of this tiny wraith.

"I...I didn't know she could play", he stuttered.

"Not that we knew", said the teacher, "She's never shown any musical interest before this....and...*banjo*?"

Life was never the same for Persipone Painestaker. people talked. Whispers followed her everywhere through the years. She became a person of wonder to the townsflok, a queer, slightly *off*, strange person; not many friends....to be honest? *No* friends. She was just too....weird. But also, it was where she lived. A lot of the weird and strange took place in this little fishing village, so she actually fit in quite well; a lonely, little girl who grew to be a lonely, weird adult.

CHAPTER 11

The Firm

AUTHORS NOTES:
   Yeah, I know....me again. The following chapter is, for the most part, related to you from Lester's extensive notes. I point this out because "extensive" or even "coherent" are not words I often use when describing his notes.
   I only discovered these because I found them all in the same leaf bag and they were on the same quality of "writing media", meaning any paper/cardboard garbage from food at PJ's, a local, famous Wellfleet restaurant. Lester hasn't always been too careful about *what* he used to keep his notes. Any time I've found some on the same, ummmmmmm, *stationary,* it meant that these were important notes to Lester.
   From what I gathered, Lester became quite upset and focused on the firm of Crouch, Diabello, Enoch and Flinch. Maybe *terrified* is a better word butnin time, terror would turn to obsessive hatred, as you will later read in my story. So here, I give you *The Firm*.

   The firm of Crouch, Diabello, Enoch and Flinch (more easily known as C, D, E & F), had/has...who knows.... been around for longer than human thought. I guess the most recent addition to the Firm, the most junior partner, is Mendicant Flinch. His roots, and I *do* mean *roots*, can be traced back to trhe Spanish Inquisition. No, Mr. Flinch wasn't of Spanish descent, so to speak, but he got involved when a "branch" of said Inquisition was opened in the New World.
   He had many "talents" but first and foremost among them, he was hired as the "defense attorney" for any who had the misfortune to come to the attention and tender ministrations of the Inquisition. His talent? He *never* won a case....for the defense, that is, probably hired him as a "check and balance", in case any defendant looked to possibly be found innocent. Once Mendicant Flinch offered his services, the poor soul had an invitation and reservation for a personal barbeque; his own.
   Mendicant was evidently good at it for a very long time

until, one day, the head Inquisitor came under the scrutiny and tender care of his buddies. Once they assigned Mendicant, the man was screwed and he knew it. After that, the remaining members realized keeping Mr. Flinch *and* his services much longer wasn't a good idea in case *they*, in turn, were ever granted his help. Mendicant Flinch met with a warm end.

But, as the stories seem to go....and yet in death, alive....or something similar. He awoke, clothes still smouldering a bit, in the boardroom of C, D & E. His first thought was that someone, (Mr. Enoch), was putting out the remaining embers and offering him a drink.

In Mr. Crouch's rumbling, rattling, tomb-like voice, he heard, "Mr. Mendicant Flinch! Welcome! We have need of a soul such as yourself in our firm. You come to us with the highest of qualifications and will make a fine addition to our family....ulness, of course....you would rather...."

Thinking quickly, with the smell of wood smoke and char still hanging about him, Mendicant Flinch blurted out, "Are you crazed? Of course I'll take the position! Whatever you want! Whatever you need, I'm your man!"

Mr. Crouch chuckled, "Of course, of course. For some reason, I *knew* you would see it our way. You will become a valued employee of our firm and, in time, a full partner." He never mentione*d how* much time or *what* would be asked. Flinch didn't care. He had motivation.

Over time, Mendicant became involved in many world issues. Several revolutions, advising certain people of their rights....much to their eventual disappointment. A trial here or there, Benedict Arnold, for one. He once advised Napoleon who, by the way, still holds a nasty grudge....ande after all this time, too. He advised many people on many, many things: attacking this, defending that. He was particularly fond of his council given on the creation of both the Edsel and Corvair....but that was simply from boredom.

He knew the late, great "King", Elvis Presley, and was still angry about that "special" sandwich he showed him how to make: peanut butter, bananas, bacon...and was it....mayo?

He couldn't remember. The man didn't have to eat them *constantly*. Needless to say, where Mendicant Flinch got involved, things happened and, in time, he became a full and valued partner.

Now, Morley Enoch was a totally different story. *He* had been around since the whole, "Tigris and Euphrates" thing; that damned fertile crescent fiasco. Morley didn't remember too much from that particular time and place. What he *did* remember concerned a band of proto-camel-jockeys he had the misfortune to work with as an "advisor".

Bad choice of job description. Worse job. Trying to kiss up to the leader of the group, Morley paid an innocent compliment to him on one of his wives. *That* was all he remembered. Ignorant, violent lunatics. It's a wonder they've made it this far, today.

He awoke, quite literally, a new person, somewhere in the Celtic world. England? Ireland? He couldn't remember. If he had thought the camel jockeys were bad, he had yet to experience the Celts. Evil tempers; argumentative would be a kind way to put them. And sense of humor? *What* sense of humor that didn't involve rape, pillage or "just-for-fun", maiming.

Once again, he made the mistake of trying to talk the local community into using his many services. These people were absolutely *not* in the mood for new marketing ideas. Whoever they figured he was in league with, the Devil, Christians, Romans, the other barbarians, it was enough to get himself killed off rather quickly.... again. So rude.

He became aware, this time, with a smiling Ishmael Crouch sitting acreoss from him at an old, well worn office desk.

"I have a job for you, Mr. Morley Enoch, that is.....if you're interested", he added wuth a crypt-like chuckle, "The ummmmmmm alternatives are so less profitable..... especially for *you*. May I call you Morley?"

It didn't take Morley Enoch much time to make an important career decision.

It beat the *hell* out of dying for one's work. More than once. He was to become the next-to-junior partner of this firm.

Now, Faustus Diabello was an entirely different story. *He* had been around a long time but, historically speaking, not around as long as the other members of the Firm. Over his *existence*, Faustus retained the same job(s) as a merchant of death and destruction; an arms merchant, so to speak.

In his time(s), he helped with the development of better steel, the dreadnaught, (ohhh, he *loved* the dreadnaught....one of his favorite ideas), things that went "boom" better than the ones he helped mproduce in earlier times; tanks, planes....you name it. Sure, he stole designs that Leonardo DaVinci had sketched out but never reailzed....but that was before *his* time.

The problem? Well, there had been several. Basically, painfully and often, his "trade" had gotten him killed, knifed, sunk, crashed or blown up. Either by his experiments or by the people he sold to. Since he never really cared *what* side he sold to, usually both sides of a conflict (that he more than likely helped instigate), this led to many untimely, unexpected removals from this earthly coil. This is why the plural(s) is used in any description of his life(s).

Strangely, Faustus always came back as an arms dealer in another more opportunistic time. He always became instantly aware.... a bit painfully,in a time that held oh, so many new possibilities. He was an expert on death and destruction and, above all else, had the ability to make "a bigger boom". He absolutely *loved* bigger booms.

Who do you think whispered in the ears of the Germans and Japanese about the outrageous idea of seventeen inch guns on bigger and better dreadnaughts? Ahhh, the combining of two favorite loves.

O.K., so what if the idiots didn't understand that "bigger and better" also made for "slower and larger" targets. What good was the ability to throw around a warhead the size of a car when you were the largest target in a rapidly shrinking ocean?

Yes, he was partially responsible for those pesky submarines and what became known as radar and sonar. *Whoops....sorry about that.* Business is business.

O.K., he made a major mistake with the whole "atom bomb" thing. Yes, he absolutely adored helping create a bigger "boom". This, however, was ridiculous in the extreme. It does no good if your "bigger boom" can totally wipe out all your clients in the process. No profit in *that*.... as he learned for himself.

He painfully remembered the whole "thermonuclear" fiasco. It went waaaaay too far. You can't plan for or survive a "biggest boom". He remembered that "Bikini Shot" as the biggest boom, (and therefore, biggest mistake of his carreer(s). Yeah, *big* mistake....made even bigger by wanting to be close enough to see his latest toy go "boom". Dumb. Normally, you only make a mistake like that once in a lifetime.

Ahhhh, but Faustus Diabello had made a few of them. It did take a while longer to recover this time. Total vaporization will do that. Hurt a hell of a lot more, too. Really dumb idea , that Bikini Shot. Oh, well. You learn from your mistakes. Or not. Yeah, O.K., maybe not.

In his most recent escapade, Faustus decided that the whole "thermonuclear thing" was a bad idea to persue as a business model for success. *This* gave him a great idea to whisper in someone's ear: "Make a bigger, more powerful normal bomb. No nuclear this or that, just make the biggest, bestest, most ridiculously largest, non-nuclear weapon *ever* imagined on the Earth!" He even came up with a catchy name for it: MOAB....Mother Of All Bombs. Yeah, he was proud of that name.

Unfortunate that it was the largest freeakin' bomb ever created and needed a biggest, freakin' monster of a plane to carry it. He had forgotten about the dreadnaught, "bigger is better, biggest is ....better...est" problem.

Not only a *very* large target for the bad guys to see but a very touchy, house-sized monster of a bomb. Oh, *yeah*!
He got too close to the first one when they were trying to load the monster on the ground. Big BOOM!

No, the military didn't report *that* to the public....just reported it as a major earthquake. They, however, kept going withn it's development 'cause they *loved* the biggest BOOM idea. Faustus didn't....not particularly. That one *hurt*, not as much as Bikini but definitely his pride was injured.

He came aware sitting in an office at a very old desk. Across from him was a large gentleman of vague age and description. In his rumbling, crypt-like voice, he addressed Faustus.

"Mr. Faustus Diabello! How nice to finally meet you. I've followed your....progress for some time. May I call you Faustus? Yes? Good! Now, if you are quite through with ummmmmm, how may I put this? Blowing the beejeebies out of yourself, I have a job for you that can provide much more in the way of career afdvancement than anything in your former life(s)."

Faustus sat there, mesmerized by the man, his presence and presentation. *Made a lot of sense, it did....but he could still think about things that went....boom. He nodded.*

"My name is Ishmael Crouch and I'm offering you a job in our prestigious firm *and* my hand in friendship." The voice rumbled, grumbled and chortled with the echos of the enduring ages. The offered hand was gratefully accepted. Faustus Diabello became the fourth member of the firm.

Wait a minute! Who havew we forgotten in this amazing firm's history? Oh, yes. One Ishmael Crouch....and *his* story is a winner.

CONCERNING ISHMAEL CROUCH
Author's notes

To begin with? Who knows? For real. Who knows anything about this....person. I use the word, *person* or *human*, loosely if only because nobody knows for sure. All these are the myriad rumors, especially from the "other-than-dead" community. That and the unique notes left behind by Lester Worthy. (Many of these were found on old Dunkin' Donut wrappers and bags.

Categorizing and filing was a nightmare, as well as probably infectious.)

The "oldest" rumor concerning Mr. Crouch is a legend passed on from the "Not-Quite-Dead" community. It is hinted at, with some awe, that he was not only present at the Big Bang, but he caused it when some business deal with God went wrong. As far fetched as this might seem, after all the stories about the Firm, there could be a hint of truth in it.   As with Diabello, Enoch and Flinch, it is believed that possibly Ishmael Crouch began life as a "real" person but if he goes so far back to have a blown business deal with God....again, who knows?

God, or whatever presides over then universe, must have a soft spot for total losers such as these four. Where else, (outside of politics and Congress), can someone **** up so badly, time and again,die, come back, die, come back and eventually "get it right". At least as far as Ishmael Crouch is concerned, I guess there is hope for any idiot, even some former or present Presidents of the United States.

Whatever Mr. Crouch was/is....he headed up the whole group. As he had, basically, all of creation to finally begin to "get things right", he must have developed a keen sense ofr what folk would eventually fit into C, D, E & F.

Somewhere along a *very* long time, he realized he could make a profit off both his failings and successes. Then he discovered the "Not-Quite-Dead" community and discovered that even they had continuing "needs", especially those with mucho money, real estate or other commodities and had deep desires to still make use of it all. Even after they "almost" passed on, they might have non-dead relatives, debts to be paid or a desire for serious payback on those who made them "Not-Quite-Dead".

Ooooh, so many reasons and possibilities to "turn a buck". Ishmael concocted a plan that worked,(unlike the Big Bang), and would give him something that anyone, especially one who had lived for eons, would want..... unlimited POWER!

Thusly, over time....and time....and time again, Crouch found "people" who could be molded to his mindset.

With such unlimited power comes both the desire to keep it and the lust for MORE. *This* is Ishmael Crouch. Again....rumors, discarded trash, even a hint or two from some kindly,(at the moment, at least) spirits,

CHAPTER 12

Dah, Dah, Dah... Dah...Dah...Dah Daaaaaaah! (What? You don't remember Deliverance?)

It was a typical November day, dark and damp. The kind of day that could head in any direction. Warm and sunny, a roaring Nor"Easter a few hours later. *So typical*, she thought to herself....*almost like Lester these days.*

Elizabeth sighed to herself at these thoughts, down in her studio creating new jewelry for the next year's show season. She was an extremely talented artist who was able to immerse herself in her creative muse under the most trying circumstances.

But *this* concerned Lester and Lester was a great artist in his own right. Sure, was also a musician, but these days, *that* was part of the problem. He could get so tangled up in what he was doing to the detriment of everything else and this was one of those times.

Lester is a good man....a good husband. He'll get it all straightened out. He always does....eventually. She thought again about November weather and how it seemed to mirror Lester's moods. It was good he found a friend in Viridian. She was a great friend to them both, and as a musician, would be the anchor Lester needed to keep from spiraling off into God-knows-what-direction.

He was so distracted these days, ever since they moved to Wellfleet. Elizabeth had caught him recently talking to thin air and mumbling about a damned cat....

At that moment, the door upstairs slammed open and Lester came storming into the house.

"Liz! I'm home! Great news! I've got great news to share". He thundered down the stairs into her studio.

"Elizabeth! We've got a job! A paying job for Whydah-Maker! Viridian lined it up for next week."

He ran over and hugged his wife.

"We're gonna play at that restaurant, Forever Clam! And ikt's good money, too!"

Elizabeth smiled at Lester. "Oh, my God! That's wonderful, Lester. About time that someone appreciated what you two do."

It was a touching scene. Neither of them noticed that the weather taking one of those unpredictable, November turns.

Across town by the harbor, Sam Bellamy sat staring off at Great Island....remembering the tavern that stood there so long ago. He too, sighed.

"Mariah....am I a good person?"

Mariah slowly appeared sitting next to him and put her arms around him. First, she giggled.

"Sam, such a silly question. First of all, you *were* a pirate, with all that entailed but, of course? You are a good person. Alright....you've had your moments but....look back at the years....and we're *still* here...together. That's a good thing."

At that the black cat appeared on Sam's left.

"Mrrrreow. Yeah, a lot of years....a *lot* of mistakes."

"Be careful, ye miserable feline. Worthy's right ta call ye names."

Sam turned to Mariah and pointed off to Great Island.

"Ye know, Lass...I have so much money....even if it's in the greedy hands of Crouch, Diabello, Enoch and Flinch. I know I can provide for any living relatives of ours out there after these hundreds of years.."

"Mrrreow....and you can handle anyone who messes with you,too, remember how you...."

"Ye damned cat, aye! I remember....don't make me happy any more, either....not like it used to."

He pointed out to the Island, again.

"One o' these days, I'm goin' to Crouch and have him buy that damned Island for me. Gonna build back the old tavern, too....get some folk ta' run it. Just like the old days."

"Nice thought, Dear", said Mariah.

A bit later found Sam sitting alone on the cliff at Lucifer's Land....what used to be part of *old* Eastham. Staring out over the waters far below, he thought....*almost the anniversary of when th' Whydah went down....just out there....April....not November.....same kind o' weather, tho....* He vaguely pointed offshore. *Just as unpredictable....and still dangerous.*

Looking up at the sky, he sniffed the air as the winds came up.

Smells like a bif storm comin' in, too....just like back then. He shook his head. *So long ago. Aye....so long....*

It was dark outside when Lester and Viridian got together for a practice.

"Hey, V! Getting nasty out there! We're in for a mean night. Good thing we're getting the work in now instead of later on."

Tuning her fiddle, Viridian smiled and commented.

"Yeah, better now than later. Got some ideas for our performance next week at the Forever Clam Restaurant. I'd like us to keep things pretty straight forward. Lets do a lot of fiddle tunes, some folk, maybe a few vocals."

"What? None of the new stuff I'm working on? Gee. I thought we could try a few."

"Les, we're not ready to do all that yet. Let's be careful and do a good job, first."

Lester didn't agree with her but wasn't about to make any waves with his new partner. Viridian added....

"Did you have to insist on that name, WhydahMaker? Sounds too dark and creepy."

"Nah, it'll be great. People will remember it and us. Just you wait! WhydahMaker will be hard to forget. You'll see!"

It was still quite early in the deep, dark morning hours; a typically dismal and dark Cape Cod morning that time of year. The wind was howling, the rain was slashing sideways, against the side of the house.

Persipone Painestaker was still up, not able to sleep. Her own storm was raging inside. So much had gone wrong recently; meeting Lester Worthy and channelling into *his* dreadful world. Sam Bellamy. Really? And those two dreeadful, creepy, ominous Enoch and Flinch! Every word they spoke hinted at terrible threats to her person.

Another night without sleep and these terrible thoughts. Maybe I should have left well enough alone and not warned Lester. No...I'm being silly.
She sat there thinking as a nasty gust of wind took out her power and all went dark.

"Damn! Just what I needed", she swore to herself. Persipone went around lighting candles and lanterns to chase away the dark.

Typical, she thought, *a creepy night, I'm creeped out and the power goes out. Perfect.*

Then, as a bigger gust hit the house, there was a tremendous BANG at the door. Persipone jumped at the sound. Another BANG at the door, only this time, it was followed by repeated bang, bang, bang, BANG!

That was no wind. Someone was at her door.... at this time of night, in this miserable weather. *Now, who could....*as the door flew open with a CRASH against the wall. In walked Mr. Diabello, followed by Enoch and Flinch.

"Why, Ms. Painestakere, how rude of you. Not coming to let us in on this foul night. *Shame* on you." He smiled disarmingly. Enoch, however, snivelled,"No, not very nice of you at all."

"At all", added Flinch. "Shame, shame, so rude." Persipone backed away from them, very unsettled by their presence and bad vibes they were giving off.

"Wha....what can I do for you? I...I'm so sorry. You.... startled me...and that wind. I...."

Mr. Diabello said, "Where are my manners? I am Mr. Diabello, Faustus Diabello, at your service. You have already met my associates, Mr. Enoch and Mr. Flinch." They both nodded in turn.

Mr. Diabello looked around the room and pointed to all the musical instrumentrs lining the walls.

"My! This is quite a collection you have. Do you mind?" He walked over and picked a ukelel off the wall, strumming it.

"You know, Ms. Painestaker, you have quite a reputation around the community. Such a handy seer you are. Well known, in fact, in many communities."

"You have *no* idea how many communities." Mr. Flinch added while snickering.

Sighing, Mr. Diabello shook his head, walking towards Persipone as she backed away in fear.

"I believe you were asked, quite nicely, to cease and desist with your *visions* and interference with a certain Sam Bellamy and his friend, Lester Worthy."

"Yes, very nicely", added Mr. Enoch.

"My firm was very clear about the need for you to, ohhhhh, how to put it? Butt out of our business! But, oh no, not you. This matter is of great concern to a client of ours."

Diabello walked up to Persipone, now becoming an seriously threatening entity. Persipone backed up to the wall with nowhere else to go.

"Look, Mr. Diabello.....I'm sorry if...."

"Too late, my dear!" With that, he swung the ukelele, smashing it against the side of her head. She dropped to the floor stunned and badly injured.

Mr. Flinch took a five string banjo from the wall and began bludgeoning her with it. Mr. Enoch grabbed a tenor banjo, as well.

"Here! Let me help you! This calls for a duet."

By the time they were done, Persipone Painestaker was little more than an unrecognizable, broken mess on the living room floor. They stopped when they realized the late Ms. Painestaker was no longer a threat...at least in *this* world.

Mr. Diabello looked with disdain at the pieces of killer ukelele he still held.

"I have always hated this instrument. Hazardous to your health," throwing the bloody pieces on her remains.

"Now, THAT was dueling banjos!"

Laughing, they exited the house, fading into the miserable night; blood running across the floor of the living room,candles and lanterns flickering weakly in the wind.

CHAPTER 13

Forever Clam (yum) and Beyond

As far as Cape restaurants go, Forever Clam was a prime example of taking a good thing too far. They didn't only offer dishes featuring clams, *everything* was based on clams. Appetizers, salads, main courses, specials, desserts, even drinks. They were known, (and I refuse to say *well*-known), for their clam stout, their clam merlot and clam reisling, (yuck). Desserts included quahog choudah ice cream(with nice chunks of clam) and their clam creme brule, (double yuck).

Hard to imagine the owners would be excited for a duo like WhydahMaker that featured Irish, folk and new age music, (not a clam influenced song to be had). Then again, maybe they were desperate to try anything. For whatever reasons, they were thrilled to get WhydahMaker.

WhydahMaker was equally thrilled to get a paying gig. Les and Viridian were so excited they had a tough time setting up without bubbling with enthusiasm.

"Les, we're going to start with some waltzs and...."

"*Waltzs*? For the first set? Are you nuts? Want to put everyone to sleep?"

"O.K., then....how about an uptempo Irish set?"

"*Now* you're talking! Let's give 'em something to get their feet moving."

And so, the night progressed; successfully, I might add. One great set after another. Happy patrons. A break and then another killer set. The audience was getting a bit rowdy but nothing a few drinks and more music wouldn't cure.

Everyone was clapping and cheering. No one but Lester noticed the figure sitting at a back table, smiling and clapping with the rest. One thing? No one at the table saw he was there. Yup, Sam Bellamy came by to listen to his newest "project", enjoying himself as he hadn't in over a century. Of course, he felt there were improvements that could be made with WhydahMaker; *would* be made, if he had any say in it.

The evening finally ended. Les and V.were exhausted, happy and even better, well paid.

"Les, they loved us!"

"And the owners want us back again."

"Amazing, isn't it? We're on our way."

"Only thing, V? Let's eat before we get here? Waaaay too many clams. Free meal or not? No way."

'Yeah, I agree on that. The clam beer? Not happening. As a matter of fact, speaking of beer, I'm hitting the Lady's Room. Be right back."

"Don't blame you,"

At that, as Viridian walked off, Sam appeared next to Lester.

"Aye, mate. Great first job! Ya had 'em dancin' and prancin', just like in the old days.....I remember a tavern that...."

"Uhhh, Sam....really? Viridian will be back any minute and it's gonna look a kinda strange, me talking to the wall here. Can't we talk about this later?"

"Sure, boyo, sure. Later....'tis I have some ideas to make things even better. Some changes *you're* going to make."

"*Changes*, Sam? Where do you get off having any say in what we do?   This is *our* band; WhydahMaker. *Our* band. You? Along for the ride, I guess....never could figure out why you think you can get involved."

Sam gave Lester a sneering smile.

"Your band? *Your* band? Who do you think *allowed* you to use the name o' my ship? There be power in tha' name. Who pushed ya ta get off yer backside and *do* somenthing for yer self? Yer nothin' wi'out me. *Nothing!*"

"We'll talk some other time, huh? V's coming back."

"By the way? This girlie, V. isn't good enough for *my* band....just sayin."

"And I don't give a damn for what you're saying." They glared at each other. Lester continued, beginning to get angry.

"You have nothing to say about anything, especially Viridian! *She* is the one who made me want to get back into music again, not some moth-eaten, raggedy-ass, old pirate ghost! You....will....leave...her...alone. Hear me?"

Viridian walked up behind Lester.

"Hear what, Les?"

Uh, nothing, V., nothing. Just mumbling to myself....going over some tune ideas. that's all."

"New ideas, huh? Sounded kind of creepy to me."

They took the last of their instruments and walked off to the car, dreaming of future gigs.

Sam sat back at the table with a look that could kill if anyone else could have seen him....if he *wanted* them to see him. As it was, some drunk went to sit down next to him. Sam waved his hand at the guy, who instantly got the idea to be somewhere else, fast. Sam was thinking.

Just you wait, boyo. You are my project. My new toy to play with as I see fit. Oh, you'll find out. You wait and see.

After dropping Viridian off at her house, Les came banging back into his own living room, as usual, instruments crashing and whacking in every direction.

"Honey, I'm home!"

"I never would have guessed. It sounded like a train wreck out here." She kissed him, giving him a big hug.

"*You* look happy. It must have gone well."

"Happy? Happy? Elizabeth, I'm the happiest I've been siknce we moved here! We did such a great job tonight. V was wonderful and we played like we've worked together for years. And guess *what*? They want us back again! For more money!"

"Oh, Les. That's wonderful. Can I come by next time and hear you while I get some dinner?"

"Uhhhh, Elizabeth....I wouldn't suggest dinner. Sure! Come to hear us....but....it's about the dinner menu. At Forever Clam? They *mean* it."

Once again, Sam was sitting at the breakwater, staring out at Great Island, thinking about the old tavern, his mates....all long gone while he was still here. For how long? Mariah appeared next to him.

"You still have me, Sam. Always have. Always will. Where you go, I go. Nothing. No God, no power will ever keep us apart."

"Never, Lass? That be a long, long time", as he turned to face her.

"Good! I got your attention from that silly, old island. Sam? We need to talk."

"Mariah, what's on yer mind that ails ye?"

"*You*, Sam. You and that poor soul Lester Worthy. Can't ye leave the poor man to find his own peace? I seen it happen a'fore with you an' yer plaything. It ain't good, Sam. Not for him an' not fer ye."

Getting angry, Sam turned back rto look at the Island.

"Tha ain't fer ye to decide, Lass. Worthy's mine, ye hear? *Mine*! I dinna get much enjoyment out a this.... this....(sweeping his hands all around himself)..... *existance*! When I be done wi' the boyo, I'll be done. Not a'fore!"

"But you will leave the poor man....*whole*, Sam? Dinna ye think he and his wife deserve *they's* happiness, too?"

"Ooooooh, he be fine, Mariah. I'll be tired o' him some day ands leave 'em in peace." Smiling and putting his arm around her shoulder, "Mayhaps, I'll get ol' Crouch and th' boys ta leave 'em something fer his troubles. How be tha'?"

Mariah snuggled up closer to Sam and they watched the sun set beyond Great island. A certain, very quiet black feline shook his head and sat slightly off, lashing his tail, not believing Sam at all. Cat's, after all, believe very little of what humans....present or past....have to say and promise.

The next weekend, the usual bang, twang and clatter took place upstairs during the WhydahMaker rehearsal. *Nothing new here,* Elizabeth thought and went back to work.

"No! Damn it, NO! That is the stupidest song I've ever heard. You want to do *that*? What happened to us doing more of our original stuff? And ukelele, too? No ****ing way!"

"Hey, Les. These are *good* songs. Even better? No omne's heard them in so long and...."

"Probably a damn good reason why, too."

"Will you shut up and listen for a change? *I* trhink these are songs that will make people remember usa and want us back. You just think these songs of mine popular will be popular....or worse? That they could like them more than yours."

"Les cut her off again. "Uke? Popular? Get over it, V. Never gonna happen."

"You can be such a fool, Les." At that, she gort up and walked away.

"Hey! Calm down, will ya?"

"I'll be back in a bit. If I were you, I'd think about what I said."

As Viridian stormed off, Sam appeared next to Lester.

"She's right, ya know? Well, in *some* ways she's got it right. In others? No way, boyo....Tha' damned ukelele thing? Gotta go. Shameful. Some of those songs? Got to go, too. Ye be right 'bout them. Sad things, those songs. She be right though about the people. Ye get the crowd to remember ye. Play songs ta rouse 'em and make 'em remember ye. Now, tha' bein' said.....I've got a list o' songs I want ye to do and...."

"Bellamy! Who are *you* to tell *us* what to play? You sorry excuse for a ghost, getting your jollies off our hard work? I can put up with you hangin' around but you are becoming an annoying pain in the ass!"

Sam glared threateningly at Lester.

"Boyo, if I be ye, I'd hold me tongue if ye want to keep it in yer head!"

"*Really*, Sam Bellamy? Mr. Big, Bad Pirate? You can't do nuthin'." Lester pointed his finger and poked it right through Sam's chest.

"Nuthin'! Ya bag of hot, stale air. Nuthin'!

Sam let out a *grrrrrrrrr*. "Boyo, ye have no idea wha I can and will do." At that he faded.

"Ooooooooooooo, I' so afwaid of the big, bad piwate."

Viridian went downstairs and sat down with Elizabeth.

"He's being an asshole, again?" Elizabeth said it with long experience.

"Elizabeth, *you* can say it. He's *your* husband."

She laughed. "Hey! Feel free. He's *your* music partner. Call it like it is. He'll appreciate you for it. Now, me? I'd shut up and not talk to him at all for a few days until he realized what a **** he was being. You? Get his attention."

They both laughed. "Well, I'd better get back up there before he decides to burn my ukelele."

Elizabeth chuckled and went back to her work. She heard the steps fading back up the stairs, then heard a loud, "You ****ing idiot! Now *you* listen to *me*!"

The rehearsal contiinued, more or less according to plan. WhydahMaker was on it's way to interesting times.

Later that evening, as the rehearsal finally broke up, Les and Viridian were heading back downstairs. Elizabeth was watching the news and looked up.

"Well, it sounds like you two got it all worked out. I didn't hear any more yelling and, from the look, there was no bloodshed."

Viridian laughed. "No, we got over it. We always do. No big deal."

"Yeah, right", Lester chimed in with a grimace. Viridian playfully punched him.

"Hey, you, get over it."

"I just heard something interesting on the news. Didn't you know a Persipone....Painestaker? You went to see her? I thought someone by that name called you about some weird stuff."

Lester stopped. "Yeah, some wack-job seer was going on about all kinds of spiritual mumbojumbo. Crazy lady. Why?"

"On the news, they mentioned that name. If it wasn't such a curious name, I would never have taken notice. The police found her murdered....beaten to death....apparently, a very bizarre murder done with a ukelele and banjo as the murder weapons. So sad. So *strange*. Here in town, too."

That shook Lester. "Painestaker? Dead? Murdered? Now who would do such a....."

It was dark at the jetty when Sam finally appeared next to Mariah.

"Sam! I wondered where you got off to."

"Oh, I was looking out for my interests.

Les and that Lass, Viridian. Sat in ta' one o' they's rehearsals. Interesting, it was. I let ol' Les know my mind. Lad has an evil temper, he does. Should learn how to speak to his elders."

"Then you didn't hear. C, D, E,&F took care of that.....problem you went to see them about. The Painestaker woman? *You* said they was goin' to convince her to back away from your....project."

"Aye, I did. They promised to scare her off, right proper too....interferin' wi' my fun, she was."

"Well, they scared her off....permanent like. She be dead. Crouch sent some of his minions ta kill the poor woman."

Sam turned to Mariah. "Dead, ye says? Dead? They tol' me it was ta scare her off, not ta kill the woman."

"Sam, you let these people go way too far. Tha woman dinna deserve ta' die. Sam? I'm getting tired of all this and how that group be doin' business. It ain't right and all. They scare even *me* an' I be dead a long time an..."

"Mariah, Lass, don' ye worry 'bout it. I can handle tha' crew, now, don' ye worry."

He put his arm around her and pulled her close. As they faded into the night, the cat sat there, thinking catly thoughts about how gullible folk can be....even after being dead all that time....Humans....Bah! Dead or alive. Never learn. Meorrrrrwwww*****!"

CHAPTER 14

Voyage of the WhydahMaker Begins

Author's notes: After all this time, it always amazes me. Yes, after all this time. The reality that so many notes have survived, disgusting as they may be and amazed that many haven't rotted away or been eaten by vermin but that no recordings of the band, WhydahMaker exist. No tapes, rehearsals, albums, nothing. I wanted to ask Lester's wife, Elizabeth, but the lady has a pretty bad temper herself, and isn't afraid to come out swinging with anything close at hand, especially where this subject is concerned. Much safer to stay away these days. I'm not exactly her favorite person. What language.

"I *know* there are some recordings out there somewhere. Maybe that can be another project down the road. I am told the band started out very good and became, as many put it, *very interesting*.

It took some time, but in such a confined area as Cape Cod, word tends to travel fast, especially where music is concerned. For Les, Viridian and WhydahMaker, the gigs began to happen. Slowly at first, most being the usual "free" gigs for cheap bastards whose bottom line always included the key word, "exposure".

That bothered Les a bit but Viridian was patient, always reminding him about how it all worked. Les, always countered that after so many years as a musician, he knew damned well how it all worked and *exposure* was just another word for *Cheap Bastard*.

V always won out....for the time being. WhydahMaker was gaining a buzz around the Cape as a "fun" group with refreshingly different ways of approaching the traditional Irish and folk music. *Fun* translated as, "not what we expected.....ever." *Different* translated as WTF? But Les and V were having a blast and it showed. The public began to adore them. Sam? Well, Sam continued to throw in his coinage to the mix which infuriated Lester more and more. Sooner or later there were going to be.... issues. And all the time, Viridian didn't have a clue other than her partner.....occasionally seemed to have a screw or two loose, muttering to himself or talking to thin air. Especially when *he* thought she wasn't paying attention.

She, however, thought, again on occasion, that she, herself was going a bit dotty. There were times....rare times....out of the corner of her eye....the edge of her vision....she could swear.....a *pirate* was standing next to Les? Naaah. Too much wine, she thought....but still....

Author's note: O.K., back again.....concerning the band, "WhydahMaker"? I believe I went into a bit of it's short history, but having rediscovered Lester Worthy's original notes....again,(see leaf bag file #133), it might be entertaining to look back.

One of the interesting factors concerning the notes? They are probably the most legible, (and possibly more sanitary) notes available to me. Originally, I thought they were done on wrapping paper from the local Wellfleet Dunkin Donuts but later realized that, besides jelly and sugar all over the "pages", there were telltale grease stains one would NOT find from DD. Research sent me to a small "real" donut shop up in Harwich that used real grease that made far less healthy but ooooh, so good donuts. Lester Worthy occasionally showed good tase. I digress.

When Lester and Viridian first realized that their group *really* was becoming a group, they had to decide on a name. *That*, in itself, caused some friction. When Viridian suggested the name, "Fiddle D.D." and "Fadiddle" as possible names, Lester almost lost it. Picking a name wasn't going to be easy.

Lester's contributions will remain unnamed for many reasons, knowing Lester and his New Jersey roots. Things better left unstated. No, the real name came about one night after a particularly great rehearsal..... good for Les and V but not particularly good for a certain pirate we have come to know.

Lester was still upstairs after V left the rehearsal, joyful and bubbling over how well they were sounding. Lester was cleaning up the studio while trying to ignore Sam, who was sitting around in various places, moving from time to time to annoy Lester.

"We sounded *really* good tonight, not that *you* have anything to say about it. You always have some nasty remarks to make."

"Here now, Boyo. This be *my* project as well as your'n. I be puttin' my coin in where I feels it best. So don' ye be gettin' all high an' mighty wi' *me*."

Lester whipped around to face Sam. "Bellamy, why don't you stop the big, bad pirate act? I know you can talk like us." He looked Sam up ands down scornfully.

"Ye may think you have to look the part but ya don't have to sound it. I mean, really, Arrrrrrrr?"

A snarl crossed Sam's face. "Alright, Lester, my good, *good* friend. If I were *you*, I'd be a little bit more careful about how you speak to your...."

"*Elders?* Don't make me laugh, Bellamy. Not much you can do to me. Ya said it yourself. What can you *possibly* do to me besides haunt me? Been there. Done that. Over and out. BOO!"

Sam hissed. "Easy, now Mr. Worthy. Arrrrr, is it? Ye may not want ta' find out what I *am* capable o' doin' ta the likes of ye."

Lester finished putting things away, stopped, turned and faced Sam. "Really? Well, g*ood* for you." A nasty look crossed Lester's face this time, along with a particularly wicked grin.

"You know, Sam? I finally got an idea for the *perfect* name for the band. Want to hear it? It so fits....along with our....friendship and your overwhewlming *interest* in the band. I'm calling us....WhydahMaker. Arrrrrrrr. How's that float your boat?"

For the first time in many, many years, Sam was shocked and at a loss for words. His face first showed it, then his smile curled down into an angry scowl.

"Here now Lester. You best not be takin' the good name o' me ship in vain. I will not brook with such insolence. Have a care, now."

Lester continued.

"Yup, WhydahMaker! Fits, too. Ya had your beloved ship? You *lost* it! You had your beloved Mariah? Lost her, too.

WhydahMaker will commemorate that you're a God....DAMNED....LOSER!"

At that, the apparition that was Sam Bellamy swelled, seemingly filling the room and with a enraged scream, he disappeared.

Lester yelled after him. "And every time we play? Every time we get applause? Each....and every....time we perfom? ME and YOU....will know that people are celebrating a TOTAL LOSER, SAD-ASSED GHOST! Haaaaaaaahaaaaaaaa. *What* do you *think* of *that*?"

Elizabeth called from the bottom of the stairs, quite concerned at the raving she heard.

"Les? Is everything alright? My God. What's with all the yelling and screaming? What happened? What is...."

Elizabeth, nothing wrong....just going over some....song lyrics to a new idea....giving me some trouble....kind of lost my temper a bit..... tried to get into the mood of the song."

"Mmmmmmmmm, if you say so. Come down soon, please?"

Downstairs, Elizabeth was worried. She feared lester was heading for a breakdown and regressing back into his former, "wacky land" faze he was in during that awful Beethoven incident. Things had been going so well here in their new home, their new town. Maybe, if she talked him into going to dinner in town....just a thought....some place with *no* music.

The name, WhydahMaker stuck. Even Viridian felt that it was a good fit....not **quite** in the way Lester explained it to Sam Bellamy, of course. That *would* have been crazy, huh?

Yes, Les and "V" as WhydahMaker were beginning to make waves....well, at least tiny ripples in the Outer Cape communities. But even considering this, they came to the attention to a *very* important set of ears; one May Potawatomi, aka March Madness, who had been listening.

As the morning show host of the Silkie and the Harpie on waaaaaay Outer Cape Cod Radio, WPDQ, she was always on the prowl for new....uhhhhhh, talent.

She knew groups like the One Chords, Deadbass, Proudfoot Roachstomper....even Kelly Anne and the Carnavegans, well known to all at the Outer Cape, were great for her listeners but she was always looking for that "new act", even if it wasn't a "new low".

Just the idea of that name, WhydahMaker, gave her a shiver thinking, *I can do something with these guys. Maybe it was time to track them down and have a listen.*

So began her search. Her music radar, as warped as it was these days, was actively pinging out towards the Wellfleet area.

Meanwhile, further "off-Cape" than one could possibly imagine....

Marie, the head secretary for C.,D.,E.&F., appeared in Mr. Crouch's office, interrupting his meeting with client Napoleon Bonaparte.

"Excuse me, sir. I'm sorry to interrupt but.....Oh! Nappy! Is that you?"

Napoleon turned with a start. "Marie? Marie, what are *you* doing here.... working for Crouch?"

"Well, yes Nappy....for some time, now."

Crouch rumbled a chuckle and cut her off.

"Yes, Napoleon. I hired your old flame Marie. I find that it's always....handy to have people around who can have an, ohhhhh, say an influence on some of our clients.... such as yourself, for instance."

Napoleon started to say something, first to Marie, then to Crouch. Instead, he glared at both of them and popped out of the office.(Yes, quite literally, popped.)

Mr. Crouch sighed, "Yes, Marie? Who comes unannounced, knocking....so to ummmmm speak, at my door?"

"It's Captain Sam Bellamy, sir. He doesn't have an appointment."

"No problem, Ms. Antoinette, please see him in. We do have literally, all the time in the world."

Sam blew into the office, immediately getting to the point.

"Look, Crouch, *you* told me you were going to take care of the Painestaker problem."

"Which we *did,* Sam.*"*

"You were supposed to scare her off, not scare her and *off* her! People are beginning to talk about it and I don't need all the wackjobs hangin' about, causin' me grief."

"Sam, Sam....she was becoming a major problem to us *all*. We tried to scare her off; twice, to be sure....but you know those banjo playing types. We had no choice. Better for us all in the end."

"Ishmael, I don't agree with your methods....not in this case. Too heavy handed for my liking."

"We'll take your concerns under advisement, Sam. Wouldn't want to cause bad....blood, so to speak, between the firm and one of our best clients. Now! Was there anything else I can help you with?"

"I want ye to buy Great Island off Wellfleet."
Crouch was at a loss for words. He stood up as if stunned.

"Sam! Are you kidding me? What can you possibly want with that old island, not to mention the *other-side* one, as well. Any way, The national Seashore has it under it's protection as an historic saite. I can't do...."

"Yes, ye can, Crouch." He pointed a finger at the head of the firm.

"Me? I got me enough gold'n silver put aside, whi' all the interest ta buy th" whole, damn state of Massachusetts! Ye can buy a lil' ol' island worth nuthin' but the crabs, bugs n' birds. It won't hurt ye none, especially if ye wants me business over the loooong future, tha' is?"

Crpouch sat down and sighed. "O.K., Sam. Alright. I'll make it happen.....but it'll take *time*!"

"Just do it, Crouch. Just do it. One las' thing? When ye get's it? Yer goin' ta hire a crew ta build somethin' fer me. Yer goin' ta build a new, Great Island Tavern, an' I'll help picks th' crew ta run it, Hear?"

"Sam, you're out of your pirate mind. This wouldn't be Mariah's doing, now would it?"

"She doesn't no a thing 'bout this. It be my surprise."

Crouch shook his head in resignation. "Yes, alright, Sam. I get it. It will be done." He pointed back at Sam.

"It won't be cheap, either, and it won't be easy. People will talk, too. It'll take time."

"Well, as ye says, we got all the time in the world, din' ya? Make it happen. It'll be fun. You'll see,.Sam popped out of the office.

Crouch shook his head. "Fun....Fun, he says.....better call the firm together for this one."

CHAPTER 15

And Now, Back to the Band

There were a few more gigs and many more rehearsals. Slowly, Lester was wearing Viridian down with some of the "new" material; again, not exactly what she was looking for, but in some way if she would admit it, she was having fun with it.

Oh, they kept building on the traditional, the Irish and the crossover, original music lester was messing around with. After Bellamy's continuing interference though, Lester began to write more....*prickly* music, if only to annoy Sam.

They had a local gig that night at the local Minesweeper Pub. Having gotten with it and it's denizens, Lester felt it should be renamed the Bomb Crater Pub, but *that* was just Lester's opinion. He was happy, though. Getting a gig at the Minesweeper was a big step up for WhydahMaker.

That night Les and V began with all their usual music; a little Ieish here, a little folk there, here, there an original piece. The crowd seemed to be enjoying it and they felt they would be invited back on other evenings. Hey! Paying gigs? Wonderful!

Suddenly, Lester realized that Sam Bellamy was sitting at the back of the pub, booted feet up on a table top, unseen, of course, to anyone else. He was smiling and beating his foot to the music. Les turned to V after the applause died down.

"V? Let's try one of the new songs, huh?"

"Les? What do you mean? Oh. No. She saw the look on Les' face.

"Oh, no! Lester, not *that* one, please?"

She was referring to an extremely obnoxious"hybrid" (a kind thing to call it), of Irish, punk and altered lyrics that would probably be shunned anywhere but here, at the Minesweeper. Viridian wasn't all that comfortable with doing it but she knew Lester wasn't going to listen to reason.

Oh, well, she thought, *we're doomed. So much for coming back here again.*

WhydahMaker tore into the new material with an exuberance that surprised the audience. The concersations quieted down as people, even the drunks, began to take

Sam? He sat up, putting both feet on the floor. His expressions was hard to figure as the song ripped into the first lyrics. Verse. Chorus. Verse. Chorus. Break. Line by line. Loud note by louder note. The audience, caught up with this new raucousness, started to cheer, clap and stomp along with the music. Les & V tore into the final chorus and came crashing to a halt on the last chord. The crowd went wild! All but Sam, that is.

Les smiled. V was in shock. They hugged, dancing around a bit. Les yelled loud enough for her to hear.

"See? I told you so! We're a hit. They *love* us!"

V couldn't argue with that. They *were* a hit, something she wouldn't have expected, but....wow!

The crowd was buzzing about what they had just played. Les turned to V.

"Let's try another one....maybe not as obnoxious as the last?"

Viridian was getting into it, though.

"How about that other one, "Bow legged Women?"

"Yeah! Time to turn it up to 11.!"

Oh, God, she thought, *I'm as bad as him!*

The hooting and stomping started as the new song began., with even more enthusiasm. People were taking notice to this band. Sam Bellamy was taking notice, too..... and he wasn't thrilled....well, maybe a little bit.....just that this wasn't *his* idea about the way things were going.

Someone else was in the audience that night who was *extremely* attentive; March Maxtor, aka March Madness, also known to a few, as May Potowatami, hostess with the.....something....of the show, The Silkie and the Harpie", there at waaaaasay Outer Cape Radio, WPDQ, (not to be confused with the far more respectable P'Town radio station).

She was taking notice to WhydahMaker and was making plans for them; *big* plans. She thought they were a *little* rough around the edges....well, many of her groups had nothing *but* edges. She had a bright idea that, with a little direction, they would fit right in. Now? To talk to the band and make some arrangements to get them on WPDQ....live.

This was going to be good....and, hopefully, the beginning of a long, long friendship.
(Little did she know....but that's for later).

AUTHOR'S NOTE: Back again. Yeah, sorry 'bout that. So much to add. March/ May sat and talked to Les & V after the show. Everyone was still bubbling about the band, even the professional drunks. You could hear the buzz: *What happened? They were pretty good...and then? AND THEN?? They unleashed musical Hell on the pub. It was love at first clash.*

Les and V were truly excited Wow! The radio....even if it *was* WPDQ. They were scheduled to be on The Silkie and the Harpie next Saturday morning. Live! Wow, again.

Sam not only had nothing to say about it, he wasn't around at all; a big plus as far as Lester was concerned. They couldn't wait. So excited, Viridian called for, and demanded, practice after practice....torture for Lester, but she put her foot down. *No crazy songs! None! Not with their big chance at the "big" time.* Of course, lester nodded in agreement....but he had *other* plans. Time would tell.

Saturday morning was fast approaching and WhydahMaker was ready for it's big debut on waaaay outer Cape Radio.

Saturday morning came as they made their way out to P'Town and hitched a ride on a local fishing trawler out to the old lightship, "The Leaky Toilet", home to WPDQ.

They were escorted to the waiting room/ practice area until Max called for them. While they were nervously tuning, they listened to the WPDQ show already in progress.

"And now, a word from one of our sponsors:
Romeo, oh, Romeo. Where for art thou, Romeo? (silence)....more insistent this time.
"Romeo, oh, Romeo. Where for art thou, Romeo? (silence)....even louder this time)

ROMEO, OH, ROMEO. WHERE FOR ART THOU, ROMEO?

"Oh, HELL!" (the window slams shut).
announcer: "Yes, is this you? Have you been failing at the dating game? It's time for you to become one of the many, satisfied people who have joined, Light My Fire Dating Service. There is a match out there, waiting for *you* to strike it! Come join us today. Call us at 1-800-GTALIFE."

Meanwhile, back in town

There they were, Elvis and Napoleon, sitting on a bench outside the town liquor store, watching the locals and tourists strolling by, totally unaware.

"Beautiful day, Nappy, whacha say?"

"I tell you time and again, my friend, eet ees no *Nappy* and eef you even think to try ,*Boney,* eensteads, you will neveh hear zee end of eet!"

"Look, lil' buddy, ah'm sorry. It's jus' what ah do with names, yuh know?"

"Oui, I know but eet is no right."

"Sh'm sorry, Lil'Buddy. A beautiful day, ain't it? Here in Pir...Wellfleet."

He began to laugh while Napoleon snickered.

"Oui, Wellfleet, yes? Ha! Even Pirate's Cove."

They both had a good laugh. Napoleon pointed to Elvis.

"And what ees thees you are eating? Eet does not look like quiche, non?"

"Quiche? Nah, Nappy, none o' tha' fairy, French food. This? A Good ol' American, peanut butter, banana and bacon sandwich. Ah've added some mayo and mustard to give it some oomph. Wanna bite?"

"MERDE!" Napoleon popped from sight. "Well, moah fuh me."

Meanwhile, elsewhere

Mr. Ishmael Crouch called the emergency meeting of the firm to order.

"Gentlemen, we are facing a unique crisis, and it's name is Samuel Bellamy."

Each member put in it's two cents to the discussion.

"Unbelievable, having us buy an entire island."

"Really, two islands, if you consider the other...."

"And the one is under the protection of both the EPA and the Historical Society. Madness!"

short note: (remember, there are two "versions' of the Island in question; Great Island in the mortal world, Really Big Island in the after/other-life)

"Do you realize what kind of bribes it took to buy the damned thing."

"Things."

"Whatever."

"The promises we had to make?"

"And rebuilding that old tavern? After all this time? I don't appreciate our firm being laughed at."

"Yes, gentlemen, a problem that grows with each, passing day. We *must* humor one of our biggest clients but we need to bring him into line. Let him have his *fun*.... for the moment."

Mr. Crouch leaned over with an expression that indicated he was about to make a *very* serious point.

"We'll let him have his island and even his tavern. Bellamy almost has as much money as *we* do after all this time....but....we will make Mr. Bellamy realize *who* controls this company and it's resources....even if some of them are *his*. Soon? Down the line, a lesson may be necessary. Here's what I'm considering....."

Back to WPDQ

"And now! One of our most favorite bands....because we're the *only* ones who will play them....and *you*, dear listeners, are the only ones who *want* to hear them! Yes! It's DEADBASS with their newest endeavor, "The Ballad of Deadbass!" Good luck."

Oh, we went out fishin' a few weeks ago....
Waaay, oh, heeey ho, bringin' four cases of beer, oh!
Went out fishing for the ol' striped bass.
Waaay, oh, heeey ho, got four cases of beer-oh.
Drank two of them on the way.
Caught more bass than we should say.
Drank the rest goin' back the waaaay....
Waaay, oh, heeey ho, no more beer is left, no!
Drunk as skunks back at the car.
Waaay, oh, sooooo drunk ho.
Dumped the bass in the trunk, it's true.
Forgot 'em there for a week or two.
Waaaay ohhh, funk ho stinkin', stankin', stunk ho!

Author's note this song goes on longer than deceny permits....ho.

Max came out of the studio.
"Guys! We're ready for you. let's go!"
Les turned to V, "Let's go get 'em, Lady....Ho!"
They played a "tame" song; a bit Irish, a bit not, way more beat than than the "tradition Nazi's" would accept. Seeing Max looking pained from the booth, Les whispered to Viridian, *I don't think she's pleased with our choice.*
"Les? Who cares? We sound *great* Leave it at that."
"Uhhh....no? Let's give 'em that punk/Irish version of "Piece of Crap.""
Viridian cringed but could do little when Lester did a quick countoff and ripped into the song. *Now* Max was smiling....and tapping....and dancing around. Before the song had ended, the phones were ringing off the hooks in the booth, keeping Max busy.

The song finally ended and, to Viridian, it couldn't have been soon enough. However, as she looked to the booth....

"Les? I think we've gotten someone's attention."

"Ya think? Ha, V. We've made it!"

The monitors came back on.

"Yes! You heard it *first*, here on WPDQ! The band, WhydahMaker! The phones are ringing off the hook here, so if you're trying to call in, please have patience. Wow! Expect to hear a lot more from this dynamic duo! And, now, yes....we must....a song from your friend and his, Proudfoot Roachstomper!"

The screeching and clashing began as Max left the booth and came to the performing area.

"Great, you two! That was absolutely *great!* O.K., O.K., honestly? That first one, unnnnnnn, not so great....bor---ing. Even that second song? Probably a little too *tame* for *our* audience....but,hey....we can work on that, yeah, we;ll work on that."

She escorted them from the room, an arm around each as she spun her web, giving them advice on what they should do next....

Sam Bellamy stood in the back, fuming. He was *not* a happy pirate, *Tha' witch? She be thinkin' ta takes my project away from me? ME? Well now, little Lady. We be seein' 'bout tha'. We be seein' 'bout tha'.*

He faded from sight, still mumbling threats....

CHAPTER 16

Aftermath, Part One

Things have been set in motion, wheels have begun to turn and will not stop until the end of this tale.

Elizabeth was sitting home. She had been listening to the WPDQ broadcast and wasn't exactly thrilled with most of what she heard. In truth, she was disgusted with it all....except for WhydahMaker. Alright, She didn't like their final song. *What the Hell were those two thinking*? They have such a great sounding duo and then....well, for sure she could hear Lester's imfluence....hard to mistake his heavy brand of sarcasm when he let it loose on an unsuspecting world.

Anyway, she was happy for them. Lester needed this. He had been drifting aimlessly ever since that Beetroot disaster, lost in the horror he couldn't dismiss. Elizabeth had thought that by moving here to the Cape, it would help bring him back to his old self.

More disturbing? What the Hell was all this going on with him? The muttering about somewhere called Pirate's Cove....and what was going on with whoever, *whatever* he was talking to in thin air?

Oh, he'd see her looking and listening; try to brush it all off as talking through some ideas....but *she* knew better. Somehting was wrong that was dragging Lester away from her. It was almost as if he was talking to an actual person. She even caught a name once or twice....Bellamy? And talking down at the floor? He says, *Oh, I'm talking to one of our cats*. Really? They weren't in the room. She sighed heavily.

My one hope has been the music and thank *God* for Viridian, dragging Lester away from all that brooding. All the time hiding in the recording studio like a hermit was no good for him. God knows, she has tried but doesn't speak "musician".

Yeah, Viridian has given him a distraction....back to the *real* world. That's what she thought....until recently. *What the Hell was going on, anyway?* She sighed again.

She had to adfmit, they had a blast as WhydahMaker and today gave them such a boost, even if that....*station* was a plague on the airwaves. If they're lucky, their live broadcast might bring them some work....*paying* work.

That would get Lester excited. It's always bugged him that, as a musician, he was always sucking down the money without contributing something back to her. Maybe now, that'll change.

She heard the car drive up, the doors slam and Les and V laughing out loud. Wow! She hadn't heard his laughter in a *long* time. This was a good sign.

"Hi, Honey! We're home!"

They both came exploding into the living room. Cases, music, equipment swinging every which way.

"Oh, Elizabeth! This was so much fun! Did you hear? Did you hear?"

"Les is right. That was *so* much fun, Elizabeth", Viridian chimed in. "We were the best music played the entire show."

"Ha! That's for sure, V. That other crap? *That* wasn't music. Get out some wine! We gotta celebrate!"

A bit later, after all the celebration and wine, things settled down everywhere *but* in Lester's brain which was still working overtime.

(Lester to himself) *Wow! This is great! We were so good....and all those calls phined in to the station! I didn't know so many people listened to WPDQ. WE WERE GREAT!!! The excitement! The power of it all! WhydahMaker is on our way. Finally! We get some respect. I GET RESPECT! All those years being ignored. Not any more. No more laughing behind my back. Now people will see what we can do.*

Thank God that Viridian got me off my butt....but now? I've got to get her to take more chances with the music. MY music. This will be great! Now, to get her onboard with my new stuff. Traditional? Boring. They loved us on WPDQ! His face dropped into a scowl.

Yeah, right. Then there's that loser, Bellamy telling us what to do; telling ME what to do. Loser! Loser ghost. Lousy pirate to begin with. Should mind his own, dead business. So he thinks he can control what I do? What to write? How to play? Ohhhh, we'll see about that!

(Now, to Viridian on her way back home) *That was so fun today. It amazes me how well we work together. I do wish he's slow down a bit.....well, a lot. All these crazy ideas he wants to try....yeah, some are fun but, really? The real crazy stuff? I don't see anyone but the rabid, WPDQ fans liking his new music. We keep this up? It's the Cape. I see disaster. I think I can get Lester to back off....I hope. Something strange is really going on with him. He almost has me believing there is someone in the room with us, even when we're out performing. Did I actually hear him mutter the name, "Sam Bellamy"? This is NOT good....for me....for him....for us. Oh, what should I do?*

(March Maxtor, still on the Leaky Toilet) *I'm gonna put WPDQ on the map! Not some third rate local station. Watch out you other P'Town station, we're gonna be number one! WhydahMaker's gonna be my ticket to make it happen!*

All I have to do is keep on that Worthy guy. He's the key. Talented? Yeah! Crazier than anyone we play here? Pretty sure but he makes crazy work for him. Lester and Viridian, together? Priceless. I gotta get to work.

(Finally, at a board meeting of C,D,E&F) "Gentlemen", Mr. Crouch rumbled, "we are in deep trouble. There is a large, negative cash flow at this crucial moment."

Mr. Diabello chimed in. "Well, we *have* had setbacks with some of our client projects. These things do happen, especially over *our* long term. It's to be expected."

Mr. Enoch retorted, "Minor setbacks are one thing. Look at our history. We've all experienced, ahem, set-backs in our past." (nods of heads in agreement around the table.)

Mr. Flinch takes the floor.

"Yes, we're strapped for cash in the immediate future but the real problem is our big client, Sam Bellamy. *He* has drained our coffers with this wild scheme of his. Buying an entire island....an *historic* island at that....*and* it's counterpart in the otherworld.

The bribes we had to pay! The hand holding. The threats, not to mention the growing construction costs. Bellamy is out of control and is losing his focus. Then you add that damned music group....WhydahMaker, to the mix. Gentlemen, we're sinking fast and after three hundred years, Bellamy is losing it as well!"

Mr. Crouch gets things back under control.

"Gentlemen, gentlemen. We will rein in Mr. Bellamy and his....how to say it, spending like a sailor. We will bring him under control....and that band of his....may be the leverage we need to get him back on track. We'll see. For now, though? We have a grave financial issue and we can't let our other clients know how deeply we have hurt their own accounts. It's all temporary, of course and, over the years, we have weathered far worse."

(All of them silently thinking of the many, painful, deadly times they had each messed up in a long, messy past.)

Crouch continued.

"We must be cautious with *all* our accounts for the time being. It will all work out, have no fear. Gentlemen? Enough for the moment. Please come up with suggestions on how we may handle this temporary....minor financial glitch. Ummmmmmm, Faustus? Would you remain behind for a moment? I have something to discuss with you."

The meeting broke up leaving Faustus and Ishmael behind. They both sat back down. Faustus looked worried.

"Ishmael, what is it?"

"Faustus, you are my oldest partner and we have been together the longest."

(What he didn't say was, that outside of Ishmael Crouch, he had been killed off for bad deals almost as many times as himself, give or take a millennia or two.)

"Yes, we have a far graver problem than I let on in the meeting. Some of our more, ummmmmm, recent dealings did not work out well. We can't blame Bellamy for all of it."

"Like the Enron disaster? Buying into the New York Jets? Dot Coms?"

"Yes, yes, *yes*! All of those and more. All unfortunate errors, but we can weather the storm until things rebound. We have to watch what we, as a firm, spend, especially as it *is* our clients money."

"Bellamy's fault?"

"No, no. A final straw, perhaps. *Technically,* we are quite fluid....if one doesn't look too closely. We simply need to direct our clients away from....overspending on new projects....for the time being."

"Like Bellamy?"

"Exactly....*especially* Bellamy. He needes to remember who is in charge of protecting his funds.. That's all for now. We'll talk more."

As they left the boardroom of C, D, E & F to fade through the door, none of them noticed a small, tuxedo cat sitting in a corner, taking it all in....

(Finally, moving on to Sam and Mariah)

They were sitting, once again, at the harbor gazing out towards Great Island where construction had begun.

"Mariah, I can't believe it's finally happening; bringing the old tavern back to life, but new again."

Looking at her, he smiled.

"We spend many happy hours there, didn't we?"

"Yes, Sam, but some hard times, too. You just don't want to recall them.

"Ahhhhh, Mariah, that was then. This will be different. Dinna worry. All ta be well. Ye'll see, Lass."

"Sam? Can we finally talk about Lester and Viridian? Won't you let them be? You ha' had yer fun with 'em. Let 'em live in peace, will ye? Thou hast had yer fun n' games. Leave 'em be, please?"

Sam scowled.

"Leave 'em be, ye say? Why, Lass, I ha' big plans fer they. This be too much fun ta let it lie. I ha'nt had this much fun in a century o' two. Leave 'em be? Fah! They be mine....ta do wi' as I see's fit."

Sam let loose all his anger and frustration on Mariah.

"Know ye all I been goin' through all these years? First, stuck workin' for me family in a dead end job, Then? I go ta sea which dinna work out so well as I

I be learnin' the trade. Then tha' mess goin' after the damned Spanish gold....already long gone. So? I tres piratin'. Damned crews and their damned "Articles"! Tellin' me, ME! What I got ta do for them! What di' I get out o' it? TROUBLE! A ship so damned overloaded....an....an...."

He looked longingly at Mariah. "An all I wanted was ta get back to thou. What a damed mess. An now? God ha' shipwrecked me here forever."

She hugged him warmly. "At least he stuck ye here with me. Sam, ain't tha' enough?"

"Mayhap, mayhap it be.." He pointed out to the island.

"I be doin' tha' for us. Our descendents will be given the chance to run the tavern I be buildin'. I be havin' WhydahMaker as tha' band....only they dinna know it yet....forever an' a day....if I can."

He smiled at her. "An' we be hangin' there, be like the ol' days, again, Mariah. Just you an' me."

"Ohhh, Sam." She sighed, rested her head on his shoulder as they both gazed out across the water to the island construction site.

CHAPTER 17

In Your Dreams!

It took a long time but Lester finally got to sleep. As he dozed off, his mind slipped into a trip to town....sort of....

Lester was strolling down Commercial Street. It was a pretty morning? Afternoon? Evening? He couldn't tell but it was nice. Lester figured to call it morning and be done with it. He passed Uncle Ernie's Bridge that connected Little Big Hill to the town.

Turning up Bankrupt Street, (named after a little bank that once tried but couldn't), he passed the spooky, old lodge and several shops, eventually coming out onto Main Street in the quaint, bustling town of....*Well, no, that's not right*...Pirate's Cove. Boy! For a busy morning it was super quiet, even with all the people, cars and bikes. *(Wait a minute! No one had any faces....well, they were all blurry.)*

Past the General Store, the liquor store,(Very popular, even in a dream), more shops. Reservation Hall and more galleries.

In a parking lot, Lester walked next to a food truck marked, "Bubba's Grub". The owner, a big, very overweight guy with a slicked back pompadore, shades and a terribly dated leisure suit, called to him.

"Yo, buddy! Ya'll want ta try some *really* good Southern-type food? Get over here. Yup, here ya go. Try this."

Lester skeptical, even in a dream, took the wrapped sample and cautiously took a bite.

"What in God's name.....this is disgusting!"

"Ahhhh, now. Be careful. You're hurtin' mah feelin's lil' buddy. That's mah new lunch wrap....bacon, peanut butter, banana, mayo an' a bit o' mustard. Great stuff, huh?"

"Uh, no?"

"Wait a minute. Wait a minute. Try this! Ah, cal this mah Hunka Burnin' Love Big Bite. It's Bacon, banana, jalopena pepper, grape jelly....an a touch o' Momma's grits. How about *that*?"

"Hell, no! You actually sell this stuff? To *people*? Wait a minute. You look kind of familiar....aren't you....him?"

Suddenly, Lester's dream takes another twist.
He found himself getting to the end of the main drag in town, still distracted by....

He knew he remembered that guy from somewhere....but where....?

Oh, well, walking on....

Lester turned and headed away from the center and off towards the harbor. He *loved* the harbor, not really knowing why, but he seemed to be drawn to it time and again, to sit and stare out at....what? That damned island?
It was an island, for God's sake. So what? A fly, tick-infested hunk of sand. He and Elizabeth had once taken a loooooong hike out there to an ancient tavern site....to see....what? A tick-infested hole in the sand? Been there. Done that. Why his eyes were always pulled to it, he couldn't tell.

Wait a minute....was there construction happening out there? What the Hell was going on? Doesn't matter, does it? Ahhhhh, such a beautiful day....morning.....whatever.... and so quiet....just sitting here....

Lester looked over at the seat next to him. A local paper was open to the headline: REALLY BIG ISLAND PURCHASED! That was it's name. Really Big Island. *No...that's not right...is it? Well, accurate, anyway...but they elft out tick-infested sand pile. People here could be so literal sometimes.* He started to read the article.

Two months ago, a mysterious consortium managed the impossible; to buy the historic, environmentally protect, Really Big island. None can figure out how it was accomplished but it happened. Money was spent. HUGE amounts of money.

Wheels were greased. All forms filled and filed. Surprisingly, to this reporter, all was approved in our town where nothing, NOTHING gets approved without title searches going back to the Dark Ages.

It appears that these parties are intending to, believe it or not, rebuild the historic, infamous, old Really Big Island Tavern that once stood on that site.

Once a gathering place to all sailors, pirates and lower types of the period, the new tavern will, at first appearances, resemble the historic records of the original.

Supposedly, besides the bar, it will feature a restaurant, live music and rooms to rent for tourists. The catch? No vehicles will be allowed. By land, one would have to follow existing trails by foot to reach the tavern. Good luck if you miss the tide change! The trails, however, will be made wider and more accessible. A large dock area is proposed for boaters to tie up and enter the pub. Sounds interesting, if not a bit remote.

Rumors are that those will will be running the new establishment will be, surprise! Descendants of local pirate legend, Black Sam Bellamy and his former lover, Mariah,(Goody) Hallett. Both had been lost in the terrible April storm that wrecked the pirate ship Whydah, just offshore. Bellamy, on the Whydah, Hallett, watching from the cliffs.

Wow! What an incredible story. I guess we'll have to wait and see how this all turns out. Could be good for tourism. It will be interesting. I'll keep you posted as details are revealed.

Lester shook his head, peering out at the island. Some of this made no sense, even for a dream, when suddenly...

His dream shifted gears, again. Now? Lester found himself walking at a local drive in flea market. The sun was shining and the place was packed with vendors...... tons of people wandering silently from booth to booth. He decided to follow them and see what was going on.

"Pssst, Buddy. hey, Buddy? Yeah, you. Wanna buy a *great* guitar?"

Lester was startled. This was somehow familiar. Here was a scroungy, smelly old derelict, no teeth, with a disgusting cigar butt being gummed from the side of his mouth.

"Got this great ol', hissss-torical geetar once owned by Jimmee Paige. See here? Signed it hisself. J-i-m-m-e-e-P-a-i-g-e. Real cheap, too. Ya know who Jimmee Paige is, ya ijit? Interested?"

Once again, Lester knew he had been here before and wasn't happy to be there, either.

"Uhhhhh, no thanks, old geezer. Definitely *not* interested. Maybe you should be interested in a better cigar? A bath? Some new teeth?"

Lester quickly walked away and down the row.
What kind of dream is this anyway? Got to be a dream.... That guy, too, there did I......

He drew up to the last booth in the row. There sat a short gentleman. What caught Lester's attention first was his clothes....a bit formal for a flea market.....pearl grey gloves, derby hat....The man spoke.

"Yes, my good man. Here you see the finest umbrellas that money can buy. Look at this workmanship. The fine, lignum vitae handle.....why, it has soooooo many more uses than just protecting the lucky owner from the rain.... or my name isn't Beetroo....."

Lester woke up screaming, covered in sweat, remembering the recent past with the evil, umbrella-toting fiend, Beetroot. Elizabeth fell off her side of the bed in shock. After they both stopped shaking....."I think we both need a drink."
Oh, well.

CHAPTER 18

In the Light of Day

The next morning, Elizabeth, Lester and Viridian met at one of their favorite breakfast places, the Wayfarer. Elizabeth was relieved, wanting to get Lester away from that terrible night of.....whatever the Hell they were. She had heard him scream out, "*BEETROOT*". She was badly shaken herself and could see that her husband was even more so by the way he was guzzling cup after cup of high octane coffee. Seeing how they both looked, V asked, "So, Elizabeth? Lester? What's going on? You both look like you had a bad night's sleep."

Lester laughed into his coffee. "Ha! Sleep? What a joke. Another night like *that* and I may never want to sleep again."

"V? He had some pretty terrible nightmares. Les was screaming, moaning and trying to beat the pillows to death. At the end, he screamed out the name, *Beetroo*t and we both fell out of bed. Not a good night at all.

"Who is this guy, Beetroot? I don't remember either of you mentioning it before."

"*Was,* thank God, not *is.* You don't want to know."

"Look, Elizabeth, I don't know anything about it but I can only guess ther music we're into with WhydahMakert has to play a part."

Viridian quickly looked to Lester. "Don't you think we should back off a bit? If the pressure is getting to be troo much, I don't mind if...."

"No! No way!" He smacked his cup down on the table, spilling coffee everywhere. " We're not giving up on WhydahMaker. We've worked too hard to get our big break. It's jusat a little stress left over from the big move up here to Pir...Wellfleet."

Elizabeth explained about the Beetroot thing.

"V, I told you about what Lester went through back in NJ before we moved. NO? The murder? The attacks? The attempts on our lives? That fiend, Beetroot? I thought getting away from there would help make it all go away."

"It takes time to forget such things. Les? You know we're both here for you, right?"

"Oh, yeah, yeah. I know we're all the best of friends I've got....If only the *others* would stay out of...."

He realized what he had started to say and shut up.

"Others? What others, Les? You've never mentioned any other people. Who's making you so crazed?"

Lester shook his head in denial.

"No, there's nobody giving me grief but me. Slip of the tongue. Last night really shook me, that's all. Bad dreams. I'd say something if there were any pewople causing us problems. Now? We're all hungry. Let's order some food. More coffee, please?"

After breakfast, Viridian went her separate way as Les and Elizabeth headed home. As they walked back into their living room, Lester stopped and told Elizabeth, "Would you mind if I went into town for a bit? You know, like I used to do when we came here on vacation? I want to find a quiet spot to play my guitar for a bit. It'll relax me and help me to forget last night."

"You sure you'll be O.K.?"

"What? My guitar gonna attack me? I'll be fine, Elizabeth."

A little later, strolling Commercial Street in Wellfleet, guitar case in hand, he started to pass Uncle Tim's Bridge and stopped. Remembering the times he used to go across and up on Cannon Hill, set up on a bench overlooking the harbor, and play for hours. There was always comfort to be found there.

He crossed the historic landmark and made his way up Cannon Hill. His troubled thoughts were still back with the nightmares from the night before. So disturbing. So vivid. So real....and the people in it. A chill ran through him as he once again thought of Beetroot. Would he *ever* be free of that monster?

Lester saw the bench was still off to the right, below the crest of the hill. He silently thanked whomever had the kindness of placing that bench there. He sat, inpacked his guitar and quietly sat....holding the instrument. Looking down at the harbor and town, he watched the people strolling the galleries and shops. Cars bustled by as usual in the tourist season madness. Boats moved in and out of the harbor as the tide was with them.

He sighed and began to play.

Every once in a while, he saw people below stop and look around, trying to find where the music came from as it floated and danced on the breezes, down the hill and through the streets. he liked that. It made him smile. He thought, *maybe this will help me forget last night*. Last night....He stopped playing and stared off into space.

Someone passing on the trail in back of him stopped to listen as he played. He surprised Lester when he spoke up. "Why did you stop? That was beautiful. Don't stop on my account. Ya know? You should try to be a *real* musician. You're *that* good."

Lester sat up straighter, startled and chuckling. "So I've been told." He always zoned out when he played. A bomb could go off under himand he wouldn't notice. Part of the "zen" he fell into while playing. "Me? Yeah. That would be something, wouldn't it?" A *real* musician." He laughed quietly to himself.

The man continued. "You really should consider it. Please? Keep playing. It's wonderful."

Lester went back to playing a few minutes for the sake of his passing admirer.He stopped again. *This really isn't working.* Sighing again, he packed up his guitar.

Making his way back down, again, deep in thought. He crossed Uncle Tim's Bridge and made a left up Commercial Street, onto the main drag in town.

Passing the market, galleries and stores, he didn't notice the two "people" sitting outside the liquor store. Well, nobody else did, either. There sat Elvis and Napoleon, tourist watching as they walked by. As usual, Elvis was stuffing his fat face. Napoleon gave him the usual disgusted look when he saw *what* he was eating.

"Yo, buddy! Nappy!" Elvis mumbled around a mouthful of food. "Ain't that Worthy? Yuh think we should say hi, or somethin'?"

With a long-suffering sigh, "Mon ami? How many times must I say....NOT Nappy....merde! No.

"Leave ze poor mortal alon', oui? He have enough problems from the look o' him."

Lester walked by, not seeing the twosome sitting there. The town was changing a bit, too, but Lester didn't notice as he kept walking. Now, passing the Lightship Restaurant, he turned left, down the street to the Wellfleet harbor.

Passing more shops, galleries and B&B's, he got close to the harbor, seeing the Minesweeper Pub off to his right, below the Bookburner Restaurant.

Lester loved the new harbor set up making full use of the views with a promenade and many benches. He picked a bench far away from the usual walking/jogging traffic, sat down and began to unpack his guitar again. Looking around to make sure he wasn't annoying anyone or that no one was going to bother *him*, he began to play quietly.

He began to work on a "piratey" thing while looking out to Really Big Island, thinking(*Really Big island?*) He was amazed at how far along the construction had gotten. He even saw where the new docks were being put in. Amazing. Really.

Abruptly, someone sitting next to him said in a very small voice. "Yes, really. It is quite amazing what they are doiung out there."

It was Mariah Hallett, Goody to some, now sitting there next to him.

"Back in *my* day? Work such as this would have taken years. This entire time has become a wonder to me." She turned to look at Lester.

"You know, don't you? This whole thing out there is Sam's doing." She pointed out to the tavern construction. "Part of Sam's latest....project. *You* are part of this project, too, I'm sorry to say. He does something.....unusual every few decades or so. Boredom, I guess.....maybe even perversity. Lester? Sam was a *good* man....but not always. There's a *very* bad man hidden in there as well, I'm sorry to say. I may be trying to entertain his wishes but, at the same time, I'm trying to make him leave *you*.... and *yours*....alone. Pirates Cove isn't for th' likes o' you."

Her voice began to change as did her clothing, going from current dress back in time. "By the way? Don't be fashed by any confusion as to where ye be. Yer between two worlds these days. Lester? Will ye tak a minute an' come wi' me? Dinna worry 'bout yer guitar. It will be safe while ye be gone."

Very slowly they both faded from sight. Nobody noticed. Lester suddenly found himself standing in a field of low bracken with the area blanketed in fog. Not far away, he heard the muffled sound of surf.

"Thee needest not....(sigh)....forgive me, Lester. I have become much more comfortable with your modern speech these days than with what I was raised with. As I wa *saying*, you need not worry. We are in familiar territory for you, I'm sure. You and Elizabeth have been here many times. We are at the cliffs overlooking the Marconi site and the ocean below." She shivered.

"In *my* time, it was known as Lucifer's Land. Anyone who did not conform to the mores of the town or the leaders or the church, got banished to Lucifer's Land.... to be forgotten....to live or die....however these poor souls could manage. *This* is where *I* was sent so long ago.

She looked off into the distance as she remembered.

"I was a healer. I could help sick neighbors and I was particularly good with animals. For *this* they called me witch. For my love of Sam Bellamy, they called me *whore*.
It was here they banished me to die. Oh, I died for sure but not in the manner they expected. Actually, I managed to survive here for a time with the help of a few friends.... both human and animal."

Lester and Mariah faded and reappeared by the remains of a broken down shanty. As Mariah talked, the remains reconfigured as a whole building; nothing much to look at but dry and warm.

"This is where I lived....for a time....and where I come time and again when I need to be alone with my thoughts."

At that, several animals appeared next to her; a goat, a fox, a dog....maybe even a familiar cat.

"*They* have never forgotten me." She smiled,

"They have been my constant companions through the years." The cat gave Lester a nasty look.

Lester gave one right back at him as he also remembered seeing and hearing a spectral goat in town.....*could it be.....?*

Mariah continued. "You see, *this* is my place. Sam has his own, favorite spot over by the harbor. That's why you find him there so often."

Lester agreed. "Yeah, he's always staring off at that damned island, whatever it's called. I never understood the fascination."

Mariah giggled. "Oh, yes. *The* island. There once was a popular tavern out there where Sam and I could meet away from unsympathetic eyes. Those *good* townspeople wouldn't be caught out there; just raiders, pirates, scalliwags and folk down on their luck. Sam and I spend many a time out there. *That* is why he has gone to all the trouble and money to buy the island and rebuild the tavern; to be a refuge for us *and* a place for our present, living relatives to make lives for themselves; a way for us to keep track of them and help whenever possible, something *they* wil*l never* know.   By the way, if you meet them some day, they are Sam Bell and Mary Hall. Sam has plans, oh, yes he does."

They faded once again and reappeared back at the edge of the cliffs. Lester tried to back away. The wind was rising and as the fog was blowing away, he could see how high they were above the roaring surf.

"Don't worry, Lester. You are safe with me." She began to speak, sadly this time.

"It was April 27, 1717. Every night I would stand here on these cliffs waiting....waiting for any sign that my Sam was returning for me." She looked from the surf below to Lester.

"He had always promised to return to me and make us both rich. I never cared about the wealth. All I wanted was Sam to come back for me. That was the night of the terrible storm. It was so foggy, you could see nothing. Even the surf was muffled."

"Then, in the distance, I could hear a ships bell. Could it be Sam? I needed to know, so I strayed close to the edge, desperate to hear, desperate to see.
The wind suddenly grew in ferocity. The fog blew away in the rush of wind. The surf became an angry beast, roaring below me. I heard voices yelling, yelling. I could swear I I heard Sam cursing the crew to man the rigging."

Mariah became very sad while remembering.

"It was then the ship foundered in the surf below me. I remember little else as the wind took me and the ground beneath me began to crumble." She sighed.

"Well, that was then. This is now....as you people are fond of saying these days. It was important for you to know all this."

They backed away from the edge. She continued as they walked.

"You and Viridian are not the first living people that Sam has taken an interest in over the centuries. Every now and then he finds the need for a new *project,* just to while away the boredom. *You* peaked his interest in the beginning....a tiny bit; a troubled soul....just his meat. When you two came up with that name, *WhydahMaker?* That was it. *You* became his."

"Oh, gee! Aren't we lucky? We have a dead pirate as our Patron of the Arts. Ha!"

"Don't be amused. This isn't good for either of you. None of his past projects have ever turned out well and, unless you are both extremely lucky? Your fates won't be either."

"Look, Mariah. Sam once told me he couldn't force me to do anything I really didn't want to do, so why should I worry?"

"Lester, what Sam told you was partially the truth but not all of it. He still has his ways and you will need to be *very* mindful. He is a powerful being and growing ever stronger with the passing time. He has plans for you and Viridian, as well as WhydahMaker. Who do you think he's been grooming to become the "house band" for the new tavern, hmmmmm?"

Lester stopped walking and stared at Mariah as she continued.

"Ahh, that got your attention. Oh, you'll be well paid and become famous in your own, little way out here on the Cape but don't misunderstand. You *will* dance to Sam's merry tune, oh, yes you will.....until he's finished with you....or gets bored."

"Viridian and me? Trained monkeys for Sam Bellamy? I don't think so!"

"I'm saying to be aware....and to beware. You and Viridian are good souls and deserve better. Be careful is all I'm saying. And for your wife, Elizabeth? Keep her as far away from this as possible. Don't let Sam get her involved, too."

"I wouldn't worry about my wife. Liz is far, too strong willed a person to fall for anything Sam Bellamy is selling. She would *never* believe in him."

"Maybe so, but there's more to consider, as well. Sam and I are, to put it bluntly, ghosts. There's not a lot we can do to influence the greater material world. We have learned to work through existing....*firms*....ones rooted in the real world but straddling the infinite. These are *not* people and they are *not* to be trifled with! When we want to get things done in your world, *they* are the ones who manage our interests. *Any* interests or wishes. Finances, living relatives....people who defy or cross those desires. Do you remember a poor soul by the name of Persipone Painestaker? Oh. I see by your face that you do. Good! *She* crossed Sam and those ....*people. You* crossed her path more than once. That caused her to become curiousw....*fatally* curious."

Lester was horrified. *Was he responsible for....?Oh, God, yes! He was ultimately responsible for the seer's death. Oh, God, no! Yey another soul on his conscience. Whern would it end?*

"Lester, there is yet another reason why you must be careful. Please? I love Sam. He is a wonderful person but there is a very, very dark, pirate side to him. There is a reason he earned the name, Black Sam Bellamy. Caution, please?"

At that, they both faded as they walked, reappearing non the harbor bench where they had started.

Mariah added, as she faded, "See? I told you. No one would even know you were gone. Even your guitar remains untouched."

She pointed. The fact that he was still holding it, bewildered him.

"All back as it was. Remember what I have said, Lester."

She faded from sight. Lester sat there staring off into space, occasionally strumming but even doing that became too miuch. He sat staring off to the Island and the construction rapidly going up for the tavern. Staring....just staring, unable to take everything in.

There was a gentle, *purrrrr,* next to him at his feet. Lester looked down.....the black cat, looking up mournfully at him. Lester was going to speak, when...

"Don't.....don't do it, Lester. Don't you *dare* call me Heathcliff....or Garfield.....my name....my *real* name....is Mikey. Mind if I come up and sit on your lap?"

Mikey hopped up, curling up in Lester's lap....unseen by anyone walking by....just some weird guy sitting....petting....the air. Both of them....staring off across the bay....one sighing, one purring. For the moment? All seemed well, maybe even contented....if only....

CHAPTER 19

Eight Months Later

The jobs started to roll in for Whydahmaker, many paying *real* money! During the day, Lester and Viridian either were practicing or were out somewhere playing.

At the LandFall Restaurant, the clientele wanted mostly Irish music. So Les and V gave them exactly that. Somewhere in ther back of the place Lester could see Sam listening, tapping his foot, *maybe* smiling, maybe *not*. It didn't matter to Lester. They loved WhydahMaker at the LandFall.

At the town Open Mike, Desolation Row, the audience was more into the folk side of things but occasionally would put up with one of Lester's musical perversions. They grew to love the band at the Row, as well. Sam was usually to be seen against the back wall, not usually tapping and *not* usually smiling, either. He didn't like where some of his music was heading. Lester noticed and reacted accordingly as well; usually to annoy Sam even more.

At the MineSweeper? Well, it really didn't matter *what* they played because not too many people were coherent enough to realize the band was playing. This gave les and V a chance to try out new stuff from all directions without too much interference from the inebriated patrons....and when they *were* listening,(you could tell because their heads were off the table and their bloodshot eyes were attempting to focus on the band), Lester would coerce Viridian into trying something *really* obnoxious. This would please Lester immensely and royally annoy Sam.

Of course, then there was WPDQ and march Madness. Viridian kept things pretty much under control. As hard as May Potawatomi tried, V kept the music they played relatively sane. Not crazy enough for May/March and *definitely* waaaaay too crazy for Sam's taste. Neither the living nor the dead approved. The rabid audience of WPDQ, however.....be they alive or whatever, ate it all up. No taste whatsoever.

After the live performance in the booth, May snagged Lester and continued her rant, trying to get him to truly sink the Silkie and Harpie to new levels of poor taste.

"Les, they love ya! They love Viridian! They absolutely love WhydahMaker! Whenever you guys perform live, ratings go through the roof....*but*....now, I'm *not* trying to tell you your business but....well, we get a lot of calls and write-ins wondering when you guys are going to step up your game and reach new heights, (or depths, depending how much your ears bleed after listening to an S&H show), for your adoring audience."

Lester wasn't really listening, well, not *too* much. He was more interested in how the whole March Madness tirade was pissing off old Sam. *That* was priceless to Lester. Thank God V had left the booth or she might have killed May....uhhhh....March....oh, Hell, whatever.

It was another dark and stormy night....(I know. Sounds impressive, though.) Well, it was dark....and it *was* night. Stormy? Not outside, but inside at the rehearsal? A different story. Viridian still hadn't arrived and Elizabeth was downstairs working, so she didn't hear the "one-sided",(seemingly to normal folk) yelling match going on between Lester and Sam.

" Look, boy! You'll do wha' yer told ta do! You'll play wha' yer told ta play! Yer lettin' that crazy radio woman get inta yer head! Tha's na' the WhydahMaker I want ta hear. Got it?"

"Oh, yeah! I got it, Mr. Musically Impaired, dead and pretty sad, pirate-type ghost. What *you* want? Not what *I* want? I let you get involved with me and V because you had some good ideas....for a dead guy....but run my life? Run our *band*? I'd tell you to get a life....but(laughter), you blew your's a long, long time ago."

"You *insolent,* pitiful meat sack! You dare to talk this way to *me*? I....I'd..."

"Yeah, Bellamy? What you gonna do, huh? Booooooo, wooooo? Gonna scare me?" Lester wiggled his fingers in an angry Sam's face.

"Baaaad Black Sam Bellamy? More like SAAAAAD Sack Bellamy. Don't make me laugh. You can't do nuthin'.....except probably annoy the Hell outa me....which, by the way, you're already doing quite well.

Ya got nuthin. Ya can't *do* nuthin'"

Sam got a twisted smile on his face.

"Don't be too sure o' yerself, Mr. Les-ter-Wor-thy. Don't ye be too sure 'bout what can or can't be done."

"Ooooooo, I'm so scared."

At that, Viridian walked upstairs, shocked to hear Lester raving (once again) to an empty room. Not the first time but she was beginning to get concerned.

"Uh, Lester? Sorry to....butt into this....interesting conversation..."

She stopped in mid-sentence, thinking about what she really needed to say.

"Look, Lester. I've put up with a lot of *weird* since we began our WhydahMaker thing....and I'd like to believe you....you know....that there really *is* another person standing there who you're holding this....argument with..."

"Yeah", he said, pointing to Sam. "Sam Bellamy.... pirate? Dead? Right there."

Viridian turned in the direction where Sam was *supposed* to be and addressed the blank space to humor Lester.

"Look. I know this is stupid....(lookijng back at Lester.... no, I feel reeeealllly stupid doing this."

She turned back in Sam's direction.

"Mr. Sam Bellamy? If you're really here? How about letting me see you, at least?" I don't have to be able to hold a conversation with you. Show me you're real and not a figment of my partner's twisted mind. Oh, I feel sooo stupid doing this, Lester."

At that, Sam Bellamy gradually appeared in front of Viridian; first in his traditional pirate garb, then a 3 piece suit. He smiled at her and Viridian fainted.

Lester quickly kneeled to help pick Viridian up off the floor.

"Well, gee Bellamy. That went over well. You had to do it, huh? Get your jollys by scaring the crap out of poor, defenseless people? Hope you're satisfied."

"Oh, quite satisfied. She *asked* for it; proof that yer not completely balmy. I gave it to her. Don't expect me to hold conversations with the lady.

You are frustrating enough to work with."

"You mean control, don't you? Good luck with that, Bellamy."

"Yeah, whatever....to take one of your charming phrases. Now? Wake her up so you both can get to work. I'll be leaving." Sam faded from sight as Viridian groaned and came to.

"Wha....that wasn't real, was it? I must have been ill or....something....that wasn't....OH, LES! Tell me that wasn't real. I must have hit my head.....or maybe a stroke....those allergy pills?"

"No, V. Sad to say, *that* was really real. Black Sam Bellamy in the ....kind of in the flesh. It wasn't your imagination. You're not sick and you're not crazy. Neither am *I*, for that matter. He's been bugging my butt since we moved up here and it's only getting worse. Now? We argue more times than not and always....*always* about the music and WhydahMaker. What a pain in the ass."

"But....Les? What have you gotten yourself into? What have you gotten *us* into? I mean, yeah, it's weird and kinda cool in a creepy way, but really? No*t that* cool."

"V, in some ways, Bellamy has helped to push us along. You know me. I'm not all that motivated and , admit it, I need someone to get me moving. Really? He's a royal pain in the ass but he *has* had a few good ideas."

"Really, Les? *Really*? You're letting a ghost....an honest-to-God ghost tell you what to do! I'm not sure I want to be involved, Les....not with Sam Bellamy's spirit and...."

"V! Give it a little more time. Do you think I'd let Sam Bellamy do anything that would harm you? Us? He can't do a damned thing to us. he said as much."

"And you believe him? A ghost....a *pirate's* ghost? Gee. The heart of honesty."

"V, just as soon as we get rolling, get some more gigs we'll dump ghost-man back where he belongs. I promise."

Viridian gave Lester a highly skeptical look. "I hope you're right; for me, for you, for Elizabeth....anyone coming in contact with WhydahMaker."

"Where do you think I came up with our name, WhydahMaker, anyway? No worries, V. How about we get some work done and forget about all this."

"Uh, Lester, I don't know. Les? That creep may still be around watching us."

"Nah, he's gone. I can tell. None of his buddies are around, either."

"Buddies?"

"Not to worry. I got it all covered."

CHAPTER 20

The Women Get Together

An evening later, Elizabeth heard a knock at the door.

"Les? Les? Can you get that?" *Oh, right. He's off wandering around the town.*

"Coming!"

Elizabeth opened the door. "Viridian! What a surprise. What brings you here? No rehearsal as far as I remember. Les is out....somewhere....doing....whatever."

"*That's* why I came, Elizabeth. Les isn't here. And, please? It's V?"

She laughed at that. "Well, perfect! Just call me Liz. A lot easier than Elizabeth but....no 'E', O.K.? Come on in."

"Wine?"

"Yeah, sure, Liz. After this week ands what we have to discuss? We'll need some wine."

"Sounds ominous. Sounds like we need the good stuff."

Liz came back carrying two glasses and a freshly opened bottle of red. She placed them down on the table between them both.

"Now! What's so all-fired important and serious that you don't want Les arfound?"

V took a long pull on her wine and began.

"Have you notices Les acting a little....odd these days?"

Liz cracked up laughing.

"Odd? Odd....Lester Worthy acting a bit *odd*?"

When she stopped choking on her wine. "Please don't do that again while I'm drinking. Lester has been acting a *lot* odd since we moved here. I'm sure he's told you the stories of what went on before we moved? Some? Not all? Well, I'll have him fill you in some day. Suffice to say, tangling with several murderers and a murder or two, can cause anyone to act a bit....off."

"No, Liz." V turned and looked seriously at Liz. "I mean *really* odd....as in something isn't quite normal?"

They both sipped their wine.

"Have you noticed Les talks to himself a lot? Holds conversations with thin air? A wall?"

"Now that you mention it? I've walked in at times when

he's been either holding a conversation or ranting an yelling but nobody's there. He says he's working things out and that he's his own worst critic. Talking through the music helps."

Liz put down her wine. "You know, though? He's been up in the studio while I'm downstairs? I could *swear* he was actually taalking to someone. He always laughs it off when I ask him about it."

"Oh, *boy*! Do *we* have a lot to talk about. Look, Liz. I'm being serious here. There is more going on here besides Lester acting a bit strange."

She took another long drink of her wine.

"He's not making things up. He's not imagining anything. He is really....*really* talking to another....uhhh, person in the room.... someone you can't see or hear. Well, not you or me....that is until the other night and I am totally freaked!"

"V?" Liz leaned forward with a look of disbelief. "You? You of all people are buying into his....his thing? I don't get it."

"It's true, oh...so true. I still don't want to believe what happened. I walked in while Les was arguing with thin air. I confronted him. What happened next scared the Hell outr of me. He turned away from me, talked to the empty room and *demanded* I be allowed to see who he was talking to.:"

"Yeah, right, V. I'm supposed to believe all this?"

"Well, you better! This....person appeared out of thin air dressed in a business suit and then as his true self....a *pirate*, Liz. Not just any pirate but Sam Bellamy....*the* Sam Bellamy!"

"A pirate. Sam Bellamy, the pirate. Wellfleet's own Sam Bellamy? Oh, V, I'm so sorry that you expect me to believe all this....and how do you know it was the.... ghost of *the* Sam Bellamy, hmmmm?"

"Les introduced me to him. Don't look at me like that, Liz! It's true."

Liz cracked up laughing, pointing her no empty wine glass at Viridian.

"And you expect me to believe you're not pulling my leg? Both legs? O.K., then. What did the ghost of pirate Sam Bellamy have to say for himself?"

"Well, he didn't say anything....not directly to me. Don't look at me that way, Liz! Les told me Sam Bellamy said I wasn't worth talking to and it was enough he even let me see him/ So *there*!"

"Oh, V....poor, poor V. So you bought into this craziness, too? And you don't think Lester is pulling one of his infamous practical jokes on you? I mean, he's famous for setting up these elaborate jokes and...."

"Liz, I know what I saw, believe *me*. If I hadn't seen it with my own eyes, I wouldn't have...."

"If I were you, Elizabeth Worthy, I would believe Ms. Viridian."

It came as a whisper from in back of them. Appearing first as a mist, then fading out from the wall came the form of a woman in her early twenties, dressed in a power business suit. As she solidified, she walked over to the two of them, both thunderstruck at what they were seeing *and* hearing.

"Please allow me to introduce myself. My name is Mariah Hallett, some say Mary, some called me Goody. I prefer Mariah."

Liz and V stood speechless, staring at Mariah.

"What? Would you rayther I dressed in the manner of a woman from the 1700's? I can do so, if you wish."

She momentarily was dressed in a simple dress and head covering of a woman from that time but quickly faded back to the power suit.

"I much prefer the clothing of this time, especially these wonderful business suits. Sam got me intrigued by them. WHAT NOW? Oh! You wish me to sound like an apparition of that time, as well? All the thee's and thou's and thy's? Boring. As I said, I enjoy this time as well as the colorful language. Please! Let's all sit down. You two? Have another glass of wine. I'm pretty sure you'll need it before I am done. Sadly, I cannot enjoy it in my present state. Pity."

Liz and Viridian sat back down and did exactly what Mariah suggested; pour more wine. Mariah sat across from them.

"I am here for a very grave reason. Lester is in deep trouble but he doesn't yet realize it. Anyone associated with him is in danger as well. Oh, it's not Lester causing the danger. It's Sam. Sam Bellamy. *My* Sam." At that thought, she smiled.

"My Sam is actually quite a wonderful person....kind, generous, too....but also...a truly evil and vicious pirate. In *his* time, that is....or was. However, people, even dead ones, don't change all that much over time. Sam is quite dangerous to Lester or, will be at some point. It's his way. I'd tell you to stay out of his way but you're already *in* his way, aren't you?" Mariah stood and walked around the room, taking everything in as she talked.

"You must understand. We've been as you see me.... for some hundreds of years now. Sam, especially tends to get bored every fifty years or so and looks for a ....*project*....to keep him amused. In an earlier time one could call it a "pretty plaything". At first, this new project was your husband." Mariah turned to look at Viridian.

"Then? *You* got involved. That WhydahMaker thing you have going. Not bad, really, but it put you, as well, directly in Sam's sights."

She stopped pacing and sat back down.

"Sam has come to love the band, by the way and has big ideas for you both and *that* is part of the problem. Sam wants a very specific set of things from WhydahMaker. Lester? Wants something else, especially if it irks Sam. By the way? The name WhydahMaker? Really annoyed Sam at first but he's gotten used to it, although he'll never admit it. Pour more wine. You'll be needing it."

As I was saying, part of the problem is that Lester and Sam have begun to actively dislike each other and are constantly butting heads." She nodded at the two women. "A game, I must add, Lester Worthy will surely lose. And so will *you.*"

Liz cut into the conversation. "But Ms. Hallett, how did this happen? Why? I don't get it.

"My Lester is a lot of things, but...."

"What you don't understand, my dear...." Mariah looked deeply into Elizabeth's eyes in wonder.

"Oh, my. You don't know, do you? Not an idea? Your husband isn't what one would call a psychic *but* he is a powerful....sensitive. I doubt he even realizes it, himself."

"But....how did this happen to my Lester?"

"The explanation isn't simple but I'll try to explain. You have moved to a very ancient area of the country with a lot of powerful history, good, bad....and violent as well. As someone put it, 'There are too many ghosts in this room'. In this case? It's true. When you moved here, you walked smack dab into ghost central. Lester? Being so sentitive and all?"

Mariah stopped and thought for a minute.

"I just thought of something. Has Lester ever talked to you about the town of Pirate's Cove?"

Liz was shocked. "Yes! As a matter fo fact, there are times I talk to him about Wellfleet and he starts talking ablout Pirate's Cove as if it's the same thing. I never know what to make of it."

"Well, you all live in Wellfleet but, to Lester, sometimes due to it's history and the spirits here, it becomes Pirate's Cove to him; an entirely different, alternate existance. At times, it becomes very real to him....*is* very real to him."

"But, Mariah, it's not *always* that way. Most times it's all normal, old Wellfleet, not Pirate's Cove."

"Well that may be, Elizabeth Worthy. Well that may be but his involvement with my Sam brings him ever closer to this other shadow existance and Sam is a *powerful* influence."

Elizabeth was badly shaken by this.

"You say Sam is a powerful influence. How badly can he do things to Lester?"

"Technically? Sam or any of we spirits hold little sway over the living."

Elizabeth breathed a sigh of relief, but a bit too soon as Mariah continued.

"But....in Lester's case? Since he *is* so sensitive...." At this, she paused, looking thoughtful.

"I don't know how much control Sam may be able to exert. You must understand....no spirit can force the living to do anything against their own, free will....and I just don't know. Sam and Lester? May be a different issue. I'm so sorry, Elizabeth. Sometimes, all it takes is a push...." Turning to Viridian, she continued.

"And you, Lady Viridian? You have become an important person in the lives of Lester and Elizabeth. Add to this, you are the other, major half of WhydahMaker. This has become a powerful talisman. *That* puts you firmly in the sights of Sam Bellamy. You are *both* at risk along with Lester."

Viridian and Elizabeth looked to each other as Mariah continued with more bad news.

"And this is very bad news and difficult to accept." Mariah giggled. "Maybe not. You have obviously come to believe in our existance, haven't you? In the afterlife, we are not alone. There are many other poor souls. We, however powerful we may seem to the living., are not the only forces out there."

She shuddered at that thought.

"There are some who are far older, far stronger and much more dangerous than any of us. It is even said that *they* were there at the beginnings of time. Several of these entities have joined forces over the ages."

Once agaln, Mariah smiled knowingly, shaking her head in sympathy.

"This is *so* hard for you to understand. Although we have passed from this mortal coil, many of us still have riches. We still have family; descendants, the living we have come to care for. It is impossible for us, personally, to do anything about all this. We need a ....service, you could say, to handle our *worldly* affairs."

Elizabeth added, "Like a financial planner or banker?"

m "Yes, I guess you could call them that. Thank you. Four of these....the most powerful. have become such a service for us. They manage our wealth, do our bidding and help those we wish to help."She paused, again.

"And, I'm sorry to admit, to punish those among you who cross us in some way."

"These beings are all powerful and can do anything; are capable and willing to do most anything."

Viridian asked, "How could any of us be of interest to them or a threat to you?"

"Simply put, you are not....at the moment....but this thing with Lester and Sam....and WhydahMaker? Some have already tried to interfere with Sam's latest project of Lester, you and WhydahMaker. You all are entertaining to Sam....for now. Already, one poor soul had begun to figure out that something *otherworldly* and powerful was taking place. Lester had approached this person when he was initially troubled by things he didn't understand. He thought he was losing his mind and came looking for help."

"And what happened?"

"Sam found out about this woman's interference. He approached these.....advisors and asked them to convince this person, a medium of some power, to cease and desist. They sent others from the firm to *advise* her."

"So? That was that, right? Oh, no! Don't tell me there's more to this. I can tell by your look there's more."

"*She* did not listen and continued to investigate, finding out more information than she should. *They* returned.... and solved the problem....permanently."

Haltingly, Viridian asked, "They....they didn't....did they?"

"Oh, yes. *She* ceased to exist in a most violent manner."

Now, from Elizabeth, "Who was this person? Do we know of her? I know I'm new to the Cape."

"Her name *was* Persipone Painestaker, a powerful, local psychic. She got in the way, too close to some truths that were fatal for her to know. Look. I can see how upset this is making you. I am upset, as well. I told you, Sam is a wonderful person but....a vicious pirate, remember? And these....*people*? They are far worse and unstoppable. You do *not* want to come to their attention. Neither do I and Sam is getting involved in a very dangerous game with them."

"I felt it was my duty to warn you. The danger to you all is real. Lester is at the center of it all and it is beginning to spiral out of control. Sam is a very stubborn soul with a bad temper."

Elizabeth broke in, "And Lester is a stubborn person with a bad temper. I'm beginning to see the direction this is headed/. We're royally ****ed, Viridian."

"Not necessarily, if I can get Sam to back off a bit and you two can calm Lester as well. There is hope this could work itself out."

"Unfortunately, I've come to understand that Lester does *not* like to be told what to do, especially with his music." Viridian pointed out, shaking her head.

Mariah nodded. "And Sam is pressing Lester to bend to his bidding with WhydahMaker."

"This will not turn out well for us all, Mariah. What can we do?"

"Ladies, I have not a clue. Not one clue. Let us all think upon this. Perhaps it will all calm down on it's own if only Sam and Lester will back off a bit."

"I think we're all so screwed." Elizabeth added, knowing Lester all, to well.

Mariah gave a sad nod, also knowing her Sam. She faded from sight. Elizabeth and Viridian looked at each other.

"We are *so* screwed."

CHAPTER 21

Dear Dairy

(really....dairy)

AUTHOR'S NOTE: I don't think it's ever been pointed out that Lester is known for his twisted sense of humor. There was a point during his "writings" when he attempted to create something of a diary. At the time, he was writing his thoughts down on the inside of flattened milk cartons.

I have included this section of the "Dairy/Diary" because it's one of the few times Lester actually wrote in a first person context. I felt it was important for you to get this perspective of Lester. This section was written directly following the events listed in the previous chapter. Well, here goes:

Welcome to my (hahahahaha) dairy. Yeah, I know. Tacky but who the **** cares? When I heard about the events from the evening before when Elizabeth and Viridian "met" Mariah and V met Sam, it gave me pause to think. I began to realize how messed up things had gotten.

Believe me when I say I had no idea that this....all *this* wasn't in my head. O.K.. I had a pretty good idea the damned spirit of Sam was real....at least to *me*. Never in my life did I think this was nothing more than a *me* thing. The next morning when Elizabeth, very shaken, brought it all up. I was forced to face the fact that this was a much, much bigger thing.

At the same time, I was forced to face the reality that I had become pretty ****ed up. I always knew that my family, those directly from Ireland, especially the women, were "gifted" as seers or sensitives. Growing up I took it for granted. The women were weird.

Sure, some of them saw their own, imminent deaths; in tea leaves, tarot cards or "spirits" who came to them the night before. It was a family "thing". The men never had these abilities but I was told it was possible for anyone.

I don't consider myself a seer or anything crazy like that but I have been forced to believe that a person can be sensitive to things *not* of this world. *Believe* me. Please believe me!

I'm not exactly happy with it. When we moved to the Cape and to Wellfleet, at first I really, *really* did think I was in both Wellfleet and Pirate's Cove. I couldn't understand the strange looks Liz gave me when I would talk about going into town(as in Pirate's Cove), to do this or that around the "Cove".

To me? The changes that happened between Wellfleet or the Cove were absolutely seamless. I never knew. I hate to admit it but I had to face the fact that all those people I met in the Cove, including that goat and damned talking cat were real....on some other level.

This forced me to believe that Sam Bellamy and Mariah were real....*really* real and that I was dealing with a demanding and pissy spirit who was getting on *my* nerves. It was bringing out the worst in me. I mean, who the **** was *he* to tell *me*, a musician, what I was doing wrong or how to write *my* music to suit him, some damned flunky pirate who couldn't drive a ship correctly? Well, I was going to disavow him of any notion he had about *that*.

Really? What the Hell could he, a spirit, do to me outside of annoying the **** out of me? Been there. Done that by far more obnoxious real live folk than he. I'm from New Jersey! I admit, I had to pause and think about that a bit. What *could* he do to me besides annoy me at all hours of the day and night.

Didn't he say he couldn't make a person do anything they didn't want to do? Or that he couldn't physically hurt me? Was there a page of fine print he didn't mention?

No, he would have rubbed it in if there was. Just his style....punk-assed pirate loser. Now, Mariah, on the other hand, seemed really cool (and kind of cute), and didn't seem to be on board with Sam's plans or interest in messing with me as his "toy-du-jour". But Sam? I had to wonder.

I had big plans myself to mess with Sam in ways he couldn't conceive. He wants music and songs to fit *him*, the pirate twit? Well, just wait until he gets an eaqr-full to what *I'm* writing! Granted, Viridian isn't comfortable with where our music is headed, but maybe now, when she knows there's more going on than me losing it, she'll understand. I hope so.

It's cool, though. I *do* hate WPDQ. March Madness is a total wacko....and some of those bands? Absolutely as demented as their music, which can make your brain bleed. Forget your ears. But....it's an outlet for WhydahMaker. We need that. The listeners seem to enjoy our stuff. Is that a good or a bad thing? And March *does* make a few good points on how to reach more people with our music....although....no, I can't go there. This new music we're doing is just a faze. V will understand and get over it once we are more in front of the public....even WPDQ's public, bless their warped, pointy ears.

And yet, again....I need to slow down and think. There's so much going on here I can't get a grip on. I sense a power here...lurking behind the scenes and I don't think Sam is even comfortable with it. Gotta think. Gotta think.

What about what happened to that medium I went to see? Persipone Painestaker? What actually happened to her? Yeah, she was killed, but by who? How? Somehow, I feel pattially responsible for her demise....no....couldn't be....could I? But....whaaaaaat....if? Have I put Elizabeth and Viridian in any danger? Me? Oh, God. I hope not. No! Put that thought out of your head. It's all that damned Sam Bellamy's doing. Forget about it. Get on with WhydahMaker. Make our *music.* Make our mark and, with a little luck? *Really* piss off one defunct pirate, Mr. Sam the Sham Bellamy!

I have a great idea for "The Ballad of the Real Sam Bellamy." Now to go convince V and get it performed on WPDQ. Then? Watch the fireworks. Surprise, Sammy Boy.

CHAPTER 22

Aftermath, part 2

The Big Bang Theory

The Final Rehearsal

The music suddenly stopped....

Viridian: "Les, this sounds great the way it is. It's our normal sound. What you want? We've got to talk."
Lester: "V? What are you worried about, anyway? We sound just fine."
Viridian: "It's about the new stuff, Les. You want us to slip this....stuff....in half way through our performance. You wrote this just to piss Sam Bellamy off."
Lester: "So? Why are you so worried? The dead, old fart can't hurt us. He let *that* slip out a long time ago. And? AND? They love the new stuff on WPDQ!
Viridian: "You actually think we should be proud of that? *This* radio audience loves us?"
Lester: "Money, V. Money and more gigs....we're making a name for WhydahMaker."
Viridian: "I'm saying, I think this is wrong in *so* many ways. Fame? Money? Gigs? Well, O.K., *maybe* we'll get a few more gigs....but tangling with Sam Bellamy? Even a *long*, dead Sam Bellamy? This is a serious mistake, Les. But... our old stuff is really, really good. I *do* hate to admit it, though, that nasty, raw edge you gave us....kind of daring....yeah, I like it...a bit....but I want us to break away from WPDQ and Sam Bellamy. We will do just fine without them. Think about it."
Lester:(quietly thinking and looking past his instrument and down at the floor). "Yeah, I know you're right....but for now? We play a live show tomorrow on "The Silkie and the Harpy". So? Let's get back to work....

    The next day, WPDQ, "The Silkie and the Harpy" show, March Maxtor presiding on the ex-lightship, S.S. Leaky Toilet....March madness/March Maxtor/May Potowatomi....leader of this merry, little show was featuring the best and extreme worst independent music that Cape Cod had to offer.
    "Yes, my good and gracious fans out here from the waaaaay, Outer Cape. Yeah, we love ya!"

"That was a new song from "Rasputin and the Happy Five"; "You Make Me Want to Fart". A blast from the past? No, my friends, a big wind from the present wafting fragrantly out to you ooooonnnnnn WPDQ, The Silkie and the Harpy! And now? The live performance from that local duo you've been hearing so much about, WhydahMaker!

I still don't know what makes them so great but, somehow, mixing Irish, folk, sea chanties and hard-assed punk? Wow! It tugs at *my* ear, I'm telling you! They'll be on right after announcements from our local sponsors and detractors."

Back stage in the former engine room

Lester turned and grabbed Viridian's shoulders.

"Look, V, we're gonna be great. Hang on and go for the ride. Oh, boy! I hope Bellamy is listening somewhere. Oh, *yeah*."

A voice calls down from above: "Alright, you two. You're on....ladder's to your left".

The recording booth was a tiny bit smaller than the "live stage"....all together, not saying too much. You could barely swing an instrument around....forget about doing any damage.

WhydahMaker began to play their first song, a nice, peaceful song about Wellfleet. The next? An instrumental sea chanty....but *that* is when things took a nasty turn to the dark side. A typical sea chanty has words...."pull this, tug that, yo ho, where's the gold " kind of stuff.

Suddenly Lester whispered to Viridian, *now*. At that, they both kicked in the effects; heavy distortion, chorus, phaser....all would have made Jimi Hendrix jealous.

The sound was now enough to shake the old leaky Toilet to it's rusty keel. Resting sea birds seemed to collectively take a dump, screech and head for shore as fast as possible.

Now? The words changed. No more *yo* or *ho* or *pull the damned rope*! Suddenly, the lyrics became about everyone's favorite, dead pirate, Sam the B.

Some of the words went like this:

"Sam the Sham. Worthless, piratey man.
Yo, ho! Watch him blow!
Got so lost, couldn't find the ocean.
Wham! Bam! He found the land
And sank just round the corrrrrrner!"

There was much more, even getting nastier. There was more to come, too.
"Thank you, WPDQ! From me, Lester and Viridian! We're WhydahMaker. We thank you so much for listening today. Now? A totally new song! "The Sam Chant. The Bellamy Rant!"

They say one can become immune to constant loud noises, usually because you become deaf. In this case? WhydahMaker took evil sounds to a new, low. I didn't know a violin or folk cittern could be capable of making such sounds without voluntarily turning to dust in shame. Then? The words kicked in. Talk about a hate-fest directed at one Sam Bellamy! Kindness and good taste force me to avoid describing them. If the ghost of the pirate was out there listening? Well, I'd be throwing a major, hissy fit heard to every corner of the globe, living or dead.

The deafening crash and clawing sound was eclipsed only by the immediate, numbing silence that followed the final, blood-curdling note.

Some said, you could hear the cheering from shore.... but this, being waaay Outer Cape, one never knows where fact and fictoin cross paths. Personally? This author thinks fact and fiction went off together, holding hands and skipping into the sunset.

Was Bellamy out there listening? Could he *not* have been out there listening? Oh, yeah....damned straight he was listening....and not....exactly....far....away.

It wasn't obvious to those in, or near the sound booth at WPDQ, mainly because Sam Bellamy chose not to appear in the uh....flesh, but in *spirit*, so to say. And at that moment? The spirit was far from happy.

Oh, it started off well enough. Sam sat back listening to the first songs from WhydahMaker and was quite pleased.

Not bad, not bad...he was thinking. *Not exactly what I have in mind but they're getting there. With a little more prodding*....then the songs changed and, just as abruptly, so did Sam's mood when the music took on a dark, ragged tone....almost the sound of souls screaming from Hell. Sam knew all about *those*. Then? Oh, yes. The new lyrics kicked in....all about Sam....and *not* in any way that pleased Sam Bellamy.

As the song continued and moved to the next song, which was even worse, Sam flew into a rage. Of course, no one saw or knew but if anything among the "living" in the vicinity felt a certain disquiet deep within their ears or brains, there was a reason why. When Sam finally faded out in a scream of rage,people felt it, then suddenly felt more at ease; not counting how this new music made them feel.

Back "stage", Viridian tore into Lester.

"Lester! I'm soooo embarrassed by this whole....thing. I am *not* happy with this new music. I am not at *all* happy with where you want our music to go. Horrible. *Horrible!*

"V? Get over it! Look. Max is beside herself with the amount of listener resaponse. She says we're a major hit! Her people *love* us!"

"Les? I don't *want* her people to *love* us. *Those* people? They aren't *our* people. You've got to understand. I don't know *what* they are, but they aren't who we should be making happy. I'm pretty close to making a break with you over this. This? Just too much for me."

"Look, V. Calm down. You know you don't mean it. Calm down. Relax and think about it. Think of the great publicity we're getting. Our name is getting out there. That means more work. More jobs. More money. Then? We can do whatever we want; our *own* music, not this crap. We get all this handed to us....and I get to piss off Sam Bellamy. It's a win/win. What could be better?"

Later on, back home....."Lester, are you out of your *mind*?" Elizabeth was raving at him.

"That was disgusting! And that terrible noise! What the Hell were you trying to do? Raise the dead? I've heard car crashes sound more pleasant than that....*that*.... whatever it was but it wasn't music. Not *your* music. Not Viridian's music. You should be ashamed."

"Well, I wasn't trying to *raise* the dead....only send them back....so to speak. You don't get it."

He tried in vain to calm his wife but it wasn't about to happen. Lester decided to cut his losses and take a walk.

"How many times have I told you? Stop this nonsense with the mortal, Lester Worthy. See what it's gotten you? I swear. *That* human is as stubborn and vindictive as yourself." Mariah was tearing into Sam, as well.

"Arrrgh, Lass! Ya dinna get it? All was goin' along well and then tha...tha...*human horses ass* got it into his head he could cross me, *Me!* No! No way! I ha' plans for tha' little rat and his girl. WhydahMaker? Bah! Just you wait. He'll get back in line....or else! Mark my words!"

"Sam. Let it lie, please? It is what it is. You need to step back a bit and stop pushing the man so hard. Mayber....giving him a bit of space...."

"Arrrgh! Yes, Mariah, maybe uyer right. We'll see, Lass. We'll see. I ha' plans and tha' little weasel be a big part o' them. I'll relax....for a bit, at least."

Things *were* beginning to calm down....a little bit. Until....Yes. Fate and blind, as well as deaf ambition took control. March Madness/aka Max Maxtor/aka May Potawatomi was running wild. She had never had such an audience response to any act before. Oh, yeah, Rasputin and the Happy Five were great, as were the Uni-cords and Proudfoot Roachstomper...bu*t this*?. Waaaay different.

WhydahMaker combined *real* talent with the added possibility of musical obscenity all in a neat package. Brillian*t Really* brilliant. And she was going to play it for all it was worth. After all, the WhydahMaker was recorded and *she* intended to play it over....and over....and over again. Then? Convince WhydahMaker to get back in the sound booth for round two. *This* was going to make *her*, her show and WPDQ famous! Oh, yeah!

"Yes, listeners! Here it is again! The Ballad of Sam Bellamy! WhydahMaker! Our local band. Played live, here on the Silkie and the Harpy....in your face on WPDQ! WAAAAAY OUTER CAPE RADIO!"

Oh, yes. This wasn't sitting well, at all, at all, with one, particular deceased pirate who had bee*n trying* to stay calm but that....sound was everywhere....EVERY-WHERE! And *he* had enough. Time to do something about it. Oh, yes. And he knew exactly where to go to get *it* done. Time to visit the folk at C, D, E and F.

Over at (wherever 'at' is), C,D,E & F, a meeting was in progress; Mr. Crouch presiding.
In his rumbling, grave-dusted baritone....
"Gentlemen, we have a minor crisis at hand. There is a temporary cash flow issue."
Mr. Diabello: "You *think*? I'd say it's more than a minor crisis."
Mr. Enoch: "Cash flow problem? How about....as in....*no* cash to flow?"
Mr. Flinch: "And what about our client, Sam Bellamy? His money is causing the *least* amount of cash flow. What is *he* going to say if he finds out the money no longer flows? *When* he finds out? How will we explain it to *him*? To *all* our clients?"
Mr. Crouch: "Gentlemen, gentlemen, please. When I say temporary, I mean exactly that. *Temporary*. We are talking a great deal of time. Mr. Diabello, how long has our firm been existance?"
Mr. Diabello: "Forever....well, *almost* forever....seems like forever....sometimes....*this* time, at least. You know, we've made some fatal mistakes in the past. O.K., to be sure, *temporary* fatal mistakes, but...."
Mr. Crouch: *Mr.* Diabello! That was in the distant past. We have learned from our past mistakes. All will be well."
Mr. Flinch muttered to himself.'Yeah, but temporarily fatal still hurts....a *lot*."

Mr. Crouch looked across the table, spreading his arms wide.

"My friends, we have nothing to fear. The future is ours. The current money issue? All due to that damned Sam Bellamy. Who could have believed he would spend so much of our....*his* money on this ridiculous project?"

"But it's *his* money", one answered back.

"But....what about all the *other* money we've lost.... albeit temporarily?"

"Squandered."

"Bad business deals."

"Gentlemen, I *said*....not to worry. It will all...."

A knock came at the boardroom door. The nervous secretary poked her head in.

"Yes, Marie, what is it?"

"Sirs....I....I hate to interrupt. There is a client waiting outside demanding to see you all."

"Does he have an appointment"?"

"N-n-no, but...."

At that, the door flew open and in barged Sam Bellamy, pushing Marie aside.

"I dinn*a need* any damned appointment! Ye damned crooked weasels owe *me* the time whenever I damned we*ll wish*! Ye all ha' been in charge of me money for hundreds....aye, hundreds o' years. I ha' the God-damned right to see ye when I damned well please! An' ye call *me* a bloody pirate?"

Mr. Crouch stood but motioned the others to remain seated.

"Sam....Sam, no need to get so upset. We're always here to help out one of our *favorite* clients. What may we do for you today? How is the big project coming? The island? The Inn? We've just been remarking about it. Things like this don't happen every day."

"*That's for sure*", Enoch muttered, quietly.

Sam calmed down a little on hearing them talk of his "project".

"Oh, it's moving along fine, just fine. Won't be long before we can open it all to the living. Young Sam and Mary will do a great job."

"Ahhhh, yessss. Family. A wonderful thing to have.... and to help.....even generations down the line. Wonderful, simply wonderful. Now, what can we do for you today?"

Calming down, Sam continued. "Boys, you've helped me with a few....problems in the past. The last being that Painestaker woman....and about that? I never asked you to *permanently* solve that problem, did I? Yes, you solved my *little* problem but by being so....dilligent....you created a much bigger one."

"Well, Sam, we aim to please. Maybe we felt it had to be handled with a bit more....force."

Sam shook his head in disbelief.

"*That* being the issue, I have another small problem but I want you to handle it with *discretion* this time. There's this woman....and her damned radio station causing me much embarrassment. Her, and a side project o' mine all ha' something to do with the *big* project. I want her to be *persuaded* to stop causing me grief. And to be honest? Every day she is allowed to continue, she is making more trouble for me. Handle it, please? Quietly?"

Mr. Enoch chimed in, "And who is this woman, Sam?"

"Let's just say WPDQ, as a whole."

"Oh, my. Not *them*."

Mr. Crouch again took contrrol.

"Sure, Sam. Certainly. Leave the information with us and we'll work out the details....with discretion....as always."

Sam added, "By the way, I'm not finished. My construction crews at the Inn have suggested some changes, just a few....through the living, of course. We will be adding an entire new section of docking to the plans. I'm forwarding the bills to the firm."

After Sam had left, Ishmael Crouch turned back to his associates. The condescending smile abruptly turned downwards.

"Faustus? Morley? Mendicant? We most certainly ARE going to work this small *problem* out but *not* in the way Mr Sam-Pain-In-The-Ass Bellamy expects!

"Ishmael, we don't *have* the kind of money Bellamy wants....not right now."

"What do you think will happen if he finds out we've....invested so much of his money....poorly?"

"Worse? How about when he learns how *much* of his money we've *lost*?"

"We're in deep trouble, Ishmael. *Deep* trouble."

Crouch stood up and beamed an encouraging smile at them, looking from one worried face to the next.

"Gentlemen, as I have *told* you, all will be well. As we meet, I have been given assurances, brutall*y stern* assurances, that the money will once again flow into our coffers. Do not fear."

"Boss?. Mendicant blurted out. "We've all....died many times throughout our collective pasts. *Painful* deaths. It's been a long time since the last and I, personally, have no desire to repeat that experience any time soon. Am I correct, gentlemen?"

Many murmurs of agreement from around the table.

"Not to worry. *Trust* me. All is in hand. However? Sam Bellamy has become a major problem and an equal drain on our resources."

"*His* finances, I remind you." Faustus quickly added.

"Well, Faustus, it is time to show Mr. Sam Bellamy *who* is in charge of those finances....for his own good. He wants his recent problems with that radio station handled in a timely and delicate manner? Well, we'll give him the firs*t; timely*. The second? Change delicate to permanent. To be honest? That pirate station....what do they call it, again?"

"WPDQ."

"Yes, that one....a disgrace to both the living, the not *quite* living as well as the not quite dead. I think it's time we make a stronger impression on Mr.Bellamy. Morley? Mendicant? Here's what I want you to do...."

CHAPTER 23

Where's the bang?
You promised a bang!

Considering the history of WPDQ and the Leaky Toilet, all was fairly quiet. Ears had stopped bleeding (for the moment), the gulls were back roosting and crapping over everything which, basically, was an improvement on the decor.

In the main office (former expanded closet off from the head), May/Max/March Madness was holding court at an important meeting.

"What do you *mean*? WhydahMaker won't do a live show tonight? What's their problem?"

The sound engineer spoke up. He had to. His hearing was impaired from the last show.

"May, Les and Viridian were very clear about it. They are very uncomfortable doing the type of music you want for the "Silkie and the Harpy" show."

"WHAT? After all I've done for them? Made the*m famous*? Made them *popular*? Helped put *US* on the map? Our ratings have soared....*soared* ever since Whydah-Maker got *down* and dirty."

"Be that as it may....May? If you force them to do the.... vicious stuff, and I'm not saying they're right or wrong, mind you....unless thery can play their original music, the music they first played here? They will *not* perform live.... again."

May put her head down on the desk, groaning around the desk blotter.

"Ohhh, I'm ruined. *We're* ruined. Here I've made this big announcement that WhydahMaker was gonna do a live set tonight. What can I tell my adoring fans?"

There was silence around the table. There was an extended, awkward moment until the electrician cautiously raised his hand...."Uh....Ms. P?"

"Yeah, what? Can't you see I'm in distress? What is it?"

"I have an idea....that might....just....work for tonight." May sat up, all attentive.

"Technically? We don*'t need* WhydahMaker here....per se. We do have the recording from their live show. We could do some of that...."

"Yeah, yeah....we could....been done before but it's not enough..."

"No, of course not. I didn't think it would be enough. The trick? We do one of two things."

He held up a finger.

"One, we play the concert footage but have some of our....*stars*....join in, live, playing along with the tapes....or, two."

He raised a second finger.

"We don't use the WhydahMaker live tapes at all. Let's bring in our top performers.....Proudfoot Roachstomper...."

"Yes! Rasputin and the Happy Five!"

"The Carnnivegans! Brilliant!"

"If we get them all in here this afternoon, we can get them rehearsing to do a major cover of the WhydahMaker material."

"Wow! A *We Are The World* event. I'm so brilliant!"

May was now up, pacing back and forth, holding court.

"Absolutely brilliant! And ya know what? If we arrange the songs differently enough? Worthy and Bean have no grounds to bitch at us. Well, even if they *do*, they can't touch us. It will be the event to end all events here at WPDQ! I'd better get started writing up the announcements for all the DJ's."

Meanwhile, below decks, unbeknown to those above, Morley Enoch and Mendicant Flinch were very, *very* busy. It had been all too easy for two, 'not-quite-dead' entities to sneak onboard and get down to business.

"I must thank you, Mendicant. *You* are the one with the most experience with explosives."

"You could say that, Morley. They *did* cause at least two of my deaths in the past."

"You never should have gotten involved with the Chinese and their rockets way back when."

"One learns from one's mistakes, Morley."

"So, dear friend, what is the plan?"

"Well, Ishmael wants us to make sure the problem doesn't continue and yet, make an impression on Sam Bellamy."

Now....I *know* our boss and I'm sure *his* idea of a permanent solution is a *bit* more extreme than mine. I wish to avoid an excessive loss of life."

"Ahhhhh, you are still troubled by the Painestaker solution?"

"At least a bit, although? Anyone who insists upon using those dreadful excuses for musical instruments; ukelele? Banjo?"

"Yes! I even saw an accordian hanging on the wall."

"Exactly! My point exactly. I *had* intended to let Ms. Painestakere off with a stern warning."

"Stern?"

"Yes, only stern....a few broken parts and bruises....but then? I saw *IT* hanging on the wall."

"What, pray tell, caused such a drastic change of heart?"

"There! On the wall? Next to the accordian? Hung a nose flute....a *NOSE FLUTE*! Can you *believe* it?"

"Horrible, Mr Flinch. Horrible. A scourge on all, living or dead."

"Well, I tell you. At *that* moment? That terrible woman must die!"

"There, there, Mendicant....the correct thing. Do not fret over doing the world a favor."

"This, however, is not the same situation, Morley. I see no reason to purposely vaporize so many because some Hell-tortured music calls this vessel home."

"True, true. We can solve the problem, bring peace to the community and give Mr. Bellamy his come-uppance all at once."

"In effect, a community service."

"Brilliant, as always, Mr. F."

"Thank you, Mr. E. Now, back to work. We have much to do before we can leave."

"Can we stay within sight to see the show? I *do* love good fireworks."

"Why, of course, dear friend. Front row seats on the shore. First? We have plenty of time. Let's go into town when we're done and have some lunch. I know a great place near the wharf."

Author's note: Yes, dear readers. I have promised you a big **BANG**. It's on the way. But....as happens in so many cases? A big bang can ignite a much bigger bang....and so on....and so forth. Things now begin to get interesting on Old Cape Cod.....or is it Wellfleet? Maybe Pirate's Cove? Can't keep track of what went on in Worthy's brain. Talk to Mikey, the cat if you have any questions.

Later that afternoon, March Madness began ramping up her rabid audience for the "concert to end all concerts" later that waning day.

"Yes! Avid listeners! In a few hours the Silkie and the Harpy show will present our *mega* concert featuring the music of your fan fav, WhydahMaker. Remember! You heard them here, first on WPDQ!. Unfortunately, dear listeners, as I am repeating to you, WhydahMaker is unable to perform today due to previous commitments. *Have no fear!* We have the tapes from their recent, live performance here on WPDQ! We will be rebroadcastin the best from that show. Then? The *big* surprise.

Many of our finest, regular musicians you have come to love and respect, will be doing a *massive*, live show featuring their versions of the fantastic music of WhydahMaker. This will be a show you do....not....want....to....miss!

"The show will be presented by our newest sponsor, P'Town's own Fuzzy Fred and his Faux Fur Undergarments....for those who really want to get *down* to their pre-historic roots! REMEMBER! Get *DOWN*! G*et FUR-RY*! Tickle your inner caveperson!"

Somewhere close by in town, sitting at an outdoor table with a beautiful view of the harbor and bay, Enoch and Flinch were enjoying their meal and the view. The restaurant, however had their radio set to WPDQ and *that* was *not* so enjoyable.

"Mr. Flinch? Can you believe there are those who are actually enjoying this annoying drivel?"

"Sadly, Mr. Enoch? I do. We live in discouraging times. The caliber of the human race has shrunken at an alarming rate."

"Well, sir, we must do something about that."

"I believe we have already taken a first step from the deep, dismal caves and into the light."

"At least, later tonight....well into the dark." Why don't we sit here, have a few drinks and enjoy the sunset while we wait for the show."

"If they keep playing that dreadful noise, it will be hard to enjoy anything."

"That is why we are continuing to order drinks, Mr. E. We will be listening to the last, abysmal show from WPDQ". He pointed out past the harbor, into the bay where one could just make out the Leaky Toilet in the distance.

"You are correct, as usual, Mr. F., an historic moment not to be missed."

"No, not to be missed."

The plans had been for the Leaky Toilet to be shut down for the night, with everyone having gone home; abandoned, silent, long before the big *boom*. Ahhhh, but the best laid plans of even the most immortal folk can go awry, as they were soon to find out.

The sun was setting. The Silkie and the Harpy was about to begin. May Potowatomi/ Max Maxtor/ March Madness....was gearing up and spooling up her insane audience for the concert that was about to begin.

"That's *right*, dear listeners! The show is about to start! What you've all been waiting for! Our Gala, WhydahMaker Event! Featuring the band itself, live...once....from their taped concert here on WPDQ! Heeeear's my favorite from that show, "Sam, the Sham, the Pirate Man."

At that, she turned up the volume as far as it would go. WhydahMaker's song began as an innocuous sea chanty with interesting lyrics but then, halfway through the song took a much nastier, edgy, loud sound. The song grew vicious teeth that seemed to gnaw their way through the airways.

Somewhere on shore, Sam was listening, gritting his teeth. Somewhere else?

Below decks, a ridiculously large pile of explosives was *also* listening. Just listening....not *particularly* interested or incensed....simply listening....twitching a bit....nothing more.

March Madness went through another song or two from the concert. She was building up to the biggie.

"Now, ladies and gentlemen of my discerning, listening public? What you've all been waiting for! The *grand*, mega-concert! The Carnavegans! Proudfoot Roachstomper and his band, Rasputin and the Happy Five, and special, added guests, The Unichords! All joining to honor the great music of WhydahMaker! Live! Here! Today....as the sun sets over Cape Cod! But first, a word from several of our fine sponsors.

Part of today's show is brought to you by Fuzzy Fred and his Faux Fur Undies....and Willies Tacky Taco Shop. Want to know where all those garbage fish go? Try Tacky Taco....for the ultimate food experience for the ultimate in recycling fans.

This went on and on for a few minutes. Below decks, the pile of explosives had settled back down, enjoying the relative quiet, *although* hearing march Madness rant on was causing some minor irritation among several of the more unstable sticks. Sadly, for all concerned, the show was about to continue.

And here they ARRRRRRRR! Performing the music of WhydahMaker! Our own, festival orchestra of *over*whelming sound!

Suddenly, across the airwaves, came an abomination of noise and screeching as the "band" plunged into *their* version of the Bellamy Chant. Ears began to bleed throughout the listening area. Birds began to leave their perches and circle the Leaky Toilet, highly insulted at what they were hearing while taking copious dumps on the poor vessel to show their displeasure.

On shore, Mr. Flinch did just that, using the toilet, that is.

"Really, Mr. Enoch? Is this torture necessary?"

"Yes, Mr. Flinch. We're listening to the last, grunting, disgusting noise. By morning? Blessed silence."

So he thought. Below decks? The explosives were beginning to take a greater interest in the proceedings above deck. Oh, they were showing signs of being insulted but nothing major as yet. Several sticks were leaking tears of nitro. They were *not* tears of joy. Still? Not a bother.

In the studio, March Madness was gearing up for the BIG finale.

"Wow! Isn't this *some* concert? WE have prepared a special, finale for you all....a previously heard Whydah-Maker song that never made their live concert. The band never knew we had recorded it during their rehearsal. The song? "Sam, Sam, the Pirate Man."

March/Max/May threw all the volume levels to eleven, all the preamps and boosters into meltdown overdrive, all red lights flashing their warnings, all needles pinned in utter horror into the red.

The sound engineer ripped off his headphones and screamed, holding his mouth open while attempting to cover his ears. The sound was epic. All the birds circling the Leaky Toilet gave up their bombing runs, squalked and abruptly headed off towards a quieter sunset as fast as their wings would carry them. Lucky them.

At the top of the decibel levels came the ultimate insult of sound from the "finest" WPDQ had to offer.

"SAM, SAM....THE PIRATE MAN....COULDN'T FIND THE WATER BUT HE SURE FOUND THE LAND...."

Some insults are simply too great to bear. Birds flew. Needles pinned. Lights flashed red warnings. Max danced gleefully around the studio, hands over ears. The Leaky Toilet shook and *did* begin to leak from every nook and rusty orifice. No matter, though.

Below decks? It was also the ultimate insult to the explosives. *Yes*, they had a job to do and they *were* given strict instructions as to when....but this? *This* was too much to bear. With a triumphant, earsplitting roar, the Leaky Toilet, WPDQ, March Madness and everyone from Proudfoot to Rasputin were instantly vaporized!

Mr. Enoch and Mr. Flinch had just dropped their fresh drinks on the floor, as did many other diners when this "new" music began.

Suddenly, there was a terrible, bright flash of light, followed by a speeding wall of sound, fury and superheated air that bellowed across the bay to inpact the shore.
BARRRRRROOOOOOOM!
The patrons were thrown to the floor by the blast. Throughout the harbor area windows shattered in unison. Walkers dove to the street, face down or thrown to the sidewalks. If this wasn't enough of an announcement of the demise of WPDQ, a small tidal wave engulfed the wharf areas, beach and surrounding buildings.

As people began to shakily get back to their feet, shaking of the dust and muck, broken glass while wringing out clothing from the mini-tsunami, they could see a large, dark cloud rising....rising....into the now, brilliant sunset

In the sudden silence, one person was heard to say, "red sun at night....sailor's delight." More silence. Then?

The town broke into wild applause and laughter, seeing that no one had been seriously injured and, even better? The plague that was WPDQ, the major thorn in the side of the town had abruptly, and with extreme prejudice, been removed from the seascape.

Mr. Enoch and Mr. Flinch regained their seats. Mr. Flinch was troubled,

"Morley? *That* wasn't supposed to happen. All those poor people? The explosion was supposed to happen later tonight after they all left, not *now*."

"Oh, Mendicant? Look at the bright side. Mr. Crouch got exactly what he wanted. In fact? I am pretty sure this is *exactly* what *he* would have done. His heart would have been in this project."

"If he had one."

"True. True. But we all reap the rewards from this unexpected turn of events."

Turning to Sam? Well, *he* was beside himself with anger. *What did that damned Crouch think he was doing?* This was going to make his own, non-life even more miserable. Instead of stopping all the grief caused by those nasty, hateful WhydahMaker songs, that damnedable concert and that terrible last song will become legend. The *new* legend of the vengeful ghost of Sam Bellamy. *Oh, this was not going to help him with his big project.* Crouch was going to hear about *this*.

    Although Lester, Elizabeth and Viridian were towns away, they still heard and saw effects from the explosion. Lester was beside himself with grief when he began to realize his music possibly *caused* this disaster. He couldn't take it. Viridian was right. Elizabeth was right, too. He had WhydahMaker on the wrong path completely and look at what *he* had caused. This was going to weigh heavily on him forever. Viridian? She didn't deserve this. She was grief-stricken for those hurt or possibly lost in the disaster and like Lester, she blamed herself. Unlike Lester, though, she was determined more than ever, to change their direction. WhydahMaker would survive but things would change....to what they *should* be. Or? She hoped so....for their sakes.

CHAPTER 24

Sam and Mary

AUTHOR'S NOTE: At this point, you're entering what I call Lester's, "Brown Period". Sounds funny, I know, but it does have significance. At this time in Lester's narrative, he had begun writing on brown paper bags with handles that, somehow, he had gotten from a local town market. The way I figure it, what Lester wrote from this time on was extremely important to him and he wanted everything he put to pen,(or pencil, crayon, etc.), to be legible.

From here on, this is the only writing material he used, and knowing what came before in all it's forms? *Very* significant.

Sam Bell had lived in Plymouth, Massachusetts for quite some time. By his nineteenth birthday, he was the last remaining member of his family....alive. This could have been a struggle for him, trying to survive dpoing the typical, low paying jobs available for one his age, but he had unexpected help.

Sam was approached by a law firm one morning and, surprisingly, told he was the recipient of an anonymous trust fund; a *very* handsome trust fund that would last him the rest of his life, *if* he were careful. A condition was that he should never attempt to search out his benefactor. Sam wasn't stupid, so he began to live rather comfortably for a nineteen year old.

Before his Mom had died, she told him the story of his dark, family history; the good as well as the infamous. No biggie, as far as Sam was concerned. That was long ago. This was *now*. Sam puttered around as most young people on their own do, (especially when *not* tied to making the immortal dollar.) He was happy for several years, working here and there, doing whatever took his fancy. Two years later, things changed.

One day, he read about the discovery of that old pirate ship, Whydah, off the shores of Wellfleet, Cape Cod. He didn't understand why, but it seriously grabbed his attention what with his family history and all. Still? He was a bit curious, that was all, or so he thought.

The entire thing began to nag at him; an itch he couldn't seem to be able to scratch.

A few months later, Sam decided to move. Wellfleet was drawing him like a magnet....to find out more concerning the Whydah, his ancestor....all that mysterious stuff.

Sam eventually got resettled in the little, tight-knit sea community and went back to doing errant jobs as before. One day, he received a letter from an unusual firm, C, D, E&F. *Please contact us at your earliest convenience. We will send a representative to speak to you. Seriously.*

Sam called at the number listed and listened to the deep, rumbling voice of Ishmael Crouch. *We will be sending our representative and firm partner, Faustus Diabello to meet with you. How does dinner sound for tomorrow evening at the Bookstore?*

Sounded good to Sam. A free meal? Meeting some dude with an odd name? Cool.

At dinner the next evening, Sam sat down with Faustus Diabello. Over a wonderful (free) dinner, in the quiet, off-season restaurant, Sam listened to what Mr. Diabello had to say. It was all interesting, especially at the end.

"Sam, you are a very special person. I'm sure by now you know all about your family history and your ancestor, Sam Bellamy. Did you know that you folks, somewhere back in time, changed the family name to Bell because he was an infamous pirate?"

"Yeah, Mr. Diabello, I knew all that. Mom told me the stories. Can't say I wasn't a bit surprised; coming from a famous, uhhhh, infamous family tree. I didn't know until then."

"I am guessing that after the old Bellamy ship, the Whydah, was discovered, you suddenly developed an overwhelming interest?"

He saw the look on Sam's face.

"*See?* I told you. *Special*. On one hand, it's due to that family history. Something awakened in you the day the ship was found. Other than that?" At this he smiled.

"I am instructed to tell you that we, the firm of C, D, E & F are the firm that manages your trust fund. We are anonymous no more."

Sam was suddenly quite interested and stopped in mid-bite. It takes a lot to stop a young man from eating a free dinner.

"Wow! I always wondered.....but as I was told? I never tried to find out who was involved."

"I know, I know, dear boy. We keep a close track on our....clients and are very discrete. You have done everything to the letter of the contract and will continue to draw on your funds. It's just...."

At that point, Faustus leaned closer to Sam, smiling.

"The firm has a rather...*small* favor to ask of you.... in return for our largess. Today is Tuesday. This Friday evening, we have arranged another dinner for you. No, not with me or anyone else from the Firm. We want you to have dinner with a totally charming young lady, around your own age, too. Don't look that way. I think you will both have a wonderful time and have *much* to discuss, Her name is Mary Hall. Here are directions to the restaurant, your reservation and her photo. She will be meeting you there. Now? Sam Bell? I will leave you to finish your meal in peace. Remember, though. You must *not* miss this appointment. Consider it....if you will....a first date."

At that, Faustus Diabello stood up and quickly left the room. Sam sat, looking between the piece of paper, the photo and his meal. He thought. *Hey! She's cute! This could be fun.* He put down the photo and went back to eating. *See ya soon, Mary Hall....*suddenly looking forward to Friday evening and the strange turn of events.

Mary Hall lived in the bustling town of Eastham, well, as bustling as it could be in the off season. Mary was twenty years old and a bit on her own these days. She knew her family history well. So did generations of her family. *That* was part of the problem.

Mary was descended from the "infamous" Mariah Hallett. *Goodie* Hallett as she had been called, a nickname for a young maiden back when Mariah had lived. Unfortunately, other names had become associated with that name; Mariah Hallett, witch, loose woman, whore.... *pirate's* whore. Nothing good.

It wasn't long after the original Mariah when the family shortened their last name to Hall. They had been living the history of the family name ever since.

Even worse? Any girl born into the family was immediately suspect as possibly following in the footsteps of one Mariah Hallett, Goodie....witch....whore....pirate's whore. It wasn't fair and hadn't been over all the generations since.

It was this familial hostility that eventually forced Mary to strike out on her own in disgust. Never looking back. Never talking , *ever* again to anyone....*anyone* in the family. Mary survived from one job to the next, menial jobs, cleaning, working in the markets, for a veterinarian (she really liked that job), always looking for any way to better herself. It was a struggle but she persisted.

One day, as fate would have it, she received a phone call from a firm, telling her she was the recipient of an extensive trust fund....to last her lifetime....as long as she *never* tried to find out who was the benefactor. This changed everything. She did exactly what she was instructed to do and began taking classes in the culinary arts; *her* idea.

The first date

Sam got to the restaurant half an hour early. He was anxious and wanted to make a good impression. Laughing to himself, he thought: *Why am I so uptight? I don't even know this woman. Stupid. It's only a business meeting. That's all.....wait....business meeting? What business? I'm only doing this because some dude told me I had to. Mysterious? Yeah, but if this guy is also responsible for all the support I've been getting? Well....O.K.... what if she's a nasty person? Maybe ugly to boot? Has a laugh like a donkey? I know...not fair....but I've known a few blind dates that....no....don't go there.....be fair. You both could have a great time....and it's a free meal!*

On the way to the restaurant, Mary was *also* having second thoughts. *Why am I doing this? The guy's probably a total dick.....probably dressed in a T shirt and dirtty jeans. Real class. Probably a midget....or has two heads or bucked teeth. I hate blind dates. A date? Is it a date? No, Mary. Call it a free business dinner with a client...or something.*

I got all dressed up for some local yahoo who goes ummmmm and uuhhhh, or....like....every other word. God help me. Why did I say yes to this? Why? WHY? This guy, who I don't know from Adam, is one of the guys who has been helping me out over the years....at least....I think he has. That's why I need to do this. Well, any way, it'll be over soon. Have a nice meal, Mary. Be kind, Mary. Be polite, Mary. Sigh.

At that, she pulled into the restaurant parking lot, wondering which car, if any, was his and if he would be late....or worse? Not show up.

She walked into the restaurant to be met by the host.

"Ms. Hall, I presume? You look *so* much like your photograph. Charming. The gentleman is already seated and waiting." As an aside, he whispered,"and very anxiously, I must say. Have a wonderful meal."

Sam stood as Mary was escorted to the table. At first glance, she knocked Sam out. *Wow,* he thought....*gorgeous. Is this a dream?*

At first glance, Mary thought much the same thing. *Oh, my....no jeans....no two heads...the guy knows how to dress, too. Definitely not a mouth-breather. This could be a fun night.*

" My name is Mary Hall. You must be Sam Bell."

" I....I must be. Mary Hall? Please sit down. *Please*."

He gained more brownie points against her "dick-o-meter" when he pulled the chair out for her and made sure she was comfortably seated. At that, they had a bit of awkward, small talk as they decided on their meals, constantly looking up from their menus to steal glances at each other. Wine was ordered and over the first courses began to warm up to each other.

"To be honest, Mary, I wasn't too happy about coming tonight. This whole thing? So bizarre. Oooooooo, the mystery man who made all the arrangements."

"You too? I felt pretty much the same way about tonight. So strange." At that, she began to laugh and took another sip of wine. Looking over her glass, she said, "Sam? You don't have two heads, do you? Just checking."

She laughed again and Sam joined in.

"No, no....only one....and you? You don't laugh like a donkey, do you?"

She was startled for a second before joining in the laughter that would continue throughout the rest of the meal.

"Mary, tell me a little about yourself. I *do* know we share some of a similar family history. At least, that's what I discovered recently."

"Yes, it's pretty unusual. Our families....their past....how they both changed their names."

"Ummmmm, all due to Sam Bellamy and Mariah Hallett. Amazing. All those years. All the stories, the hatred and embarrassment. My family? I guess they shortened it to Bell after generations of mistrust....not in the beginning but after histories about pirates became popular."

"Kind of the same for me, Sam, only being a local family, it has been difficult to escape the Hallett name. The Hallett women were always looked on with fear or suspicion. The whole witch thing? So unfair."

Taking another sip of wine, she looked directly at Sam and continued.

"Up until I went off on my own, *I really* wanted to be a veterinarian. I was *so* good helping animals in need. When my parents found out about this? They went ballistic. No more thoughts of veterinarian school. Another reason for going off on my own. And I never understood why it made them so hostile until I read some of the Mariah Hallett legends. That poor woman."

"Yeah, Mary. I *do* understand. God forbid if I ever mentioned the sea or wanting to be a sailor as a kid. Not that I ever *had* such a desire. I *did*, however have many dreams while growing up." Sam eaned closer to Mary as he warmed to the subject.

"In the good dreams? I was a sea captain and great hero, surviving many battles with the enemy. In the bad dreams? I was always running from people determined to catch me. I was an evil criminal and always woke up screaming and covered in sweat. I never *dared* mention those to my parents."

Mary finished her glass. Sam drained his.

"Oh, look. I think we need to order another bottle. Interested?"

"Oh, yes."

They sat staring into each other's eyes as the wine steward hustled off to get the wine.

"And here we are."

"Yes, here we are...in Wellfleet." They clicked their glasses and laughed.

"All because someone neither of us knows wanted us to meet."

"Disappointed?"

"Not in the least. You?"

"No way! Interested in going out to dinner, again?"

"Soon. Yes, *very* soon."

The conversation continued through the wine, the rest of the dinner and dessert. Unknown to them, although with their family history, they might have sensed something....if they weren't so into each other. Standing nearby were Sam Bellamy and Mariah Hallett, holding each other close, both smiling.

"Oh, Samuel. This is wonderful. Thank you for setting this all up."

"Part of the plan, Lass, all part of the plan." Pointing to the young couple, "And *they* are a major reason for it."

"Sam, the deserve what we never had."

"Mariah, we may not be part of their world any more but we *do* still have each other."

She sighed and leaned her head against Sam's shoulder. "But it's not the same, is it?" Looking up at him.

"It will have to do, though, won't it, Sam?"

"We can make a good life for them, Mariah. All part of my plan."

At that they faded from view, the event totally ignored by Sam and Mary who sat and talked for hours. Thankfully, the restaurant wasn't busy that evening. The host and wine steward both smiled knowingly to themselves.

Sam and Mary went on that second date. They talked on and on; about themselves, each other, their families. All the things both alike and different. They went on a third and then a fourth date, not sleeping together until after the fifth. That following week? Sam moved in with Mary. Her place was much better than his. All was going well. Then?

One morning, a Mr. Diabello showed up at their door with a rather large portfolio for them.

"Mr. Diabello." Sam said with some surprise. "How did you.... what can we do for you this morning? We've done everything you've asked, haven't we?"

Smiling widely, he put his arm around Mary, hugging her.

"As you can see, it's all worked out well for us."

Mary joined in. "How can we ever thank you?"

In answer, Mr. Diabello held out the thick portfolio.

"Well, first of all, please take these documents and read them well. They are very important and concern both your futures."

They both looked over the papers they were handed, a bit skeptical at what they read.

"Our futures? Really? *That* important? Why us?"

"Since we first met and you took us up on the offer to meet, that event set things into motion you can't comprehend....but you will. It all depended on how things progressed after your first meeting. *Please*. I'm serious. Read all the papers carefully. Discuss them. If you agree to it all, contact me at the number provided and we will set up a meeting with the head of our firm. You don't know it but you have some powerfully interested benefactors; interested in your futures....together, But...."

As he prepared to leave, "If you choose *not* to agree, we will never ask you again. Nothing will change except for the opportunity offered in these documents. Will.... not....be....repeated, so, I strongly suggest you think it all over with care. Have a good day and if you choose *no*, have wonderful lives together. Good day."

After Faustus Diabello had left, Sam and Mary had much to read and discuss over the next few weeks. Life became....complicated.

CHAPTER 25

Concerning Pirate's Cove and Several of it's Denizens

It's me, the author once again. The next few pages concern things not directly taken from the notes of Lester Worthy, although a lot of this has been hinted at. These are *my* observations, suspect as they may be.

Concerning the "supposed" town of Pirate's Cove. I've been up and down the great town of Wellfleet and stopped by all the shops and areas Lester mentioned had existed in the "Cove" under their other namers.. Not *once* have I gotten a glimmer of these places from his "alternate existence". Maybe it's only a thing a clairvoyant or sensitive can sense. Not me, *that's* for sure.

I have sat by the harbor for hours checking things out. I must admit, the construction that had gone on out on the Island was quite some project. At least, *that* was real while it lasted. More on that particular part of the story as it will unfold.

I've never seen the ghost of Sam Bellamy or Mariah Hallett, even though Lester said they both had come to Elizabeth Worthy and Viridian Bean. Elizabeth refuses to talk about it at all, not that I can blame her.

Although none of these things have become apparent to me, every once in a while? I keep hearing the bleating of that damned goat....somewhere...but never see it. I don't think there *are* any goats here in town.

And there's this very sneaky black cat I can see out of the corner of my eye sometimes....watching me....until I turn and....suddenly, it's gone. Nah, it couldn't be that cat, Mikey, Lester talked about....could it? Nah.

In all my research, wading through bags and bags of Lester's crap, the names Napoleon and Elvis keep popping up. I mention them at all because Lester did and this is *his* tale, not mine. I only have to be willing to more or less "dumpster dive" through his (ha) manuscript and bring it all to light. It's been an interesting adventure, to be sure.

What *do* I know for sure? Both Napoleon and Elvis.... or should I say the "not-quite-dead" Napoleon or Elvis had one thing in common. According to Lester, they were both clients of C, D, E & F. No, there are no records fo such a firm anywhere but Lester swore to their existence.

If you notice, I have used very poor linguistic skills to bring out Napoleon's "supposed" conversations as written by Lester. I do not speak French nor wish to. I'll leave the actual language to those of you who show an aptitude for it. I did notice Lester's mention of a chance meeting at C, D, E&F with the secretary, Marie (as in Antoinette), and that Napoleon was rather shocked to find her working there. My guess? He didn't expect to see her with a head. I don't know...just an interesting observation.

Elvis? I have no idea how *that* came about, how or why he would show up in little, old Wellfleet in "not-quite-dead" form. I *could* imagine from Lester's notes, Elvis getting so interested in a food truck business for the "not-quite" customers. Everything peanut butter, jelly, bananna and bacon? I shudder....but, again...Elvis, so who knows?

I can't fathom how any of them became fast friend over the years. One of those things that only made sense to Lester.

There is, however, another character that keeps making an important appearance, that being Mikey, the black, "not-quite-dead" cat. I did some research on "Mikey" and such a cat, Mikey or otherwise, actually did exist at one time. Sadly, according to legend, the poor little guy died in a closet at an early incarnation of the present day Orleans Inn; one of several ghosts said to still roam the building. Again? I've never seen any of it, but if Miley does exist in some form, according to Lester? He's a pretty cool cat.

Finally, I need to bring up a character who has been an important part of all three books about Lester Worthy. That is his wife, Elizabeth Worthy.

I consider her to be the unsung heroine of the books. She put up with Lester's sorry ass and shennigans in the first book, "In The Out Door". She literally *saved* his ass in book two, Opus 133", in true "Wrath of God" fashion, blowing away an evil, old villainess before she could blow away our hapless "hero". She is a Beast, our Elizabeth, when it comes to getting her riled up.

No, not a Rambo-type. She is a quiet, very friendly, successful artist who has a questionable, soft heart for Lester Worthy, (wherever and whenever....more on that later....why spill the beans so soon?) All in all? Elizabeth Worthy is and has always been a woman to reckon with and not a person to ever, EVER take lightly!

    To this day, she remains as she always has been; steadfast, true and supremely talented....although her belief in that sad fool, Lester....I don't get it.

    Now! I've gotten these things out of my mind, explained, confused or whatever and we can return to the story, which is about to seriously heat up and go BOOM, yet again....but not to give it all away too soon....later, later. Read on.

CHAPTER 26

Trouble brews..

Big Time

Sam sat at the harbor watching the construction out at Really Big Island ,(the *other* Great Island), with great interest. It was, after all, his pet project of more than a century. He was very pleased. Construction was moving along at a rapid pace. It was good he kept after those four crooks at the Firm. They could nickel and dime on every detail, no matter how small, but thinking about it, maybe that's what made them so good at what they did investing and protecting his money. He wished he didn't have to pitch a fit at them so often but he wanted things dine *his* way. If plans had to change? So be it.

Right now? He was contemplating names for the new inn. "Sam's Place"? "The Pirate Inn"? "WhydahMaker Inn"? *No....that one would make that little, self-satisfied shit, Worthy too....no, not that name.* Any way? Worthy had no idea his band was destined to be *the* band for the Inn. In time....in time.

This was to be such a surprise for his distant re-laitves....and Mariah's, Sam and Mary. He planned for this a long, long time. As he sat there thinking, he peered over at the dock area that was almost complete. *Wait a minute,* he thought. *With the size of the Inn, land access and parking, there weren't enough slips for the number of boats that would surely come....those penny-pinching....*He sighed. *Well, it looks like I be payin' another visit ta them four pirates who never be learnin' ta do what I ask the first time. I'll take care o' tha.*

Meanwhile, elsewhere....
Speak of the devils....Elvis and Napoleon both showed at the offices of C, D, E & F. They figured "strenght in numbers". Any way, Ishmael Crouch was one , scary dude and they needed each other for courage.

They walked past secretary Marie Antoinette, barging up to Crouch's door.

"But sirs, you can't go in without an appointment. I'd be glad to..."

"Marie, cherie, do not lose your head. We are here on pressing business and will see Ishmael."

He smiled back at her as Elvis opened the door for them both.

Ishmael Crouch looked up a bit startled, from his massive desk.

"Gentlemen, this *is* a surprise! I don't see you listed on today's appointments. What may I do for you?"

"Ishmael, whe last we talked, we both requested some money for ongoing projects. You said you would take care of things as soon as possible. Well? *As soon as* was several weeks ago. We need our money. Me? Aaah've got me a new food truck to finance; food to get, advertisin' ta do. See?"

Elvis smiled at Crouch.

"Nappy? Ahh don't know whuh he's a-doin but I know it's important tuh him, too."

Napoleon gritted his teeth at the name, Nappy, and whispered to Elvis, *How many times? Do not call me Nappy!*

"Oui, Monsiour Crouch. We both have ze things to do. We are in need of our funds."

Ishmael Crouch stood slowly, still smiling broadly at the two of them; the kind of smile one would expect from a shark that also sold used cars..

"Gentlemen, gentlemen. I am so sorry. There has been so much going on here at the office that your requests were lost amid the piles of firm business. Money, money, money." He opened his arms as if to show how "much" money.

"Money is flowing in from all directions and at the same time? We, at C, D, E & F, are handling all our clients requests as soon as physically possible."
(Notice he did *not* use the word, human.)

At that, he put his arms around both of them and herded them out the door.

"As a matter of fact, I am meeting shortly with the rest of the partners and, trust me, we will get it all straightened out. You can expect your funds....shortly."

He bum-rushed them out the door and glared at his secretary as if to say, *want to keep your head....again?* The guys left a bit bewildered but convinced they did the right thing and would soon see the money flowing in as promised.

Crouch stormed back into his office, sitting down heavily at his desk, grunting. *What a day*, he thought to himself. *Let's see....who's next on myt appointments....oh, no.... NOT Bellamy. What did I do to.....*The knock came at the door as marie peered cautiously in.

"Sir", she flinched, "Sam Bellamy is here to see you. He is your next appointment."

Crouch sighed and pasted on a fake smile.

"Yes, Ms. Antoinette, please show Sam in."

Sam strolled into the office with a purposeful gait, walked directly up to Crouch's desk and sat before Crouch could offer him a seat.

"Well! Sam Bellamy, what can I do for you today? Obviously, you have something on your mind. What's up, old friend?"

Sam smiled back at Crouch. "Let me cut to the chase....*old friend*. You are well aware of my ongoing project."

Crouch smiled knowingly, but inside he was cringing,...*Oh, no. No that damned project, again! Now, what is it?*

"Yes, Sam! Of course.... the Great Island/ Really Big Island Inn Project you've spent so much time on....*and money*, he thought....*money we don't have....alright, now.....damn it, Bellamy! Damned risky martket, too!*

"Ah, yes Sam. A *wonderful* project as soon as it's done. I'm sure the money will come rolling in. *Excellent* project." *What the **** is it, now, Bellamy?* He thought.

"Good! Right to the point. I like that, Ishmael. Yes. The point. I need to make a few changes to the plans."

"But *Sam*! Look at all the money already put into the project! When will it be enough? You keep changing things....and the bills keep growing."

"Yeah? Well, I've *got* the money so I might as well use it, right?" He gave a chuckle. "Well, any way, *you've* got all my money....and this project *will* get done....no matter how many damned changes I want to make."

"Yes, Sam, yes. I fully understand how you feel. What is it *this* time, hmmmm?"

Sam, leaned forward and put his hands flat on Crouch's desk. It almost looked to Crouch as if Sam was hinting, *See? I have no weapons*....Crouch was relieved at *that* thought.

"Well, remember the docks and boat slips I had put in?"

"Yes, of course. That part of the project went *way* over budget as I remember."

"Well, budgets be hanged. I was wrong. The demand from the bay side is going to be much greater than I first thought. I need to double the size....no, let's say triple it."

Crouch almost fell from his chair in shock, sputtering.

"But....but...Sam! Be reasonable! How much will ever be enough for you? How much? It may be *your* money, but *we* have the job of protecting your assets! Even from yourself."

Thinking, panic-stricken, *protect us from you finding out....WE....DON'T....HAVE....IT....at the moment, at least. We will...we will....but right at this moment? Crap!*

"Sam", he said, forcing a smile, "Sam, we have a lot of money going out at the moment. It may take me a day or two to draw the funds you'll need. Do you have any idea....how much you'll need?"

At that, Sam handed over an estimate from a contractor, (who worked through a really-quite-alive-third party.)

Lokking at the figures, Crouch felt he was holding a vicious, poisonous snake. Trying to contain his shock,

"Well! Sam.....ummmmm, yes, I *see*. This is quite an expansion on the original project. I may need more than a day or two. Give me a week, at least, to move around your funds and get them available for you. You know how it is with investments. Very little is actually *liquid* at any one time."

Sam stood and gave Crouch his nastiest, pirate sneer. He had many years to practice it.

"Ahhhh, aye, Ishmael. Well, ye better get a move on. Me projects a-waitin' and I ha' little patience wi' details such as these. That be your problem. Things be gettin' close ta' finishin'....soooo ye better get to it."

Sam turned to leave and said as he opened the door. "Ye'll be gettin' me meanin' aye? Course ye do."
At that, Sam left the office and faded out past the secretary.

Crouch sat there looking worried. So worried. Reeeeeally worried and he had every right to be. He got on the intercom.

"Marie? Call the partners....yes, all three of them. We need a meeting....now.....*immediately*."

Later in the boardroom

Diabello- "Look, Crouch, this is a disaster! We warned you!"
Enoch- "The clients will be beyond angry this time!"
Flinch- "Yes! I haven't died in a long time and I'm telling you, I am *not* in the mood to die again,. any time soon, thank you!"
Diabello- "Flinch is right....no one wants to die again.... and it hurts...a *lot*."
Crouch "Gentlemen, gentlemen. No need for all this talk about dying. All will be well. It's all being taken care of. Money from recent investments will come pouring in any day now."
Enoch- "Like with the Enron debacle?"
Flinch- "How about the dotcom scam. *That* really went well, too. How much did that mess set the firm back, hmmmmm?"
Diabello- "You may not remember the angry crowds.... the torches...."
Enoch- "The pitchforks."
Flinch- "The guns....don't forget the guns."
Crouch- "I am *telling* you not to worry. It will all work out in a few days."
Diabello- "Ishmael....do we even *have* a few days? What of Bonaparte? Presley?"
Enoch- "An even more pressing problem, Bellamy! Talk about money being flushed down a toilet."
Crouch- "We have enough funding to take care of all three demands...for now."

"Bonaparte and Presley are small potatoes. They aren't asking for much. Bellamy, on the other hand? We barely have enough to cover this latest outrageous upgrade. From what I see? Th*is should* be the last before he opens that Inn. If not? Welllll, I have some contingency plans for Sam Bellamy if *that* problem persists."

Flinch- "Bellamy could be the final thing to bring everything we've worked for over the centuries crashing down."

Crouch- "Trust me, gentlemen. Sam Bellamy will not be a problem. There are ways to let him know his own boundaries, even as a client."

Diabello- "Our largest client at the moment...."

Flinch- "And if the money *doesn't* appear in time? Then we're broke, correct?"

Enoch- "Busted."

Flinch- "Facing an angry mob....again."

Ishmael Crouch stood, confidently smiling at his worried partners.

"I *said* all will be taken care of. We are not *presently* broke, nor are we insolvent. It is being all taken care of and...if not....well, no one will ever find out how close we came to having a cash flow issue. Relax. The meeting is adjourned."

As they all faded from sight, they did not notice a very concerned black cat standing off in a corner. Mikey, the cat had much to think about....

CHAPTER 27

Several Months later

Things were moving along quite well with surprises all around. First of all, Sam Bell and Mary Hall discovered they were the proud owners, free and clear, of the newest Inn on the Cape, (whether in Wellfleet or Pirate's Cove), Bellamy's Pirate Inn" located far out on Great Island/Really Big island (depending). Mary had always dreamed of being a successful chef but dreams weren't supposed to really happen. Sam" He was going to handle the paperwork, guests and "front of house" stuff. He was looking forward to the coming challenges.

Both of them found they had been given courses in all aspects of the project; chef school, Inn management, etc. by their mysterious benefactors. All to much to believe it was true.

Author's Note: Look....before you ask? I have absolutely *no* idea who or *what* was going to run the Pirate's Cove version of the in out on their Really Big Island. Use your own imagination. I gave up.

On top of that? Over the months, Sam and Mary had grown to be a major "item", with plans to marry soon after the opening of the Inn and it's success. And success it was projected to become, if all the publicity in the local news was to be believed. A new, major Inn? On a distant, formerly inaccessible location? Where an historic, pirate inn once stood? A B&B? A restaurant? Parking *and* dock access? Local jobs? Wow!

The two lovebirds had such high hopes for the Inn and it had so much going for it, too; run by descendents of two historically infamous, local families. Add that here was a brand new Inn being built on the site of the original tavern from their ancestors time. It was important that the original ste was being protected. In time, visitors would be able to visit the ongoing archeological digs, all funded by Sam and Mary. Good food, (they hoped), good access by road or boat, rooms to rent, the B&B *and* live music provided by local band, WhydahMaker. What could possibly go wrong? It was exciting because, if the In was a big success, they would be wed here, at the Inn before the year was out.

At present, though, things were still a few weeks or months away from an actual opening. At the same time as all this good fortune? Lester Worthy and Viridian Bean,aka WhydahMaker, received a formal letter that informed them, if they accepted the terms of the agreement, the house band for Bellamy's Pirate Inn. The only condition? They could not perform any of the horrendous music that was still featured on WPDQ, (in memorium, of course by another disreputable pirate station).

Both Lester and Viridian knew exactly who drew up these papers and conditions; one, not-quite-dead, Sam Bellamy. Hey! It was a good paying, steady job. They weren't idiots! So what if a ghost was setting the terms of their employment. WhydahMaker was back to work, practicing music that, while original, was a bit more acceptable to their "boss". Another part of the agreement? Sam Bell and Mary Hall were never....*never* to know who was really behind the whole thing. Lester could dig that. The dead, old bastard really did have a heart....somewhere, even if it hadn't beaten in centuries/ Family looked out for family.....*and* a paying gig, to boot! No problemo. Again? What could *possibly* go wrong?

Two words could quite possibly answer that question: Sam....Bellamy. Oh, this was his big project he'd planned for ages (really). Keeping track of his latter-day family made it even more rewarding. The only problem? Sam was never satisfied with the progress and insisted on "tweaking" the construction, much to the growing aggravation of C, D, E & F, who's coffers were running dangerously low, thanks to Sam. It was making it more difficukt for them to hide the fact that the successful investment firm for the "not-quite-dead" was in serious financial straits.

Not that they hadn't ****ed it up many times in their historic past (leading to multiple death threats and actual deaths over the centuries). But, hey! The funds from the latest investments were coming to the rescue, shortly. Weren't they? As stated previously, what could *possibly* go wrong?

Whatever. Sam and Mary were happy. Lester and Viridian were, too. Elizabeth Worthy was overjoyed not to be running into any more ghosts....or wharever *they* were. *What were they, anyway? Oh, well. If it involved Lester? Could be anything.*

Trouble was brewing with otherr clients of the Firm who were growing concerned for their *own* projects and a little black cat named Mikey, was about to make them even more concerned. Funny thing about cats that can talk.....and are good at snooping around.

Somewhere else

Elvis was working on his food truck plans. Napoleon? He was enjoying watching Elvis, dreaming how he was going to convince someone....*anyone*....to attempt another coup in France. This would be *the* one. *He* had a foolproof plan and he didn't like the road his old country was taking in this modern time. It would take money....a *lot* of money. Until then? Maybe he could help Elvis and the food truck menu......maybe convince him to accept a touch of French cooking to that.... that *menu*.

He shuddered at the thought of all that peanut butter, bananas and bacon, not to mention all those other ideas. Elvis. What a redneck rube!

In the middle of that thought, who popped in, literally, but Mikey. As far as a cat could do, he was trying very hard to get their attention. Cats *are* able to show excitement but showing extreme consternation? Not usually in the cat playbook. Elvis was the first to notice Mikey.

"Hey, Lil' Buddy, what's up? Why ya'll dancin' round like ya gotta use a litter tray, huh?"

Mikey stood there staring, as only a cat can do, then finally said, "Meow this, Bozo! You guys have some big problems and you don't have a ****ing clue. You talk all these big plans but, you're **** clueless! Meow!"

Napoleon looked down at the cat, but when you consider their relative height and all....not that far to look down, at all.

"Mikey, mon chat, what has you so....fluffed up? Clue? Whit is zis clue you talk of?"

"Napoleon? Elvis? All this talk, talk, talk....dreaming away.....what are you using to *pay* for all this dreaming, huh? *Meow, hiss.* Where's the money coming from, huh?"

Elvis chimed in, "Lil' Buddy? Ya'll don't have to worry. We got plenty of money packed away at C, D, E &...."

"*HISS!* That's what *you* think! I was over at Crouch's office....wandering around, you know....what us cats do. (Cats being the curious, nosey, busybodies that they are.) I happened to be in their boardroom when a meeting was going on....minding my own business, of course. Guys? I heard *stuff*. Not good stuff, either. Those guys? The ones you trust with all your money? It sounds like.... *hiss*...they're broke!"

Elvis lost his smile. "Broke? They *can't* be broke. They's some kinda financial geniuses, ain't they?"

"Elvis, mon ami, there have been rumors, even legends....yes, l*egends* among our ...type. Rumors about their past....way past...and the many mistakes made by Mssrs. Crouch, Diabello, Enoch and Flinch....past lives....past disasters....but....I always thought they were simply, pardon the expression, whispers from the grave....so to speak,"

"*HISS, YEOWL*, rumors? Maybe....but from what I heard? Old man Crouch is on the ropes but counting on some *BIG* money coming in to bail them out. Seems they made some pretty bad investments.....reeeeally bad ones...with all our money. *ALL* our money. They've been covering it up until this cash rolled in to save their butts."

"But Mikey, mon chat? Zis cannot be. The Not Quite Dead have trusted this firm....for centuries. This surely is not true. We must waitg and see. Time will tell."

Elvis growled, "We gotta find out, but Nappy's right. They's always been talk and rumors 'bout the Firm." He shuddered at the thought. "Ah may not be all that alive anymore, but *those* guys? They are some scary dudes. We gotta be careful....think this through."

Mikey hissed one more time. "Scary dudes? Yeah, they are that but remember whose money is also involved? One *very....scary*.....pirate dude."

"Oh, merde. Sam."

""Bellamy. Oh, man."

"Hissss, yowl."

Meanwhile, the pirate in question was staring out at the construction on....whatever Island you wish to call it.

"Hmmmmmmm, I see it , now. The docking facilities.... still not big enough....and we'll have to upgrade the roads from the mainland. Sandy trails won't cut it. Something else I decided? Enoch, we need a ferry service from here at the harbor, over to the Inn. What if people don't have boats? Not everone is as rich as we are."

Cringing next to him, Morley Enoch flinched at each new idea. With every word, he saw dollar signs, growing wings and flying....flying away....money they *still* didn't have. *Oh, my! Pleeeeease let it be soon.* Finding the words difficult to get from his mouth, Morley said, "S-s-sam? These are all *wonderful* additions to the plans.... but... do you really think you should go ahead with these changes so....soon? I mean, the Inn hasn't opened yet. You don't know what you may or may not need to change. It could take months to..."

"Morley, that's *exactly* why I wan gt these changes made *now*! I have many more ideas for improvements once the Inn *is* up and running. For now?"

Sam pointed over to tie island.

"For now, I want this done, understand? Morley? Done! No more excuses. Get it *all* done."

Sam slapped Morley on the back, laughing.

"What's all that money for, right?"

"Of course, Sam. Ha ha. Of course. *What* was I thinking?" *(Another painful, embarrassing death, I'm thinking if Crouch doesn't come through....oh, not again.)*

CHAPTER 28

Conversations

The emergency boardroom meeting: D, E & F

Mendicant Flinch- "Gentlemen, *I* have called this emergency meeting. Ishmael Crouch was *not* invited.
Morley Enoch- "You have concerns, Mendicant? What could be so important to have us meet here behind Ishmael's back?"
M.F.- "No...*we* have concerns....serious concerns and yes, we're meeting this way *because* of Ishmael."
Faustus Diabello- "It's concerning the money, I assume? The money Ishmael has promised the firm? Hde told us there would be no problems; not to be concerned. You're saying otherwise?"
M.F.- "Oh, there's a problem, Faustus, possibly a *fatal* problem....as in....*no* money."
M.E.- "There cannot be a problem, Mendicant! He promised and he's never been wrong before."
M.F.- "Really*? Never* been wrong before? How long has Ishmael been around? Eons? How many times has he died because of....problems? And how many times have you, Morley, suffered that painful indignity due to....problems, hmmmm?"
F.D.- "Personally? I would rather not suffer the consequences of such a ....problem. How about *you* explain your concerns for bringing us here behind Ishmael's back. He *is* the leader of our firm."
M.E.- "Most powerful."
F.D.- "Most dangerous."
M.F.- "Most *wrong* at times, if you get right down to it. Look. Those funds were promised many days ago. I became concerned enough that I decided to look into these investments that were going to miraculously save our firm....and *us* from our many clients."
M.E.- "I'm not going to die again. I remember the last..."
D.F.- "Stop whining, Morley. You're not going to die just yet....again."
M.F.- "Don't be too sure, Faustus. As I said, I've done some research and here's what I've found concerning our recent investments."

    Mendicant brought out a folder. He began to read.

"First, we have several millions invested in an Alaskan bridge....on top of what he dumped into it years ago."

M.E.- "What's wrong with bridges? I *like* bridges."

M.F.- "One that goes nowhere? Not even a highway or a dirt track in sight that connects? Let me continue."

He flipped to another page.

"Ah, yes. He invested even more millions in something called social media and internet."

F.D.- "Wasn't there just a major meltdown with one of those social media things? Something called Facebook?"

M.F.-"Yes. Total meltdown thanks to the Russians....and he invested in many of *their* projects, too. There's this golf course...."

M.E.- "I like golf."

M.F.- "An 18 hole golf course in the middle of Siberia? Trust me. Putin is laughing at *that* one. And that is not all, speaking of golf courses, he has invested, heavily I might add, in that big scandelous organization that builds them, towers and casinos that fail like a cheap watch."

F.D.- "Oh, my God! Not *that* disaster. What was he thinking?"

M.F.- "Finally, our leader has purchased] controlling interests in....brace yourselves....most, if not *all* of the failing mega-malls around the country."

M.E.- "But...but....there are reasons all these mega-malls are failing. Why? What was he thinking?"

M.F.- "Believe it or not, his concept was sound but not an overnight money maker. Ishmael had the idea to gut these malls and turn them into condo villages, with a wide range of interior apartments, services, restaurants, healthcare, mail, shopping."

F.D.- "*That* doesn't sound half bad. What's wrong with it?"

M.F.- "Ishmael made a series of *very* bad choices in exactly what stores would be put into these communities and he invested in *all* of them! SnackFest! StayHome! Booze R U! Fancy Pants! To name a few of these losers."

M.E.- " But...but....even I knew they'd all go out of business! With *those* names?"
F.D.- "If not before some of them opened a single store. What *was* he thinking?"
M.E.- "I don't want to die....*again*....and so soon!"
M.F.- "Gentlemen, we're not dead yet. We can still extricate ourselves from this....mess."
F.D.- "But *how*, Mendicant?"
M.F.- "We lie....a lot....to our clients until things sort themselves out. Who knows? Some of these terrible investments may just make us enough money to save us, even by delcaring them losses."
M.E.- "As long as nothing more goes wrong."
F.D.- "As long as no one else comes demanding money for a long, long time."
M.E.- "We can only hope. What more can possibly go wrong?"

Meanwhile, at the Wellfleet harbor
    Lester and Viridian stood on the dock as the temporary ferry approached. Sam and Mary were onboard, the owners of the soon-to-be opened Inn on Great Island. As the small ferry bumped the dock,they both hailed them.

"Les! Viridian! I hope we're on time.This isn't what the real ferry will be but it's all almost finished. Hop aboard and we'll go back to the Inn."
    It wasn't a long trip. Along the way, Sam and Mary explained about the Inn, the entire project and the important role WhydahMaker was to play.
    "Les, you and Viridian...."
    "Please, Sam. Call me V."
    "Sam laughed. "Alright, V. You and Les are going to be key in pulling this all together And help make it a great success. A nedw n for the town. Great food and lodging. The history. What better group to provide the music for a famous pirate's Inn than a band named WhydahMaker?"
    "Uh, Sam? You mean *infamous pirate*, don't you?" Lester chimed in.
    Mary gently put her hand on Sam's arm.

"Les? Don't mind Sam. He's so excited. Of course, we understand; *infamous pirate*, but the legend of Black Sam Bellamy is ingrained in the town's history. Why not use it?"

Lester gave a twisted smile.

"Oh, I understand about making use of a legend. V and I *both* understand *very* well. By....the ....way? You both said you have this mysterious benefactor working behind the scenes. Sounds almost like a fairytale."

Mary was so excited and jumped at the chance to answer.

"Oh, Lester...V. You have *no* idea. It has been such a whirlwind! Right from the start! Sam and I, both? We had this anonymous donor who, more or less, sponsored each of our lives as we grew up. Sam and I? We never met until representatives of this person got us together." She smiled warmly at Sam.

"We hit it off *so* well. Next thing we knew...."

Sam joined in, smiling back at her.

"Next thing we knew? We were an item. Then we were planning our marriage."

He turned and pointed in the direction of ther Island and Inn.

"Then? This.... and now? Well, you two are now part of it. as well."

"It's like a dream." Mary added. "And all due to our Fairy God Mother, whoever it is."

Lester laughed wickedly. "Oh, he's a *real* Mother, alright. By the way? From what I understand? Definitely, I think, a He. We have a bit of similar history with a *benevolent* sponsor. Gee! Ya think maybe we have the same one? Ow!" At that, Viridian kicked Les in the shin.

Mary gave Lester a confused look, not quite catching the sarcasm.

"The same benefactor? How could that be possible? I never thought of that....." Her thoughts trailed off as they approached the new docking facility which had already been remodeled, thanks to Bellamy's demands.

"Well! We're here. Pardon the mess. For *some* reason, ther decision was made to expand everything."

"Mary and I thought it was fine the way it was but, oh well. Who are we to agrue with such a gift?"

They all stepped from the ferry. Sam spread his arms, expansively, turning to the almost completed Inn.

"Welcome to Bellamy's Pirate Inn!" Sam proudly exclaimed.

"This is our new home and *you* are welcomed as our first guests."

Mary added, "*And* as WhydahMaker, an important part of what will make us a success!"

They all stood, quietly taking it all in.

In awe, Viridian said, "Wow! I am....I don't have words for this. Amazing? Comes to mind. Wishing you all the luck in the world? Of course. The idea that Les and I can be a part of this? I have no words."

Lester added, for once humbly, "I hope we can live up to your expectations. V and I have worked so hard to make a name for ourselves as WhydahMaker."

V turned to Lester. "Yes, we have...and worked *so* hard to earn us a *good* reputation. There were moments."

"Yes! We heard about those, mmmmmmm concerts you gave at that *unique* radio station, WPDQ. I grant you, some of what came over the airwaves was horrifying. Even though, so tragic what happened."

"But", Mary added, "That was how we first heard of WhydahMaker, so it wasn't *all* that horrible."

"We both apologize for that shameful episode in our growth as WhydahMaker. We were having a *slight* disagreement with *our* sponsors. Lester felt we had to.... make a statement."

"How interesting. However, it *did* bring you to our attention. It was the name that got our attention: WhydahMaker. Sam and I assume you know the history of the Whydah? And how we discovered our lives have become intertwined with the legends. By ther way....you repeatedly mentioned your *own* mysterious benefactor. What do you know about yours?"

"Ohhhh, I think you'd be surprised. Ow!" Another kick in the shins. "I mean, it's truly amazing, isn't it? *You* have a mysterious backer. *We* have an anonymous backer, too....whoever *they* are."

"And here we *all* are. Welcome to Bellamy's Pirate Inn."

They stood on the front steps of the impressive building.

From the outside, it had the look of an old, rustic Inn, one you might imagine had been in this place for all these centuries, only this one was brand new. It smelled of cedar and tar and the sea. Inside, it also had the look of an old Inn, beamed ceilings, multiple fireplaces and a bar that looked like it was part of a ship's hold.

Everywhere lanterns, candles, tables and an impressive stage. Rustic but rich and inviting. Lester and Viridian could see that this was going to be a hit, especially when the tourists discovered it. The locals? Well, it might take *them* some time to come to grips....but if the food was good? If the *bar* was good and if it all helped put money back in the town coffers? They would come.
Sam began to explain in a short tour.

"You're obviously standing in the main dining hall, the bar, the stage and ther main desk. We have rooms on the main floor, down the hall as well as enough rooms upstairs. All the amenities. We've spared nothing to make our guests stay here a happy, memoral one."

Sam was so proud of their Inn. Mary took over the conversation.

"And even better? Beyond the Inn, itself, we're setting up a museum and archeological site around the original tavern site. Visitors will be able to learn the fascinating history and the town will be pleased that *we* are respecting that history for all time."

"It's a win-win situation as far as we can see."

"There *were* some issues with the road leading to the Inn."

"And with the docking facilities."

"But when they realized what we were planning...."

"And with our *own* family history?"

"They eventually saw it our way....or that of our benefactor. We understand he could be *quite* persuasive.

"You have idea."

"Let's show you the rest of the place."

"In about a week, you'll be able to come out here to rehearse and get a feel for the main room. It's so exciting, isn't it?"

And everything came to pass as they hoped.

From the docks, back at the harbor, the other Sam and Mariah stood watching as the ferry faded off towards the island.

"I've waited a long, long time for this Mariah, my dearest." Sam held Mariah close to his side.

Mariah sighed and leaned her head on his shoulder.

"Sam? Don't you think it's time for us....you know.... to move on? Now that you're getting what you've always wanted ; a secure future for our families. Isn't it your fondest wish fulfilled?"

Sam smiled at Mariah. "And just where do ye wish us to go? Move on? Into the light? Or wherever God sends us? Me? I've grown content here. I dinna ken why you want to leave. Our lives have been so tied to this spit o' land, I can't imagine us leavin'. Think about it. We can stay and watch our families flourish and grow as *we* never could. Ye never know. There could be new dreams to chase and all the time in the world to chase them. Think about it."

Sam waved his arm over the bay and distant island.

Mariah sighed again. " I guess you be right, Sam, my dear. So much that was bad has happened to us here but so much good as well. We *are* together, after all."

"For all time, Mariah."

"For all time and beyond, Sam."

The ferry carrying the others faded to the island as a bit of fog moved in, as it usually did, to hide them.. Behind them, and sitting as quietly as a feline, especially a ghostly one can be, Mikey sat there purring softly to himself. It wasn't all birdies and fishies to him, though. At the moment, he *might* be purring but his tail was lashing.... back and forth....back and forth.

Mikey was troubled by all he'd seen and heard recently.

How much should he really tell Sam about Crouch and his gang Ohhh, he had to tell him some of it but he knew Sam's temper. He wasn't called Black Sam Bellamy for nothing. Oh, yes. This would take some thought.

At that, as the fog continued to roll in, three beings, not visible to anyone walking the harbor promenade, faded slowly into the mist; two happy and a bit sentimental, one....a bit worried.

Back at the Inn, Viridian turned abruptly to Lester. "Oh, Sam....do you think we can rehearse here?" Excitedly, she turned to Mary.

"Mary, will that be alright?. I don't mean to be pushy but how soon can we begin? It's a wonderful place. We can really get into our music. Les? Can't you feel it? Practicing here will be so much more fun than back home."

"Oh, yeah. A lot better. Out here We won't be bothered by....*people* barging in on our work." He smiled at young Sam. "You know how it is, Sam? Sometimes you don't have a *ghost* of a chance to, OW! Damn it, Viridian!"

She had once again kicked him in the shins, this time, not too subtlely, either.

"Oh! Sorry, Les. I didn't see your leg there." She kicked him again. "*Now,* I do."

Sam and Mary both laughed.

"Oh, it's going to be fun having you two playing out here. You are *so* funny together. Give us a few more days to get all the electrical work done. Then? You'll be more than welcome. By then the real ferry will be running on a regular schedule in preparation for the opening. Let's go have a drink or two to celebrate."

A few days later, at C, D, E & F, there was a *minor* confrontation among the firm members and a few of it's clients, led by Elvis and Napoleon. Elvis began.

"Boys, we have heard disturbin' rumors 'bout what ya'll have done managin' our money."

"Oui! I am also certain you gentlemen will allay our concerns?" Napoleon attempted to be the charming half of "good cop/bad cop".

"All we need to know? Is our money safe? Our finances secure? May we draw funds when needed?"

At that, there were a number of vague murmurs from the clients behind them. Ishmael Crouch stood up and blustered, good-naturedly.

"And *who* has been spreading these terrible falsehoods about our firm? Our good name is everything and has been for centuries!"

Behind him, Enoch whispered to Flinch. *"And that's about all we have at the moment."*

"Shut up, Morley!" Faustus hissed back.

"Every so often, as a responsible investment firm will do, we look at the portfolios of our clients and make decisions; make changes and reinvest in more....lucrative opportunities."

"Yeah, like Fancy Pants."

"Shut up, Morley!"

Crouch continued, unconcerned by the small talk behind him.

"So! Of course, whenever we do this; make some of these changes....for your own well being, of course...."

"Yeah, of course!"

"Shut up, Morley!"

A sigh and smile from Ishmael Crouch.

"Of course, during this *very* short window of time, funds may *seem* to be unavailable."

Grumbles from the clients.

"But, in reality, when you actually *need* them....*if* you need them? Funds will *always* be forthcoming. *We* simply ask you to be patient for day or two. At present? We can handle small amoiunts, if needed....but....but only for a day or two. Then we're back to normal operations. As always, we remain....successful guardians of your fortunes. Now? If there are any other concerns, you can see our secretary, Marie, outside. Good day , Gentlemen and Ladies."

As they all faded out to harrass poor Marie, "Well! *That* went better than expected."

"Chief, where's the money"
"When will the funds start *rolling* in?"
"We're gonna die again, aren't we, Faustus?"
"Shut *up*, Morley!"
"Gentlemen, relax. All we have to do is dole out what we still have put aside for just such contingencies. Your jobs? Keep the money moving out....but slowly, cautiously....as needed to keep our clients quiet until all this passes."
"We're all gonna die, again."
"Shut *up*, Morley."
"*sigh*....Oh, give me a break."

Two days later; the same office

In strolled Sam Bellamy, (well, more like *mists* into the room). Demanding and arrogant, Sam hands Crouch a bill.
"Crouch, I said I'd be back if I needed anything more. Rumors or no rumors, here's the bill for the latest upgrades."
Ishmael looked down at the paperwork as if it would bite him.
"And *what* do you expect me to do with *this* on such short notice? I warned you to be sparing in squandering your fortune, *especially* during our reinvestment campaign....on **your** behalf, I might add."
Sam glared at Crouch. "Dinna give me tha', Crouch! Here's what I've done and here's what ye owe me.... Now? Deal wi' it! It be your job, ain't it? *Do* it!"
Sam faded out. Crouch immediately called another emergency board meeting. All anxiously were in attendance.
"Gentlemen, we face a minor crisis. And Morley? Shut up about death, please? Sam Bellamy is proving to be a problem and is pushing his demands too far. The money demands have become intolerable. Even if we weren't caught a bit short for the moment, his wild, frivolous spending would cause us to put the brakes on his spending."

"For his own good."

"Yes, exactly. For his own good."

"As well as ours."

"*We* must do something to show Mr. Bellamy....who actually is the boss around here...and it is *not* Sam Bellamy. Time, gentlemen...time for us to....*help* him understand this crucial fact."

CHAPTER 29

Welcome to the Old Pirate Inn

or....

The Plot Congeals

As posted in the Outer Cape Cronicle:

Grand Re-opening! (After several hundred years waiting)

In one week, THE OLD PIRATE INN will open it's doors. Located on Great Island near the site of the original, Samuel Smith Tavern, it will be the first time in hundreds of years that such a business will exist at the location.

This will not follow in the footsteps of the original Inn, which catered to sailors, whalers, the occasional pirate, smuggler shady characters and, as legend has it, the infamous, local pirate Sam Bellamy.

Interesting enough, the Inn is the brainchild of two descendents, infamous or famous, to Cape lore; Sam Bell, related to Sam Bellamy, and Mary Hall, related to Mariah Hallett. History and legend has the two ancestors as star-crossed lovers. Today, Sam and Mary truly are lovers, planning to marry soon after the opening of the Inn. We wish them great happiness and success.

The new, Old Pirate Inn will not simply be a tavern. Oh, no. It will have a full restaurant along with tyhe tavern, featuring live, local music weekly. The house band will be Wellfleet's own, WhydahMaker.

The duo features Lester Worthy and Viridian bean, both "transplants" or "washashores" but who cares? The music will be great!

The Inn will also feature vacation lodgings in a popular, historic locale. Still not enough to interest you? Off-site parking will be available with new, ecologically friendly roads and transport to the Inn. Boat docking will be another exciting feature.

As part of their commitment to the community, Sam and mary are building a museum around the site of the historic, old tavern, continuing the archeological study that has been going on, too slowly, perhaps, for years. People visiting the Inn will have access to the museum as soon as it is completed.

All in all, this is an exciting develpoment that will benefit all of us, not only Wellfleet but the entire Cape, as well. Congratulations, Sam and Mary!

This article was much more than the usual reporting that appeared in the Cronicle. As a result, interest and excitement was growing in anticipation of opening night. Sam and Mary were run ragged with all the final details; employess, wait staff, chefs, menus, etc..

Meanwhile, Les and V were using their time to get used to the stage area and sound system in the tavern. Yes., it was an exciting time. All were working hard to make it happen. Les and V were *so* involved, they totally forgot about two, "not-quite-dead" folk who continued to monitor the procedings. They, two, were excited and Mariah was doing all she could to keep Sam from interfering.

"Just let them be, Sam. They be working it all out. You should be proud of what you helped to accomplish."

At that, she slipped her arm through his and hugged him. "And *you* are responsible for bringing these two wonderful, young people together. You have given them what *we* never had."

Mariah was saddened at the thought. Sam smiled back, knowingly. "Oh, Lass. We did na get the chance ta marry but we *are* still together.....after all this time. Tha' means a lot."

They looked on silently, as everyone went about their business. It was a glorious time filled with anticipation for the opening. All *must* be perfect.

All *was* perfect. Before the official opening, people were waiting at the doors to the tavern. Boat slips were filling. The land shuttle from the Great Island parking lot was in full swing, as was the harbor ferry servive. Sam and Mary were amazed at the response from a single news article. Mary had been busy all day at the Inn desk.

"No, sir. The Inn isn't ready to take room reservations for a few weeks. Yes, I'm sorry, too. Please leave me your contact information and we *will* call immediately upon making reservations available."

She turned to one of the new Staff.

"Phew! Is it ever going to stop? I know. I know. This what we were hoping for but I wish we were fully up and running. This is insanity. I *must* be patient."

At 5 P.M., the doors opened for the first time. All was ready. The tavern and restaurant filled rapidly. They watched it all fill with curious customers.

"Well, here we go. Let's make it work!"

This being opening night, WhydahMaker decided to start playing early, celebrating the event. After this, music would begin at a Cape-dignified 7 P.M. on Fridays and weekends.

Lester faced the audience, grinned and yelled, "ARRRRRRRRRR! Welcome, mateys to opening night here at the Old Pirate Inn, where allllll the old ghosts of local pirates and scalliwags come to party. ARRRRRRR! I'm Lester Worthy and this be my partner in song, Viridian Bean and WE....ARE....WhydahMaker! Get yer pirate on!"

At that, they ripped into a traditional Irish jig done "their way". The diners and bvar crew all were having a great time. Many would join in when they heard a song they knew. The drinks flowed and everyone began to loosen up. It wasn't long before the dancing began in earnest to the liovely music. Old songs, new songs, war-horses, original ones from the band; all received with rounds of applause. A few brash souls from the WPDQ fan base were there and kept calling for the Sam Bellamy song. V looked worried but Lester smiled, answering over the mike. "Hey! Sorry, guys. We don't play that stuff here.... might upset some evil spirits. Ya never can tell."

At that he looked past the crowd to where Sam Bellamy stood, watching and liastening intently. He had been enjoying himself until some idiot called for *that* song.

Oh, well. He thought, *Worthy handled that heckler. Nothing to get concerned about.*

All in all? A perfect opening night, passing all expectations. At closing, when the final customers had gone, Sam and mary were exhausted but excited with the response to the first night. Les and V, as well, were exhausted, their voices ragged and their playing arms aching but, it was worth it.

V said, "Wow! That was so fun. Les we really made it, didn't we?"

"Yeah, we're finally....*finally* on our way. Now, people have to respect WhydahMaker."

"Oh, Les. I hope so. That whole WPDQ thing didn't do anything for our credibility."

"Well,. Lady, we don't have to worry about that now, do we?"

"ARRRRR!"

"ARRRRRRRRRR!"

They both laughed as they packed. What a night. What an experience. Sam and Mary felt the same way.

"We're going to make soooo much money, Mary. It'll all be smooth sailing from now on."

At the back of the Inn, unseen,(on purpose) were both Sam and Mariah. She smiled, saying, "Yes, Sam. Smooth sailing, right? You shoiuld be proud. I know *I* am."

"Aye, Lass, fair weather and smooth seas. What could go wrong? We've planned well....for everything."

Maybe.....not. It is, after all, Cape Cod and things.... *tend* to work differently in our small town. The first indication there might be a problem came early the next morning. Sam was handling the phone call.

"Wait a minute. What do you *mean*? We have to provide and pay for police presence at the Great Island parking lot during hours? People were doing *what*? Out in the open? Really? O.K., how much will this cost me? What? You're kidding, right? No? Damn!" Sam slammed the phone down.

Mary handled the next call, from the harbor master.

"Hello, yes, sir. I am the co-owner here. What? *What*? Complaints? What complaints? About our ferry service? No! Oh, the dock? Not big enough for the traffic it causes? We need to do *what*? That much bigger? How long do we have.....by *when*?" Unlike Sam, she politely put the phone down.

"Oh, Sam. It sounds like we have so much we still have to do. I never expected so much trouble, so fast."

"Don't worry, Mary. Just a few bumps in the road. It'll all pass soon enough."

A knock came at the door. In walked an officious looking man holding a rather large clipboard.

"Good morning. You are, I assume, Sam Bell and Mary Hall? My name is Reginald Ephram from the Cape EPA. You folks have some problems to correct before you can reopen. The docking bays? Not wide enough. Not enough of them *and* you've got to provide protection against possible environmental contamination. The nearby shellfish beds need to be protected."

Sam sighed. "I understand Mr. Ephram. We had no idea. Exactly what needs to be done for compliance? What, when and how much will it cost?"

Next came the local historical society.

"Mr. Bell, Ms. Hall? We applaude your intentions for the archeological site of the old Smith Tavern. Truly, we do.....However? You are not moving rapidly enough to contain and protect the site while the museum is being constructed. Do you know we found beer bottles at the dig? Someone even peed on the "No Trespassing" sign. Unacceptable! Here's what we require you to do, *soonest*."

Next? Came the guy from the Grand Island Conservation and Protection Trust.

"You call what you put in a *road*? Laughable! All you did was cut a path from the parking lot to the Inn, one that will disappear in the first nasty weather."

"But....we did exactly what you *told* us to do!"

"Maybe, but things change and we saw how much traffic there was going to be."

"We have been very careful, using only electric vehicles to do all the transporting.....what if we did more to stabilize the sand and...."

"*Totally* unacceptable! Before you do anything like that? You must prove to us the chemicals used will be environmentally safe."

Mary sighed. "And *sir,* will *that* be enough? If we do all this?"

"Sadly, Ma'am? No. We have a serious complaint from the local "Green" club. According to them, you have encroached on the site of the last, living home of a nearly extinct slime mold."

"You're kidding, right? An endangered....what? Even Mary was beginning to get annoyed with the constant barrage of bad news. She got louder.

"Just *what*, sir, does this....worthless slime mold contribute to the town that makes it more important than the tax dollars we will be bringing in? The tourists?"

"It's a concerned group."

"How many and *how* concerned?"

"Not important. *They* have a concern and it *is* nature we're talking about."

"Nature has been wrong before. And Darwin had lot's to say about *some* people."

Sam broke in. "Sir? Tell us what we have to do to protect....to satisfy....*sigh*....O.K., how *much* does the slime mold need to make it happier and how long do we have?"

Oh, in true fashion, it went on and on. The circus of people, hands out, papers waving, indignant and concerned this and that. By days end, Sam and mary sat down, trying to work it all through.

"Mary, as far as I can figure, they're at least giving us enough time to make all the changes."

"That may be, Sam, but this is costing us a lot of money. *Money* we don't have as yet. And if these... people hAve their way? They will suck us dry and spit out the husks."

Sam rubbed his neck, a major headache coming on.

"You're right, so right. Well, there is one thing we can do. I'll get in touch with our contact to the mystery benefactor. Maybe he or they will help. I have his card somewhere....here it is....strange name, Faustus Diabello. Let's give him a call."

The next day, Faustus Diabello met with the young couple at the Inn.

"Mr. Diabello, thank you for responding so quickly. All of a sudden we are in quite a bind."

Faustus looked around, taking in the unique "pirate tavern" decor.

"Well, I must admit. I've heard so much about the project and your incredible opening night. I *had* to come and see for myself. You have made such an impression here. Our firm and your benefactor are all so impressed. Now, what may I do for you besides applaud?"

Mary commented. "Applaud? Yeah, we had a great first night....until next morning when all Hell broke loose! *You* name the complaint? *You* name the official. *You* name the angry group? They were all here....in force. All with gripes and demands that scream, **more money**! "

"Mr. Diabello, we need some serious help. We've sunk every cent we've got into making this a success. These.... people....came from nowhere like a proverbial plague. To the point? We need money. A *lot* more money. And we've been given a month to get everything done that's been demanded, or (Sam waved to the Inn), all this? Will be history when they close us down....permanently. Now, Mary and I don't know who our mysterious benefactor is and we're ashamed to come begging after all you've done."

"But we're in *deep* trouble, Mr. Diabello. Deep trouble and you folks look to be the only ones able to dig us out of this mess."

"Mary's right. This is a mess but from what you've heard, we can and will make this business a big success. Any money we require will be paid back, no doubt."

Faustus sat there quietly, expressionless, sweating slightly as he gripped the edge of the table and tried to remain calm.

"Well, this is terrible, absolutely *terrible*. Such a great beginning. Such a bright future, too."

He stood up straightening, and with a fixed smile on his face, said, "I must get back and consult my collegues at C, D, E & F. There should be something we can do to help you out of this bind. It's just....(he paused, smile still fixed), it's just....at the moment, we are in our own financial crunch. No, nothing for you to worry about. We occasionally get caught a bit....short while we wait for investments to bear fruit. All I'm saying? Have patience for a few days. You say you have a month? No problem. It may take us a few days to get the money together, that's all. Now! Do you have the figures on what all these penalties will cost?"

Sam handed over several sheets of figures. Diabello took a look and began to sweat even more, gthe smile rapidly leaving his face.

"My dear God! How much....why, this is almost a million dollars, maybe more. Are you sure that....?"

"*Absolutely* sure, Mr. Diabello. As sure as death and taxes. If we're lucky, that is, and no more nasties come knocking at our door."

He cringed at the word,"death", especially death.... thinking about Mr. Enoch's constant whining.....it was getting to him.

"Ahhhh, aruuuum, yes. I have to bring this back to the office so we can discuss how to handle this....*small* inconvenience."

He gave a fake, hearty laugh. "Believe me, ha ha, this is simply small change to a firm such as ours. All we have to do is scrape up the small change for you. We'll be back to you shortly."

He quickly headed for the door, turning one last time.

"Shortly....we'll be back....shortly."

He left the Inn in a big hurry. Sam shook his head and asked Mary,

"Am I reading too much into this or did we just get the bum's rush? I mean...he *sounded* sincere....up to a point."

"Sam? Did you see him sweat? The more he tried to sound confident, the more sweat....and that smile? Didn't inspire *my* confidence."

"A couple of days, he said, Mary. A few days. Maybe we're reading too much into this. He *is,* after all, a lawyer-type."

"Yes, Sam. They *all* seem to be on the slimy side of things....and he left quite a slime trail out the door.. I'm worried, Sam. Sorry, but I'm deeply worried."

"Don't be too much, Mary. Look at all they've done for us so far." He took her hand in his.

"And they *did* bring us together."

She smiled lovingly. I know *you*, Sam Bell. You want to move the wedding up, don't you?"

"All I'm asking is we wait until this money issue gets settled. All we'll need is a week or two. Then? Everything will be O.K., and we'll *have* that wedding. I promise. Right here....at the Inn."

"And we'll invite *everyone* from town?"

"Whatever you wish, darling."

All seemed better to the two love birds. All did *not* seem well to Black Sam Bellamy, who had been standing there, out of sight, listening to the whole thing. His thoughts becoming "blacker" by the second, he was seething over that weasel, Diabello.

What was that band of crooks up to, any way? Where is my money when I need it? Oh, yes. It was time to pay a visit to those four bandits and get to the bottom of it!

Sam faded from the tavern, leaving Sam and Mary still holding hands. It was Sam's intention to get a hold of more than someones hand.....maybe a neck or four. There would be answers *and* money or there would be death.

In the C, D, E,& F boardroom/emergency meeting

"But we *can't* afford this! *Any* of this!"

"We've been hanging on by the skin of our teeth! We barely scraped enough together for the last upgrades Bellamy ordered."

"They're going to find out! They're *all* going to find out!"

"Skin us alive!"

"No! I don't want to die....again!"

On and on it went, the panic setting in with the reality of the situation, feeding the fear of the three partners until Crouch stood up and bellowed.

"No one's going to die! *Especially* not us! It's all going to work in our favor, as I said it would. Simply put, it just....is....taking....a bit more time than I expected. I will hear no more of this panic, defeatist attitude."

Ishmael Crouch continued. "Yes, things have been much worse than this in the past, so relax."

At that Flinch started to speak out but Crouch shut him down.

"No! Don't even try to say something about dying or you'll have *me* to worry about!"

Suddenly, Ishmael Crouch and the rest were startled by clapping coming from behind them. It was Sam Bellamy, Napoleon Bonaparte and Elvis. Leaning casually against a wall, Sam was laughing as well as clapping.

"Bravo! Bravo, gentlemen! It is so *good* to hear that the gentlemen charged with protecting our fortunes are doing such a *fine* job." Sam's smile turned to an evil scowl.

"And I'll be tellin' ye all....'tis a good job ye better be doin'.....fer us all."

Napoleon added, "Oui! I am as concerned as my friends."

"Somethin don' smell rhaat, boys. Ahm agreein' with mah friends, heah.(That being from Elvis, of course).

Sam continued. "Crouch? Diabello? Enoch? *Mister* Flinch? Do we all detect a problem here? I, for one, am concerned, having a major project in the works...."

"As do I."

"Me, too."

"Over the many years, we've asked very little of this firm, confident in the knowledge that our funds have been safe and well cared for."

"Is this not true, Mon ami?"

"I think it's time for a bit of an accounting and...."

At that, Ishmael Crouch not only stood back up, but in a terrifying rage, seemed physically to expand to the ceiling, filling the entire space around him; the semblance of a violent storm. In a booming voice that rattled the building, causing all present, except Sam, to cringe in fear.

"THERE IS *NOTHING* WRONG WITH THIS FIRM! HOW....DARE...YOU! THERE WILL BE *NO* ACCOUNTING FROM THE LIKES OF *YOU*! YES! WE HAVE BEEN HERE FOR YOU FOR CENTURIES AND WILL BE HERE FOR-EVER! DO....YOU....UNDERSTAND?"

At that, Crouch shrank back to normal, yet, still an imposing figure. All were quaking, except for Sam, who still stood leaning against the wall.

"Bravo! Bravo! Nice effects, Crouch but I'm not so easily impressed."

Sam stared each of the firm members in the eyes, as if giving each notice.

"Tha' all may be well, Ishmael...and truth it *may* also be.... but I be tellin' ye. We be puttin' this firm on notice. If we find ye be thinkin' o' playin' pirate with *our* money? We will make sure that each....and every....client of this firm be comin' knockin' at yer doors....and *they* will na' be so cheerfully inclined."

Sam turned to leave, motioning for his two friends to follow. Looking back at the four, "Have I made myself absolutely clear? Good! Gentlemen? A good day to you all." All three faded from the room.

"We're all gonna die! I tell you! We're...."
Crouch glared at Mr. Flinch and forced him into silence. In a quiet, but evil rumble, he said, "I *do* believe it is time to show these clients that *we* are in charge of their money. *We* are. *We* have been. *We* will be."

Looking at each member of the board, he continued.

"Yes, I believe...no, I *know* it is time. Long time coming....to teach an important lesson and I believe we start with Mr. Sam Bellamy, pirate. After what I have planned, the rest will hear, observe and quickly fall into line."

Sitting back down and folding his hands, the partners listened closely to him.

"Here is what we are going to do. Mr. Enoch? Mr. Flinch? I have a very special project for you and the talents you have proved yourselves to be *so* good at. Here's what you are going to do....."

CHAPTER 30

Piece-Full moments

Lester and Elizabeth were happily....and calmly, I might add, strolling peacefully through Wellfleet. Taking in the stores, gallereies and sights. They didn't have a care in the world.

At least to people who saw the happy couple, that's how it appeared. Lester, however? Keeping a happy face on for his wife and doing the best to enjoy the day, he couldm't stop thinking back to that morning....

"Gee, Liz? Let's take the day off and go into town. We need to have some fun. I know, I know. I've been so wrapped up with this band thing. I haven't really been here for you and that's wrong. Let's go take that walk, O.K.?"

Elizabeth was taken by surprise. Lately, between Lester's obsession with the music and all the weirdness.... she was still pretty shaken by the whole "ghostly" thing. This sounded like a great idea. Maybe, just maybe Lester was snapping out of this....whatever it is.

"Lester, that sounds absolutely *wonderful*. Let's go." So, here they were, taking in the town, hitting the stores, browsing the galleries, even planning to stop in one of the many restaurants for some lunch. Lester had to admit, it felt good to get out and away from it all. This whole....mess had shaken them both badly. It seemed to him he couldn't get away from all the death. First, the murders and death surrounding the Opus 133 affair. *That* shook him; being so close to death, himself at the hands of that old bat of a woman, only to have Elizabeth come from nowhere and rescue him from that crazy Nazi bitch.

Of course, her blasting a murderous, antique Nazi bitch to Hell wasn't how he wanted to remember his wife....or the murder in *her* eyes while doing it.

Now? Here in beautiful, laid back, picturesque Wellfleet, once again Lester found himself being dogged with death and destruction. He *still* felt he was in some way responsible for the Painestaker death. He shook it off and went back to checking out the stores, smiling to his wife and holding a conversation. His owed this, and more to his wife.

It wasn't *that* easy, of course. Lester was easily confused, thinking one second Wellfleet, the next, Pirate's Cove. Back and forth, back and forth making his head spin like he had a flock of little, cartoon birdies circling 'round and around...

One minute, the shops of Wellfleet, the next, different shops in Pirate's Cove. It was making him jumpy, too. At every strange noise, he was looking for ghosts or for that damned elusive goat; that damned cat, Mikey, too.

Nope. Nothing out of the normal, whatever the Hell *that* was. Real folk doing the same thing, wandering in the early summer crowd of quasi-tolerant locals and obnoxious tourists.

They just passed the restaurant with a lighthouse on the roof when he thought....at the curb? *Oh, no. Was that Elvis and his damned food truck? Nah....get a grip, Lester. Get a grip!*

That got him thinking about Elvis. How, even dead as an overweight doornail, *he* was still having better luck than Lester. And that horrible food truck! What was the dude thinking? Everything P,B&J? Yuck! Only Elvis. No! He lectured himself. Stop it! Enough! Enjoy the day, out with your wife. He turned to her.

"Liz? Where do you want to go for lunch? So many places to choose from now that the season has started." Thinking to himself: *Yeah, depending on what freakin' town I'm in....a lot to choose from.*

"Oh, I don't know. Why don't we try the Bookstore? We can look out over the harbor, then go sit there afterwards."

"Sounds like a plan. Let's go,"

At that, they continued their stroll through town and headed down towards the harbor and restaurant. All the while, Lester was surrepticiously watching things from the corner of his eye....for things....sounds....ghostly inhabitants of that *other* town. His head was a mess, so confused but he wouldn't let on to Liz how bad it was for him.

Happily, they had a relaxed, enjoyable meal, looking out from the balcony out, over the harbor.

Such a welcome distraction; no ghosts, goats, cats or phantom food trucks. Firmly planted in the seaside, historic, *real* town of Wellfleet. A beautiful moment on a beautiful day.

"Let's go down and sit at the harbor and then walk around a bit." Elizabeth was enjoying herself. "We can watch the boats coming and going."

"Great idea, Liz. Let's fgo. I can't think of a nicer thing to do with my wonderful wife on this spectacular, summer day."

Elizabeth laughed.

"God, Lester, don't get all soppy on me." he hugged him. "But it's good to hear it from you. Let's go."

They spent the latter part of the day relaxing,(really), on one of the many benches looking out over the harbor.. In the distance, they could see the sun beginning to sink behind Great Island. The Old Pirate Inn was clearly visible, outlined in the shadows, giving Lester a chill. *That place....was going to give their band, WhydahMaker, it's big break and steady job. Something, though....was giving him chills. Something wasn't right....or soon wouldn't be.* **** *that,* he thought. He knew Viridian was thrilled, as was Elizabeth. Finally! After all these years of trying, he was going to bring some money back into his house. All the time Liz backed one crazy music scheme after another. It felt good that he could really be successful at something. Still? Every time he looked ba*ck to the Island? It gave him such a chill of forboding.* **** *it*, he thought again.

Further down the harbor, unseen by the couple, stood Sam,(the elder) and Mariah. They, too, stood arm in arm looking out over the same scenery.

Mariah laid her head on Sam's shoulder. "Oh, Sam.... we may be dead, but I consider ourselves *so* lucky. No... now don't give me that look. Of course I'm *not* happy we're not alive but we've seen so much. You know we both love the Cape and our own little part of the world. You've given two wonderful, young people, *our* descendants, a future together *and* set them up for life. I'm so proud of what you've done."

Sam smiled. "Aye, Lass. An' if we ha' lived? None o' this might have happened. I canna guess. We still have each other, no matter what, when or even if, someday, we move on. Aye. I'm happy."

On Great Island, Sam and Mary were sitting at the dock, looking to the west, over the top of the Inn. The setting sun was painting everything golden; one of those early, summer evenings that the painters attempted to capture on canvas, photographers framed and poets waxed about. Sam commented as they looked on.

"We are so lucky, Mary. Who would have believed any of it possible? Our families with their dark history? The chance that, not only do we both have anonymous benefactors but they brought us together."

Mary added. "Yes, Sam. It's a dream. And we were given all *this*! We surely are living the dream. Look at all that's happened. Days ago? They were going to shut us down unless we made all those changes."

"Yeah, Mary, enough money thanks to the efforts of Mr. Diabello to help us keep things up and running; granted, not everything but enough....for now, at least. Yeah, we're so lucky."

They sat close, holding hands, nothing more to say; the perfect end to a perfect day.

Back at the harbor, again, unknown to anyone else, just down from Lester and Elizabeth, sat Elvis and napoleon, basically doing the same thing; taking in a picture perfect end to a summer day.

"Nappy, Ol' buddy? It doan' get much better than this, do it?"

Napoleon sighed, avoiding the desire to correct Elvis, not to call him Nappy. "Oui, old friend. Amazing, yes? The living get to see only a finite number of these. We get an infinite number to watch."

"Bubba? Ain't too bad bein' dead, huh?" At that he put his arm around Napoleon.

"Oui, King. Oui." As the sun set over the horizon, all was welkl....for the moment.

Oh, what? Mikey? Mikey, the cat was doing what *all* catly creatures do; sit, look inscrutible and, ever so slowly, lash his tail back and forth, back and forth....as he sat watching the sun set...*not* looking *too* interested. Catly....you understand.

CHAPTER 31

Big Storm's A-Comin'

It was the next morning. Out on Great Island, Sam and Mary were working hard, excited to be reopening. All that was stressful enough but trying to fit all the pieces of the puzzle so they could reopen in a day or two? Insane!

Thanks to Mr. Diaberllo and their anonymous benefactor, enough money flowed in to complete work to satisy the town and variety of inspectors. With only a few more to go, things were looking up again. There was a knock on the door of the Inn.

Sam opened it to find Mr. Diabello and two others waiting to see them.

"Mr. Diabello! What can we do for you? By the way, we can't thank you enough for all you've done."

"Sam! Mary! It was nothing, really. Nothing less than a good investment banker would do for some of his favorite clients. May I introduce Mr. Mendicant Flinch and Mr. Morley Enoch? They are members of our firm and are in charge of doing the final construction checks on everything.....even after the normal inspectors go through. Now *don't* look so worried. They are only here to make sure the other inspectors didn't mess anything up. You never know if they might come back later to find a problem that wasn't there in the first place...if you get my meaning?"

Enoch and Flinch both had hardhats on and large bags of equipment.

"Mr. Bell? Ms. Hall? Don't you worry about a thing. We'll be in and out of here so quickly, you'll never realize we've come and gone."

Morley Enoch added with a giggle. "Oh, yes. We'll be gone in a flash!" While they both proceeded to the basement, Sam, Mary and Faustus sat at a table to discuss the grand reopening.

Downstairs? Our two forces of mayhem went to work, studying things.

Let's see....Morley? If we place several pounds of C4 here....under the main beams....cover it with some of that left over brick....should be fine."

"Mendicant? how about more over here? Behind the heating and cooling? No one will look there."

"Excellent choice, Mr. Flinch, outstanding! Of course, we're just mapping this out for later tonight when we can get back to finish. Keep a running tally of everything on the computer plan we mapped out."

"I've found a perfect spot for the stack of overfilled propane tanks!" Mendicant chuckled. "Right next to the normal ones. Perfect!"

Enoch warned Flinch. "Under the circumstances, we can't rightly use accelerants; too messy and the smell would attract undue attention."

"Right you are, Mr. Enoch! Right you are. We must be *very* careful to do things properly."

"Oh, so true, Mr. Flinch. We *are*, after all, *professionals.* Make a note of everything!"

"Yes, Mr. Enoch. I think we're done down here, for the time being, but if you think of anything else to improve on the results, write it down for later. Let's move upstairs to the kitchen, shall we?"

"Yes, we shall."

On the way, they passed by the trio talking over cups of coffee. Mr. Diabello broke off the convewrsation for a second.

"Mr. Enoch? Mr. Flinch? How go the ....inspections?"

"Oh, absolutely *wonderful*, Mr. D. There will be no issues with *this* basement. Now, you folks just sit and chat. We're off to the kitchen and then upstairs to the rooms. Got to be thorough! Done shortly."

In the kitchen, Mr. Enoch started a pleasant conversation.

"You realize, Mr. Flinch? People think most accidents happen in the bathroom but, in reality, it's the kitchen where things can go horribly wrong."

" So right, Mr. Enoch! Fires? The stove? Explosions? Sharp objects, such as knives? My favorite? Electricity! So many nasty things. And if they accidently get mixed? Disaster! Lovely!"

"Now, now, Mr. Flinch.Do not let your exuberence carry you away. This is a *job*, not a *hobby*!"

"But surely, Mr. Enoch? An art form! Combine many of ther elements I have mentioned? You get art of the *highest* order. Let me write down what we'll need for tonight."

They quickly moved on to the upstairs and attic spaces.

"So much to do and so little time.....more C4 over there? Next to the main beams? We'll set the timers so that just after the walls blow out, the roof will let go....a second or two after that, the basement vaporizes..... aaaaaand, I think....that should do it."

"If we make our lists and print out the plans? We should get everything accomplished in under an hour. *Plenty* of time!"

Enoch and Flinch went back down to the three, still relaxed in their conversation.

"Gentlemen! How does it look? All in order?"

"Certainly! To everything there is a place and to every place....there *will* be a thing."

Mr. Diabello smiled. "Mmmmmmmmm, Mr. Enoch and Flinch *tend* to get carried away sometimes with the joy they show in their work. I think what they mean to say, is that everything is perfect. *Am I correct, gentlemen*?"

"Oh! Yes. Sorry. Of course. All is in order. I don't see any issues to keep you from having the doors fly off tomorrow night. Your opening should be a blast!"

"Well! In that case, Sam, Mary? I'm sure that what my business partners mean is that your opening will be an incredible success!" Here, now. We've taken up far too much of your time. You have so much to do before tomorrow evening."

As they were leaving, Faustus Diabello turned back at the open door to ask Sam and Mary, "Now, I assume no one will actually be here in the building before, ooooh, say 3 P.M.? I only ask this....in case....something comes up and an inspector or two makes an unscheduled visit. You never know with *that* type."

Mary looked siurprised but quickly answered, looking at Sam. "I....never thought of that, Mr. Diabello. If you ssss s think it would be best, we can finish up most of the details tonight and stay away until after 3 tomorrow."

"Yeah, it'll be tough but we can get it done. As long as it ensures we'll have no more problems."

"Oh, I think I can guarantee that, Sam. Mary? Good day to you both."

The threesome walked off towards the docks while Sam and Mary went back to work. So much to do! They figured the tavern would be in full swing tomorrow night with bar food from the main menu. The restaurant would also begin taking dinner reservations as well as the Inn, itself, for vacationers. It would be busy.

On the way to the docks, Mr. Diabello growled at his companions.

"Are you two *idiots*? I'm convinced you enjoy doing this stuff far, too much. We'll go over things more completely back at the office, but first? And *most* important? The timers must be set to go off at 2 P.M., tomorrow. *Not* before! Not be...fore!To avoid casualties. *Is that clear?*'

Neither of them had been listening, quietly going over their arrangements.

"Oh, yes, Faustus. Civilian casualties. Got it. It'll be at four....no worries. We'll finish setting it up tonight."

"Before. Got it?"

"Yes, Faustus.....by four. Got it. Don't worry about us."

"Yes, gentlemen....before....no later, no earlier. Two."

Later that night.....

"Morley, this is exciting! My kind of work."

"Yes, Mendicant, we get to show off our real talents."

"Get to blow things up....again."

"People, too."

"I was a bit surprised at that, but...if that's what Faustus wishes."

"Now, remember what Faustus said. Set all timers for 4 P.M.....*not* before."

"Of course, Morley. I'm *not* an idiot."

"Again? I was a bit shocked when he said to off the owners, too. *Not* his usual style."

"But? An added bonus for us."

"Well, (sigh), back to work so we cen get out of here. Remember! Set those timers...." *(Yes....idiots....dangerous ones)*

CHAPTER 32

Lowering the BOOM!

It was, as usual, a busy morning at the Worthy home. Both Elizabeth and Lester were hard at work for their art/craft business. Morning people, and all that.

Lester's mind was on his latest creation in progress and not on the grand reopening coming up tonight. Oh, yeah, exciting, for sure, but he and V were in "push button" mode. No way they would mess up tonight's show. They were *too* good at what they did. He did chuckle, though. He knew Viridian all too well. She was probably home, practicing her fingers off. *God forbid*, if she played a wrong note or forgot a song. He did it all the time.

Well, anyway, they *always* forgot something. They would laugh it off, improvise something. By then? The customers were usually *too* far gone in their drinks to notice. He was looking forward to the show. Any show that paid good money *and* on a regular basis? *Their* kind of gig. He did understand V, always trying to be a better player; give a better show, keep *him* in line. That was V, alright and he loved her for it. Maybe.... a little later(as a flicker of doubt fluttered past), he would warm up a bit, as well. Couldn't hurt.

While Elizabeth worked at her bench, she was thinking....about all that had been happening. Lester, acting stranger than usual. Those damned ghosts? Who believed in ghosts? Well, now. *She* didn't have much choice these days, did she? Mariah seemed nice but that Bellamy character gave her the creeps. He was more dangerous than Lester realised. She *felt* it....a deep, dark power there, brooding below the surface. maybe, it was the whole pirate thing. Who knew? As far as *she* was concerned, Sam Bellamy was a threat, not only to Lester, but to her and their future, as well.

Maybe, once Les and V got into a performing routine, (and a good one, at that), things could settle back to normal. She could only hope. They had been through *so* much over recent years. A break in the action would be welcome.

Viridian was doing exactly what Lester had thought; practicing her fingers off. She was determined that WhydahMaker was to be *perfect* tonight.

Lester could be such a dick about that at times. He loved performing but this thing about keeping things....interesting. She shuddered at what *that* could mean, thinking back to WPDQ....the *evil* WhydahMaker. Sure, it was fun....well, *some* of it had been fun, but this? Now, *this* was good....and sane.

Back to practicing. She realized she was so wound up, she wouldn't be able to relax before tonight. Instead of practicing and pacing around the house like a caged animal, it would be better if she got all her stuff together and went out to the Inn early. She could get the sound system up, do some sound checks, get the feel of the stage....and, of course, a bit more practice. She'd surprise Lester by having everything ready to go. Yes! That was what she'd do!

1:30-Lester was doing a lot of "something/nothing". You know, when you're doing a little bit of a lot of things but, actually, accomplishing very little? He was determined not to fall into the trap of practicing like a crazed person until it was time for him to go to the Inn.

Oh, he practiced enough to keep his brain and fingers craving more. Doing what V usually did with her type of practicing, left him without an "edge" come time to perform. He needed that edge.

He checked his watch, laughing to himself, thinking....*1:30....If I know V, she's still working on the music. I'll bet by 2, she'll be deciding to head over to the harbor to get a jump on things.....just like V.*

2:00- Viridian finally had enough of practicing, imagining what Lester was probably thinking, *Yeah, well too bad, Les....someone has to keep on top of details and it isn't you! O.K., time to head to the harbor. Sam and Mary must be already there.* The same as her, they wanted to get a jump on the reopening. She'd surprise them, get the sound system up and checked, get ready for Lester, and yes, get some more practice using the sound system.

Making two trips to her car, the trusty Christine, she

got everything loaded and headed on the short trip to the docks to call for the Inn Ferry, if it wasn't there. yet.

2:30- The C, D, E&F conference room- All in attendance, Ishmael Crouch presiding.

"Gentlemen! All is well. Our financial issues are now under control and we are fully back in business. No more worries!"

He looked over at the wall clock.

"Any time, now, the other major thorn in our sides will have been removed. Hmmmmmm, Mendicant? Morley? I believe we should have heard a rather large *BOOM* just after 2 P.M.. Isn't that right, Faustus?"

Looking over at Morley and Mendicant, Faustus, with a questioning look said, "Yes. That's right, Ishmael. They had *strict* instructions; 2 P.M., or thereabouts. Well, guys?"

Mendicant tried not to look worried.

"W-w-w-ell, yes....of course. Everything under control. M-m-maybe a ...tiny problem with the timers."

"They can be a bit touchy and inaccurate at times." Morley added quickly.

"And that means what, *exactly,* gentlemen? Ishmael responded.

All three answered at the same time.

"No problem."

"Any time....soon."

"Wait and see. No worries."

2:45- Viridian stood at the docks as the ferry pulled in to pick her up. "Hey, Viridian! Gettin' out there a bit early, ani't ya?"

She laughed at the pilot. "Yeah, a bit. You know me by now. Help me load all the stuff. Better early than late. Bet Sam and Mary are already there, too."

The pilot laughed with her. "Gee. Guessed that, did ya? I hear tell they was supposed to stay away until at least 3 but they just couldn't wait. Been out there since noon. Come on, let's get out there. I know you're itchin' to get to work."

He started the engines and they headed out into the narrow harbor to where they could eventually throttle up. Directly ahead of them, in the afternoon haze, stood Great Island. As they grew closer, the new complex of the Old Pirate Inn loomed larger and larger as they approached the new docks.

3:00- Back in the boardroom- Ishmael Crouch: "O.K., *gentlemen*! What's going on, here? The EX-PLO-SION was supposed to happen a half hour ago. See the time? Can you explain what is wrong with all this?"
   "Well, Boss....I'm not quite sure, but...."
   "Hey! These things happen. Has to be a small glitch."
   "Yeah, all this state-of-the-art demolition stuff."
   "There's still time for it to go off."
   "No worries, Boss. It'll happen."

3:30-back at the Worthy home-"Liz? Hey, Liz? I'm all set to head over. Gotta get there and get set up for the opening."
   Liz Worthy came into the room.
   "Sure, Les. I thought you'd be gone by now. You tend to get wirey and edgy long before this."
   "Yeah, well....this time? I left all that for V. I figured to give her a few hours to get it all out of her system and she'd be calmed down by the time I got to the Inn. Gotta be going. I'll call you from the Inn and let you know how it's all going. Should be a tremendous blowout, tonight. Love ya."
   Liz laughed. "Yeah, well, don't get too blown out. Be careful and have a good time."
   She kissed him goodbye and he headed to the car. She watched as he drove away. Shaking her head, she sighed and thought, *musicians....never will figure them out. Viridian is just as bad as he is.*
   She went back down to her studio to work. There was another show coming up. *Come to think of it? Artists are just as bad....only quieter....most times.*

3:30-the Old Pirate Inn-"Viridian, welcome! I see you couldn't stay away, either. I suppose we'll all get in trouble with Diabello and Company. Well, too bad. It's not *his* life's dream, now is it?" Sam hugged V as did Mary.

"Look. Sam and I still have much to do before we open at 5. The stage is yours. The sound system is ready for your gentle touch. Go! Have fun. Knock yourself ou until Les get's here."

3:30-back in the boardroom- A very angry Crouch with three intimidated partners trying to find excuses....

"Gentlemen, where....is....the....*boom*? You said there *might* be a slight delay with the timers....how slight, please?"

When no answer was forthcoming from the two bomb 'experts', Ishmael turned his glare to Faustus Diabello.

"Faustus? I believe I gave you explicit instructions, did I not? 2 P.M. was to be the time of the explosion that ended our problems, *not* create more? Two....P.M..Oh, look! It's *not* 2 P.M.!"

"Ishmael, I made it *very* clear to Morley and Mendicant. *Two P.M.! That* was the time for the bombs to go off som no one would be harmed. The building would be empty."

Morley blurted out, "T*wo?* You told us *four!*"

Mendicant added, equally upset, "You said we could kill people, too!"

Faustus abruptly stood, slammed his fist on the table and roared, "YOU TWO IDIOTS! I *said* to set the timers for *two*, not **before**! *And* I told you to *avoid* injuring any people, *too!*"

Indignant, Mendicant added, "Well! You weren't clear, now were you? Otherwise we wouldn't have gotten it all confused. It will work out in the end, won't it? What's a few more bodies flung around, anyway?"

Crouch was beside himself. "Do you know what will happen if any of those people at the Inn get injured? Killed? Especially, if the victims are named Sam Bell or Mary Hall? *DO YOU?*"

Crouch began to pace the room.

"It may not have dawned on you but those two are near, and *very* dear, to the hearts of Sam Bellamy and Mariah Hallett? Did you also forget that Sam Bellamy is one of our largest clients? And....AND, to make it perfectly clear to you two idiots? *Black* Sam Bellamy is no person....alive, dead....or otherwise....to mess with? Besides *me*, he is one extremely powerful and dangeruos being. *Do-you-begin-to-understand*?"

"Not to worry, boss. There's still time. Anyway? They were all told not to come back to the Inn before four P.M.."

"All will be well."

3:55-at the harbor-Les Worthy was unloading his car. the ferry was in but Les was stuck hauling all the equipment by himself, muttering at his rotten luck. *Damn....How come I always get stuck with the grunt work?*

The ferry pilot saw his look and laughed.

"Well, first of all, you ain't as pretty as Ms. Viridian.....and you're pretty ugly, to boot. So? Suck it up and get a move on. Time's a-wastin' and it's almost 4. Stop your bellyachin'."

4 P.M....the witching hour- Sam and Mary were at tghe main desk answering calls for reservations, which were beginning to pour in.

Viridian was finally satisfied with her playing and the sound system. She walked over to shut it all down until Lester got there.

He was in the process of stepping off the pier and into the ferry, thinking....*damn, heavy crap....got to be an easier....*

Sam was answering the phone, yet again.

"Yes, we do hasve a room available for all of next week. Your name is....?"

Viridian was thinking, *Where is Lester, anyway? He's got to pick today, of all days, to get lazy and....*

Time is such a transitory thing. It seems to drag on forever, going nowhere at the slowest pace. Suddenly?

It goes by in a flash....and you wonder, *what just happened? Where did the time go?* Until much later, when you can't get what happened from your mind....ever, again.

This time? It all went by in an enormous flash! The entire sky lit up, the whole island as well as the town of Wellfleet. In the non-town of Pirate's Cove they felt and saw something entirely different happen; flashes in and out of existance. They knew something terrible had happened.

In that first microsecond, not a single thought or word was finished; not by Viridian, not by Sam nor by Mary. They, as well as everything they had worked for, was gone in a flash.

In the boardroom- Even there, the flash lit up the office. Ishmael stopped in mid-rant and grabbed the table. The three partners fell to the floor with what came a split second later.

At the Worthy home- Elizabeth caught sight of the incredible flash of light through the window, even though it was facing away from the blast. Her first thoughts?

My God! What just happened? What happened to Lester? What did he do this time?

At the harbor- Lester had placed one foot into the ferry when the monsterous flash temporarily blinded him.
In the next second, he, the pilot and ferry were thrown through the air like pieces of scrap paper. As a mushroom cloud of smoke, flames and debris went up over the now obscured Great Island, the tsunami followed the roar of the blast. It traveled across the narrow bay at great speed, building in height as it hit the shallows.

Whatever the shockwave hadn't destroyed, the tidalwave certainly did. Every boat moored in the harbor was shattered and thrown through the air all the way to the far side of the small cliff that protected the homes up there, although not a window survived.

The roar, blast and wave sent debris showering down all over the town of Wellfleet, which also suffered quite a lot of damage. Not much survived the impact.

At the harbor in Pirate's Cove-Sam Bellamy suddenly grabbed his chest and fell into Mariah's arms.

"Sam! What is it, Sam? What ha...." At that moment, the seriousness of what happened even affected this not-quite-real-town, as well. In shock, Mary realized, "Oh, no! Sam! They're both gone! Sam and Mary.....I can feel it! Oh, please....no!"

Also at the harbor-Or harbors....depending....a black cat with an interesting vocabulary, was also taken by the immensity of it all but not physically affected.

"Oh,F***! Meow, S***!"

Back at the Worthy home-Even from such a distance, Elizabeth saw and felt it all. The house shook. Windows cracked. "Oh, no. Lester!" She had enough with the life of her husband to comprehend that *he* had to be involved in *some* way. All she could do was hope and pray.

Back to the boardroom-" YOU INCOMPETENT IDIOTS! You have destroyed us all! How much explosives did you use?"

"Well, you see, Ishmael....you wanted the job done right.....nothing left behind thet they could rebuild?"

"Send Sam Bellamy a strong message?"

"Oh, you *fools*! You have no idea of what Sam Bellamy is capable of!"

Mendicant, in a tiny, quvering voice, added, "Are we....g-g-going....to....die? Again?"

At that, Ishmael turned on Mendicant Flinch, grabbing him by the throat.

"Oh, yesssss, Mendicant. It is *entirely* possible that you....will....die....*again*! And if I don't kill you for all your stupidity, first? Count on Black Sam Bellamy to help you along."

He let Flinch go, who fell back in his seat, choking. Sighing, Crouch motioned for everyone to take their seats, again.

"Look. I don't know how we're going to solve this....*if* we can....I need to think....*we* need time to think."

Morley Enoch tentatively raised his hand. "Maybe.... maybe Sam Bellamy won't know it was us who did it?"

"We can only hope."

The townsfolk of Wellfleet were deeply in shock; the explosion, the shockwave, the tsunami, not to mention all the shrapnel and debris from basically, everything that was on Great Island, raining down on the town.

Those who *could* see the Island as the smoke and dust began to clear saw....nothing. Absolutely nothing remained standing on the Island. Not a wall, not the historical site, not a tree; stripped clean with a mighty crater in the middle....until it eventually would fill with water seeping in from the bay. In the near future, it would be named, Great Island Lake.

For now, however, the only thing on the minds of the people was to help the injured and try to figure out what, in God's name, happened. Was it a terrorist attack? If so, why Great Island? Could it have been a forgotten stockpile of old munitions left there from the days of the old target ship? Was it the Inn? If so, what was in there that set off such a terrible blast? Rumors flew around town. What caused this disaster?

One particular....being.....a small, unseen (by most) black cat, had been, as they say, "all ears" at many a board meeting of C, D, E & F. Oh, Mikey, the cat had a pretty good idea of *what* and *who* were responsible. Now? He had to find Sam Bellamy and break it to him. Oh, he was sure Sam was already suspicious, but *this* cat had a lot to tell him.

What, you ask? Lester Worthy? No, I haven't forgotten about dear Lester who, at present, was half-drowned and buried under pieces of boats, harbor buildings and noxious sludge....but he was alive and not badly injured although, at present, it didn't feel like that to *him*.

He regained consciousness and his hearing after an hour or two and immediately began screaming and beating on anything to make a racket. Luckily, by then, many of the townsfolk had worked their way down to the remains of the harbor, looking for survivors.

Lester was one of the only few who wound up buried under muck and mire. Even better? No one in town had been seriously injured. A few cuts, bruises and ringing ears, but all in all, not bad for the amount of damage everyone could see. Lester was hauled off to the local medical facility to get checked out, cleaned up and patched back together. Elizabeth was alerted and rushed to his side.

"Mrs. Worthy, don't worry. Your husband is more shaken up than anything else. He was extremely lucky. His hearing may take a few days to return to normal, though. Like almost everyone in town, extremely lucky."

"*Most* everyone? There were bad injuries? People died?"

"Look. I can't go over that with you. Families must be notified. I'm sorry. When you see your husband, he may seem a bit distracted; muttering a bit, some nonsense about names I cvan't quite make out, pirates, a ....talking cat? I'm saying, don't be surprised. He's badly shaken up but there's no head trauma. It'll all pass. Be aware. that's all."

"Thank you, Doctor. I want to go to him now."

"Good, Mrs. Worthy. Actually? You can take him home as soon as he's ready. He has amazing luck."

Elizabeth passed a few other townsfolk in the process of getting patched up. She came into Lester's room, shocked to see him lying back in bed, covered in bandages. Not as bad as she feared but there was a vacant look about him.

"Lester? Les? It's me, Liz. How are you feeling? My God! What happened? That explosion was terrible. You were *so* lucky to get out alive."

He turned to his wife but didn't acknowledge her questions and began to mumble softly.

"All my fault. All my fault. Whatever I do, wherever I go. People get hurt. People die. Innocent people. All my fault....all my fault."

At that, he finally recognized his wife and grabbed her arm, suddenly yelling, "Liz! Viridian! She's gone! Dead! So are all those poor people at the Inn! Sam and Mary! The ferry pilot and...God knows who else. All my fault. All my fault. Viridian....dead. All...my....'

"Les", she stopped him. "Viridian...dead? Why is it your fault? *Talk* to me, Lester. Snap out of it!"

"Liz, I should have been there, too. Maybe if I had been? This horror wouldn't have happened. Those poor, poor people. My dear friend, Viridian."

"Lester, honey? The only thing you would have accomplished would have been to get blown up with V. How can that *possibly* be your fault?"

"You don't remember? Back when we taught? All my friends who died? My *friends*. The Beethoven mess? All my fault. My fortmer students who almost were killed? My fault. My buddy, Tadpole? Dead. Dead, dewad, dead. On and on and on and on..."

She couldn't get through to Lester. Growing concerned, she paged the doctor.

"Let's wait a few hours before we release him. I've given him aomething to calm him down. I'll casll you in a few hours. Really, he's fine. He needs to rest and cope with all that's happened. I understand he lost a good friend in the blast. That, alone, will be a heavy burden for him to accept but he *will* be fine. He needs time. As I said, I'll call you as soon as he's calmer."

CHAPTER 33

Living in the Lost and Found

Days after the "event" as it was being called, things were progressing as they usually do in a town such as Wellfleet. The locals were "making do", repairing damage and getting on with their lives. Luckily, in town at least, there were no deaths as there were on Great Island. It was no longer being called a "terrorist attack"; too many unwanted connotations with the idea, Oh, the rumor machine was in full swing, from the benches to the bars and the restaurants. That was normal.

The tourist, however, were another matter, entirely, playing themselves up for what the locals expected.... and *that* wasn't very attractive. Always in the way, taking too many pictures and "selfies", with the Great Island remains in the background. Loud, entitled, pontificating upon their favorite "theory-du-jour". Tourists. Still, considering? It was the normal thing for the summer, "silly season" and normal was good after all that happened.

In the "non-town" of Pirate's Cove, *those* residents went about their business, whatever that might be for the dead and almost-but-not-quite-dead folk. The difference could be felt, though, by those capable of feeling such things. There was a distinct, sombre note to daily...life. People here,(*please*, let's just call them people for now.... far easier), were waiting for something dire to happen.... a shoe to drop....the calm before the storm....you get the idea.

Some of the living, relatives of long dead residents, had been killed in a most violent and unfair manner. Such things were not taken well. There were rules, even among the dead. Even worse? These deaths were related, in part, to one of *the* most powerful, respected and dangerous of Pirate Cove inhabitants; Black Sam Bellamy.

If they had been capable of holding their collective breath, they would have, waiting to see what Sam, and possibly, Mariah. might do in response to ther dastardly deed. The firm of C, D, E & F might be a most powerful, dangerous entity in it's own right but, had anyone *ever* seen the full fury of an enraged Sam Bellamy? No, not ever.

There were rumors and more than a few legends concerning those who had crossed him over the centuries, but never....*never*....did any involve the murder of a living relative. Things could get very interesting.

Around town,(the Cove), people talked softly among themselves. Some we know. Elvis, Napoleon and their small friend, Mikey, sat down by the harbor discussing many, many things and Mikey had a lot to say. They sat, deciding on the best course of action.

Back to the real world. Pretty banged up and a mess, more mentally than physically, Lester moped around the house, taking naps, wandering aimlessly, a total waste of time and space.

Elizaberth found him packing up all his instruments for the umpteenth time.

"Lester? Packing it all, again? Giving up, *again*?"

"Liz, why should I try any more, huh? Every time I thinlk....well, maybe I'll get on with my music....I think of V...and....oh, Hell. I pack it all up, again."

"It wasn't your fault, Lester, it wasn't...."

"Yes, Liz. It was! I'm not sure what I did that caused All this but, ever since I got involved with those lunatics a WPDQ, and Sam Bellamy....and thinking....we could *be* something? Yeah, I see it as my fault V is dead. I can't get over it and don't think I ever will."

He finished packing the last of the many instruments. Turning to Elizabeth, "Look. It's on *me* and I can't get away from that. There's no more room for the music while I carry this burden. I'm going for a walk."

Liz couldn't think of anything to console her husband. She saw him slipping away from her and the world, ingeneral. What could she do to snap him out of it? Right now? She didn't have a clue and let him head out the door. As always, he was going to wander around the town for a bit before coming home. Maybe it was doing some good. *She* wasn't, *that's* for sure! All these years. They had gone through *so* much. The good, the bad, the tragedies and, yes, even the deaths, (and a murder or two....or three), but this? This....she shook back some tears and gently closed the door as Lester wandered off.

Whatever happened, she'd find a way to snap him out of it. Even if it took years, yes, she would. Lester was a lot of things, good, bad, obnoxious, at times unbearable, even stupid...but he was *hers*! Damn it! She wanted him back.

Lester wandered through the town, not taking notice to anything, fading in and out between Wellfleet and the Cove. One after another, superimposed, at the same time, back and forth. All part of that "sensitivity" to the "other" existance Penelope Painestaker told him about. *Curse her! Another person dead because of him.*

Wandering about, his thoughts kept returning to Elizabeth and all the harm he was doing to her. He understood but couldn't control all that was spinning around in his brain. Elizabeth, Viridian, Penelope, all the folk at WPDQ, that damned, old Nazi bitch, his old buddy.... even that insane Beetroot. (See book two, Opus 133). All his doing.

Lester passed the Wellfleet Market, (which suddenly faded to be the Cove Mercantile and back again). He passed a gallery with an obnoxious owner, (which turned into a general store with another, even more obnoxious entity running it).

The Lighthouse Restaurant became the Old Pirate Bar and Grill. Back and forth, back and forth. The living. The dead. The living. The almost-but-not-quite-dead. He finally found himself down by the harbor. Which one? He didn't give a damn. He noticed one of them was under repairs.

Looking down the walkway, he saw three "almosts" he knew quite well by now. as a matter of fact, still deeply in conversation; one overweight Elvis, the diminutive Napoleon and a small, black, furball.

"Hi, guys....you, too, Mikey."

At first, they didn't seem to recognize he was there and talking to *them*, but then again, that was the whole, "guess what world I'm presently in", thing.

They paused their debate. Being as polite, and respectful as they could be,(difficult for Mikey), they all greeted Lester.

"Hey, Lester. How are you doing after....O.K.,how are youi doing? We know it's been hard on you."

Mikey chimed in, "******! For all of us. Trouble's brewing, (meow), and you're gonna ****ing see it first paw when it comes. I'm here to tell you!"

"Look, guys, I don't know what you're going on about and, really? I don't particularly care. All I want to do is forget....*everything*."

Elvis chuckled, "Well, Bubba? Ah tell ya? You in th' raht place tuh ferget stuff. Thas fuh sure."

Mikey hopped onto Lester's lap.

"Look, Lester, don't listen to that *meow* idiot! We're all beeh here a *long* time. You get over stuff. Time....that's the thing....time."

"He's right, mon ami," Napoleon added. "Time....and it's all.....pfft...gone."

"Wow, guys, philosophy lesson; not needed. Didn't come here to get one." He got up to leave. "See you guys later. Garfield? Later little dude."

"****you, Worthy and the mouse you rode the ****in on. Later."

Lester decided it was time to wend his way back home. His head spinning from too much deep thinking and the kalaidescope of shifting landscape. Wellfleet....Pirate's Cove.... Wellfleet. His head spinning even mpre, he sat down on a bench outside the Wellfleet Liquor Store until, he hoped, his troubled mind would calm down.

It was getting quieter, but then, he realized things got *really* quiet, far *too* quiet. That's when he noticed Sam Bellamy sitting next to him.

"Lester, we have to talk."
Some time earlier, Sam and Mariah were at the harbor in a heated argument.

"Look, Sam, I know you're intent upon revenge", as she held his hands tightly and stared into his stony face.

"You know these...these...people who did this. Even *you* can't match their power. They are oh, so old, Sam and so dangerous. Please! Reconsider. We still have each other and I don't want to lose you."

"Mariah, I've tried. I'm not going to let this go. Aye, we have each other. Forever and always....but....we would have watched our *living* family grow as we continued to help them be successful. That was taken away from Mary and Sam. *They* were taken away from *us*. This? I can't forgive."

"And Sam? What about the others? What of Viridian? And Lester? What of his wife Elizabeth? The way Lester is acting, she may be on the way to losing her husband. Will revenge help all of them, too?"

Sam gave her a cold, twisted smile before replying.

"Mariah, I *will* have my revenge. Nothing you, or anyone else says, will change my mind. Aye. I know how old and powerful those four are. I have a plan to make me their equal or even stronger."

Really smiling now, he continued while they held hands.

"Dinna worry, my Lass. All will be well. For me, for us and for the Worthy's as well. Wait and see. When we be done, many, many things will change *and* for the better."

"We? Not you and me. I'll ha' nothing ta do wi' your revenge, Samuel Bellamy."

She paused for a second, reality dawning on her.

"Ye don't mean me, do ya. You be talkin' bout someone else." Her eyes widened. "No! You mean to involve poor Lester Worthy in this plan of yourn. Am I right?"

"Yes, ye be correct. When I talk to Mr. Worthy and get him onboard, nothing will stop us."

"Oh, Sam. This is so wrong, whatever ye be planning, it's just terrible. I'm sure."

"Lass, as I've promised. I will have *our* revenge and all *will* be well. Remember? Ye fell in love with a pirate; one of the best. *Black* Sam Bellamy....and I intend ta live up to it."

Back at the Worthy's, Elizabeth heard the door close.

"Les? Is that you? How was your morning?"

She already had a good idea but felt she had to ask.

"Oh, just another walk through the towns....town, trying to clear my head. Didn't do much good."

As it had been since the explosion, Lester sounded totally downcast. Showing little emotion in his voice,

"Another day, another walk. Nothing new." A sigh and he went to kiss his wife.

"Some day, it will be different...better. You'll see." She hugged her husband. "It always gets better with time. Why don't you go upstairs, unpack some instruments and work on some music? How about doing some work for the business?"

"*Music*? Nah, why bother? I'll go down and get some work done in a bit. Now? I'm tired. Gonna sit down and see if anything is on the TV,"

So ended another day at the Worthy household.

The next morning, much the same as all the ones before, Lester could be found wandering through whichever town his tortured mind led him. He came out of his funk and found himself back at the liquor store bench. At that time in the morning, none of the locals were around to talk to. *Good!* He thought. *Why bother?* Better to be alone with his thoughts.

Lester stared at the sparse, early morning traffic. Once again, he found a smiling Sam Bellamy sitting next to him, all in his pirate finery.

"Mr. Worthy. Morning to ye."

"Well! Aren't we all dolled up for Halloween. A bit early, isn't it? *So*, it's *Mr.*Worthy today, is it?"

Yes, Mr. Worthy. It be that....and *I* be *Captain* Black Sam Bellamy....at yer service. We have things to discuss; important things and I *think* you will wish to hear them."

"Well! Captain, is it? Go right ahead. It's your dime. From past experience, I know there's no way to shut you up when your mind's set."

"My dime,is it? Quaint jargon. I never thought in dimes. Fine, boyo. Here goes. I know how badly you're hurting. You lost dear Viridian and all those poor innocent, unnecessary deaths. *Me*? The loss of my Sam and Mary will pain me for centuries. The tavern and all my well laid plans for those two....all blown ta Hell. Now, *Mr.* Worthy. I knows who be responsible for this tragedy and I be pretty sure ye have a good idea as well.

"I know enough to mention the names, Diabello, Enoch and Flinch. Are there more?"

"One more, the leader, the most powerful and dangerous member of the firm; Ishmael Crouch. All four of them. What ye don't ken is that this gang of murderous thieves be nearly immortal and damned hard to kill."

"Big surprise. *Nearly* immortal? Hmmmm. Close enough, I assume where you or I can't make much of a difference."

Sam smiled a knowing smile.

"Aye, that be mostly true, but there be a way to give us an edge on 'em, nearly immortal or not."

Sam inched closer, lowering his voice to speak confidentially.

"I am suggesting we join forces."

"And *what* the Hell good will that do? What difference will working together do?"

"Dinna jump to conclusions, damn it. Of course, just working together won't make a damned bit of difference."

Sam clamped his hand down on Lester's shoulder.

"When I says working together, I really mean.....*working together*....as one."

Lester was startled,

"Wait a minute....as one? You mean....*literally*...as one? One *being*? Wasn't it you who told me the "not-quite-dead" couldn't influence the living; make us do whatever you wanted?"

Sam smiled. "Technically, correct....but there *are* extenuating circumstances when some things are....possible."

"O.K., Sam Bellamy. I'm curious....horrified, but curious. I'll bite. Please explain."

"Lester Worthy, first of all, we are of a like mind. WE have both lost people dear to us."

"Correct, as far as it goes."

"Second, even if ye don't wish to admit it, ye want revenge as much as I and *that* is an important detail."

"Yes, sadly, I guess you're right. Revenge? Oh, I'd consider it. It won't bring V or anyone else back but I *would* get *some* satisfaction in revenge."

"Third...and most important. Ye can see me, talk to me, Mariah and others, and ye can see Pirate's Cove. You have a power not many of the living can claim to use. You don't understand it and I guess you don't want to, but you *have* it. A good deal of it, too. Working together would give us an edge, as you would say.

Fourth? You, Lester Worthy, are *not* a vengeful or bloodthirsty human. *I,* however, am a pirate of much repute. Black Sam Bellamy has no such problem with murder or revenge."

"Sounds scary."

"Not at all. Trust me. Finally, while I can't force you to do anything against your will, with enough common interest between us? In one body, together? Oh, we can accomplish what is important."

"And that is?"

"Revenge. Pure and sweet. Cold and bloody. Cold.... satisfying revenge against those who have done us evious wrong.. Be ye interested*, Mr*. Worthy?"

Hesitantly, Lester nodded yes.

"There are some, not so minor details, as well. Not being of your world any more, I cannot influence the living *in* this world....and before you annoyingly ask it, I *can,* as you know, drive you crazy until you *do* my bidding. That is not my intent. These four entities we're going after? They are very, *very* different being in both worlds at once. They can affect both the living *and* the dead. *Very* dangerous. A good thing, though, Mr. Worthy? They claim to be immortal, and in some ways, they are *but*.... they can be killed and quite painfully. The bad news? Eventually, they will come back. The best news? Never in the same place or time, good for us as their kind tend to hold grudges. Our job will be to make their deaths *so* painful and memorable, they won't be back for a long, long time."

The more Lester heard, the more upset he got. This idea of revenge was getting worse and worse. What was he getting into?

"Mr. Worthy! Lester. I can see you are upset with all I'm telling you.

"Be at ease because there there is something else of vital importance concerning Crouch, Diaberllo, Enoch and Flinch. They have tended to be highly successful over the great span of time but....and *this*, my friend, is something they have always tried to hide over the millenia. In spite of all they have accomplished? These four are *raving idiots*! Sooner or later? They mess up....and I mean fatally. *This* could be there time, again. We can be the ones to make them pay. We *will* make them pay for all their crimes against us and ours."

Lester sat looking down at the pavement.

"Look, Sam? I need a little time. This? A lot to take in. I need until tomorrow to think it through. The whole "ghost thing"body takeover"....reminds me of a movie."

"Ye damned fool! It be nothing like a damned movie! Get it out o' yer head. Just trust me!"

"Fine. I'll be back here in the morning with my answer."

At that, Sam faded. Lester sat there alone for a few minutes, watching the few tourists walk on by. Finally, he got up, stretched as if he had the weight of the world on his shoulders, and headed back home.

CHAPTER 34

Final Plans and Deliverance Can Suck, Mr. Flinch!

Elizabeth heard the door quietly close.

"Lester, I'm assuming you're home." In other times, it was obvious when her husband entered the house. He was like a tornado, slamming through the door, yelling about something or other and generally wrecking havoc. These days? Much different.

"Yeah, Liz. It's me. I'm going up to read for a bit. Don't worry, I'm fine...really. Got a lot to think through. Be down in a while."

Liz Worthy stood chewing her lip. This was *not* her husband; the eternally boyish, boisterous, happy, angry piece of work she knew for all these years. The series of diasaters ending with the horrible explosion and loss of his friend and partner, Viridian. It all pushed him into a dark place. She was deeply concerned. Well, she could do nothing until Lester was ready to face it and talk about it. Knowing him, it was all she could do and wait for him to make the first move. Wait and see. Wait...and see.

After all they'd been through, working together forever, through the improbable to the impossible, she knew her husband. He'll' find his way....find his way back to her. She sighed, thinking, *just another day living with Lester Worthy, damn it!*

The next morning found Lester sitting on the same bench outside the Wellfleet Liquor Store, gathering place for the local, wanna-be politicians, world-problem-solvers and nay-sayers. Not this morning. Lester sat alone, waiting.

"I knew you would return, Mr. Worthy", said Sam bellamy, appearing next to him. Lester didn't acknowledge his presence but spoke.

"Look, Sam, If we're doing this....thing, whatever it is, shouldn't we be back on a first name basis?"

"Right, ye be....Lester....Les."

"O.K., how does this work? Wave your hands over me? Sing Kumbayah? Fairy dust?"

"Les, it be real simple. Watch and learn."

At that, Sam faded from being next to him to melding with Lester.

"See? That simple."

"Wow! *That* felt so strange. Hey! I can tell what you're thinking....your past....Oh, crap! You really *are* a blood-thirsty pirate!"

Bellamy sighed. "At your service. Was....Lester...*was* a pirate. Guess you can say I retired as few centuries ago. By the way? You don't have to speak out loud to me. We're of the same mind, so to speak. Ye don't want folk to stop an' stare at the weird guy, do ya?"

"Well, it *is* Wellfleet. Kinda normal for here."

"Try....anyway? It's embarrassing, otherwise."

O.K.....Sam, I'll give it a try....wow! Cool. It works.

See, Les? Cool, it is. Now? We have many things to plan. My suggestion? We take the partners out, one at a time. Give the others time to sweat and worry about what happened. Not knowing and fear are great weapons.

Sam stopped for a minute, listeneing to Lester's thoughts.

Damn! Lester Worthy! An' ye call me a bloodthirsty pirate? Ye have some pretty interesting ideas for revenge I would never ha' thought of.

Lester gave a twisted smile. Passersby had no idea what nastiness was being plotted, just a local staring scornfully at the tourists.

Ohhhh, Sam. I've had plenty of time to stew over what I would do if given half a chance. I never realized how much power you, yourself had. You're no slouch, either. We can do some vicious things together.

Lester, remember. I can't use this power you mention, on the living, not in the usual way. That's where you come in. With your abilities and anger? Oh, we're going to have a time, we will.

Mentally, at least, Lester turned to talk to Sam.

I have some satisfying thoughts on what do do and who to start with. Let's start backwards from the bottom of the food chain to the top, beginning with a certain.... Mendicant Flinch. Here's my idea.

Lester went over his plan for the fourth member of the Firm. Sam smiled and laughed.

Oh, yes! Lester Worthy? I am relieved I wasn't your enemy in real life. You, sir, have an evil and nasty mind!

A little later, Lester/Sam walked on back home. He opened the door but, this time, Elizabeth heard the door slam.

"Lester? That you, Dear? What happened? Something wrong? Doesn't sound like your usual arrival home.

"ARRRRR, honey. My mistake. Didn't know my own strength, arrrr."

"Arrrr, Lester? Why, in God's name are you talking like that?"

"Ummm, sorry, Liz. I was thinking about going to the Whydah Museum and was reading some pirate stuff, you know?. As in: Arrrrr, aye, matey! Ye be walkin' the plank....stuff like that. Sorry. Got caught up in the moment." (He heard Sam groan and make a nasty comment).

Liz met him in the hall, looking deeply into his eyes.

"I don't know. The way you've been acting since the explosion? This isn't like you....almost....like you're someone else."

"Someone *else*? Don't be daft, woman!" He caught himself and laughed. "Hey, I was having a bit of fun with you, Liz. remember? *Fun*? Been so long, hasn't it?"

"Well, maybe....but *woman*? Better watch it, Lester?"

"I'm O.K., really, Elizabeth. I finally got my (our) head (s) together and I'm beginning to work my way back (*after I kill off a few miserable bastards who deserve killing.*)

The rest of the day went by more normally than it had for weeks but there were times that Elizabeth Worthy felt she was dealing with two totally different people. She shook it off as another, normal day living with Lester Worthy. Normal being a word that rarely came up on a regular basis.

The next several days was a bit of a rollercoaster ride with the "new" Lester, until one morning, Lester announced, "Liz, I've got to go out for a few hours. I've (*we've*) got things to attend to (*murder*). I (*we*) should be back in the afternoon. Plan for dinner at our usual time. Hey! Instead? Let's go out to dinner. Maybe celebrate.... oh, I don't know....me returning to normal...

(*after we ruin Flinch's day....for good*)."

"Wow! That *is* a surprise. Les? I'll be looking forward to it." She kissed him. "Love you."

"Love you, too. Be back in a bit. Got places to go (*stalk*), things to do (*kill*)."

He walked out the door, not slamming it this time....talking to his "other" self.....*here's what we're gonna do....first....*

Back at the boardroom

Ishmael Crouch was presiding over the first major meeting since the ...."incident".

"Gentlemen! Please sit down. It is my distinct honor to report to you that, as of today, C,D,E&F is once again completely fluid and funded."

There were cheers and applause around the table, as well as sighs of relief. Crouch continued.

"Yes, *I told* you the funds would get here eventually. They took a little longer than expected, but they *are* here. And the whole Bellamy fiasco has been dealt with. No more major drain on our funds and balance sheets."

Mendicant Flinch raised his voice.

"Speaking of Sam Bellamy, aren't you afraid he'll come after us? What if he finds out what we did?"

"Not a problem, Mendicant. Rest easy. Sam Bellamy knows *nothing* about what really happened. Even if he did? Well, don't you think he would have acted by now? Since all is quiet, I don't think we have fear of reprisals by Mr. Bellamy."

At that, secretary Marie Antoinette, knocked and entered the room.

"I am sorry, sirs, but I received a call from one of our confidential informants...one of the living. The local police have received some new information about the Painestaker murder. I am informed they will be heading to the Painestaker home sometime tomorrow checking on newly discovered evidence."

Ishmael stood. "Thank you, Marie. Gentlemen, I have no idea what they could have found. Mr. Enoch? Mr. Flinch? You *did* take care of everything, I presume?"

Both shook their heads in fervent agreement.

"Well, then, Mr. Flinch? I'm sure you won't mind going back to the Painestaker home later tonight and make certain, hmmm?"

Mr. Flinch wasn't happy about that. He, and the deep, dark night, didn't see eye to eye, especially when alone.

"Yes, sir. I'll do it around midnight. Have no fear. There is nothing they can find."

"All right, then. gentlemen? I call this meeting adjourned. Good day to you all."

Close to midnight, on a lightless road, coming up to the darkened outlines of the old Painestaker residence, Flinch wasn't happy. After all this time, police barrier tape still wrapped the place. It was a bad night to be out with rising rain and wind. Mendicant huddled down against the weather, thinking, *Crap! What am I doung here? Why can't Crouch do his own dirty work? Crap, crap, crap! And he knows I hate the dark. Well, let me get this over with and checked out so I can get home.*

At that, he noticed some of those police tapes were torn, flapping in the wind.

Damned kids....got no respect for the dead, these days... He thought that while chuckling to himself over the little, private joke, remembering back to what he had done to the Painestaker woman.

Suddenly, he stopped in his tracks. First, a single light came on in one of the front windows. Following that, he heard something..., *What the..? No! Couldn't be.*

Yes, it could. The sound of a banjo picking out....dah, dah, dah, dum, dum, dum, dum, dum dah...Yup. The opening of that damned, Deliverence song. Flinch always hated that damned song, even more, the banjo.

He sneaked up to the door and silently opened it a crack. There was just enough light to see a single chair in a pool of light, empty, except for a portable sound system playing that awful tune.

O.K., someone's playing games, here, he thought. Stepping boldly into the room, he called out, "Funny! Real funny! I almost laughed."

"Whoever you are? Get the hell out of here before I call the cops....or worse!"

From nowhere, the heavy end of a banjo came swinging around the door, connecting directly with Flinch's head.

"Crack! Twangy, twang!", went the banjo. "Thud!" Went the banjo strinking Flinch. "Blonk!" Went Flinch as he hit the floor.

"Yesssssss! A homerun! Yaaaaaaay, for the home team!"

It took some time for Mendicant Flinch to come to his senses, wishing he didn't. He found himself bound and tied to the chair and that damned music was still playing in the background. The pain in his head, combined with the sound of that damned song made him groan.

Peering up, he saw....wait a minute....he *knew* this guy holding the banjo.

"You! It's Worthy, right? Lester Worthy? Wh...why are you doing this? I've done nothing to you."

Lester stood there holding the banjo, hovering menacingly over Flinch.

"Really? You've done....*nothing* ....to me?" He walked around in front of Flinch and bent down to look him in the face, laughing at a private joke.

"Are you so sure of that, Mr. Flinch? What about the former owner of this house, Persiphone Painestaker? Remember her? Yes, I thought you might."

Mendicant Flinch focused on what Lester was saying.

"Wait a minute. I don't know anyone by the name of.... what did you say?"

"Painestaker", he hissed. "Oh, I think you should try harder. Do you need your memory jogged some more?"

At that, Lester stopped playing the banjo and, once again, held it like a bloody bat.

"Uhhh, *no*. No! Please! O.K..I remember the woman.... lousy banjo player....busybody psychic. Yeah, I remember now."

"Maybe you also remember that you and your buddy.... was it Morley Enoch? Came to have several chats with Ms. Painestaker? The last one being an extremely final conversation."

"Ohhh, I don't know....just like *this* one?"

At that, Lester began to swing the banjo at Flinch's head, stopping short, as Flinch began to moan.

"No, please! Don't. Yes, I remember now. We were following orders. *Please*, don't kill me!" He begged, pitifully.

Lester lowered the banjo, looking sympathetically down at Mendicant Flinch.

"Mr. Flinch, you may not realize this but I, personally, have more than enough reason to see you harmed in the *most* permanent of ways....but I am a kind and peaceful person who woul*d never* harm someone, even as disgusting as you or your friends."

At that, Flinch began to look hopeful. Lester gently patted his cheek, almost tenderly. Horrified, Flinch looked up at Lester as his face took on a drastic change. No longer was Mendicant looking into the eyes of Lester Worthy, but the fiery, angry eyes of Black Sam Bellamy.

"Arrrrr! But I, Mr. Flinch? I have more than enough reason to see ye harm! D' ye forget San Bell and Mary Hall so soon, damn ye? An' all th' other mischief you an' yours ha' done to the likes o' me an' mine? Look into the eyes of your Reaper, Mendicant Flinch. Ye have one....last.....look....an' th' last damned thing ye will see? Black Sam Bellamy!"

At that, Sam/Lester took a mighty swing at the head of Mendicant Flinch, ending his present life with a sickening crunch.

Lester/Sam stood over the body. As Sam dropped the broken, bloody banjo, he said, "May ye rot in Hell, Mendicant Flinch....'though I know it will na' be permanent. I'll be damned certain ye will na' forget,*ever*!"

At that, Lester was given full control back to his body. Horrified and sickened at what he had done, he ran for the door. Outside, in the raging and wind, he stood there retching and gagging against the side of the house. Sam spoke in his mind.

"Now, ye be a part o' this. Now? It begins."

As they left the Painestaker home, Sam continually whispered to Lester, calming him, making him feel more like himself and more like this was all a very bad dream.

"Alright now, Lester, as we be done for the moment, we can go our separate ways."

Lester, stood mournfully, the rain falling on his upturned face and body.

"Ahhhh, Mr. Worthy. I knows what be botherin' ye. It was me doin' the killin' not yerself."

Lester turned, saying aloud to the rain and wind, "Yes, but I was the one doing the actual killing, no matter what you say."

"Well, boyo, tha' be true. But ye couldn't ha' done what I wanted if somewhere deep down, ye really wanted ta do it."

"Sam, that's what worries me the most....that deep down, I am capable of such a thing."

"*It was revenge, true and sweet. Ye canna' fash yerself. These....beings? They ain't like you....or even me. They are gettin' wha' they deserve. Maybe? They be learnin' a lesson to take to the next life, somewhere down in time. Now? Head back home and by the time you get there, all will begin to feel normal again. I promise. Come morning, we'll talk about the next project, and really? You had a brilliant idea for the likes of Morley Enoch. Ye be an amazing human, Mr. Worthy. Such an untapped talent for evil and violence. My! How I wish I had met ye back in the day. We'll talk in th' morning. Now go home to yer pretty wife and get some rest. We ha' work to do!*"

In a daze, Lester made his way back home. It was early morning and not wanting to scare Elizabeth, he quietly knocked at the door. It took several times before he heard her at the other side of the door.

"Lester? Is that you? It better be you!"

"Yes, Liz. It's me. Please, let me in. I'm cold, wet and so tired."

She opened the door to her bedraggled and soaked husband, standing there so pitiful in the rain and wind.

MY God! Where have you *been*? I've been worried sick It's the middle of the night."

"You said a few hours. It's been the whole day and half the night. What have you been doing all this time? Get in here!"

Lester placed his soggy hand on her shoulder.

"Liz, I'd kiss you but I'm a mess. I was trying to work things out when I ran into that damned Bellamy. We had a long, *long* talk. Hours went by and before I knew it? It was night and I was sitting in the middle of this storm. Look. I'm exhausted. Can't we talk about this in the morning? I need sleep. I promise, Sam helped me work things out....a bit, at least. He wants to talk some more tomorrow. Really! It's a good thing. he's helping me come to terms with....things. In the morning, really. We'll talk."

As the books states, it was a dark and stormy night; in the air and in his soul.

CHAPTER 35

Morley Enoch:

Time Trials or Beat the Clock

It was a bad night for Lester Worthy. All that Sam Bellamy had said was true. Revenge, pure and true. Anyway? These creatures weren't human; even close to being human. God only knew *what* they were. And they'd be back again, sometime hopefully, in the far future. Maybe? They learned a painfully important lesson this time. Maybe not. Who knew?

What Lester *did* know was that *he* did have that kind of violence in him. It didn't matter that Bellamy told him it wasn't his fault. As far as he was concerned, he felt damned; damaged and permanently scarred.

As the sun came up, he was still laying there, wide awake and tired as Hell. Sighing, he thought, *I might as well get moving and face the day....face Elizabeth, too.* Another sigh and he dragged himself from bed. Elizabeth, must have been up already, probably making breakfast for them both.

Elizabeth was heading for the table whewn Lester dragged in.

"My God, Lester! You look terrible. I know you didn't sleep much but somewhere around four, you dozed off. You muttered a lot. Incredibly bizarre stuff, too. What *did* happen last night?"

"Liz, I made a deal with Captain Bellamy to help get retribution on the ones who did this to Viridian and so many others. It was a deal with the devil, I'm sure, but I'm involved now. One down and three to go."

"*Captain* Bellamy now, is it? One down? Three to go? Lester, you're scaring me. What *have* you done?"

"Look, Liz, not me, as much as what Bellamy has done....*is* doing. All I'll say is these four...individuals are nothing like you or me or even Sam Bellamy, for that matter. They are old, strong, evil and much more terrible and damned near immortal. With *my* help? Bellamy is making them pay and pay dearly. All you need to know....all you *want* to know."

"Les, I don't like the sound of this. You have to stop."

"Can't stop, Liz. Too late for that. Not until all of them pay for what they did. The die is cast. Signed and sealed. Until it's done with.

"Don't worry. All will work out in the end. You have to trust me."

"Trust you? I don't trust *him*."

They sat down to eat and nothing more was discussed. They ate in an uneasy silence.

In the Boardroom

"Why haven't we heard anything back from Flinch, gentlemen? Faustus? Morley? It was such a simple task, even for Mendicant. Go and check out the Painestaker place. Make sure nothing had been left behind that could lead back to us. Come home. Simple. Well?"

Morley sniggered, "Well, boss? It *is* Mendicant Flinch we're talking about. He can blow stuff up better than anyone but he's afraid of the dark."

"He hates rain". Faustus added.

"Put them both together? Who knows *where* he is. I'll bet he's holed up somewhere dry, waiting for daylight. I agree with Faustus. It's Mendicant we're talking about."

Faustus laughed. "Ooooooooo, I hope we're not going to die.....again. You know how infuriating he is."

"I agree with Faustus. I'm amazed how far he's gotten in the Firm. What a wuss."

Crouch wasn't placated at all.. "You *will* keep me informed. We must know what happened to him. The moment he contacts either of you, let me know. I *must* know!"

The day passed slowly for all concerned, except for Mendicant Flinch, of course. Late in the afternoon, Lester prepared to meet Bellamy, this time down at the harbor.

"Liz, I'm heading out. Don't save dinner for me. I'll be late."

Elizabeth took his hand and held on tight. "It's Bellamy, again, isn't it? Don't go. I see what this is doing to you."

"Liz, I must. I must help Bellamy finish this. If I don't? Who knows what could happen? They could even come after *you* and I won't have that. No way. I have to do this; finish it. Once and for all."

"Be safe, Les. For me. I'll wait up whenever you come in. be careful."

At that, Lester kissed his wife goodbye, turned and walked out the door into the late afternoon. Over at the harbor, Lester sat on one of the many benches overlooking the bay and out towards the remains of Great Island.

Next to him, he heard, "Yes, don't forget what they've done, Mr. Worthy. Steel yourself."

"Hello, Sam. I've done a lot of thinking since yesterday and I have some ideas for Mr. Morley Enoch. I *think* you'll approve. Care to join me?"

At that, the ghost of Sam Bellamy, once again melded with the body of Lester Worthy.

"Oh, Lester! I had forgotten how it feels to be more in the real world."

"Well, don't get too comfy, Captain. We've work to do. After that? Buh bye Bellamy."

Sam/Lester sat staring out over the bay as they quietly went over Lester's ideas.

"Damn, boyo! I was right! Ye would ha' been one dangerous pirate back in *my* day. Ye do have a creative and diabolical mind, Lester Worthy. A plan fitting for the likes of Mr. Morley Enoch. I *am* impressed. It will be dark soon. Let's get to work. This will be fun!"

Night had fallen and Crouch, Diabello and Enoch were still in the boardroom, waiting....waiting....waiting.... anything that would put them at ease concerning Mendicant Flinch.

Crouch's secretary, Marie, knocked and entered.

"Mr. Crouch? There's a call waiting for you on line one."

"Thank you, Marie. *Now*, gentlemen, that has to be Flinch. I can't wait to hear his excuses." He picked up the phone.

"Mendicant, is that you?" The voice at the other end wasn't that of Flinch, though it was as hesitant as Flinch could be.

"Sir? No. Mt name is....Scruggs, sir. I *am* calling for Mendicant Flinch, though."

"What are you talking about, Scruggs? Where is Flinch? Put him on immediately."

"Is this Mr. Crouch? He told me to call you, sir. I am sorry. Mr. Flinch is here, sir, true....but he's asleep; been that way most of the day, sir, sleeping like the dead. I decided it was better to let him rest until I could get in touch with you."

"Scruggs? What is all this? What's wrong with Flinch? I demand to know. Put him on!"

"Sir....I *told* you....he's resting.....for now. Here's what happened. Last night? I was heading down Painestaker Road....so dark, the rain and all. I almost didn't see the man Flinch until I almost ran into him. Soaked to the bone he was...and raving so...a total madman, he was. Raving over and over....*I can't get that banjo out of my head!!!!!*Over and over. Such a state he was in, sir. I got him into my car and brought him home with me. He did manage to tell me where he left his car....not too far away, either. I got him quieted down, gave him a few drinks to help and he muttered off to sleep. Not before saying over and over, *call Crouch. Get Enoch to come pick me up.* He gave me your number. I waited until he calmed down, got dry and warm. Then he fell into a deep sleep....sleeping like the dead he is, sir."

"This is unbelievable, Scruggs! I can't thank you enough for helping our partner."

"Sir? It was the *christian* thing to do. Mr. Flinch is still out, so why don't you let me come in his car to pick up Mr. Enoch, as he begged me. By the time we're back here, he'll be ready to join you. Please, sir? Give me your address and I'll be out front waiting for Mr. Enoch. I'll honk twice so you'll know it's me."

"Thank you, Mr. Scruggs."

"Just Scruggs, sir. The address, please?"

"Certainly, Scruggs....and thank you, again, on behalf of Mr. Flinch and the rest of us at the Firm."

Morley Enoch stood outside the offices of the firm, growing impatient until an Uber vehicle pulled up and honked twice. As Morley opened the door, he recognized the driver.

"Hey! Aren't you Lester Worthy? Driving for Uber, now?"

"Yeah, funny world, isn't it? There's not much to keep me busy these days, so this gives me a chance to get out and make a few bucks. You look familiar, as well. Mr. Enoch, isn't it? You did work to....*for* those poor people who died in that terrible explosion. Just terrible. Small world, huh? Me being your driver, and all? Where to, Mr. Enoch?"

Morley settled into the back seat, grumbling at the inconvenience of being recognized by an old fool like Worthy.

"You know where Painestaker Road is? Good! Take me to this address. I'm meeting someone there."

"Oh, you mean Scruggs. Yeah. He called me and gave me the job. I'll have you at your destination.... before you know it."

Lester/Sam gave a small, twisted smile to the rear-view mirror and drove away. At the next stop light, when he saw no one around, he turned to Morley Enoch.

"Say, Worthy....what's your problem? Keep your eyes on the road and get me there. Don't waste my time with chitchat."

Lester smiled aiming a tranquilizer pistol at Morley. In Sam Bellamy's voice, he said, "Ye dinna have ta worry, Morley, old friend. Ye be in *my* care from now on. Relax, boyo. What? Can't relax? Well, this will help."

Lester/Sam shot Morley Enoch with enough tranquilizer to astop an elephant. Knowing *these* creatures, he wasn't taking any chances.

"Beddy bye, Morley Enoch. Sweet dreams....few a few minutes, at least."

Lester drove away, out of town and past the Orleans traffic circle to the dark area un-fondly known as "Suicide Alley".

Eventually, Morley woke up, extremely groggy, but awakening fast as soon as he felt he was restrained by....something.

"Wha....what are you doing, Worthy? What's the meaning of this? I'll have your hide for this insult or even worse, once I get free."

Lester/Sam stood over Enoch. Suddenly, Lester's face took on the visage of Sam Bellamy. Morley sat up in shock, pulling as far away as he was able.

"Ahhhhh, ye know who ye be talkin' to, aye, Morley? Good. Oh, right. It's about a hide to be payin' but that hide be your own. For what you did to Sam and Mary. Remember them?"

Sam's face disappeared, leaving only Lester's to stare down hate filled at Morley Enoch. "And for what you did to Viridian....and all those other innocent people you killed and maimed. Payback, you bastard....whatever *you* are."

Walking around a bound and tied Morley, Lester/Sam continued. "Please notice. You are cuffed to this stake and electronic device. *If* you're awake enough now? You should feel a comfy vest locked to your body. Yes, that's right. Look down. Should be familiar, you being an explosives wiz and all." Sam took over the conversation.

"Ye like yer bombs, don't ya? BOOM! Oh yes, ye loves yer bombs. Well, Morley? This be a biggie. *Big* boom....and *you,* me old friend....will be it. I'll let Lester explain it all to ye. It be his brilliant idea."

"Here's how the game will play out, Morley. Tick, tock. Tick, tock. Now, listen carefully because, (laughing), your life depends upon it. Two minutes after we leave, your cuffs will release. Noooo, now, don't get any ideas. Hear me out. At that moment, a buzzer will sound. You will have thirty seconds, no more, no less. In that short time, you must run all the way across Suicide Alley. I *love* that name, don't you? So explicit, so *true*....to life, yes?"

"To continue....run directly across the highway....and be very mindful of the traffic. A few feet from the road, back in the trees, is another post, identical to the one you're presently attached to. You have those thirty seconds....to press the large button on the top. *That* deactivates your vest. Trust me, you *really* want to deactivate your vest. That gives you another thirty seconds to make it back across to the button right over your head. Then? It repeats. Over and over and over, again.....well, until you tire of the game."

Then? BOOM! End game." Morley looked on in terror.

"Don't get us wrong, Morley Enoch. We're not quite the murderous monsters as you and your buddies. We intend to give you a bit of an *out*. A breather? After, and *if* you complete the first four go-rounds, you get a gift.... an additional ten seconds. Believe *me*, you'll think those extra seconds are sent from Heaven. Each additional crossing completed? Add another ten seconds. Until you hit a full minute. Wow, a full minute! Now, Sam and me? Well, we could be real bastards....kinda like yourself....and start to cut back on the seconds again, but no, we're not like *you.* Given a minute each time? We think you'll be able to keep going and going, (Lester's face returns to Sam's), and goin' and goin'. Mayhap? Someone will come along and help ye to find a way out.
Or maybe? Ye will just give up and....BOOM! Not our problem. Oh, by the way, your buddy Mendicant? Had a bad run in with a banjo. Sound familiar? Have fun.... and remember....tick tock....tick tock."

At that, Lester looked at his watch and walked off into the woods. Once out of hearing, Sam began to laugh.

"I was *right. Thou* could have been one Hell o' a pirate in *my* time. A right *bastard*. Brilliant. Absolutely *brilliant.*
Ye left the poor fool wi' a bit o' hope. So evil, Worthy."

Lester answered...himself. "Yeah, well? So what? The bum will get to one minute thinking of ways to get out of his mess. Hope is a nasty bitch, especially when it isn't *really* hope."

Sam answered, laughing. "And as he nears the end of the first, full minute? When he sighs relief an' pushes tha' button? BOOM! Ye be a right bastard, Worthy."

Lester answered himself. "Boom. Buh bye, number two. Two down. Two to go,"

Sam answered himself. "I canna wait ta' hear what ye have planned for those other two demons."

They continued walking back to Lester's car. At the end of around eight minutes, as they were driving away; an enormous flash of light and BaBOOM from the area of Suicide Alley.

"Guess Morley took a breather, huh? I guess so.. Let's get back to the harbor and we can go our own ways.Let's make it two days, this time.
Let's take two days off. Let you calm back down, Lester. Relax a bit and let Diabello and Crouch sweat, not knowing what has happened to either of their partners." Bellamy spoke again, in his own voice as they separated. "Ye know what they say? Revenge a meal best served cold...."

Back at the harbor, Sam departed and faded, saying as he left, "Two days....here....same time."

As he left, the impact of what they had done overtook the joy Lester had initially felt when he was mixed with Sam's spirit. Now? He sat in the dark, head in hands, groaning softly. "What have I done? What am I *doing*? Oh, God, V? This one was for you. Rest in peace, dear Lady."

Lester slowly got to his feet, feeling years older than he did a few, short hours ago. He dragged himself to his car and drove slowly off into the night, back to a darkened house; except for one light burning in the bedroom.

CHAPTER 36

FAUSTUS DIABELLO

The Return to Lucifer's Land

The next morning....

"Coffee", he muttered, then smiled. "Coffee....good. Need coffee. Food good, too."

He shuffled to the table and sat to a steaming cup of coffee.

"Lester? Be careful. That coffee is scalding hot and...."

Not listening or even aware, Lester drained the molten cup of coffee in a few large gulps. He never noticed the heat.

"Better....much better....more, please? Damn! That was hot!"

"I *told* you."

The hot coffee focused Lester, becoming aware of his surroundings, giving Liz a wan smile.

"Mornin', Liz. Honey, thank you for the coffee. Hey! The breakfast smells great I'm hungrier than I thought..."

His voice faded as he stared into his cup, lost in his thoughts.

"Les, *this* has *got* to stop. Whatever you and Bellamy are doing is killing you in front of my eyes. *You* can't take any more and neither can *I!* If this is a revenge quest you're on, stop it now."

Upon hearing this, Lester's face became stern.

"Look, Liz, we're almost done; two to go....two....to....go."His voice fading on the final words.

"Les? What are you doing to these horrible people? Killing them? Oh, please! Tell me you're not involved in murder!"

Lester chuckled. "Liz, don't be absurd. You can't *kill* creatures like these. Well, you can....kinda...for a while,at best and you *can* make them remember. Sometime in their futures? Remembering what *we're* doing to them? *May* make them think about *never* doing what they did, ever again.. Basically? That's *all* we can do to them in the long run. Revenge? Revenge in *any* form is good. Please, trust me. With Sam's help, all will be well. Not much longer to go and I'll be free."

"Les, you can't *last* much longer. *Please* give this up."

"No can do, Liz. No can do. The die is cast. All is in motion. All or nothing."

"At least, Lester, take today off and rest. Relax."

He chuckled at that, laughing into his coffee. "Relax.... hah."

The coffee and food revived his body, if not his aching soul. He decided to take his wife's advice and rest, if possible. Bellamy didn't expect him until tomorrow. Why not rest? He had plans to make for Mr. Faustus Diabello.

Next day when it was time, Lester waited for Sam Bellamy. Sitrting on the harbor bench, Lester stared across to Great Island, thinking of all that had happened and would *still* happen before he was done. That was when he realized Sam had materialized next to him.

"Mr. Worthy. Deep in thought, I see. What nasty plans have you devised for Mr. Diabello? You left me with a few interesting thoughts the other day."

"Well, if you're so interested, come aboard, matey and we can discuss things."

As Sam melded with Lester's body, both appeared to take deep breaths.

I'll never get used to that, Sam.

Neither will I, Worthy. After a few centuries, you tend to forget how the real world feels. By the way? That one toenail of yours seems to be hurting, again. When are you going to trim it? God, man! Take some care of yourself.

"Bellamy? You're not my Mom. Don't even go there."

They sat quietly. All any walkers saw was Lester Worthy sitting, contemplating the horizon while internally continuing an enthusiastic conversation.

Mr.Worthy? Brilliant. I wondered how you intended to lure Faustus Diabello from his lair. An evil, devious, sadistic plot as well. My hat is off to you, sir. Devious! Evil! So fitting. Using Lucifer's Land, as well. You are truly an artist. If we're in agreement, let me contact Elvis. We can use the big guy and I think he will be thrilled to get involved. MIKEY! Where are ye, little furball?

Mikey appeared next to Lester, looking annoyed as usually the case.

"Yes, meow @!!#####****!What the #### $@@! is it?"

"Go find Elvis and bring him here. He's probably at that

infernal food truck of his, feeding his face and trying out new recipes."

Lester shuddered ay that thought....so many disgusting things to do with peanut butter, jelly, bacon, bananas and....ugh.

At C, D, E & F, secretary Marie interrupted Mr. Crouch who was sitting alone in his office, his world crumbling around him.

"Yes, Marie, what is it? Any good news, yet?"

"Well, Sir, I have a message for you from Mr. Elvis. I think it could be important information concerning the whereabouts of Mr. Enoch and Mr. Flinch."

"Finally! Quickly, Marie, give it here!"

He snatched it from her hands and waved her from the office, anxiously reading the note from Elvis.

Mr. Crouch. The word is out you need to find Mr. Enoch and Mr. Flinch. Rest easy, my old friend. I know where they've gone and maybe even, why. I heard a rumor going around that investigators were headed out to Great Island after going to the Painestaker house. They may have found some evidence. I saw both Morley and Mendicant heading out there on the bay taxi. That was yesterday. They may still be out there. You know how hard it is to get messages back from there to here....especially after...well, you know. Oh, and Mr. Enoch said to tell you he was totally blown away with what he found. I hope this puts your mind at ease.

After placing a call, Crouch slammed down on the intercom, bellowing for his secretary, "Marie! Get me Diabello....and fast! I've got a job for him."

"Yes, Boss? What's up?"

"I just got a message from that fat fool, Elvis. He saw Enoch and Flinch heading out to Great Island yesterday. Seems the police have found something that interests them. Head on out there and give those two a piece of my mind. Get 'em back here, pronto!"

"Right away, Boss." Diabello hurried out, clearly on an important mission.

Faustus Diabello was in luck. When he got to the harbor, the island ferry was sitting there at an idle, while the captain smoked his cigar.

"My lucky day! Am I in time to get out to the Island, captain? There's important business."

The ferry captain slowly looked up from where he sat, stared at Diabello for a few seconds, turned and spat over the side showing great contempt at the request.

"Yeah, buddy, well, these days, we ain't got much call fer a-goin' anywheres, so I guess yuh can call it lucky. Give me ten bucks and hop onboard. That's my new rate. Don't like it? Bug off. Ya see I'm busy?"

"Ten dollars? Robbery....oh, what choice do I have.? Let's go and hurry up."

Faustus jumped on board. Handing the captain the ten dollars, he looked closely at his face.

"Hey! Don't I know you? Worthy, isn't it? Are you the new ferry man?"

Lester smiled. "Yeah, Diabello, that's me...the new ferry man....*your* ferry man....to Hell!"

Lester quickly pulled his now, well used tranquilizer gun and shot his passenger. First surprised, then with a blank stare, Faustus fell to the deck. Lester smiled down at him as he put the gun away, looking to be sure no one had been around.

"Yeah, buddy, I'm your ferry man....and you didn't even need a silver piece for the journey. Thanks for the ten spot, though. "Preciate it."

Lester revved the engines and headed out for a mre secluded spot where he had a truck waiting.

It wasn't a long drive to their final destination but it *was* off the beaten path. Yes, it may be in a National Seashore area, but one to be avoided except by ticks, mosquitoes greenheads and more. Faustus Diabello awoke in a daze with an aching head. First, he realized he was hearing the roar of the surf. Next? That he was securely bound to....something sturdy and metallic. Finally? He realized when the wind hit him, he was butt naked. All told, he then came to his senses very quickly.

"What the....who are.....Worthy? Why am I....what's all this sticky stuff?"

"All in due time, my dear Faustus Diabello. Let me refresh your memory. I am your captain and good friend of some former clients of yours who met with a tragic, untimely end."

Lester gave a formal bow and backed up.

"Right now? I have a friend of yours, and mine; a long time client of your Firm, and I believe he has something to say to you."

At that, suddenly, seperating from Lester was the form of Sam Bellamy, solidifying to his full, pirate glory. Grinning at Faustus, Sam took a stroll around the bound prisoner.

"Thee knows me well, Faustus. A long, long time, now. Yr also knows I'm not the person ta mess wi'."

He stopped, once again facing Diabello.

All of you have made some very....bad....mistakes recently. Corrections are in order. Oh, yes. We began with tha' fool, Flinch." He circled around Diabello, again.

"Next, we made Mr. Morley Enoch understand that' he was a very....bad....man." Again, he circled Diabello, who was desperately trying to keep track of him.

"And now? Now, we get's to *you*. Thou art a very....very, bad person. It be time ta' pay th' pirate."

Sam turned away and spread his arms wide.

"Look at this wonderful view. Amazing, isn't it?" Again he turned back to Faustus.

"You should really thank Mr. Worthy for your punishment today. He has an exquisite sense of irony and creativity. You see? This place? They used to call it Lucifer's Land, an area so ominous and dangerous, it was once used long ago to banish anyone the locals found ...undesirable, comdemning them to live out whatever life the Land left for them. It wasn't usually much or for long."

Sam turned again, spreading his arms wide.

"Look around you. Well, as far as ye be able in yer present position. Lucifer's Land; scrub ands na' much else. Far, far away from humanity. See? That's why we didn't gag you. No one can hear you....

or come save your pitiful soul. As you can see, you are perched precariously close to the edge of the cliffs. These cliffs? A very unstable place to stand."

Sam stood quietly for a moment, remembering his fate centuries ago, as his ship foundered below these very cliffs; and painfully, the fate of his beloved Mariah, who fell fell from the same area during the violent storm that claimed himself....while she was waiting for him to return for her.

"Yes, Faustus. Many memories here, all bad. If you could see around you,there? In the distance and the fog? The remains of a wee shack where many unfortunates of local *justice* attempted to survive. O' couirse, it's na' really still there. You can get the idea."

Once again, Sam peered into Diabello's eyes.

"Not for *you*, though, Diabello. Mr. Worthy has come up with a much more....*interesting* plan for your demise....slow.... demise. I do believe I will let him tell you all about it."

Sam melded back into the body of Lester Worthy.

"Thank you Captain Bellamy. Well, now. Let me explain. We have an exciting time set for you. Such choices. So many ....*uncertainties*. First? Obviously, you're naked. The weather here? Brutal. Dangerous heat by day, bonechilling cold by night. Hmmmmm. Death by exposure? A possibility. Slow. Maybe, maybe not.

Oh, yes? The sticky, smelly stuff? You're covered in a concoction of my own making: honey, blood, fish guts and other good smells. Sam mentioned the wildlife here?"

"Ticks, msquitoes, nasty, blood-sucking flies, many, many coyotes, to name a few. Maybe you'll get slowly drained by the lil' critters, may get eaten by the bigger predators....all attracted by your unique perfume, Eu Du Morte, I call it."

Sam and Lester were enjoying this. They stood laughing.

"No, we're pretty sure *this* will not be your end, though it would satisy both of us....not *you*, of course."

"No, we don't think this will be your end. The next possibility? With this, Mother Nature has lent us a hand. There is a *major* storm rolling in, in fact? *Very* soon. Oh! That's right. You can't see the evil clouds billowing up behind you. Pity. We guarantee you'll hear the thunder and feel the wind, soon, enough."

They took a turn or two around a worried Faustus, even as he struggled against his bonds.

"You....you can't do this, Worthy! Bellamy? You're both insane. When I get free...."

"Trust us both, Diabello. You won't. We planned this all out so carefully. Nothing has been left for chance....well, except which way you will die...and you *will* die, Faustus Diabello, just as sure as you killed those near and dear to us. Let us continue, please? So impolite to interrupt." We have placed you at one of the ost fragile, unstable and suspect areas of this cliff. Sam knows *that* so well. As the storm rages and the rain pours down? There is every chance that the cliff beneath your feet will crumble, throwing you to your death in the surf below. If that happens? Buh-bye, Faustus."

Sam took over the conversation, enjoying himself as much as Worthy.

"Then, again, Faustus? I doubt *this* will be your end. Look up. Strain your neck a bit. Oh, sorry. can't see? Let me describe it to you. You are bound to a twenty foot, steel pole. They call such things l*ightning rods*. Ah, yes? Familiar with the term. Good. Well, you, by far are now the tallest object found here in Lucifer's Land. By the way, this storm is turning into a beauty; a real howler, severe weather warnings everywhere....especially for lightning."

Lester/Sam backed away, Sam once again separating from Lester. They stood side by side, both grinning at Faustus Diabello. They took turns speaking to the condemned "man".

"Such a dilemma."
"So many ways to die."
"Which will it be?"
"Slow?"
"Fast?"

"Painful?"

"Oh, I hope so."

"Anyway, Faustus? When you think about it? You'll be back....some day."

"Sadly."

"Goodbye, Faustus Diabello. Happy Trails."

At that, Lester turned to Sam.

"It's time we leave, and quickly, before join the Diabello BBQ."

They had just reached the truck when the rain and wind came crashing down. Lightning blanketed the area. Above the rain and wind, they heard screaming.

"Do you think...?"

"I don't know....could be anything."

There was an even bigger flash of lightning.

"Wow! Now *that* was close. Do you think?"

Sam stood, listening carefully. A smile spread over his face.

"I do believe that last bolt of lightning had Mr. Diabello's name on it. Pity it was so quick."

"Yeah, Sam. Pity. Oh, well. Three down, one to go."

"I'm sure you have some ideas..."

"Oh, yes. Fitting, too. It *is*, after all, Wellfleet."

Sam faded and Lester made his way back home through the raging storm. As he drew further away from the influeence of Sam Bellamy, the weight of what he had done crashed down on him; his own private storm beginning to rage inside. All the guilt, anger and revenge he had been part of...crushing him.

All he had to look forward to? The end was in sight. He began mumbling to himsewlf as he neared home.

One more....one more to go....one more....

CHAPTER 37

Ishmael Crouch

Farewell and Ado

Elizabeth Worthy was now seriously worried about her husband. There had been many times in their marriage when Les went off on some unpredictable project or had an idea she'd listen to, only to wonder what mayhem would come of it. Fortunately, or unfortunately in some cases, the ideas worked, with either good or dire results. She admitted that, the ones that *did* work well....were worth the trouble.

This time? No way! Until she had actually seen both Sam Bellamy and Mariah Hallett, Elizabeth thought Lester totally off his rocker. She shuddered, remembering the first time she saw and actually *talked* to them both. At first, she felt sorry for them both but ever since Sam got her husband wrapped up in this bruhaha, he was falling deeper and deeper under Bellamy's spell. Lester wouldn't explain anything nut she saw the changes in him and she was scared.

Take today, for example. She and Lester had always been early risers, up and about before the sun. Since this all began, Lester had been wandering more, sleeping later and doing nothing constructive that *she* could see.

Today? Well, forget today. It was already almost dinner time and Lester was still in bed. He hardly moved at all and unless she saw the covers move slightly, she coiuldn't tell if he was still breathing. All of this *had to stop!*

She sat in the kitchen, head in hands, crying softly. Then she felt a hand caressing her shoulder. Lester was up and about.

"Liz, honey, I didn't mean to startle you."

"Well, at least you're up in time for dinner. You *do* want some dinner, yes?"

He thought for a minute. While she waited, she was shocked at how wraith-like her husband had become.

"Yes! Why not? I've missed a few meals, haven't I? Yeah, I guess I'm hungry."

He gave a hollow laugh, ringing with the sincerity of a policeman's promise. They got to work making dinner together, as they always had before....this. At dinner, she tried to draw Lester into a conversation, *any* conversation.

"By the way? Dinner is excellent! I'm sorry I missed so many. I hate saying this, but sometime after dinner I have to go out again."

At this pronouncement, Elizabeth bristled, but Lester continued.

"Now, please. Please hear me out. This is the last time. By tomorrow, by early evening, probably just after dark? I'll be home....for *good*. This will all be over and our lives can return to normal."

Elizabeth was distraught. "I guess nothing I can say will change your mind?"

"Dear, I started this....thing....and I have to follow it through to it's end. It all ends after this. *All* of it."

She got up and hugged her husband, looking him sternly in the eyes.

"Lester Worthy, you *biggest* idiot. You damned well *better* come back to *me*. In one piece, too. Do you hear me?"

Dinner was finished in relative quiet, if not calm and peaceful, as close to normal as they had shared in a long time. Later on, they hugged, again.

He kissed his wife and turned to go. At the door, he turned, smiled and said, "Don't wait up for me. I'll be back for you. Wait and see. You can't get rid of me *that* easily. Not even the ghost of Sam Bellamy will keep me from coming back to you."

As he closed the door and slowly walked off. he thought, *Well, I hope that SOB can't do that.* He walked off into the darkened night to meet with the Captain. Hopeful this would be the final time. Lester was worried, though, because he was to meet Bellamy and a few others over in Pirate's Cove. Oh, he'd been in and out of the Cove many times but that had been done on a subconscious level and he was never *there* for long. This time would be different, purposely *willing* himself to pass through and visit that other side of Wellfleet.

While he walked, he closed his eyes, imagining he was there in Pirate's Cove. As he began to hear the baaaa baaaa of that infernal goat he never saw, he knew he was in the Cove.

All was quiet....except that damned goat. He stopped by this town's version of the town liquor store and sat at one of the benches.

It didn't take long. First Sam appeared, then Mariah and finally, to his surprise, Elvis and Napoleon. He wondered, *O.K., where's that damned cat, Mikey? Might as well have the whole set and...*

"I'm right here, mrrrrrrow, look down you dumb....yowl, hissssss, meow!"

Sam cleared his throat.

"All of you, thank you for coming. This will be the final act in our revenge against this horrible gang o' murderin' thieves. We all have our parts to play. Mariah, ye be in charge o' gettin' th' vessel we be needin' in a few hours."

Yes, Sam. I can do that, *if* I can influence the right person back in Wellfleet."

"Mariah, Lass. I knows ye be more than capable. No worries."

"One last time, Sam, I am voicing my disapproval of this entire revenge of yours. It's not the way for us to do things."

"Might not be yourn, Mariah, but it sure be mine! Next? Lester and I will be headin' to the offices of C, D, E & F". He began to laugh.

"I do believe the Firm needs to be shortenin' their name a bit. We'll be approachin' Ishmael Crouch very carefully, confront him a mite, scare him a bit....then we'll be relaxin' ol' Ishmael. Lester, that will be your job. Elvis? Noapoleon? Crouch will be too much for Lester an' me to haul."

Elvis answered. "Not to worry, Bubba. Me and Nappy can handle it. It ain't like the old bastard is of Lester's world., so we can handle it."

"Mikey? You'll be stayin' with Mariah."

"**********!

"Too bad, furball. Get over it. Let's get together and finish this thing, once and for all."

Back at the very much smaller firm, only Crouch, to be exact, there was a knock on Crouch's door. It was his secretary, Marie, who peeked in, cautiously. The boss was in a terrible mood and ready to attack anyone not careful enough in their approach. After the last few days and the unresolved, missing partners, Old Man Crouch was acting like he was juggling rattlesnakes and nitroglycerine while blindfolded.

"Mr. Crouch, sir? It's only me, Marie."

Crouch was pacing around his enormous desk, seeming even larger now that he was the only one there. Pacing one way, then the other, sitting, standing again, fidgeting....a total mess of nerves.

"Oh, yes. Marie? What is it? I'm busy."

"There's a person here to see you. He *says* you may know him and that he has important information concerning the whereabouts of Mrrs. Diabello, Enoch and Flinch."

"Why didn't you say so! Send him in....immediately!"

Lester walked into the officewith an authoritative gait. He exuded power and confidence. He held out his hand.

"Mr. Ishmael Crouch! My name is Lester Worthy. I believe you *may* know of me."

Crouch shook his hand, peering into Lester's eyes, searching his rattled memory.

"Worthy....Lester Worthy....seems I know the name from somewhere....beside the point. Marie tells me you have information concerning members of my firm who are missing"

"Well, Mr. Crouch? It's not *really* beside the point and I have much to tell you. Why don't we both sit down and I'll enlighten you."

They both sat, Lester in a chair, Crouch on the edge of his desk, arms folded, impatient to hear what Lester had to say.

"First, you know me through some people your firm has had dealings with, Sam Bell and Mary Hall. I once worked for them."

At that, Lester began to scowl. "For a *very* short, *tragic* time."

Crouch's expression began to harden upon hearing those names.

"Worthy, yes, I knew those two young people. Very sad, what happened. Yes, tragic."

"Yes, I'm sure. You didn't know, however, my dear friend, Viridian Bean. *She* died in that same, *tragic* explosion."

"Oh, I am so sorry, Mr. Worthy...but you were going to tell me about..."

Lester cut him off, suddenly getting angrier, as well as louder.

"I suppose you *also* don't know anything about the people killed from the radoio station WPDQ....or all the local folk who died or were badly injured in that *tragic explosion*, am I correct?"

Now Lester stood, pointing a finger accusingly at Crouch. He began to yell.

"You also didn't know a Persipone Painestaker or that you sent your *associates* to shut her up, too. Remember? REMEMBER?

Before Crouch could respond, the form of Black Sam Bellamy separated from that of Lester Worthy and, in a rage, stood toe to toe with a terrified Ishmael Crouch.

"Well, Ishmael, if you do not, I most certainly do! I remember all those people quite well. Ye forgot my dear, relatives, Sam and Mary, too? All due to yer greed, ye thievin', lyin', murderin'....and they called *me* a pirate! My God! I thought I be the pirate here. Ye ha' done worse than anything I ever did."

Crouch backed up against his desk as bellamy advanced.

"But Sam....Sam....you don't understand...it was...."

"Dinna think ye can tell me...it *only* be business. Ye and yer kind ha messed with the accounts of so many of us over the centuries. We all trusted *you*! Ye crossed a fatal line killin' mind an' so many others. I be sure it ha' happened many times before, ye damned villain."

Sam returned to Lester, fading back into his body. The difference this time was that Lester's face became blended with Sams.

"Now, *Mr.* Crouch! To get to the point, as you put it. Your buddies?

Faustus Diabello? Morley Enoch? Mendicant Flinch? All dead....or, at least as dead as your kind can be. Painfully, too. Trust us both? They suffered untold agonies. Maybe to the point that, someday in the future when they return to their miserable, rapacious existences? They'll think twice afore doin' something so bad, again!"

Lester quickly pulled out his well used tranquilizer gun, pointing it at Crouch.

"Don't worry, Ishmael. You'll soon be joining your buddies."

Lester's voice changed to that of Sam Bellamy.

"Aye, ye be joinin' 'em presently an' it be a shame there be no way ta' keelhaul ye as in *my* time."

Back to Lester's voice. He now had a big smile on his face.

"However, you are now in *my* territory and time. Here, in Wellfleet, *not* Pirate's Cove. *My* idea for you is something *much* more appropriate, especially these days."

At that, Lester shot Crouch with the tranquilizer gun. Crouch stood there, unbelieving for a few seconds before the massive shot sent him falling to the floor, unconscious.

"O.K., Elvis, Napoleon? Your turn. help us with this fat bastard."

The two appeared and helped Lester/Sam pick Crouch up and haul him from the office, passing a terrified Marie Antoinette. Napoleon smiled devilishly at her as they passed with the unconscious Crouch.

"Oh, Cherie, I will be back for *you,* later. Au revoir for now."

A short time later, as the old lobster boat was cruising out from the bay, Lester/Sam was happily singing, "Yo ho, yo ho, a pirate's life for meeeeee! Hahahahahahaha. Hey! Crouchie, you awake? Must be. I see you cringing. Don't like the song? Too bad. It seems kinda appropriate, don't it? No? Well, too bad for you. Good enough for Johnny Depp. Good enough for the likes of you."

Crouch lay there on the deck, bound and groggy. The small boat rounded the point at Provincetown.

"Yo ho, Ishmael! Just keeping you posted, we've actually crossed into the Atlantic Ocean.

Can't you feel the swells building? No? Pity. Remember those Johnny Depp pirate movies? Huh? What did you just mumble? Oh, yeah. Sorry about the gag. Yeah, you're right. The first one was the best. What's that? Can't understand you. Never saw any of the movies? Shameful."

Lester/Sam closed the throttles, letting the boat glide toan unsettled stop. Lester looked down at his/their captive and grinned wickedly.

"Bet you know about another movie, though. Jaws? Filmed right around here, too." Lester/Sam stared out over the waters.

"Yeah, historic movie. Scared the crap out of me, *that's* for sure. Never thought you'd be in a live reinactment of it, did ya? No? Well, you're gonna be the new star.....well, maybe....more like the bait....and who knows *who* the real star will be?"

Lester took the time to attach a long, heavy line to Crouch's wrists. He continued explaining.

"Ya see, *this* is called trolling. *You* are going to help us see what beastie might be out here with a poor enough taste to want you for dinner."

At that, the visage of Sam Bellamy superimposed itself on Lester. Also continuing to grin down at Crouch, he cheerfully kept the conversation going.

"Here. Let me help you up, Ishmael. Ye ha' been layin' about for too long. Time to enjoy the sea air and salt water. From vast experience? I can tell ye, this be far better than keelhaulin', tho' thinkin' 'bout all ye been doin'? Ye deserves far worse. Well, anyways? Time to meet yer damned partners in whatever Hell ye be visitin' for a bit. Not sorry to see ye go. Yo ho an' all tha'."

Sam/Lester picked Crouch up, pulled off his gag and dropped him over the side as he begged, pleaded and threatened.

"No one can say Captain Sam Bellamy ain't a charitable man, takin' off yer gag ta say a few words, maybe catch a breath or two on the adventure of a lifetime. What's that? Can't rightly hear ya wi' all tha' sputterin'. Oh, well. Have fun and good fishin'."

Lester went back and pushed the throttles forward, just enough to begin a slow troll, thinking, *A troll for a Troll.... fitting.*

Lester/Sam slowly headed out into deeper waters, dragging a sputtering, yelling, gurgling, cursing Crouch behind them.

It took a good twenty minutes for the first interested party to show up. It hung around, following Crouch as he panicked, yelled and kicked. They guessed the shark wasn't all that interested in the questionable food they were offering.

"Sorry, Crouchie, guess you smelled bad to the beastie or it had better taste. Well, try, try, again. Don't give up hope."

They kept trolling, back and forth, faster and slower.

"Well, boyo! Lookie there! Now that be a prime specimen of carcacodon carcarious....great white shark if ye be interested. Damn! Boyo, he's a big 'un, too. To be fair? At *that* size, could be a female of the species. Wonder if she be hungry? What d'ye think? WHOOPS! Damn! In one bite, too. Farewell, an' ado....ye damned monster. Dinna rest in peace."

Lester looked and felt a bit drawn and tired. To himself, he trhought quietly, I*t's done. Finished. I want to go home, now.* He left the wheel and cut what was left of the line, returning to the helm. Sam once again separated from Lester and sat quietly, staring out at the open ocean as the afternoon light began to fade. He sighed.

"I miss it sometimes. Beautiful....and cruel, too, Mr. Worthy. Don't ye ever let it fool ya. It did *me* a long, long time ago. Let's head home."

They returned the boat they borrowed back to it's slip. Lester wearily dragged himself from the boat to the dock. Waiting there were Mariah, Elvis, Napoleon and even Mikey.

"It be done. Once an' for all, it be over an' done.Now, we move on to the rest of the plan."

Thery walked off while Sam did all the talking. Mariah stopped, turned and looked back at Lester, who sat on a harbor bench, head in hands.

"Sam? What about Lester? He doesn't look too good."

"Ahhhh, Lass, he'll be fine. let him rest a bit." At that, they moved off, discussing what would come next.

Out here, at the Cape, darkness fell fast and absolutely. A fog began to roll in and still, Lester sat there staring off into nothing. The gathering moisture began to drip from his face, his thought in such a turmoil, he never noticed. Grief and despair filled his mind. Mariah returned and gently sat next to him.

"I thought you would still be sitting here.Look at you! Getting all soaked in this fog. You'll catch your death and I can't let you go home looking like this."

She brushed the water from Lester's hair and clothing. Sam? Well, you know him. A pirate, always a pirate. Folks like him? Ye get used an' forgotten. Not by the likes of *me*. You did good things for my Sam, and for a lot of us. It may sound false but we *all* will be *forever* grateful at what you did." She looked sadly at the forelorn and torn Lester.

"And you can *not* go home like this." She realized there was something seriously wrong with Lester. Uncommunicative, staring off at nothing. She was concerned that Lester was totally burned out by what he went through, poor devil.

"No! We will not send you back to your wife like *this*. She would hate the likes of us forever....and *that* can be a very long time. Take it from me. You will be coming with me. Me and Sam? We'll heal you until you can go home once again."

Mariah gently put her arms around the shell that was Lester. They both faded into the foggy evening.

CHAPTER 38

Loose ends and Such

Back at the Worthy household, Elizabeth was beside herself with worry. Where was Lester? He said he'd be back home within a day, at most. Now? Closer to two days and not a word. Wildly distraught, she went into town asking if anyone had seen her husband lately. Some did while most didn't. There were "Lester sightings" but that was always the way in a small town. The most reliable had been shellfishermen having seen Lester down by the harbor. One said he saw him taking out an old lobster boat two days ago. Who could she believe?

Elizabeth was ready to call the Wellfleet police to report her missing husband, when she felt a presence behind her. It was Mariah Hallett, whom she recognized from their previous conversations. Mariah held up a hand.

"Elizabeth Worthy? Please don't be afraid. I can only guess how worried you are about Lester." She had a very sad look on her face as she said this.

"So long ago, I felt the same way concerning....Sam. I'm here to ease your worries. Lester is fine....well, in *time* he will recover. It's nothing physical. He was damaged....in other ways."

Elizabeth looked searchingly at Mariah.

"What do you mean *damaged*? Recover? What's wrong with my husband? How has he been hurt? What! What? Tell me!

"Excuse me, Elizabeth. I chose my words poorly. Physically, Lester is in perfect health. Mentally? He's hurting so badly, all the way to his soul. What he had to do, what he *did* do with my Sam, got them the revenge and closure they both needed. They helped so many others who are now safe from those monsters. You do *not* want to know all the details."

With deep regret, she added, "I felt the need for revenge as well, and I'm not happy about what was done but it *had* to be done."

Well, when can I see my Lester? Please, let me see him."

"No, Elizabeth, that isn't possible. Not now. You would not want to see him this way. Sam and I, as well as several others? We're helping to gently bring Lester back into this world of the living where he belongs, as he *should* be....with you. It could take a few days, even a few months. He took so much damage. We have him in a special place where he will recover his senses and well being. When he's ready? He *will* be home, again. I give you my promise. Be at peace until then."

Mariah faded as Elizabeth stood there, dumbfounded. First, she was angry, then, terribly upset and finally, crying piteously, "Oh, Lester, you big dummy! Come home to me!"

Shortly thereafter, there was an important meeting going on at the former offices of C, D, E&F. In attendance were Sam Bellamy, Mariah Hallett, Marie Antoinette, Napoleon Bonaparte, Elvis Presley,(sandwich in hand).... but no Mikey the cat. (He had better things to do.) Sam called the meeting to order.

"We meet here at a new beginning. Gone are those four lying, cheating, murderin' monsters....an' good riddance to 'em! All of us here have been at the mercy of those four rapacious rats for far, too long. We're not the only ones, either. Many others have accounts here that need better management."

They all nodded agreement.

"I have a plan to make our new organization better than it ever was, putting it back on a road to profitability for everyone! Marie? Since you have been the one closest to what went on around here, you belong in charge of all operations. Don't worry, you'll have Mariah as your second in command. She has more common sense than any of the rest of us. Napoleon, Elvis and myself will sit on the board and work closely with you both, offering any advise you feel is worthy."

He stopped for a minute, thinking, "By the way? How is Lester Worthy doing? I was pretty hard on the Lad."

Mariah gave him an update. "Lester is resting back at my *old* place. You remember where."

"Good, good. We owe Mr. Worthy so much. The least we can do is return to full health and back to his wife. Now? Back to our futures...."

Napoleon slid over next to Marie, putting his arm around her.

"Ahhh, cherie. It will be so exciting to be working under you." He leered at her.

She sighed, shook her head, thinking....*all I need is another, horny, old ghost.....well, maybe.*

The scene: in the heart of Lucifer's Land, near the roar of the sea and close to the cliffs.; somewhere between the worlds of Wellfleet and Pirate's Cove. Sitting in a ramshackle hut that had been there, (unknown to most), for centuries, there sat Lester Worthy. Alternately looking down at scraps of paper, writing, then staring out to sea. Around him was a menagerie of animals Mariah had rescued and cared for over time. Among them? A *very* vocal goat, occasionally baaaaaaa-baaaaaaa-ing in the background. Lester would mumble, *damned goat.....always knew I wasn't imagining it....shut up, goat!*

Then, he would go back to work writing on whatever was available. At various times of the day, he would be visited by one of the many he was getting to know better, especially Mariah, Sam, Elvis and Napoleon.

He stopped and wondered. *I haven't seen that damned cat Garfield in some time....or was it Heathcliff? Fritz? Oh, yeah....Mikey. Wonder where he got off to?*

Funny thing about that. One morning at the Worthy home, who appeared in front of Elizabeth but Mikey, the cat. Startled, Elizabeth could only say, "Oh! You're one of *them*, aren't you?"

"Meow! @###$$$$****! Meow! Yessss, Mrs. Worthy, ****, I am!"

"Figures, a talking, cursing , spirit feline. What else?"

"Hey, Lady? Give me a ****ing break, will ya? I'm here to keep you company until that **** Lester is ready to come home. I can report on his progress, too....all that ******* stuff."

In reality? Mikey the cat was lonely, though he would never admit it. He hadn't had a *real*, live family in *so* long. The Worthy's seemed as good as any to grace with his presence.

"Hell! Why the **** not? Welcome to the asylum."

"!@###**! Thank you, Mrs. Worthy. My name is Mikey....no matter what that ****faced husband may have called me. *Well*, who's this?"

At that, the Worthy family cats, Shadow and Critter showed up to supervise what was going on.

Mikey was pleased. "Meow! Company! My name's Mikey, (in cat talk, of course).

Critter purred and brushed up against him. Shadow, on the other paw, gave Mikey a withering look down his white nose and yowled, !#####*******###!!!, then walked away.

"Well! I never! What language! Huh! *This* is going to take some time."

Mikey followed after them at a safe distance from Shadow.

A loose end

During the final editing, I discovered a page I was originally leaving out of the story. Why? It wasn't necessary to the tale of Lester Worthy. Reading it again, however, I realized *this* was one of the few "scribbles" left behind by Lester written in the "first person".

So much of what he left in his notes seemed the ravings of a truly disturbed person, but this? Lester spoke to *all* of us from this forgotten page. Here are *his* words from his time in Lucifer's land:

I have truly come to love the sound of the sea. I think I always felt this way but being here, close to the edge of the world, the wind and surf speak to me as never before. My time here? Thanks to Mariah and even that bastard, Sam, I've had to face myself and all the harm I've caused.

I have wanted to get back home to Elizabeth for so long. I'm not ready, yet. How do you face the monster you became?

I mean, sure, I didn't actually do all that bad stuff on my own but I could have. I was a party to it all; all done at my hands.

Even scarier, after Viridian and those I also knew were lost to me. I began to enjoy the idea of revenge. How do you face yourself after that? I had become, in part, the monster that Sam Bellamy had been in real life.

Well, that's not fair, either. Sam had his own reasons for his rage. Also, he had been a bloodthirsty way back when....so he had skills. He loaned them to me.

I've had time to think and maybe, work it all out. Maybe. I **so** want to go home. Am I ready? I don't know. I'm not lonely here, in spite of what you might think. Mariah has visited every day, as have those other two characters, Elvis and Napoleon. What an unlikely pair.

Even that damned goat of Mariah's is kind of cute. Damn! I must really be getting homesick. Mikey visits now and then, too. He tells me about home and what goes on there. Gotta laugh sometimes; how Shadow and Critter, our two real cats, treat him, especially Shadow. Good! Mikey getting some of his own medicine...ha!

I do love the sound of the sea. Said that, already, huh? Well, it's true. Maybe I could just stay here. Lucifer's Land isn't all that bad most times. Maybe I could... Wait a minute! Mariah just popped in. What? **She** did what? No! Oh, no! Evidently, Mariah went back to the Painestaker place and brought back an instrument for me. A friend of mine suggested it. **She** says I've sorely missed having one to play and it will help in my recov... Oh, crap! Oh, no! Not a damned ukelele. Mariah says Viridian gave her the suggestion and says it's all I'll have until I decide to go home. Crap, crap, crap! Gotta think about this....

Another loose end

Some months later....(I've always wanted to use that line in a book, too), it was a dark and stormy night. The rain and wind being typical for an early Autumn evening on Cape Cod. Lester Worthy slowly walked up his driveway towards his front door. The porch light was on, as it had been every night for months.

Pulling his coat collar up against the weather, he cautiously knocked at the door. Elizabeth was there to open the door and pulled him into their home....at last. Home, at last.

The obligatory, short epilogue

Sometime in the future, in a galaxy far, far away, (I always wanted to use that line, too), on some strange, inhabited planet, there sat one recently reconstituted Ishmael Crouch, conversing with the head honcho and his court; typically unusual creatures, all....they have to be, don't they? In their equally strange language, (I'll translate). Crouch was explaining to the leader, who sat there, imperious and a tad annoyed.

"You see, your_____(whatever), I am offering you the chance of a lifetime! I can invest your wealth in any number of ways. What? I have no idea what that is. Is it some form of wealth? Oh, really? Never would have guessed. Well, any way, I can double, even triple whatever *that* is in a single year!"

The Imperious Leader was impressed and much whispering was bandied back and forth among his court. Crouch became emboldened with what he supposed was a positive response to his financial planning strategies.

"What's that? Your _____? You agree? Why, that's absolutely wonderful!"

Crouch thought he had a live one here, so he decided to go a step further. One never knew until one tried, did one?

" Now that is all settled, before I draw up the contracts, I have to add one more,minor detail. When this much.... wealth, is involved, I must insist on a policy of Life Insurance."

As the translator looking horrified at what Crouch said, relayed the information, Imperious Leader stood screaming! The entire court drew their weapons, all aimed at Ishmael Crouch. Imperious Leader screamed some more, all sounding *very* official and, to Crouch's ears, rather threatening.

The translator, now equally angry, spat an answer back at Crouch.

"Wait a minute! What? I insulted you, how? The entire court? I said what? No, no! I had no idea....I didn't mean....I didn't *know*!"

The royal guards grabbed Ishmael Crouch and threw him at the Leader's feet. Standing over the terrified Crouch, yelling and pointing, he finally gave a wave of dismissal.

As they dragged Crouch away, he was heard screaming, "What? The *gravest* of royal insults? Life Insurance means *what* in your language? Death penalty? How? NOOOOOOOOOOO!" As they dragged Ishmael Crouch off to his fate, yet another time in his very, very, very long, and sometimes painful, existance.

The Universe works in mysterious ways.
Uhhhhhh, uh tha, uh tha, uh that's all folks! (Always wanted to use that somewhere, too.)

WhydahMaker completed(again), 12/24/19

John Best
Art work by Elizabeth Best
Thanks to all who unwittingly were used as "character references" for my story. To all those who have followed the Lester Worthy saga, Lester will NOT be back for another book. Special thanks to my band mate, Jean and associated occasional pirates, in my band, Black Whydah.

To the town of Wellfleet? You are a wonderful place to call home. All of us are grateful each and every day to be part of it.

To the future? A new book is gradually taking shape, "Cape Lands". You know it can't bode well for anyone or anything that leaves my pen. Keep tuned. Lester says Hi!